About the Author

Colin Wheeler lived in England's Home Counties, for most of his life, and currently resides in Suffolk, East Anglia. Grammar school educated, he spent most of his career in marketing, sales and advertising — both as a copywriter, and later, as an account director. He has also dabbled in graphic design and computer art over a number of years. Now retired from working life, he and his partner, Ann, spend much of their time in their beloved vegetable garden. He began writing novels as a 'useful way of passing time' and hopes to complete many more.

The Coming (Past Imperfect)

Colin Wheeler

The Coming (Past Imperfect)

Olympia Publishers
London

www.olympiapublishers.com
OLYMPIA PAPERBACK EDITION

A CIP catalogue record for this title is
available from the British Library.

ISBN: 978-1-80074-257-4

First Published in 2022

Olympia Publishers
Tallis House
2 Tallis Street
London
EC4Y 0AB

Printed in Great Britain

Dedication

For Annie,
Your fantasy, faith and
Forbearance, are
what made this possible

Acknowledgements

In almost every book I have read, there has appeared a list of people to whom the author has offered his or her thanks, and acknowledgement. Until now, at the completion of this, my first book, I had not realised just how important all these people were to the author, and to the successful publication of their work. Now, so do I. so it is with enormous gratitude, that I would like to thank the following people.

To my brother, Dick Wheeler, for making the time to read every last word, and offer his encouragement, every step of the way.

To my dear friend, Janet Woods, for stepping out of her comfort zone to read, advise and encourage me on the writing of my first novel.

To my proof reader, Jo Barlow, for a thoroughly professional job, coupled with unsolicited encouragement.

To Kristina, for shepherding my work through the production process, and making it as painless as possible.

To everyone at Olympia Publishers, who has been connected with producing this book. Thank you all, for your efforts.

Prologue

The man looked steadily at the screen, upon the scene of utter devastation that appeared before him. Where, only moments before, it seemed, there had been a beautiful blue green planet, vibrant and alive with endless activity, purpose and hope, now there was simply a dead, ugly, grey, brown circle of meaningless rot. A source of noxious and poisonous gases that permeated the entire atmosphere of this once glorious globe, completely blocking the life-giving rays of light from this system's sun. Then the gases seemed to clear, leaving only the transparent vacuum of space between him and the planet, now a reddish-brown colour. Dead, utterly lifeless.

'*How could this have happened?*' he asked silently. What was the point? In a matter of a mere six thousand cycles or so — a moment in his lifetime — this entire race of beings would contrive first to develop their intellect, to construct magnificent buildings and monuments from the materials around them, to build civilisations and advance their scientific and artistic abilities, to understand a little of the universe that surrounded them. And he would be a part of that. A small, but effective, glimmer of hope that tried to lift them above the drives of their own natures. For a while he thought he might have saved them, redeemed them from an inexorable fate, but then finally, he saw, they would destroy themselves and their planet around them. '*What was the point,*' he asked again?

He could only wonder at the short-sightedness, arrogance and stupidity that surely must have led to this devastating moment. These creatures had contained within themselves a great capacity for learning, for understanding, for compassion towards each other and to the other flora and fauna occupying their world. Some — not all he conceded — would show a willingness to adopt responsibility not only for their own welfare but for that of the entire globe. Yet there was also a darker side to their natures. One that fed on conflict, destruction and death, which gloried in their ability to destroy, believing instead that they were finding a way to create. A dark force that they could not escape.

Would this part of their psyche finally subdue all reason? Would their logical thought processes finally sink beneath a roiling emotional turmoil of hatred and hostility to one another? He had thought them better than that. And yet, the notion entered his head — and became a conviction which he could not dispel; was not he himself at least partly responsible for this catastrophe? For would they not die with his name, or what they understood to be his name, upon their lips?

As he continued to stare at the viewing screen, the uncomfortable idea grew and finally crystallised into the one conclusion he had not wanted to reach.

"The plan finally fails then, Father? There is no redemption for them. Is this what you are showing me?"

"What you have seen is only one of any number of possible outcomes, but it usually happens this way, yes. Huge over-population, massive pollution of land, sea and air, greed and lust for wealth and power coupled with lethal technology. Generally, it is all of these factors."

"Then what was the point of it all?" asked the man again.

"The point, was that you gave them a choice and a chance to save themselves. Without you, what you have seen would be a certainty."

Around him, the huge ship hummed with a constant very low-pitched note, seemingly oblivious to the devastation he had just witnessed, yet at the same time somehow aware of his distress. It seemed to be trying to soften the blow of reality as the intensity of its life-giving vibrations lessened and the hum sank further into the background, almost as if it desired to ease his grief.

After what seemed like a long time, but was actually only a micro-cycle or two, he turned away from the screen, which immediately faded, seemed to harden and become opaque and gradually melded into the same colour and texture as the rest of the walls of this office.

The man sat on a bench seat, placing his head in his hands and began to weep.

Chapter 1

"The results of the planetary survey look pretty much the same as the other five we have conducted in this sector, sir. Blue/green planet; standard oxygen/nitrogen atmosphere; sixty per cent oceanic with the land mass broken into a number of major continents and numerous island land masses varying in size from large to miniscule. Age of the planet is eighty million cycles, and again, the dominant life form to develop is humanoid."

Having chaired so many of these meetings and heard much the same story so many times, the director could not prevent his mind from wandering…

He recalled the tragic, and devastating event which had led them here in the first place. The death and explosion of their home star happened so suddenly, at the end, that only their own and a few other discovery ships managed to escape the effects of the all-enveloping supernova. So, their race, their civilisation was effectively wiped out. The discovery ships sought new homes and new beginnings.

It was really pure chance that had saved the Eldorans from destroying themselves with their own weapons. A few people had developed telepathic abilities and it became clear to them that exploration and expansion of the mind and its pathways was the route to ultimate fulfilment. One of those telepaths, the famous Thamos Etrel, had such acute and advanced ability that he was actually able to affect many things around him and exert persuasive power on the minds of others. He had persuaded the leaders of their diverse nations to come together and thrash out the question of total unification. He had used the power of mass media to help quell people's fears of living together in harmony instead of conflict. But even then, he might have failed had it not been for the attempted system takeover by the Xavos and their monstrous weapons— the only species they knew of, for whom militarism had become a successful end, in itself.

Xavos. Even now, the very word sent a chill down his spine. These creatures were born to war. As a species they had become all powerful. What they could not conquer or dominate, they would destroy without a thought. Apparently alone amongst militarist, domination-led races, they had survived their own self-destructive crises and had developed both technically and intellectually to the stage where they had intergalactic travel coupled with the means to subdue or eliminate anything in their path. Their aim was, quite simply, conquest or destruction of the entire universe. And they seemed quite capable of achieving it!

United against this common external foe, the Eldorans had fought and repelled the Xavos on both the inhabited planets in their system. But it wasn't just their fleet of ships or their weapons that had defeated them. Had that been so, the ultimate cosmic war would have been fought — an event the Eldorans were determined not to bring about. Again, he had come up with a solution so simple and yet so all-encompassing that it almost defied belief. He simply wiped all awareness of the Eldorans, their system, and even their star, from the minds of their enemies. The Xavos simply forgot about them and continued on their search for other star systems to conquer. A grateful people had called him The Etrel from that time onwards.

Left alone, the peace loving Eldorans had developed and prospered in terms of understanding themselves and their cosmic environment. Peace and harmony had given them the freedom to effortlessly develop technology and art as well as their minds and that situation might have continued — but for the suddenness of the final catastrophe.

Unwilling to go over the tragedy yet again, it was with some considerable effort that he dragged his thoughts back to the present...

The Defence Prefect laid the tablet on the smooth, opaqued conference table and looked steadily around him at the others assembled for this briefing. The General Operations Director occupied a lone chair at the head of the table. Opposite the speaker sat Medical Overseer, Gaveri and Education Secretary Maikel, an unusual choice for such high promotion because she was female. Beside him sat Engineer Saecra, a reliable ally when it came to discussions of strategy and central philosophy. *We five,* he thought, *have the future of mankind in this galaxy to direct and control at our whim. These primitive sentient races we have encountered present no threat to us at all at present — in most cases, they will never be so as the galaxy would be many thousands of cycles older before they ever achieved the ability to leave their own planets. During that time, we will establish which could be most useful in our cause and thus allowed to develop through the normal militarism principle. Those who we predict will not be of any help...'* Well, the director would, he was certain, show a sure-footed approach to that problem. *'And yet,'* he pondered, *'he has always shown a reluctance for direct action when, at times, it seems to me, it was necessary.'* But such speculation should wait, perhaps, for a more appropriate moment.

"Thank you, Lucian," the director replied. "Does the report cover the current cultural status of the sentient people? I am rather interested in their artistic, engineering and religious achievements as well as the militarist status. So often, we have found the more peaceful potential of a race's development almost completely subdued in favour of militarist driven development. It would be interesting to find at least one that is a bit different."

"Not a lot to report there, sir," Lucian followed, "as the total population numbers only a few millions of individuals. Certainly, they are tribal in nature, and strength and aggression drive the current dominant empire — the Thorians, I believe they call themselves. They have conquered around two-thirds of one of the major continents and there is no obvious obstacle to their eventual occupation of the entire land mass. Weaponry is their primary means of technological advance, as you would anticipate, and this is quite sophisticated at this stage with steel hand weapons, personal armour, siege engines of all sorts, wheeled vehicles and so on. All pretty normal for this period. Military organisation is very advanced. In fact, their whole empire is founded upon the strength and needs of their armed forces.

"However, shipping is at a fundamental stage, little more than inland lake navigation and the occasional inshore foray from the coast. The oceans seem to frighten them. Artistically, they are distinctly lacking in scope and direction. Engineering achievements such as roads, habitation, communication and so on, are about as we expect. They have gods for just about every important aspect of their lives, the main ones being war and agriculture. No surprises there."

"What about the other major continents?"

"Not quite such a clear picture, sir. The continent occupied by the Thorians spans only the northern hemisphere of the planet. The others stretch across the planet's equator, from north to south in roughly equal proportions and occupy the mainly temperate atmospheric zones. Whereas some parts of the extreme north of the Thorian empire are virtually uninhabitable, due to the intense cold near to the pole, the other continents and their peoples have only relatively narrow equatorial zones, where the atmosphere is hottest, to contend with. Because of these conditions, the Thorians' drive for dominance stems, in part, from pressure on living space.

"No such pressure exists on the other continents, so they are, at the moment, relatively peaceful with no clear-cut dominant tribe or race. Minor, inter-tribal conflicts only for the most part. Their major enemies are not so much competing tribes as other animal species. There exist a number of carnivorous predators occupying plains, forests, lakes and rivers which the humanoids must be wary of. But by and large, they seem to be in a state of relative inertia. Many of their artistic achievements show marked superiority over the Thorians. Colour and design seem to play a big part in the things they make and the clothes they wear. Their engineering and scientific progress seems a little slower than on the northern continent, though most do have roads, domesticated animals to pull wheeled vehicles and they have managed to build bridges to span waterways of some considerable width in some cases. Trade is quite well developed almost everywhere, and as in the Thorian empire, communications through established trade routes and centres has developed spontaneously, leading to exchanges of opinion and information which, presumably, has helped drive what cultural progress has been made. What the indigenous peoples seem to lack is a sense of purpose and direction."

"In your opinion, Lucian," interjected the director. "But that does not automatically make it so."

"Quite, sir," the prefect replied, a little peeved at what he saw as yet another unnecessary rebuke from his superior. "If I may continue, their religious beliefs are largely the same as those we found on the northern continent — gods for everything! There is one tribe, however, who present an interesting anomaly in that they worship only one God who, they believe, governs and controls every aspect of their daily lives. They call themselves and the land they occupy Juhl. Strangely, given their location quite near to the equatorial region, this god is not the sun that they see rise and set every day, but is an intangible being whom they believe to be omnipotent."

The director leaned forward in his chair, a sudden interest evident in his demeanour.

"Now that is interesting, Lucian," he said slowly. "What more do we know of this tribe?"

"Little beyond that which I have mentioned, sir. They appear to be semi-nomadic, herders of domesticated animals which provide food, drink, clothing, shelter and even transport. They do not seem to form alliances with any other tribes — indeed it is not unknown for them to raid adjoining territories from time to time, though this seems driven only by need. Most of the time, they live in relative harmony with their neighbours. They have domestic skills such as weaving, pottery, carpentry and so on, but little use for metals to any degree beyond domestic and agricultural. This behaviour and level of development seems typical of most tribes on this continent although, as I said, they are the only monotheistic group."

The director sat quietly, digesting the information, thoughts running through his head leading to other thoughts, some harnessed, some discarded. Clearly, he had encountered some key piece of data, although its nature and purpose were as yet unclear. The others sat in silent anticipation, anxious to hear his thoughts.

"Gentlemen," he began, "I am considering a course of action which will undoubtedly come as a surprise to you. Indeed, the vast implications of what I have in mind give even me pause for thought. But before I share this information with you, let me tell you what has led me to this point.

"Man was not meant to live in space. It is a hostile and dangerous environment, despite our mastery of its vast expanse, and I am determined that we shall find a more permanent way to exist and explore our future. That is why I brought us to this younger part of the universe. The stars here have much longer to run in their natural cycle, giving us at least a chance of long-term survival.

"Throughout our travels in this galaxy we have encountered many different life forms on many different planets. Only a few could truly be said to have developed true intelligence that has enabled them to move beyond their simple, instinctive needs to a state of self-awareness and intellectual progress. The militarist principle of cultural progress we are familiar with from our own past history is, it would seem, one of the abiding laws of the cosmos. But whilst it is undoubtedly effective in driving the progression and advancement of civilisations, I consider it also cruel, wasteful, inefficient and utterly pointless as an end in itself. The Xavos are the one, cursed, exception that I am aware of.

"Conflict and war are merely the vehicles that drive scientific, artistic and economic progress. Unfortunately, most sentient races and civilisations manage to destroy themselves before they ever discover the true benefits that militarism can ultimately bring. Almost inevitably, the power of the weapons they invent far surpasses their wisdom in resisting using them against each other. When the method of self-destruction reaches that level, it should become apparent that its use, and even its very existence in the absence of extra-planetary threat, is totally without reason. This realisation is very rarely reached. In my opinion, the galaxies would be better served if militarism could be replaced by something else."

The director paused, deep in thought for a moment which grew longer and longer. The others at the table grew concerned. All of this was open-book history to them, why should the director be bringing it all up now? Gaveri thought that, perhaps he had detected the presence in this sector of space of the Xavos, although they had not been heard of for many hundreds of cycles! Now that was something which chilled the soul.

Defence Prefect Lucian could sense that something of real importance was about to be revealed, and with some trepidation, considered the director's words. In truth, he held a hint of admiration for the Xavos, the one race that had proved the veracity of the militarist principle. How could the director dismiss the importance of their achievements so easily, as to suggest, as the written histories would have them believe, that they were simply gullible to a mental trick? He himself had long been a devotee of the militarist principle. Surely their technological advances alone were testament to the viability of their approach to progress? He quickly put the thoughts from his mind as the director stirred at last.

"I'm sorry, gentlemen, I digress," he continued. "Of course, you are all only too painfully aware of the circumstances that brought us here. What you are not aware of is the mission I was given prior to our escape from home — to find and nurture any and all sentient species in the universe that I can find who might be relied upon to continue, prolong and develop the finest aspects of our own civilisation. Free will, drive, ingenuity, creativity, physical capacity to develop and harness the mind's own development, these are the qualities that I perceive to be our finest and they are the ones that I seek in our planetary surveys.

"I presume the directors of other ships were asked the same thing, though I do not know if there was time so I cannot be sure. Of one thing I am sure, though. The militarist principle has only very limited veracity and I am determined to find an alternative — a shortcut if you will — that might just mitigate against some of its worst effects or, perhaps, even eliminate them altogether. So, I am going to interfere."

The silence that followed this announcement was pregnant with a wide spectrum of emotions, ranging from satisfaction through doubt to pure awe. It lasted for about ten seconds, which seemed like forever, until everybody began to speak at once.

"Quite right and overdue in my opinion."

"But we don't know what effect it may have — it could destroy the civilisation."

"A stroke of pure genius. Why haven't we thought of if before?"

"Wow, that is right out of the blue. Are you sure of your premise, sir?"

"Under our rule, there is no telling how many thousands of cycles we may be able to shave from the natural course."

"How can we justify interference when we ourselves rejected it?"

"Have we found a new home then?"

"How can we eliminate conflict when its effect on technological advance is so important?"

"Enough!"

The command pierced the jumbled mass of voices like an arrow, and all was immediately quiet. Each man turned toward the director, who studied each face in turn as if trying to determine the effect his words had had. What he perceived from his study was evident only to him, but each officer was convinced that he had been tested in some way, although quite how was a mystery.

"I understand that you will have many questions, gentlemen, indeed I would be disappointed if you did not, but I am still working on some details of my plan. I therefore propose to postpone any further discussion until I have had time to formulate my strategy. We will reconvene on this matter in one hundred cycles. That is all."

* * * * *

Back in his quarters, Gaveri stretched out on his sleeping platform and pondered the events of the past meeting. Whilst the director's announcement had come as a surprise at that moment, he could not honestly deny that he had thought something like it could be coming. The director had seemed somewhat distracted for a while now and he sensed a growing disappointment with the endless reports, all saying virtually the same thing. 'What is he up to now?' Gaveri mused. But he could find no answers. He was sure of one thing though — he would support the director's decision, whatever that might be.

Maikel walked slowly along the passageway leading back to her quarters. She was, of course, aware of her unique position as the only female senior official on the ship, although there were a number of female crew members. In truth, she saw these women as her responsibility, in part, their voice in the corridors of power on this ship. At times, this felt like a heavy responsibility, but she tried to carry it out to the best of her ability. So, what would her fellow crew members think of the director's proposal? Did it really concern them all that much? Did it even concern her?

Not for the first time, she wondered exactly what her role on this ship should be. As education secretary, her tasks were largely tutorial — her other skills and expertise extending only as far as an ability to navigate the ship unsurpassed by any other crew member, and as an effective arbitrator when disputes arose. Otherwise, she thought herself quite unremarkable. However, she had always been loyal to the director and saw no reason to question that loyalty now, at least until she knew more about what he intended.

Lucian and Saecra were deep in conversation in Lucian's quarters, the dialogue becoming more and more excited.

"Saecra, I do believe the director is planning something totally at odds with the established rules that govern the universe. What did he mean by interfere? Surely the only way to do that is to do what I have suggested to him many times. If he wants to manipulate the development of these inferior beings, then he must impose his will on them. Otherwise, they will simply wander about, aimlessly killing each other — the good with the bad — and get nowhere fast. And speed of development is, to my mind, the key to getting the right result. But it didn't sound like he had anything like that in mind. So, what is he up to?"

"As long as it doesn't affect the safety of this ship, I don't know that I'm all that concerned," answered the engineer, himself in some confusion over the director's speech.

"Consider the possible reappearance of the Xavos. As we are now, we would be easy to pick off, one ship at a time, wiping out the entire remnants of our race with little or no effort on their part. So, if we are to bother with these inferior beings at all, what possible reason could we have other than the development of worthy allies in our struggle?"

"If the Xavos were that close to this sector, I don't see how interfering with the development of inferior races will lessen the threat. There simply wouldn't be time."

"I agree with you, my friend. Even accelerating things by use of militarism could not achieve the necessary level of technological advance in time, and his continual leanings towards pacifism as a realistic alternative are laughable to say the least. So perhaps there is more time than we thought?"

Lucian looked expectantly at the engineer but could not discern what he was thinking.

"Think, Lucian, think!" he exclaimed, as much to himself as to Saecra. "I'm sure there is no question of a Xavos attack, not for a while yet. Don't forget, they are still under the influence of the mind intervention of The Etrel and therefore unaware of our existence. This sector of the universe is of no interest to them — yet. In time, of course, they would look to conquer it as soon as there is something worth conquering. Which brings us full circle. How do we gain the necessary time? I'm sure pacifism is too slow, if it can be made to work at all, which I doubt. The alternative…?"

Lucian stopped in mid-sentence as an idea suddenly occurred to him. As it grew in his mind, he became more and more excited.

"Show them their gods!" he shouted. "Send them a god-leader. Use their own obsession with deities to bring them onside. Once there, we can control the rate of advance, establishing our own superiority at the same time. It's brilliant, don't you see? Effectively, by taking over a few worlds such as this one, we can accelerate technological development, bring them up to and even beyond our present level and be prepared to meet the inevitable Xavos invasion head on with sufficient manpower. And we can do this thousands of cycles before they expect it. Brilliant!" Lucian almost jumped with glee as his theory developed.

"We can use the dominant Thorians. Barbaric now, of course, but they will be brought to a state of enlightened dominance with our guidance over a few hundred cycles. I could even give them a taste of what is to come right now."

"Is that wise, Lucian? Let's not get ahead of ourselves. After all, despite the implications in his briefing, we still don't actually know what the director is planning. It could, conceivably, be something very similar to your own idea," said the engineer

"In which case, Saecra, he will thank me for using my initiative and getting the ball rolling. The director is no fool, but he does employ a little too much caution sometimes and I am not convinced that he is on the right track. No, I am going to speed things up and in the right direction."

The engineer said nothing, not even to enquire what the defence prefect had planned, but he left with a sinking feeling in his stomach. A feeling that, somehow, a huge mistake was about to be made. The trouble was, he did not know by whom.

The next officer's meeting, promised to be quite eventful.

* * * * *

Emperor Tyrsis awoke with a start, unsure exactly what might have interrupted his sleep so suddenly, but certain something had. Slowly, his right hand moved toward the dagger resting beneath his pillow. If this was another assassination attempt, he would make whoever it was pay a heavy price. Grasping the weapon, he sat up suddenly, waving the blade left and right in quick succession but met no resistance.

"Whoever you are, know that this is your last night of drawing breath," he growled.

Nothing moved, no one answered, no intake of breath as a result of his challenge. Time passed. Could he then have been mistaken? A sudden gust of wind, perhaps?

"No, you are not mistaken, mighty Emperor, though your weapon will not help you here and now."

"Show yourself then, arrogant one, and we shall see what help I may, or may not need."

Tyrsis looked around the dark room, seeing nothing clearly, though his night vision enabled him to verify the contents of the room were as they should be. Then he found what he sought, in the far corner of his room, a darkening of the shadow, the vague outline of a man. Fear crept up his spine. How did this intruder get in, past all his guards?

"Oh, do not concern yourself, Emperor, I am not here to kill you. In fact, I am not really here at all in a physical sense. Though, make no mistake, should I choose to do so I could easily accomplish both. You need only check on the state of the guard outside your room."

Not a man to be easily frightened, Tyrsis decided to play the game and wait for a suitable opportunity to unmask the intruder.

"If not murder, then for what other reason do you disturb my sleep?" he asked.

"Emperor Tyrsis, great as you think your achievements and those of your ancestors might be, viewed in purely mundane terms, you should be aware that there are — things — way beyond your knowledge or comprehension that could be used to destroy all that you have built in an instant. Shall I give you a demonstration?"

At once, the whole room erupted in flame, enveloping everything. The emperor lifted his arm to shield his face from the inferno, felt the searing heat strike his skin, blistering and sizzling until he thought he could stand it no longer. Then, just as suddenly, the flames were gone, only to be replaced by — nothing. He looked down and saw only white clouds and knew that he was falling inexorably to his death. The wind whistled past his face as he looked down and saw the ground fast approaching. Panicked, he screamed as he plummeted downwards until...

Just as suddenly, he found himself back on his bed and the room resumed its brooding silence. He felt the covers of his bed and found that they were not scorched, yet he had seen the fire with his own eyes. But then, he was falling to his death, he remembered. How could these things be?

He lifted his head and once again regarded the deep shadow, vaguely aware that, in his panic, he had dropped his only means of defence but knowing, suddenly, it would not be nearly enough to stop this stranger from doing whatever he wanted to do.

"How did you...?" he began but was cut off in mid-sentence by the stranger's voice.

"How is beyond your knowledge, Emperor, and it is but a very small demonstration of the power that we wield. The important thing is that you know we can destroy you and your empire if we choose. Are you convinced, or would you like another example?"

"No," the emperor answered, aware now that this was no simple assassination attempt, but also growing curious. "Are you a god then?"

There was but a moment's hesitation before the stranger answered. "Yes."

"It has been many generations since any member of my family has believed in the gods. As far as we are concerned, they exist merely to help keep the population in line."

The emperor paused, considering his last statement and his own, present, vulnerable position.

"Yet, here you are, with power I have not come across before. So, let us assume, for the moment that you are, as you say, one of the gods, then what purpose is served by coming here, now, to me? There is surely some reason, otherwise you would not go to all this trouble."

"Well observed, Emperor. There are a number of reasons, as a matter of fact. Firstly, you needed to be convinced of our existence. Secondly, I am sent to make you a certain proposition. We can give you dominion over this whole world, if you want it. All you have to do is accept the advice and — certain gifts — that we have to give, and you can achieve conquests you never even imagined possible. Your empire, and that of your successors, will encompass the entire world. Would you like that?"

"Who would not," answered the emperor, now somewhat calmer after his experience. "But that does not fully answer my question. Why do you do this? Why me and why now?"

"Why not?" answered the stranger, clearly becoming agitated. "The ways of the gods are not for you to question, mortal one, but I can tell you this. You and your empire are mankind's hope against an uncertain future. We have decided to nourish that hope."

With a bravado he did not entirely feel, the emperor replied, "My empire already stretches almost from one end of this land to the other, with the small exception of the Bolgs who, I promise you, will not stand in our way for much longer. Uncertain? I would have said that our victory was about as certain as it could be. So, I ask again, with all respect, why me and why now?"

"Fool!" the stranger exploded, revealing his anger. "Still, you question matters which are not your concern. Your small mind cannot possibly grasp the importance of our intervention in your affairs. We are here to redeem your entire race from its ultimate fate. Did you think that there is only one continent on your world? More than this concerning your future, I will not tell you. Simply be ready when we call upon you."

The outburst caused a renewed fear in the emperor. Suppose this creature really was a god — who was he to question its instructions, especially when, he was convinced, this 'god' or these 'gods' — for had he not said 'we' — could as easily strike him down as let him live?

Reluctantly, he answered, "I will be ready when you call." In his mind, he thought, '*But do you really exist?*'

"Oh, we exist, and you should not underestimate our power. You can either benefit from it or be destroyed by it. The choice is yours."

With that the shadow disappeared and silence resumed. Tyrsis sat, quite stunned by his experience. Had he really just encountered a god? And what was that about more than one continent? Everyone knew that the endless ocean simply stretched to the edge of the world. Beyond that? Tyrsis could not fathom it out. And how had the intruder known what he was thinking? Exhausted, he sank back to his bed and was asleep at once.

Lucian arrived back at his personal planet shuttle thinking that the encounter had not gone entirely as planned but satisfied that no harm had been done. He would have to see that the next 'vision' this emperor had was a more tangible — and frightening — one. Whatever the director's intentions, he felt that the groundwork of his own plan had successfully been laid. All that remained was to convince the director to follow it instead of his pacifist nonsense. No easy task, he felt, but as military leader on board the ship, his responsibility was to ensure their safety and survival — at any cost. Nothing was going to get in the way of that.

Chapter 2

The second briefing did not go entirely as planned for a number of reasons. At the appointed hour, the director, Gaveri, Maikel and Saecra resumed their places at the conference table but there was no sign of the defence prefect.

"Where is Lucian?" asked the director. "It is most unlike him to be late for a briefing. Saecra, have you any idea where he is?"

"N-no Director," the engineer replied, clearly uncomfortable at the direct question. "The last time I saw him, was mid-last cycle, and we did not speak at length."

The director held his gaze for a moment or two before looking down at the tablet in his hand. An almost imperceptible nod of his head was the only thing that betrayed his thoughts, as if something unpleasant had just been revealed. Yet nobody had said anything.

His face was impassive as he digested the situation.

"Very well," he began. "We will start without the defence prefect. Perhaps he will put in an appearance at some point.

"As I announced at our last meeting, I have decided to intervene in the development of life on the planet below us. Indeed, I have already begun to do so in small but significant ways. I know this is contrary to the principle we have adhered to so far and it is not a decision I have taken lightly. However, alone amongst all the other planets we have surveyed so far, this one seems to me to hold the greatest promise of a positive outcome to what I can, in truth, only describe as an experiment."

He had their attention now. His ability to read faces and discern reactions told him all that he needed to know about the officers around him.

"In fact, we are going to give the sentient race below us access to some of our technology over the next two hundred or so cycles by sending them a leader who, whilst one of us, will also be one of them. I plan to use the pacifist-oriented situation on one of the continents to combine their talents so that they may direct their development of technologies in a peaceful, harmonious environment, thus avoiding the waste and bloodshed of militarism."

"But won't the Thorians have something to say about that, sir?" asked Saecra, "after all, their technology is already more advanced than that on the other continents."

"This is true, my friend," the director confirmed. "But the Thorians, thankfully, are an ocean away from the other continents — and they are frightened of the deep water according to the survey report. I estimate that it will be anywhere between one hundred and two hundred cycles before they overcome that fear and have sufficient large, ocean-going ships to despatch a significant invasion force across the sea. Do not forget, also, that they have yet to conquer all of their own continent. Apparently, at least one stubborn race — I believe they call themselves Bolgs — are still giving the Thorians a very hard time. In fact, there seems to have been something of a stalemate in existence for the last fifty cycles which will hold the Thorians up for another five to ten cycles yet.

"We have time, therefore, to make the experiment work. During that interval, technological and mental advances can be made which will allow the indigenous, united peoples to peacefully subdue an invading force, buying yet more time — though not much — for them to develop their capacities to the extent that they can repel all invading forces. Do not forget that the leader we send them will have power way beyond the capabilities of any invading force, partly due to our technology.

"There is, of course, an element of risk, and as with any experimental plan, any number of things could go wrong. I am satisfied, however, that, should it fail, the experiment will not have adversely affected what would have been the 'natural' direction of events, only the timing."

"May I ask a question, sir?" said Saecra.

"Certainly," replied the director.

"Have you decided who to send them as leader?"

Just as he was about to answer that question, the door to the conference room slid open almost silently and Defence Prefect Lucian walked in.

"Director, I am so sorry to be late, sir. I was unavoidably detained in the chart room. A rogue asteroid appeared on the scanner quite suddenly, and when I plotted its course, I realised it would pass very close indeed to this planet — in fact, it appeared to be headed directly for us. I decided not to take any risks and pulverised it before it could get too close. I hadn't realised it had taken so long and I apologise once again."

The director considered for a moment. This was the first time he had detected an outright lie on the part of his defence prefect and it gave him momentary concern.

"No matter, Lucian," he said. "I trust your judgement in these matters. Now let us bring you up to date."

Lucian listened intently as the director repeated the salient points of the meeting so far. As he listened, he became more alarmed, realising that, far from entertaining any discussion of alternatives, the director was clearly planning, and had already started carrying out, something which made no sense at all! Unless, of course, he was the one chosen to become the leader, in which case he might yet salvage some semblance of order from what could otherwise be a complete mess.

"Don't you agree, First Officer?"

"What? Oh, I am sorry, sir, I was distracted."

"I said that sending one of us would, in my view, be a mistake as, aside from the personal risk due to bacterial infection, the trauma involved in revealing ourselves to such primitive people could actually set the plan back rather than advance it. Their natural fear of such obvious intervention would introduce far too many unquantifiable factors."

This statement took Lucian completely by surprise. Not one of us? Then who? The scheme already sounded crazy enough, ignoring all the basic rules, and now he proposed sending someone else? How could you impose your will without revealing yourself? He regretted not having followed up his visit to the Thorian emperor, Tyrsis, especially since it was now his successor, Tyrson, who they would have to deal with. The son had even less regard for 'gods' than his father had.

"Then what exactly do you propose, sir?" the defence prefect asked, in some dismay.

"Simply that we send them a leader who is, to all intents and purposes, one of their own. Whose 'miraculous' birth will be attributed to their one God, and who will grow up amongst them, becoming accepted quite readily, gradually revealing the powers and technology which can help them. This will achieve three things. Firstly, it will avoid the trauma of apparent extra-planetary interference in favour of divine intervention. Secondly, it will provide the means of introducing useful technology more quickly and will make it more readily accepted. And thirdly, their conviction in their invincibility, founded in faith rather than science, will be strengthened beyond measure. The confidence this will give them in using the new technology and developing their minds will be enormous. I must admit that I do hope that some form of true telepathic ability will manifest itself in the short term, though this cannot be predicted with any degree of certainty. What can be predicted, however, is that peaceful development, allowed to proceed uninterrupted, can knock thousands of cycles off the accepted norm. They need no more interference from us until and unless they are ready for it."

"Then we may not, strictly speaking, be intervening in their affairs at all if one of their own leads them," said Maikel. "We can simply allow them to try to achieve in a few cycles what it took our race many thousands to do."

"That is essentially the plan, yes," replied the director.

"How sure can you be of the experiment's success, sir?" asked Gaveri.

"With something of this magnitude, there can be no absolute guarantees, but I have already paved the way," the director stated. "Making use of their seers and prophets, I have planted in their culture the idea that a leader, a messiah if you like, will be born to their race and will lead them to eventual peace and prosperity. Long winded, perhaps, but at least it does not directly interfere with their progress at this stage since their free will allows them to believe or disbelieve as they will. Interestingly, though they are now but farmers and traders, they have, in their past had kings who led them in battle and conquest. In fact, their 'royal' line is still unbroken, and I want to use that to reinforce the leader's authority. There is much study still to be done and the timing must be right, of course, but I estimate a seventy per cent chance of its success, which is by far the best odds that have presented themselves so far."

"You have considered this before, then?" Saecra said.

"Of course, Saecra. With every planet we surveyed. I was simply waiting for the monotheistic/pacifist combination, along with a relatively stable environment before I could truly consider this action. This is the first time it has occurred."

"But — forgive me, sir — but why do we need to do this at all?" the engineer insisted.

"In order to give the sentient races in this galaxy, and others, a chance to survive their own stupidity and the inevitable invasion of the Xavos," replied the director patiently. "Although I do not anticipate that event for many thousands of cycles, come it will eventually. These young races need all the time they can get to develop technological and mental powers the equal of what the Xavos will become. This is a kind of shortcut to achieve it. Otherwise, I believe they will fall as have all the rest, other than ourselves. And let us not forget that most sentient races end up destroying themselves. Even if they are not equal to the Xavos when they come, at least I may have saved them from self-annihilation."

Lucian had heard enough. Contending with his own disappointment, along with the apparent senselessness of the proposal, finally became too much for him. His fist banged on the table.

"Director, I must protest. What you propose is madness which cannot possibly succeed. Why do you choose to ignore the one major principle that has been proven to direct and promote all forms of development? If we are to intervene, surely it would be more sensible to 'adapt' that principle, make use of it, and in so doing ensure its enhanced and accelerated performance in allowing the sentient race to reach the required stage of advancement in the shortest time possible. Any other course seems, to me, a complete waste of time."

The room went quiet. Outbursts of this kind and outright disagreement with the director were almost unheard of.

The director sat back in his chair and studied the defence prefect. He had been aware of the other's headstrong tendencies and almost unreasoning fixation for some time but had thought that these traits could be brought under control with some help and guidance, which he had tried to offer. He saw now that the effort had, so far, been largely wasted, and that his once most highly-valued colleague, was committed to a course of action that he himself, could not, and would not, contemplate. He allowed himself the briefest, gentlest foray into Lucian's thoughts and was appalled at the recent memories he found there. He was more taken aback by the mental block that was suddenly thrown up to prevent him from penetrating the other's mind further. He decided not to pursue the intrusion any further.

"So, Lucian, you do not agree with my proposal. You have presented some arguments against it which, at first glance anyway, carry a certain logic in keeping with your duties on board this ship. Can we presume that you have a plan of your own? If so, perhaps we had better hear it."

Lucian knew that he had been invaded, that the director almost certainly knew of his past actions, and he realised that there could be no turning back. Having himself broken the non-intervention rule, he was, unconsciously perhaps, but irrevocably, committed to the course of action leading from it. He could, of course, simply apologise, accept the director's admonition and the embarrassment it would cause him, and for a moment, he was tempted to do just that. But something held him back.

Had he not successfully blocked the director's invasion of his mind? Did this not mean that he was, probably, as powerful mentally as him? This may be his ship, but did that automatically make him right? By what right was he in control of the ship anyway? The more he thought, the more the bitterness built and the more convinced he became that the time for a change was now. Starting with this chance to get the others on his side.

"You want to hear my plan? Very well then. Your attempt to penetrate my thoughts, feeble though it was, has probably revealed much of it to you, but for the benefit of my brother officers, I will tell you." Lucian spat the words as years of frustration finally reached their peak and he stood up to present his case.

"The tools of my plan already exist. The Thorians are ideal masters who, through conquest, can be relied on to bring all the other races on the planet under one rule — all we have to do is add the all-important ingredients of divine guidance and superior technology. Once relative peace is established, with only minor resistance, sabotage and terrorism to worry about, their mental capacities can be guided and devoted towards development of superior technologies, scientific and engineering advances, weaponry development, strategy development, medical advances. There is always the small and ongoing risk of rebellion and counter-conquest, but with our help, this can be minimised and easily overcome. The resulting civilisation would develop in, I estimate, no more than a few hundred cycles as opposed to the few thousand cycles it would otherwise take.

"There is minimum risk of failure here and we would end up with a powerful ally to use against the Xavos when they come. Who knows, we would probably have enough time to repeat this entire process several times before they arrive, provided we can find enough inferior beings to start with. Thus, we will establish our superiority here, as gods, and we create the means whereby our enemy can be defeated once and for all — without the intervention of a supernova!"

The defence prefect sat down and looked at each of the others in turn. He could read little in their facial expressions, but he was satisfied that he had presented his plan as well as he could. He was convinced that it highlighted the futility of the director's proposal. But just in case, he thought, perhaps a little mental nudge would help.

He started with Gaveri, preparing to enter his mind — and found that he could not! But Gaveri was not telepathic, and was not therefore, capable of repelling him. So how had he been stopped? He moved on to Maikel. The same thing. How was this possible? Saecra, then. The blocks remained. He had not expected this from his fellow officers. Their silence and stillness confused him further, until he finally looked at the director once more. His expression told Lucian all he needed to know.

The director spoke, "No, Lucian, I cannot allow you to interfere with their minds because, just like you and me, they have free will to make their own choices — and I will not allow you to interfere with that in any way. They can hear all of this conversation and will remember it. And their decisions will be made by themselves alone, I shall not attempt to influence them.

"You, on the other hand, seem to show nothing but disdain, not only for the self-determination of your fellow officers, but also for the right of those sentient beings on the planet below us to decide their own destiny. You refer to them as 'inferior' beings, but just because we are more advanced than they are, does not make us superior to them. Who are you to decide who might conquer and rule whom? Who are you to grant or deny them access to our technology simply to achieve your own ends?

33

Who are you to decide who shall lead and which beings shall be declared their mortal enemies?"

"But you plan to do exactly the same thing w…"

"No!" the director exclaimed. "That is exactly what I do not plan to do. I am intervening, yes, but in the smallest possible way. I will present them with a phenomenon in the form of a being who may or may not become a leader. Both he and they will make up their own minds on the matter. And that goes for future generations too. They may accept or reject him, but they cannot deny his existence. One small event, brought about by our direct intervention, bolstered by small and indirect visions and prophecies, is all I plan — certainly until they reach a stage of awareness of extra-planetary beings such as ourselves. Should they fail to achieve that, should they destroy themselves as so many have, should they reject that which I send, these decisions are entirely up to them. Otherwise, the whole exercise is pointless, don't you see that?"

"Pointless? Futile? The whole thing is utter madness, Director. Think of the inordinate amount of time you are about to waste. I want no part of it," declared Lucian.

"Then you shall have your wish," said the director sadly. "You are dismissed, Lucian."

* * * * *

Lucian made his way back to his quarters seething with anger. How dare the director embarrass him, in that way. It was as if the man had set a trap for him and he had blundered into it, quite oblivious. That the altercation could simply be a result of his own impulsive actions, coupled with his disappointment at not being appointed a leading role in the experiment, did not occur to him. All he knew was that his faith in the director's ability to drive events in this galaxy was completely shattered. Almost before he knew it, he had made his decision. He could no longer serve under the director's command. This was influenced, not least, in the knowledge that the director's telepathic ability was at least the equal of his own. This was not something he wanted to test any further right now, so he needed to get away to give himself time to think.

Having reached this conclusion, he was at first nonplussed as to how to proceed. There were so many things to consider, so much to plan. Should he declare his rebellion openly? If so, could he take over the ship? He quickly discounted that idea, the other officers and crew would not join him, he knew. Except, maybe Saecra? And with that thought, a plan began to form. One that just might get him that which he craved — power — and spike the director's plan as well. *'You're not so omnipotent old man. We'll see who can make intervention work,'* he thought. All he needed was to know the exact timescale the director was working on. Saecra could get him that information, as he was obviously no longer a party to the plan itself.

* * * * *

Maikel hurried from the meeting having decided to go after Lucian, intent on nipping this matter in the bud if she could. She could not explain why, but she had been quite impressed with the way he asserted himself. There was no doubt that he was physically attractive, and she found that, almost despite herself, she was drawn to him in some strange way. She hurried down the passageway, passing the office of the general operations director before descending towards the lower decks. After a while, she realised they were heading toward the boat deck and began to wonder what the defence prefect was about. She increased her pace and gradually caught up with him on number four deck.

"Lucian," she shouted. "Lucian, may I speak to you a moment?"

Lucian stopped and turned towards her. He had often wondered why she had been appointed to officer level. After all, what did she contribute to the command and running of the ship? Very little in his estimation. Though she was, he supposed, a decent enough voice for the female members of the crew, not that it mattered all that much as men and women were treated almost the same on the discovery ships. She did have a certain physical grace and charm, handsome rather than beautiful, he thought, but other than that, no special qualities that he could discern. Strange that he had not really noticed her obvious physical attributes before. But now that he did, he began to wonder about the future of their relationship. Yes, he was interested to hear what she had to say.

"Unless you have come to offer to join me, Maikel, I suggest you dispense with the formality."

Such an abrupt opening caught her by surprise. Had things gone so far then? Was there no hope that he could be persuaded to change his course of action?

"Join you? I don't understand," she answered, nonplussed by his directness.

"I would have thought it was plain enough, even to a teacher. I have decided that it is time for a change. Our leader has clearly lost sight of the realities of our situation. We have no home of our own, therefore we must find another. Our almost limitless lifespans give us natural superiority over other life forms. And those of us with telepathic abilities can, if we are prepared to use them alongside our superior technology, direct and subject those life forms to our own ends quite easily. Result? We can lay claim to just about any planetary system that we want, and we can look forward to eventual victory over the Xavos and thus to our survival as the supreme race in the universe. Only that way lies eventual peace.

"Since the director cannot see that, it is up to me to ensure that this future comes to pass. But it will be easier if more of us commit to this cause. So, are you with me or not?"

"I... no, you see... I was not expecting... I thought to ask you to reconsider your decision, to give the director's plan a chance before..."

"The director's plan has no chance," he interrupted. "And I will not waste what could amount to many thousands of cycles waiting for verification of what I already know. There is no turning back, Maikel. Make your decision. Either come with me or return to your comfort zone. That is all."

Not convinced by his argument, Maikel nevertheless felt almost overwhelmed by the power of his conviction. She had thought her decision would be an easy one to make, but faced with this sudden onslaught, she became less sure of herself. What if Lucian was right? What if there was no other way? How would they defeat the Xavos with so few unless they were able to create strong allies? On the other hand, the thought of exerting that much control over younger races repelled her a little. What right did they have to do that? Who was the arbiter where that sort of power was involved? Would this not lead, eventually, to corruption, deceit and failure?

Then another thought occurred to her. If she were there, could she not help to ensure that the end did not become corrupted? Even without telepathic ability, surely, she could exert some influence over Lucian in an effort to prevent the worst excesses from happening during the development of the younger races. She could even, perhaps, offer alternatives to the less savoury events that might be about to come. She had not measured herself as a woman in a relationship with a man since her very early years. She well remembered the fumbling attempts at physical relationships, most of which ended in exasperation or laughter. Some, a few perhaps, she had found more fulfilling, but she had never thought to use her womanhood as a tool or weapon. But that, she realised, was probably the only way she might influence Lucian.

The atmosphere between them underwent a subtle change as they both seemed to become aware of the other's physical presence. This was something she had not anticipated. And yet, what had she hoped to achieve by going after him? Again, she considered the man beside her. Calmer now, despite her earlier misgivings, she realised that, whilst there may be several advantages in joining him, not the least of which would be to learn something of herself, she could not bring herself to disregard the director's arguments. That would be tantamount to betrayal. Tempted as she was by the sheer power of the man before her, nevertheless, she decided, she belonged at the director's side. Her mind now somewhat clearer, she observed Lucian closely.

"And what would be in this for me if I... offered my services?" she asked maintaining a coy exterior.

Lucian regarded the woman. Perhaps this rebellion could be a lot more enjoyable than he had at first thought. He too wondered what she had thought to achieve by chasing him. She was not, after all, his equal and could not hope to control him. On the other hand, there was more to life than making big decisions. Every leader needed a little diversion from time to time. But even without reading her mind, he could see from her face that she had decided to stay and that his fantasies were to remain just that.

"You know, Maikel, you could make somebody a great partner someday. A pity, because I'm sure I could have thought of some way to satisfy your needs," he said with a knowing air. "However, we will never know now if we had a future together, will we?"

With that he turned and walked away. This could actually work out very well indeed, he thought as he made his way towards the boat deck. Upon reaching his personal shuttle, he began his pre-flight checks and was so engrossed that he did not see the security guard approaching from his station against the wall.

"Excuse me, sir, but as you know, you are not allowed on this deck without authorisation from the director. I don't recall receiving an instruction allowing your departure. Would you mind halting what you are doing while I check?"

"No, of course not," replied Lucian, somewhat startled, despite his outward calm. "You go ahead, and I'll wait."

Later, he did not recall exactly when, or even why, he had made the decision. He just found that his personal phasegun was in his hand, and almost before he knew what was happening, he had pressed the trigger. The guard simply ceased to exist. All that was left was a pile of ash on the floor. The realisation of what he had done suddenly hit him. Frightened and angry now, he completed his pre-flight. Using his telepathic power, he depressed the switch in the security office that opened the boat deck outer doors and launched his boat, setting course for the planet below.

* * * * *

After the defence prefect's dismissal, the director released all telepathic restraints on his other officers.

"I apologise for that mental intervention, but I felt it was necessary. You all heard, and you must all make up your own minds regarding the wisdom or otherwise of the defence prefect's assertions. As I said to him, I shall not attempt to influence your decisions in any way. However, with a matter of this importance, I do feel that it would be inappropriate to continue the meeting until it is resolved. I therefore propose that you should all take whatever time you need to make up your own minds. I fear, however, that Lucian is lost to us. He will carve his own way from now on. Whilst that makes me sad, I cannot say that it is altogether unexpected. I need to consider who will be appointed defence prefect in his place. I will see you all later, but for now, dismissed."

The others filed out of the room and the director went to stand in front of the observation window. Once again, he marvelled at how clean and blue the planet below him looked. If only they could all stay this way, he thought, knowing full well that they so rarely did. Ultimately, the inhabitants would almost certainly find a way to poison the planet or blow it up. Sadly, he reflected upon his chances of saving this one from the fate of so many others, knowing that this was just one of a number of very important, and pressing, issues which he had to resolve.

He left the conference room and made his way down to the hydroponics deck, where the elements of food that the crew needed for survival were nurtured, using the recycled water that they harnessed. Though their physical need for sustenance was light, still the crew could not survive entirely without food and drink, and the director often liked to just watch the plants growing, to feel the life pulsing through their stems and roots, though he could discern little actual movement.

He had been studying the hydroponic operation for a while when the door opened behind him. Medical Doctor Gaveri walked in and stood beside him.

"I thought I might find you here," he said softly.

"Indeed, and how is that old friend?" the director inquired.

"I have noticed you studying the plants on a number of occasions when you have important matters to consider," he replied.

They both stared at the plants for a while until the director spoke again.

"Do you remember much of Eldor, Gaveri?" he asked.

"It has only been a mere two hundred or so cycles since we left. How could I forget in so little time?" he confirmed. "Eldor was a beautiful planet. Green and vibrant with natural life, both animal and vegetable. Even though I had little choice, my heart ached when I was told the day had arrived when I would need to leave it and join the discovery ships. I did not think then that I would never see it again."

"I miss it too, Gaveri," the director said gently. "Do you know what I did on Eldor before taking command of this ship? I was, amongst other things in my youth, a gardener, charged only with trying to keep my little part of the planet as green and colourful and healthy as I could. My telepathic ability was a bit limited when it comes to plant life, so I found it a suitable challenge and an end in itself. If I could help make things grow using only such skill and knowledge as I carried in my hands and my head, I considered that a suitable reward for a life's work.

"A simple seed, for example. You plant it in the ground. You water it, you feed it, you protect it from harm with your labours, and it rewards you by springing to life, sending its roots down into the soil and a green shoot upwards towards the light. Ah, but that is when another miracle begins to happen, for not content with simply reaching the light, the seed, which has now become a plant, is impelled to grow and grow and keep on growing for as long as it is able. Sometimes, from that one seed, a huge tree will emerge, its branches spreading everywhere, its foliage providing nourishment for itself and shelter for anything that might need it. Its roots spreading beneath the ground to gather more and different forms of nourishment and so it continues until it reaches its full capacity for growth. And during its lifetime, it produces yet more seeds so that it may reproduce endless copies of itself. A wonder, don't you think?"

"I do indeed, sir," answered Gaveri. "May I ask, did any of the telepaths manage to communicate fully with plant life?"

"Truly, I don't know," said the director. "Perhaps they could, though I doubt anyone paid the matter that much attention, but I don't suppose we will ever really know.

"Come, my friend, your time of deliberation is passing, and you have an important decision to make. You should seek what counsel you may."

"Oh, my mind is quite made up, Director. There was never really any doubt of the outcome."

The director regarded the other, knowing at once that his loyalty was complete and unequivocal. That had never wavered over the years, and he had not expected it to be in doubt now.

"Then accept my thanks and I will ask you to be careful not to try to influence the others. The only loyalty worth having, is that which is freely given."

"Don't worry, Director, I am sure you have the complete loyalty of the whole crew."

Chapter 3

"Is this the Bolg?" asked the man seated on the ornate throne.

"Yes, Majesty," answered the soldier. "Prepared for your interview as ordered."

The creature that had once been a highly respected engineer lay sprawled upon the polished marble floor, unable to move much without severe pain in all its limbs, its face almost unrecognisable now, covered in blood and bruises. Slowly, the head raised itself off the floor, turning to take in the magnificent surroundings in which the man found himself.

"It's not very big, is it," said the emperor.

"No, Majesty. None of his race are tall in stature, sire, but they fight like demons all the same."

"Yes, Hadrin. I am well aware of that. How a people so small have managed to stall our mighty armies for so long was a bit of a puzzle, though, don't you think?"

"With respect, Majesty, as you know, it is not only their fighting skills that make them such formidable opponents. It is their ability to construct defences — castles, redoubts, even ordinary palisade walls — that defy attempts to break them down, they are so well built. They also make better war engines than we do. Our most effective heavy weapons are those we have captured from them. And they always seem to be one step ahead of us."

The emperor was well aware of the tortured progress his armies had made against the Bolgs over many years, and of how long it had taken them to find an answer. And he was uncomfortably aware that they would not even have achieved their victories had it not been for the intervention of Ares, the name they had given to their god of war. He had to admit that he was in awe of the sheer power of the strange machine the god had first brought with him to the seemingly impregnable ramparts of the Bolg towns and cities. For two years they had laid siege to a border town named Pell without success. Its walls seemed to emerge from the very clifftop on which the city was situated, and it backed onto the ocean, flanked on one side by deadly jagged rocks and strong, swift ocean currents that produced enormous waves, constantly breaking upon the rocks, and on the other by a mountain that had proved impossible to climb. The Bolgs had chosen well. The only way to take the town had been by frontal assault. How many men had they lost in fruitless battering against those defences?

But then Ares had come. He remembered his father had told him of a nocturnal encounter with a creature who claimed to be one of the gods. He had put the tale down to a simple nightmare, until it happened to him in a similar fashion. Awakened by something, he had not known what, he saw a shimmering figure standing at the foot of his bed. Man shaped, but surrounded by a greenish luminescence, the figure announced itself and told him that his father had told the truth about his encounter and proceeded to prove it by putting him through the same ordeal. Like his father, Tyrson was still not entirely convinced that he was dealing with a god, but he was astute enough to recognise raw power when he saw it. And besides, the 'god' was willing to prove his claim and invited Tyrson to go with him to the walls of Pell to see for himself how victory could be delivered into his hands. The strange chariot driven by the god made no noise, nor did it require horses or, indeed, any visible means of propulsion. It did not even appear to touch the ground, but the speed at which it travelled defied belief. In but a few hours they had arrived at the front where the besieging army was encamped.

Tyrson smiled inwardly as he remembered the looks on the faces of his general, Alexis, and his other officers when they saw their emperor step down from the strange chariot, accompanied by a shining, man-shaped figure. When they had all entered the general's tent, he, Tyrson, turned to them and said, "Gentlemen, meet the god, Ares, who has come to us to crown our efforts with success."

The astonished looks turned to murmurings and scratching of heads as they looked first at him, then to one another. Then, quite unexpectedly, Ares had spoken in a loud and utterly compulsive voice.

"Bow down, mortals. None, save your emperor, who is beloved of the gods, shall stand in my presence!"

The effect had been immediate. Every man in the tent, except himself of course, knelt before this shining, compelling vision. Despite himself, Tyrson had been impressed. The sheer power and arrogance of the creature! With one line, Ares had established his divine influence on the Thorian army, and incidentally, reinforced his own hold on the throne of the Thorian empire. Any assassin would think twice before upsetting the gods!

Having briefed his officers, who prepared the besieging army for an all-out assault, he had again entered the strange chariot, which Ares had driven almost to the walls of the town. Using strange hand motions on the flat top in front of them, he produced, from the front of the chariot, an intense beam of light that travelled in a dead straight line aimed directly at the wall. The effect was devastating as the walls simply began to crumble, and yes, to melt into nothingness. What before had been an impregnable fortress now stood totally unprotected by its huge wall, which had simply gone, leaving a one-hundred-foot gap. The defenders who once stood upon the ramparts lay in grotesque death at the foot of the wall, through which the Thorian army now poured, seeking to kill every Bolg that they could find.

Ares himself had then done a strange thing. Almost as if he had been caught up in the heat of the moment, he had stepped down from the chariot and ran with the soldiers to the breach. Grabbing a sword from a dead Bolg, he had proceeded to hack and chop his way through the defending army in a frenzy of action, oblivious to anything, it seemed, but the killing. He ignored the small tears in his luminescent skin and the cuts he sustained from enemy soldiers until, at last, his energy seemed spent, and he returned to the chariot, a triumphant look on his face.

"Do you see, Tyrson?" he shouted. "Do you see what your armies are capable of given the right encouragement?"

The strange light seemed to go out of his eyes just then and he gradually became aware of the small injuries he had sustained. He let go of the sword he had still held in his hand and staggered slightly.

"Are you, all right?" Tyrson had enquired, sensing that all was not quite as it should be.

"Perfectly," the god had replied. "Now go and lead your army to victory and leave not a single Bolg alive. We need to plan our next assault and we do not need enemies at our backs."

And so, he had gone, leading his soldiers, sacking the town, sparing none of the inhabitants. Yet, there was the strange thing. They found plenty of soldiers, of course, most of whom sold their lives dearly, but there were nowhere near the numbers of civilians they had expected to find, nor were they able to capture any members of the ruling households of the Bolg town. As the reports came in, so they began to realise that their quarry was not here. So where were they? He had looked to the god, then, and seen an unusual look on his face.

"You said you could deliver the Bolgs to me, but without their leaders, I have nothing," Tyrson said accusingly to the god.

He would never forget his reply.

"My, my, how small-minded you creatures are. The reason you do not have them is because they have escaped. Quite some time ago, actually"

"But how, and where to?"

"Didn't you know? They do not only travel by land, but by sea. They build ships, you know. Big ones. Some will undoubtedly now go from this land and build themselves a new home across the sea, but for now they are of no further threat to you. As for what I have delivered to you. Tell your men to be careful who they kill. You will need all the engineers you can get, because you are going to build ships, too, with their help. And with them, you are going to conquer the world. THAT is what I have given you this day."

Tyrson allowed the events of the last few hours to sink in, and at last, he began to believe that, just maybe, the Thorian empire would encompass a world he had not even dreamed existed. And he, Emperor Tyrson the First, was going to build that empire.

The next few months saw victory after victory and as more Bolgish engineers were captured and either persuaded or tortured into helping them, so their weapons improved and so the art of warfare seemed easier and easier. As for the god and his chariot, he used it in one or two more sieges, but seemed more and more interested only in killing, a kind of madness seeming to take control of him whenever he entered a battle. He had taken to wielding a personal weapon similar to the light emitter on the chariot, only on a smaller scale. With it, he was always in the vanguard dealing death and destruction to all his enemies. He did, however, teach his generals more about strategies and tactics that proved superior to anything they had previously tried.

Gradually, however, the god appeared less and less often. This was not too big a problem as Tyrson offered sacrifice and prayers in the temple he had built to Ares who, in his physical absence, nevertheless spoke to him through shadows and dream-like encounters, always pushing him on to the next battle, or advising him how to make use of the latest bit of information given by the Bolgish engineers. He himself took to leading his armies and so became the focus of his soldiers' loyalty and adoration. Still, he thought it strange that the god did not appear. Soon, the Bolg nation would cease to exist. But what then, he wondered? Where would the god Ares have led them?

And then, Ares had stopped talking to him altogether. At first this scared him a little. After all, the morale boost given by divine approval was almost inestimable, whereas without it? All right, he thought, perhaps you have gone altogether, but my armies don't need to know that. Where he could not be himself, he could send one of his priests of Ares to inspire his armies with messages and exhortations from the god himself. As some of those priests, were in fact, convinced that the god did speak to them, that made it all the easier to convince simple soldiers that their god led them into battle and that they could not lose. And so, the victories continued.

His mind returned to the present and he regarded the pathetic figure on the floor in front of him.

"What kind of an engineer are you?" he demanded, leaning close to the Bolg.

All resistance gone from the man, he whispered, "I am a shipbuilder."

* * * * *

The gentle knock on the director's door was expected.

"Come in," he ordered, as the door opened admitting his trusted friend and colleague, Gaveri.

"Welcome, my friend. What news do you have for me? Has there been any improvement in his condition?"

Gaveri pulled a grimace as he seated himself in the soft chair in front of the director.

"I'm afraid that is not a simple question to answer, Director. His physical condition has stabilised, although he will never again be fully mobile. The sheer strength and speed of the bacterial and fungal invasion that his body suffered when his enviro-protective was pierced has put full repair beyond even my reach. It is what we have suspected all along that our virtual elimination of infection and serious disease back home, many thousands of cycles ago now, although it gave enormous longevity, also made Eldorans dangerously susceptible to alien infection. Essentially, we are cut off from direct contact with alien races without suitable protection.

"In Lucian's case, because he did not seek treatment for his minor injuries right away, a severe form of sepsis began quickly and virtually took over, invading most parts of his body, reducing him to the physical wreck we have now. The only thing to have escaped impairment, it would seem, is his telepathic ability. If only that could give him the power of self-regeneration, there might be some hope. I do not know if such a thing is even possible," Gaveri finished sadly shaking his head from side to side.

"I do not know its limits either, Gaveri. I know only that Lucian's abilities fall far short of biological regeneration, especially when he is being attacked by totally alien bacterial species. Let's face it, we have not even needed to consider the question until now. Our medical knowledge and the skills contained within the hands of doctors such as yourself have been sufficient to ensure their continued health and well-being. The question of alien infection is still relatively new to us. To develop such telepathic powers might take generations, if indeed it can be developed at all, but in the meantime the enviro-protective is the only protection we have. "He is still in isolation, I presume?"

"Yes, of course. I dare not expose any other members of the crew to possible infection. His body has undergone a physical change which may not be reversible. I am not sure exactly how this will affect his lifespan, only that it will shorten it considerably.

"There is one other thing, Director. Though his telepathic power is intact, his mind has been changed along with his body. To call it a madness would be too strong, and too narrow, a definition. He has become fixated on war, death and destruction, not as a means to an end, but as an end in itself. I have tried various psychological techniques on him, but all they show me is that he is perfectly lucid and coherent in all respects, except for this utter and complete conviction. The continual fermenting and nurturing of war for its own sake is his entire reason for being. It consumes him to the exclusion of all else."

"Is there absolutely nothing you can do?" asked the director sadly.

"Nothing. It is as if we, Eldor, everything he once knew, have ceased to exist for him. He sees only the world below us. And he has an obsession to rule it," answered Gaveri, wishing that it could be other than that, but equally sure of his prognosis.

The director only looked at his friend, a deep but unwilling acceptance of the reality gradually settling on his mind.

"Has all other evidence of contamination been removed from the planet?" he asked suddenly.

"Yes, Director. The rescue crew saw to the recovery of Lucian's personal sled, and they could find no artifacts other than those carried in the vehicle as standard, all except his hand phasegun. Fortunately, the crash site was a long way from any human habitation, so they are quite confident they were not seen, and they are continuing to search for the weapon. As far as the Thorians are concerned, their 'god of war' has simply gone to his home, wherever that is, and will reappear as and when he chooses."

"Unfortunately, in the meantime," said the director, "a great deal of harm has been done and unnecessary bloodshed inflicted on a harmless but extremely talented race of people. The Bolgs are so good at what they do, and the borders of their lands were so well chosen, that they could have held the Thorians up for many more cycles yet before they would eventually have to surrender their lands to the invaders. During that time, it is conceivable that they could have made good their escape from destruction in their ships. Incidentally, how were these vessels missed in the original surveys? Had their existence been known, it could have altered many things."

"Apparently, they were not missed, Director," answered Gaveri as a new hardness entered his manner. "They were 'omitted' from the report, delivered by Lucian."

"Omitted? By whom?" asked the other.

"By Lucian himself," said Gaveri. "This only came to light when we were investigating his personal files looking for clues as to how we might heal him. We came across a previous version of the report showing that the Bolgs were far superior to the Thorians in engineering, shipbuilding and technology in general, despite the fact that the Thorians were the more aggressive race, thus bringing doubt to the theory that only ardent militarism could produce technological advance. We presume Lucian decided to hide this evidence because it undermined his argument in favour of supporting the Thorians."

The director was clearly surprised at this revelation of Lucian's betrayal of his trust as, until now, he had never had cause to doubt the integrity of every single member of his crew, especially his high-ranking officers. Of course, he had realised Lucian had decided to go his own way as a result of their disagreement, but he had presumed that was an honest manifestation of Lucian's conviction. Now he knew that subterfuge had been employed, it threw a new light on everything. And that was before he even considered the question of the missing, presumed killed, guard on the boat deck. Were there signs? If so, how could he have missed them? Perhaps he had been concentrating so hard on solving the bigger problems that he had failed to notice the change in attitude on the part of his defence prefect. Was there something in Lucian's make up that he had failed to see when selecting him for this mission? He did not think so. After all, despite Lucian's efforts to hide his telepathic ability, the director had still been aware of it. Yet, he had not taken him for a murderer.

Well, it was too late for speculation now, it would seem. The immediate question was what to do about the situation Lucian had created on the planet and how did it affect his own plans. He turned once more to his friend.

"Are you absolutely sure there is nothing more that can be done to recover his mind?"

"Yes, Director, I am," Gaveri answered. "I have exhausted the limits of my knowledge and skill and beyond. He is lost to us, and I fear, cannot survive for much longer.

"And the phasegun must be found. He may have disguised it and thrown it away, or he may simply have lost it. Either way, it must be found. The consequences, should it get into the wrong hands, could be disastrous."

"I cannot ignore his betrayal," began the director after a while. "Nor can I ignore the nagging conviction that he had something to do with the disappearance of Gareth, the boat deck security officer. Yet I cannot bring myself to condemn him completely for what he has done. I will give the matter some further thought, Gaveri. Kindly give me some time to myself and I will inform you of my decision."

"Of course, Director," whispered the other, realising that the look he saw on the director's face was not just sadness, but real pain.

Gaveri rose from his seat and left the room. As the door slid quietly closed behind him, he wondered what would now become of his charge. The decision, he knew, was out of his hands.

The director sat for a moment, wondering whether to wander down to the hydroponics deck to seek — what? — inspiration perhaps? As the full implications of what had happened began to take shape in his mind, the enormity of the many faceted problem became clear. Lucian needed to be punished for his crimes. To execute him was out of the question, yet he was already doomed to die. So, what punishment would be suitable? He had promoted the existence of state sponsored religion, as opposed to a spontaneously growing one. Unwittingly perhaps, but nevertheless it was so. That this religion existed in an aggressive and barbaric race like the Thorians was bad enough in itself, but he had openly declared himself to be the god of war. This meant that their rulers, politicians, merchant houses, military leaders and everybody who claimed to be part of the ruling body of that nation, now had the support of a church and a priesthood, dedicated to the pursuance and ends of war. No matter that their 'god' was not there to guide them in person — they could simply invent whatever 'messages' promoted their own ends. The potential for corruption, destruction and death was almost overwhelming.

On top of this, Lucian had shown them weapons from their distant future, had given them knowledge in a few centicycles that should, perhaps, have taken them many cycles to attain and had added to the catastrophe by forcing them to capture engineers and scientists from a conquered race who would undoubtedly improve and strengthen their own technology — specifically in shipbuilding — in leaps and bounds.

That this would accelerate, and make almost certain, the Thorians' conquest of other parts of this world could not be doubted. But was this a good thing, or just another inevitability? And how did that affect his own carefully laid plan for the planet's future? Did it mean abandoning his efforts here and moving on to another planet where he might, perhaps, be able to start again?

He realised, of course, that he had the power, both in technology and in his own mental capabilities, to change completely almost everything that was currently taking place on the planet. But what, he considered, would that achieve? He could not turn back time, and anyway, the thought of wholesale direct intervention, the virtual enslavement of the people on the planet, appalled him utterly. Though his plan involved a minor intervention, he was prepared to accept its uncertainties because the very foundation of the plan was to leave the planet's inhabitants to make their own choices. The thought of taking away their free will was abhorrent to him in every way. But the need to contrive a more peaceful way of solving everyone's problems was equally pressing.

No. The experiment must go ahead. Too much rested on it. Besides, they were here and had already interfered. That could not be changed. But could that interference be turned to his advantage? As the director pursued that line of thought, a plan began to take shape. There just might be a way to limit the damage done so far and solve a number of problems at the same time. He moved to his work surface and picked up his tablet, pressing a communication button.

"Engineer Saecra? Could you spare me a little of your time? I have a problem which I would like you to help me solve."

* * * * *

Lucian was walking through a never-ending mist. Vague shadows moved in and out of his peripheral vision, sometimes threatening, sometimes merely curious it seemed. He kept looking straight ahead where a strange bright but blurred vision, like a burning blade suspended in the sky, was beckoning him on and he knew it was really important to touch the blade. But every time he got close and reached out, it seemed to move further away from him. Images of faces that he vaguely remembered floated into and out of view, some would speak soft words to him, others seemed to accuse him of something, though he could not think what it was. Then he was running, the shining blade in his hand, towards an unseen enemy, suddenly revealed in their thousands. He shouted, 'Come with me Tyrson, this is your future,' though he did not know who Tyrson might be, only that it was important to kill as many of the enemy as possible, so he ran on, swinging the blade wildly left and right, each swing severing a head or a limb. He exulted as more and more blood flowed all around him, into him, through him, drowning him, down and down until …

He sat up with a start, sweat pouring from his face and body. It was the same dream he had had countless times. Looking around him, he realised he was unfamiliar with his surroundings. He was in a bright, warm room much larger than his own… somewhere … The room was comfortably furnished without being opulent. Hardly good enough for a god, he thought. Puzzled, now, he rose from the bed on which he had been lying and nearly sat down again as the vertigo struck him. Looking round, he noticed a white robe draped over a bench seat near one wall. For the first time, he realised he was completely naked, so he moved to the bench, picked up the robe and put it on, at once feeling its softness surround him. So much for creature comforts, he thought, but where is everybody? He stopped then, realising that he wasn't exactly sure who 'everybody' was. The thought made him stop and sit on the bench, his eyes firmly on the floor, trying to remember…

He didn't remember anybody entering the room — he had not noticed a door anyway — and yet there stood the imposing figure of a man, undoubtedly of middle to advancing years, tall and erect, clean shaven and dressed in a floor length white robe similar to his own. The face was very difficult to read, at once stern and yet gentle, a smile played on his lips, yet there was a sadness there too. The man spoke.

"Hello, Lucian. How do you feel?"

"Lucian? That is not my name. I am… Ares. Who are you and where is Tyrson and my soldiers?" he asked in increasing confusion.

"They are gone, Lucian," the man replied gently. "Though you may find you can still speak to Tyrson from time to time."

The man paused before continuing, "As for who I am? I am the director, your ultimate superior."

Lucian considered this reply but could make no sense of it. "You are mistaken, old man, I have no superior. I am the most powerful person in the world, and I will rule it all. Where did you come from anyway?"

The director studied the broken man in front of him, remembering how he and Gaveri had tried to penetrate and sort out the jumbled mess of this man's mind, and decided to try once more.

"What do you recall of Eldor?" he asked.

"I know no one of that name," replied Lucian firmly, though he thought he should know the name for some reason. "I know that my armies are superior to anything they have encountered, and we will be victorious."

The director sighed as he realised that Gaveri had been right. Not only was Lucian's body poisoned beyond hope, but his mind was completely gone as well. Worse, they had realised that the bacterial infections that had invaded him thrived and mutated easily in the atmosphere aboard their ship, so Lucian could no longer stay there. They had had to return him to the planet where the sepsis that was killing him would, at least, work more slowly, extending his life by a little more at least. Fortunately, Saecra's skills had allowed them to build this hideaway, which also served as a prison, where all the necessities for sustaining Lucian's life were provided and where the atmosphere of the planet could be purified, allowing in only minimal amounts of the lethal bacteria. Situated in the cold, uninhabited northern region of the continent, there was little if any chance of the prison's discovery by any of the sentient peoples. And even if they did explore the region eventually, the prison had been effectively hidden deep within a mountain cave, the entrance to which had been blocked.

"Lucian, listen to me," the director told him. "It would be useless to point out to you the crimes of which you are guilty since you cannot remember them or their significance. Nevertheless, I cannot allow them to go unpunished. Neither can I allow you to attempt to influence other members of the crew. I have decided, therefore, that you shall spend the rest of your days here, away from everyone else, but where no one can harm you. I am sad that it has come to this, but I see no viable alternative. This is the last time we will speak, Lucian. Events have been set in motion whose outcome we can only predict in general terms. I cannot allow you to influence, and therefore jeopardise, those events any further.

Goodbye my friend."

With that, the old man began to fade from view, becoming at first translucent, then barely visible before disappearing altogether. Lucian did not understand what was happening. What 'crimes' had the man referred to? Punishment? What events did he speak of? Perplexed, he rose and began to pace up and down the length of the room. Try as he might, he could not relate to anything the old man had said.

He was Ares, god of the... Thorians...! he realised, with sudden delight at the revelation of this new piece of information. Now there was someone he needed to speak to, but he could not, for the moment, remember who. Perhaps, if he put his mind to it...

* * * * *

Emperor Tyrson stopped in mid-sentence, taking General Alexis and the other gathered officers completely by surprise.

"Majesty, are you, all right?" the general enquired. "You seem distracted, sire."

For a moment he received no reply, and he became increasingly concerned as the silence lengthened. Emperor Tyrson, on the other hand, slowly began to smile and nod his head, gradually becoming more and more agitated until, at last, he simply burst out laughing and threw his hands in the air.

"Fornius, send for the surgeons. The emperor is ill," ordered the general.

"No!" came the cry from the emperor. "I am not ill, Alexis. In fact, I have never felt better. I have just spoken with the god Ares."

Momentarily stunned, the general hesitated before voicing his next question.

"May we enquire what he said, Majesty?"

"Oh yes, you may," answered the emperor. "He said that little Bolg shipbuilder we captured is going to deliver us a stunning victory and that I am going to rule the world."

"Of course, sire," said the general indulgently. "But we have first to reduce the Bolgish nation, surely..."

"Ships!" interrupted the emperor. "We are going to build enormous ships and sail across the great oceans where there are other lands just waiting to be taken. The Bolgs are nearly finished, anyway and we can just about afford the extra manpower for a fresh invasion army. All we need are the ships. Send the Bolg to me — and this time, I want him treated, kindlier. A man cooperates better on a full stomach and with full health than straight after a beating."

"Yes, Majesty," answered the general, but he could not prevent the doubt that he felt from creeping into his voice.

Turning to his officers he issued the orders that would immediately change the actions of the Thorian armies, and the course of a nation.

* * * * *

It was a mere three cycles later that Adrian, the officer the director had appointed to be the new defence prefect, knocked on his commander's door.

"Come," the voice said from within the room as the door slid open.

Entering the room, Adrian was struck once again with the simplicity and sparseness of the furnishings. The director did not go in for obvious opulence or unnecessary decoration, preferring instead simple lines and soft delicate colours on all that surrounded him. Table, chairs, couch and low table were all that the director seemed to need. Forcing his attention back to the matter in hand, he cleared his throat nervously.

"Director," he began, "I am sorry to trouble you at this time, but I have some news which I thought you should know right away."

"What is it, Adrian?" said the director softly. "You seem a bit agitated and that cannot be good."

"Sir, it's the Thorian fleet — the one we have assumed they were going to use to outflank the Bolgish defences."

"What about it?" the director enquired.

"It has landed on another continent, sir. About three millicycles ago as far as we can determine, and the army has already disembarked. No opposition has been sent to stop them, or to see what is going on. Sir, they look set to overrun the indigenous population with little or no effort at all."

For a moment, the room was absolutely still. Nothing and no one moved and there was no sound. Adrian thought that the director might explode at the news of this catastrophe. Instead, he was shocked when the director replied in a perfectly even voice.

"How did we miss this, Adrian?" he asked. "Are our scanners not working? Have you been sending scouts to the planet?"

"The scanners are fine, Director, and scouts go out at regular intervals, though I limit these incursions to night-time only. It lessens the chance of discovery. I'm afraid the failure is mine, sir. Having been instructed to monitor them, I was simply looking in the wrong places and I have misread the signs that I did pick up. I am so sorry, Director."

He was not sure exactly what kind of reaction he had expected on delivering his news, but he was surprised at the apparent calmness with which the director seemed to take it in. At last, he broke the silence.

"Be sorry that we overlooked this important event, by all means, Adrian, but do not feel sorry that it has happened. If anything, the fault there lies with me, for I see the hand of Lucian in this, and it is I who have allowed him to live on the planet's surface with his telepathic power intact. Do not forget that the Thorians have free will as well — notwithstanding that they are currently being directed somewhat — but we will not take that away from them, no matter what the cost. Nor will I add to the misery of Lucian in his imprisonment, because, in the end, he can only watch while others achieve what he himself desired."

"But your project, Director," protested the other. "Surely, this throws severe doubt on whether it can succeed, especially since Lucian knows at least the outline of the plan."

"It certainly alters the conditions somewhat, but we are close now to locating a suitable subject host and I am determined to see it through, Thorians or no Thorians."

"Yes, Director," said the prefect. "What are your instructions now, sir?"

After some time, the director looked straight at his defence prefect.

"The Bolgs already made the journey to one of the other continents, did they not?"

"Yes, sir. The royal family, one or two of the ruling houses and a few thousand others have settled the lands to the north of the same continent, but from the eastern shore. They have been migrating there over many cycles now and have established a whole new nation in that time."

"And how long, do we estimate, would it take the Thorians to tackle this Bolgish nation?"

"If they ever do, sir, it will take their army a good one or two cycles to even reach the Bolgs. The wide mountain range running roughly north to south, effectively separating the Western side of the continent from the eastern, is a formidable barrier to mass movement and the Bolgs have already build outer defensive positions within the mountains. With their skills and the unforgiving terrain, any army, no matter how well equipped at their current level, would find it nearly impossible to invade from that direction."

"But what about smaller groups, up to, say, ten people? Could they make the crossing if they had to?" asked the director carefully.

"There are passes through the mountains, of course," said Adrian, "but it would be all too easy to become lost and trapped in such terrain without a guide, especially for a small group who could not carry enough supplies to sustain themselves for that journey."

"And the Bolgs. What are their chances of preventing an invasion of their new land from the sea?"

"Though we cannot be certain, Director, we do not see that as a realistic proposition for at least another ten to twenty cycles. Even the Thorians have limits to their resources and it has already taken a great toll just to build this one fleet. Their invasion of the western shore caught us by surprise, I will admit, but they now have barely sufficient resources of every kind to both sustain the invasion and hold their positions on their home continent. This will change given time, of course, but that is the situation now. Their progress will be relatively slow on all fronts."

"Good," said the director. "Then we must let time be our friend, and make it work in our favour. Adrian, I want you to concentrate on finding a route through those mountains for a small group of people — say only three or maybe four. If a guide can be found, so much the better. The trail must be marked clearly, but once it has been used, it must be effectively hidden until we need it again. You have little more than a cycle to complete this mission. Can you, do it?"

"I will, sir," Adrian replied. "Even if I have to guide them myself."

"Then let us hope that, in the meantime, the Thorians do not slaughter every man, woman and child that they find."

Chapter 4

Marin hummed gently to herself as she pulled at the rope, gradually lifting the, now full, pail towards the top of the well. She did not consider herself particularly pretty or, for that matter, well-endowed physically, but she was happy in the knowledge that her husband to be, Jespeth, was a kind and gentle person, good at his job making and fixing almost any wooden object that the villagers might require. In fact, he had even designed and made one or two interesting and useful items — like the pulley wheel on the well — that made life a little bit easier for people, especially the women!

As she walked back to her parents' cottage, she thought about her life here in Wilet, humble though it was, even humdrum at times, but she was content to be surrounded by friends and family who clearly loved her as she loved them. They were quite lucky, she supposed, in that the Thorian occupation had not affected them very much, apart from the occasional appearance of an army patrol en route to somewhere or other, and the regular appearances of the tax collectors, always accompanied by soldiers. But it was a million miles away from the life she imagined her great, great, great forebears might have led. After all, she was descended from kings and queens who must have lived opulent lives in great palaces and cities, like the capital, Tevalem, surrounded by servants and beautiful things, worshipping The One in posh marble temples, unlike the simple, one-room building in her village. Sometimes she liked to speculate and imagine what that must have been like. Most people from families like hers — simple but devout followers of The One — would, at some time in their lives, make the pilgrimage to Tevalem to pray and make sacrifice at the great temple which was supposed to have been built on the site where Abrin, the father of the Juhl race, had been ready to sacrifice his son, Ishtal, to The One. Their history had it that The One had ordered Abrin to stop just before the act was completed, satisfied that the man was indeed faithful, and thereafter, God 'blessed the fruit of his loins' in abundance. In gratitude, the devout were required to sacrifice regularly at their local shrine or temple, and at least once in their lives, to make the pilgrimage. It would be nice, she thought, to see how the other half lived and worshipped just once.

Of course, the grandeur was all in the past now, her people shackled by ruthless occupation by a foreign power, the hated rule of a puppet king from a neighbouring tribe who had been brought in to oversee purely domestic matters. Prevented from determining their own future by the strict rule of imposed martial law, they were forced to simply husband their lands, moving on if it became necessary, becoming a semi-nomadic people where tradition and its maintenance became an end in itself. Even Tevalem, so she heard, was no longer the great city it had once been. The rulers and priests of the temple too stuck in their ways to consider bringing about any change or to foment any hint of rebellion. They had obviously struck up some kind of understanding with the Thorian governor, and the puppet king. They allowed the priests to continue worshipping The One, and accepting the sacrifices from their people, in exchange for their guarantee to keep the population under control.

But there was discontent, she knew, amongst the young, and she heard, a number of organised resistance groups had been formed who achieved very little except to be a constant thorn in the side of the occupying forces. She and her friends had often discussed the possibilities of breaking away from tradition, of putting their minds to the invention of new and wonderful things, of righting the wrongs that were sometimes done to them by the Thorians and others, even by their own rulers, of using once again the weapons of warfare that their parents seemed to have forgotten, to protect themselves. They often discussed the coming of the great leader, promised by prophets now long dead. The stories and prophecies had been told and repeated so many times that it was easy to imagine that they were just another part of their folklore. And yet, something kept the hope alive, especially amongst the young, that the leader might come. Well, she thought, there could surely be no better time than now. What would life be like without the yoke of Thorian rule, she wondered.

She rounded the corner and entered the short street on which she and her parents lived, waving hello to her neighbours and smiling as she went.

As she entered the cottage, she was assailed by the pleasant smells of cooking coming from her mother's kitchen. She carried the pail through the dividing curtain as her mother turned to greet her.

"Thank you, Marin dear, just drop it by the wall there won't you?" she told her happily. "Your father is still out in the field, and I don't suppose he'll be home for a while yet. Perhaps you would like to help me prepare the evening meal?"

"Yes, of course, Mother," said Marin jauntily. "I saw Sara and Tirsa at the well today and we were discussing what colours they should wear for the wedding."

"That's nice dear," said her mother, clearly not really listening. "Could you pass me that pan on the shelf, please?"

As Marin pulled the indicated object from its hook, the body just dropped from the handle and clattered onto the wooden floor, rolling under the table. Marin was left holding only the wooden handle.

Her cry caught her mother by surprise.

"Oh, Mother, I'm so sorry," she cried. "I don't know what happened there."

She bent to pick up the now handle-less pan and put it on the table.

"Oh, that dratted handle," her mother cried. "It's been loose for months. It's not your fault, dear. Perhaps you could ask Jespeth to fix it for me? He's coming here this evening, isn't he?"

"Yes, Mother," answered her daughter. "I'll ask him."

"Thank you, dear," said her mother. "Now go and see to your brother and sisters while I carry on here."

The evening meal was eaten in comparative silence as usual after thanks had been offered up by Marin's father. Another ritual, she thought, that only seems to occur because tradition demands it. Afterwards, when Jespeth called at the cottage, Marin mentioned the pan to him, and he took a look at the pieces he was offered.

"I'll see if I can't make a stronger joint to hold the handle," he offered.

"Better still," offered Marin's brother, Andrew, "why don't you take the pan to the smith and get him to melt it down and remake it into a sword. Then at least it could be put to proper use by killing a few Thorians."

"That's enough, Andrew," said his father sternly. "You know very well where that sort of talk will get you, so hold your tongue, unless you want some Thorian to come along and cut it from your head."

"But Papa," Andrew began, "I'm only saying what we all feel. They've been here for four years now and it's time these…"

"I said enough!" exploded his father. "Now listen to me, all of you. I will not allow any of you to bring trouble with the Thorians to this house. Let others play revolution if they want. Our only job is to survive until they leave. We get through this the best way we can."

"The messiah will come, Papa…" began Andrew again.

"Not in my lifetime, he won't," answered his father. "It's all nonsense, the crazy ravings of madmen and hermits who spent too long under the desert sun, that's all your precious messiah is — a myth. Now sit down and eat or go to bed. I care not which, but I will have no more of this, messiah talk."

The meal continued in an awkward, embarrassed silence until Marin's mother tried to settle things down.

"Well, just so long as I can use it without it falling apart in my hand will be fine. Thank you Jespeth," she said

"You are most welcome maam," he replied.

"Mother," said Marin. "Jespeth and I are just going to sit outside and enjoy the evening air."

"Don't be too long," she replied. "You know how chilly it can get."

Both youngsters realised what she really meant. It made no difference as they exchanged knowing glances and smiled at each other. Outside, they sat together on the wooden bench that Jespeth had made for the family long ago, not speaking, just content to hold hands and be with each other. Jespeth looked up and stared in wonder at the ink blue sky dotted with uncountable lights.

"Your father really had a go at Andrew didn't he," he said mildly.

"Father is frightened, just like everyone else and Andrew is too hot-headed for his own good sometimes," she answered him. "Please don't be like him, Jespeth."

"Who, Andrew or your father?" he quipped.

"I'm serious, Jespeth," she came back. "I don't like what the Thorians do to our people either, and I do believe that a messiah will come, but somehow, I just feel that Andrew's approach to the problem is wrong. I don't know. On the one hand, I cannot believe that The One would just let us suffer like this interminably, but on the other short of killing every Thorian in the world, I do not see how He can save us. Like papa, I am frightened. I just think it's all too… big… for the likes of us. Please don't be tempted to get involved Jespeth."

"I won't, don't worry," he reassured her, "I'm just a simple carpenter, trying to make a living. As long as the Thorians stay away from me, I'm happy to stay away from them."

The night grew cooler, and the only sound was of the insects who inhabited its dark domain. The pair remained still and quiet.

"Have you ever wondered what the stars really are?" he asked her suddenly. "I mean, did The One just put them up there so that we could enjoy evenings such as this, or are they something we could not imagine?"

"Like what?" Marin answered.

"Oh, I don't know," he came back. "It's just that, well look at it, Marin, I mean, it looks so BIG from here, as if the sky goes on forever."

"Why Jespeth," she said with a grin. "You're not just a dull wood carver, after all. You have a romantic soul."

"What?" he cried, "who said I was dull? Now look, I didn't mean… I was just speculating… you know… I wouldn't."

Marin let him splutter on for a while before she stopped him with a gentle finger on his lips.

"I was just teasing, silly. I don't think you are dull at all — as a matter of fact I think you are quite bright — for a simple carpenter, that is — and…"

"Oh, that's not fair," he cried. "I don't know, sometimes, what the people of this village would do without my skills to help them out of trouble. And anyway, what's wrong with asking questions about things outside of our experience?"

"Nothing," she said, "nothing at all. In fact, it's one of the things that makes me love you so much."

"Oh," was all he said, not quite knowing how to handle such a direct declaration. "Well, I love you too, Marin. Actually," he began, summoning a courage he had not known he had, "I love you so much that nothing else really matters to me. Only that I can marry you and be with you for the rest of our lives."

"Well," Marin replied. "We had better discuss the practicalities of that, then, hadn't we?"

They talked on, clearly comfortable in each other's company, until at last they heard her mother call and knew that the meeting was over.

"I'd better go," said Jespeth. "I'll see you tomorrow, my love. Tell your mother I'll get her pan back to her as soon as I can."

With that, Jespeth made his way through the small garden and out onto the street, whistling tunelessly as he went. What a lucky man I am, he thought.

Watching him go, Marin waited until she could no longer hear his whistling and turned to go inside. As she did so, a slight movement in the shadows under a tree caught her eye. She stared into the darkness, trying to make out what it might be. Slowly, the shadow moved, and as she looked, it took the shape of a man — no, a woman — but dressed as she had never seen anyone clad before. Instead of the floor-length robes or loin cloths she was accustomed to seeing on everyone, man and woman, this woman's shape could be clearly seen, almost as if she were naked. Only the fact that her covering was as dark as night convinced her that the woman was indeed dressed — but in what?

Her curiosity turned to fear within seconds, and she opened her mouth to shout to her parents for help but did not quite manage that before the figure spoke.

"Marin, do not be afraid, I am not here to hurt you. In fact, I am sent to give you great and exciting news."

Something in the gentle quality of the woman's voice held Marin spellbound for long enough to prevent her calling out. Still shaken, she asked tremulously, "Who are you? What do you want with me?"

"Ah, that is not easy to explain," said Maikel. "But I will try."

* * * * *

Marin could not seem to take it all in. She could just about accept that the woman facing her was, indeed, a messenger from The One, but that did not help when she considered the enormity of the message. Maikel had said that she, Marin, had been chosen from amongst all the women of her race and that, somehow, she was to give birth to a child who would become the long-awaited leader, the messiah and redeemer, of her people. Her brother would, in one way, be delighted at the news, she realised, but her father would be horrified. Come on Marin, she told herself, this is no time for idle speculation of that sort. This woman was clearly serious, and Marin had to face up to that fact. Desperate to give herself time to think, she spoke as soon as the thought came into her head.

"But I have not laid with my husband to be, nor will I, until we are married, and I have no intention of going with any other man. So how can I get with child, and furthermore, why? Jespeth and I are just ordinary people. Ordinary people don't produce great leaders!"

"Good questions," said Maikel. "And I will answer you directly. The One God has promised your people a redeemer for many years. His prophets have borne witness to that. The Chosen shall be no ordinary man, however. God intends to send his own son. But the child will need a mother and a surrogate father so that he may grow as any other man, eventually to lead his people to a state of freedom and enlightenment such as your world has never known. You have been chosen to be his mother."

"But I still do not understand," said Marin. "To do as you ask would involve both Jespeth and myself becoming outcasts from our own community. No one would ever believe that I have not been unfaithful to him if I become pregnant before we are married."

"It is true that some in this community may condemn you for what they see as unacceptable behaviour. Unfortunately, this cannot be avoided. That your reputation is presently unimpeachable, as is that of Jespeth, is an important aspect of this situation. People must be able to accept, from the outset, that your child is begotten of the One God and not created by man. He is, in every respect, to be the Son of God. The actual circumstances of his birth will be seen as further proof of this.

"You will both have to leave this place, of course, but you will have time to plan your journey and you will know that God will always look after your welfare.

"Much that I cannot tell you rests on the outcome of this event, and you may, perhaps, never know the full importance of what is being asked of you. However, I can tell you this. The One does not demand anything of you. He asks that you be the mother of his son, with all the pain and uncertainty that might entail. I can tell you of the importance of this child, but only you can decide if he will be born. Do you believe in God, Marin?"

"Yes," she answered without hesitating. "But I am very frightened by what he asks of me. You said I have been chosen, which means there is no other suitable woman, right?"

"That is correct," said Maikel.

Marin paused to let what she had just heard sink in. Her mind screamed at her, told her that none of this could really be happening. This could all be just some joke, surely. It was true that she had secretly longed for some sort of change to what she saw as life in a somewhat hidebound society, lived under the occupation of a foreign army working for a foreign ruler, but she had never imagined she might actually be involved. And what of Jespeth? If this was real, then the decision she made here and now would directly affect him and his future. Could she commit him to this level of uncertainty? Would he even support her when, perhaps, all others including her friends and family, might desert her? Her mind became a jumble of conflicting questions and suppositions and she sat down on the bench to try to sort out the mess. At the end, though, it seemed to boil down to one thing; did she have faith and was it strong enough?

Again, the fear of the unknown, the knowledge of the enormity of what was being asked of her rose to the surface. She had been chosen to do the bidding of her God but was, herself, free to choose whether to obey or not. The decision was indeed hers to make then, or was it? What if this was some sort of elaborate but vicious trick to make her be unfaithful to Jespeth? But again, she asked herself, who would do such a thing and why? No answer came to her mind. She looked at the woman standing before her, her mind still in a turmoil.

"Who are you?" she asked again.

"I am Maikel and I serve the One God," answered the other. "I wish that I could allay your fears, Marin, but I cannot. It is of concern to me that so much is being asked of you and you are given so little time in which to decide. Truthfully, I do not know what purpose your pain and sacrifice will serve. But like you, I believe in Him, and it is He who asks this of you."

And it was this that finally helped her make up her mind. The guileless honesty of this woman could not be doubted. She looked up at Maikel.

"If the One God is prepared to put his trust in me," she said quite deliberately, "then I will put my trust in Him."

"Bless you, Marin," said Maikel. "I can see why He has such confidence in your people. I can put your mind at rest on one thing, anyway. You will know nothing of what is about to happen. You will simply go to sleep tonight and tomorrow, when you wake up, you will be expecting your first baby."

* * * * *

When Maikel returned to the ship, she immediately removed her enviro-protect and swapped it for a robe. She then reported directly to the office of the director. There she saw that Gaveri was already seated and that they had obviously begun the meeting without her.

"It went well?" he enquired of her as soon as she entered his office.

"Very well, Director. Marin is not only devout but also a very personable young woman with a bright, enquiring mind worthy of her background., but if I may say, sir, she is a member of a primitive people and so, quite easy to manipulate."

"This is true, Maikel, and it is why we must be very careful how we proceed. I can sense from your tone, however, that you have misgivings?"

"Not exactly, sir. It's just that we ask a great deal of this woman and I saw the fear in her eyes. The terror and uncertainty passing through her mind., and to be frank, though I have no knowledge of either childbirth or parenthood, I can sympathise with her."

"Maikel," the director began, "in my experience, which is, you will agree, extensive, I have encountered many women of many races. And though I see and understand many things about people that others do not, the intricate workings of a woman's mind are never-ending in their variety, independence and complexity. It is one of the more beautiful facets of this universe that we travel, and even if only for that reason alone, must, in my view, be nurtured and encouraged. It is why I sent you to Marin rather than Gaveri here, or any of the others. It is precisely

65

because you empathise with this woman that she has agreed to what I have asked. Of this, I am sure. You can argue that I am guilty of, perhaps, the worst kind of manipulation — that based on the loyalty and faith of others — and I concede the validity of that argument viewed from a certain standpoint. But there are many factors at play here and I am content that I have not infringed my own golden rule. I have not usurped either her freedom of choice or yours, and though I have not made clear to you, or anyone, the full intricacies of my plan, yet I ask for your faith and loyalty with a clear conscience."

Maikel was both reassured and troubled by the director's statement. She could detect no falsehood in what he had said — in fact, there was a measure of understanding which surprised her. Yet she could not shake the feeling that, as the director had said, she had been a part of a piece of deep human manipulation, which, she had to admit, made her feel uncomfortable. Nevertheless, she decided to put those feelings aside for the moment.

"I am sure you're right, Director. And I am sure she will be able to persuade her husband-to-be to participate in the plan, even if not entirely willingly. Having spoken to her, I am equally convinced that she will prove a reliable mother."

"I hope so," answered the director. "So much is riding on this, I cannot begin to tell you how important the child's upbringing will be."

He turned to the Medical Doctor.

"Are you ready to carry out the operation, Gaveri?"

"Yes, Director, though I am not too happy about having to perform the operation down there instead of on the ship."

"How long will it take?" enquired the director.

"Not much more than a couple of millicycles. It is a relatively simple extraction, fertilisation and re-implantation procedure. Perhaps, Maikel, you would be good enough to assist me?" said Gaveri.

"Certainly, Doctor," she confirmed. "Then, should she wake up, she will at least see someone she recognises and not panic."

"Have no fear," said the director. "I shall ensure that no one in the house, nor even the entire village, shall wake up while you do your work. You have my seed, Gaveri?"

"Yes, Director," answered Gaveri.

"Good, very good. Then let us proceed."

* * * * *

The operation went according to plan, despite the less than desirable conditions under which it was performed. Gliding the three-man sled — a misnomer since the vehicle was in every way an enclosed environment shuttle-craft — silently to land on the edge of the village, the three made their way to Marin's house under cover of the dark, cloudy night. In truth, there was not much chance of their discovery since the director's telepathic power was enough to shield them from all prying eyes. Nevertheless, they proceeded with caution until they finally reached their destination.

There, Doctor Gaveri, assisted by Maikel, carried out the one medical procedure that might decide the ultimate fate of millions. Unhampered by the reality of that assertion, they laboured on, under the watchful, protective eye of the director, whose quiet effort kept a whole community of around one hundred and fifty souls in a state of untroubled rest while they worked.

At last, they were done, and Doctor Gaveri announced himself satisfied with the result.

"She is indeed pregnant," he said. "I see no obvious reason why, in approximately seventy-five centicycles, she should not give birth to a healthy baby boy."

The director smiled as he approached the sleeping girl.

"Bless you, Marin," he whispered. "You are one very brave young woman."

Maikel, too, smiled. Convinced at last that the director truly cared.

* * * * *

Alone in his quarters, the director sat mulling over the events of the past millicycle, almost unable to believe that his plan — his experiment he reminded himself — was actually now underway. All his careful preparations, the expectancy he had planted in the minds of the people below — the Juhl as they called themselves — all the hopes he had raised, all the speculation he had instigated with his messages, all were about to be tested. He had taken great pains, over many cycles, to ensure that no pertinent detail had been ignored. And there was now no turning back.

But there was always, it seemed, the unpredictable at play. He once more considered the unforeseen invasion of the Thorians and wondered again if he might have prevented it. But to what end, he mused? To interfere, even with the free will of the Thorians — or at least their emperor — was as abhorrent to him as any other form of interference. But he could not escape the reality that rampant militarism, the greed and thirst for power among the few, was, and always had been, the most likely route taken by planetary civilisations. It was the easiest choice, given the nature of mankind as an animal, and in many ways the most natural, requiring only greed and ruthlessness on the part of those who would rule, and fear, acceptance and obedience on the part of the mass of people. Perhaps, therefore, he should have foreseen it? He had not, and that was a fact that had to be dealt with. Certainly, the Thorian occupation of Juhl lands made his task more complicated, but not impossible, he mused.

Again, he considered the effects of militarism. It was a messy, cruel, destructive route to technological advance and did not, in his experience, lead to eventual happiness, peace and contentment for everyone, but only covetous satisfaction for the few who attained the power to control and dictate the lives of others.

No. His own people were an example, perhaps the only one for all he knew, of what could be achieved through pacifism and development of the mind. Admittedly, they too had a somewhat militaristic past and they had always been aware of the need for their own defence against outside attack. But they had paid a price for their development for which no amount of longevity of their lifetimes could compensate. Even so, he was convinced, if chosen at an early enough stage in the development of a civilisation, that race could become far superior and far more able to face and defeat the Xavos threat. It might even hold some hope for his own people, he thought briefly, but then put the thought away as if by exposing it to consciousness he was afraid he might destroy it.

All in good time, he thought.

* * * * *

Lucian was aware only that a powerful telepathic force had been used. Where and by whom he had no idea because he was still somewhat disoriented, not knowing exactly where he was. All he knew was that he had found no way to escape from this — prison — though he could not deny that it contained everything he needed to survive — food, water, warmth and a degree of comfort. Nevertheless, he was unhappy that, though he could talk through dreams and visions with this petty emperor, Tyrson, he could not actually see him or speak directly to the soldiers of his army who, he knew, would follow him into battle without hesitation.

Battle? he grimaced. He could not stand for any length of time just lately, his body was becoming a bit weak. Who had done this to him, he raged for the umpteenth time? He was destined for great things until… someone… had taken away his strength, had imprisoned him in this place. But who? WHO?

An image came into his mind. An old man who had told him he was guilty — of what? — who was he? If only he could remember. Must concentrate. *The name is there, I just have to find it. Must direct my mind …'* the director. That was his name! And having identified his quarry, he found it easier to locate the source of that powerful force.

This was his enemy, he knew, but how could he fight him from this lonely place? Did Tyrson know? He must get some information from Tyrson's head. Find out what was going on. Only then could he plan his strategy to defeat his enemy.

So, he sat and concentrated, sending out his mind to contact that of the sleeping emperor. He found that he could now do this with ease, having 'spoken' to him in this fashion so many times now. He discovered memories about the battles and ships — ships! — in which the Thorians had crossed the great ocean, overcoming their fear of the water. They had invaded another continent!

They were racing through the countries surrounding where they had beached their ships, beating all opposing armies into submission and occupying the lands for miles around. And they had encountered a strange race who called themselves the Juhl. They were a bit livelier and more resistant to occupation, than some of the other tribes around there, but what made them strange, was their worship and belief in only one

God, who they named The One. Now, why was that so significant? He racked his brain but could find no answer. Never mind, he thought, it will come.

He searched further through the emperor's mind, identifying the governor he had sent to rule the new Thorian province of Juhl, and — clever move Tyrson! — the 'king' that they had installed on the Juhl throne. A savant who could manage internal affairs and be a useful scapegoat if anything went wrong. Oh, yes, my little emperor, you have done well, he thought. I will rest now.

Chapter 5

Marin shifted uncomfortably on the makeshift saddle that had been thrown across the donkey's back so that she could ride instead of walk. Though grateful of the slight rest, if the truth were known she could not get comfortable at all, whether she was walking, sitting or lying down. Oh, the joys of pregnancy, she thought, when a woman looks like an overstuffed bag of vegetables, waddles like some kind of demented duck and feels altogether wretched for a lot of the time. And the constant rocking motion of the steady donkey did very little to alleviate her suffering.

She remembered, once again, her all too willing acceptance of her role as mother-to-be and smiled ruefully as the various encounters it had involved paraded once more through her mind. The shock on Jespeth's face when she told him, followed shortly by his acceptance of their fate and gentle reassurance that he would be with her all the way on whatever journey they embarked upon; the unexpectedly gratifying support of her mother; the harsh words of her father who could not come to terms with his daughter's decision and still had not by the time she and Jespeth left home. Her brother, Andrew, had not believed a word of her story either, and had left home altogether, too ashamed of his sister's obvious indiscretion to be able to face his friends again. The last she heard, he had joined one of the terrorist groups, which made her very afraid for him, not to mention the rest of her family.

Paradoxically, the situation had put their immediate wedding plans out of the question as no priest would preside over the wedding of an already pregnant girl. She and Jespeth had wondered whether and when to leave their home, but in the end, the decision had been made for them when, about a month before she was due to deliver the baby, a small Thorian patrol had ridden into the village and their officer had announced the latest in a long line of decrees from the emperor. This time, they were all to be counted and classified, like sheep in a pen she had thought, and every man woman and child had to return to the seat of their forefathers to be registered. Because they were now betrothed, and therefore, Jespeth's lineage took precedence, they were faced with travelling to the north-east corner of Juhl lands, to the town of Bazel, the traditional seat of the house of Daer, one of the greatest of the ancient Juhl kings. In the case of her own family, the royal line was traced through her mother, and was therefore ignored in favour of the lineage of her father, a commoner.

They decided to leave sooner rather than later, in the hope of finding somewhere safe to reside in Bazel where she could give birth in reasonable comfort. But their progress had been very slow, due to her difficulty in walking and so they found themselves not yet at their destination but with her confinement imminent.

"Jespeth, I am tired," she said.

"Yes, I know, my love, and I am sorry for your discomfort. But we don't have far to go now. In fact, we should be there in an hour or two. I'll find us somewhere to stay and then you can rest," her partner told her. He was growing increasingly concerned by her condition, not least because he had not the first idea of how to deliver a baby.

"Jespeth," she murmured.

"Yes, Marin?" he answered, the concern showing in his voice.

"Do you remember the night you looked up at the sky and wondered about the stars?"

"Yes, I do, why?" he asked, anxious to take her mind off their immediate problems.

"You asked what their purpose was, didn't you," she said.

Despite his concern, he smiled then, thinking back to the event.

"Have you worked it all out, then?" he joked.

"No, but I have been wondering about that new star that seems to have been moving at the same pace and in the same direction as we are. Is it just my imagination or is it some kind of sign, do you think?" she asked him.

Jespeth had noticed the star too, but had kept his own counsel on the matter, still a little unsure, even at this late stage, of Marin's 'divine involvement' as he had called it.

"I'm pretty sure it follows us, as you said," he answered. "But what it could be, I'm afraid I just don't know. And I haven't speculated on it in case I got accused of being a daft romantic again."

She laughed, then, the first time she had done so in many weeks. So, they continued until, at last, Bazel came in sight.

* * * * *

"Are you sure this is wise, Director," asked Maikel from her position at the navigation controls of the ship. "After all, we are clearly visible now from the surface."

"Indeed, we are," answered the director. "But only as a moving light in the sky. A mysterious star, which is all. But this star's sudden appearance is all part of the plan.

"And, to satisfy your curiosity, our position serves two purposes. Firstly, it puts us directly on hand when Marin is due to give birth. We can reach her quickly and help her deliver my son. Secondly, the appearance of this 'star' will be noted by many and a few will be curious enough to investigate."

Although she accepted the director's assurances, nevertheless, Maikel was uncomfortable at the thought of their close proximity to the planet's surface, not to mention the upcoming problem of how to get to the place where Marin and Jespeth would be staying, assist with the birth and then get out again, all without being detected.

"I know your concerns, Maikel," he told her lightly. "But you must not get too worried. I have planned this part of the operation well in advance, though I had not thought it would take place here, but thankfully, the geography is immaterial. We are going to give the inhabitants a little show. Not huge, to be sure, but just enough to start the ball rolling, as it were."

Maikel thought she even detected a slight chuckle in the director's voice. Now that was unusual, she thought.

"You and Gaveri will assist directly with the birth. I am also sending Adrian and a couple of his security team on a separate mission. Please ensure that your enviro-protects are adjusted to emit a white light instead of the usual luminescent green. We want them to be impressed."

"Aren't you in danger of taking this a bit lightly, Director?" Maikel asked.

73

"I am sure that's how it appears, Maikel, but I assure you, nothing could be further from the truth. There must be witnesses to this birth. They must be convinced of its importance and reliable in their reporting of it. This is no mere spectacle we are planning. It is the single most important event affecting every single person on that planet," he affirmed with unusual intensity. "No, Maikel, I am not taking this lightly."

* * * * *

"The stable?" asked Jespeth incredulously. "That's all the room you have left?"

"Take it or leave it, friend," said the burly innkeeper. "You should have been here earlier if you wanted rooms."

He saw the despondent look on Jespeth's face and cast his glance again towards Marin. She smiled at him, despite her obvious discomfort, and he was moved to pity.

"Look, I'm very sorry I can't do any better for you, but you will find it warm, and your wife will be able to rest there. Tell you what," he added suddenly, "you can have it free of charge. I'll even send some food out to you later, though I'll have to charge you for that, I'm afraid."

"Thank you, my friend," said Jespeth, too tired now to argue any further. "We'll take it, with thanks."

Jespeth was turning away when the innkeeper spoke to Marin.

"Will you be all right, ma'am?" he asked. "Only you look all done in, and if I'm any judge, it won't be long before your baby's here. If you like, I can have my Sara come and help with the necessary when she brings you some food."

"You're very kind," answered Marin. "That would be very helpful."

Jespeth turned suddenly towards her, fear and alarm in his face.

"Are you really that close, Marin?" he asked, suddenly reminded that the constant travelling from inn to inn in the town looking for lodgings cannot have done anything for her well-being.

The serenity with which she appraised him came as a complete shock. Quickly he led the donkey bearing its burden round the building to the stable which, thankfully, looked clean and freshly scrubbed. There were already a few beasts there, but they left plenty of room for the new arrivals. He set up a few bales of hay, laying covers over them so that Marin might have somewhere reasonably comfortable to lay for the next few hours.

"I am so sorry, my love," he whispered. "You deserve much better than this."

"Don't worry," she said, with a calmness that took him completely by surprise. "We're going to be fine. The One God will help us."

"How can you be so sure?" he asked, becoming more agitated.

"Haven't you noticed?" she asked. "The moving star has come to rest directly overhead."

* * * * *

"Doctor Gaveri," said the director to his intercom. "You and Maikel are about to be required on the planet's surface."

"Yes, Director," answered Gaveri. "We are already on the boat deck. I'll check in when I have something further to report."

The director knew exactly the 'something' to which Gaveri referred as he reflected again on the relative speed with which events had taken place. While the Thorian census had taken him by surprise, he knew that it would not materially affect the course of events. Even the appearance of the three scientists, one from a very long way south, had not been unexpected. He had spread his messages and prophecies far and wide and had anticipated something of this order, although he could have wished they had not been to see Harag, the 'puppet' king, on their way. Still, that he had been made aware of the birth could not be helped now. The director resolved to keep an eye on that situation, something his considerable telepathic power made easily possible.

This night, though, his attention was focussed on the town below and ensuring that none of its inhabitants would interfere with, nor even be aware of, the tasks his crew members were about to carry out. None, that is, except those he wished to be witnesses. On a whim, he decided that the innkeeper's daughter should be included in that number.

"Prefect Adrian," he addressed his intercom, "is your team ready?"

"Quite ready, sir," Adrian replied. "Though I am still not too sure about my theatrical ability, even if the inhabitants are a bit rustic."

"They are the only ones who need to be awake at this time during their night Adrian," answered the director. "But what could be simpler than persuading a few sheep farmers to go and witness the birth of a child. You simply offer to leave one of your team outside to look after the flock. They are both curious and kind hearted, these farmers. They will be a willing audience, have no fear."

So, it was that a couple of hours later, Janus, his brother, Aaron, and their neighbour, Maniso, looked up from their small campfire and could not believe their eyes, as what they saw was simply not possible. Three large silver lights glided across the meadow, no noise accompanied their movement so that not even the sheep were disturbed. As they came closer, the lights seemed to arrange themselves into three man-like shapes, but these were like no other men they had ever seen. Clad only, it seemed, in a silvery light, they could not make their features clearly. Transfixed with fear and trepidation, they could only stare open mouthed as the three apparitions came to a stop right in front of them.

"Don't be afraid…" one of them began.

At this, all three leapt away from the fire, seeking their crooks and staffs with hands that seemed to have a will of their own. They were, of course, terrified. They were quite prepared to protect the animals from wolves and foxes, but this? How were they supposed to protect the sheep from magic?

'*Oh dear*', thought Adrian. '*This isn't going to be easy, is it?*' Silently, he offered up mock thanks to his director, then decided to try again.

"Do you believe in the One God?" he asked.

The ensuing silence said something, at least, for the character of the men before him. They were afraid, that was obvious, but they were equally determined to protect their sheep.

Adrian decided to continue his line of approach.

"I am a messenger, sent by Him," he began. "And I bring good news of great importance to you and all men."

At last, one of the shepherds spoke.

"We believe in the One God, but why would He send a message to us? We're only poor farmers, we're not important people."

Adrian saw his opening and took it with an assurance he had not known he possessed.

"All of his people are important to The One," he began, inventing and improvising as he went along. "This night, you have been chosen to bear witness to the birth of His son, whom he has sent to be a leader and saviour to his people. Follow me and I will show you where the baby lies."

"How do we know this isn't some sort of trick just to get us to leave the flock?" asked Aaron.

Adrian realised the time for theatre was past. He regarded the men before him and softened his tone.

"I can only assure you that it is not a trick," he said. "As hard as it is to believe, the long-awaited prophesy is fulfilled tonight. The messiah is born. I am offering you the chance to see him and believe your own eyes."

Something in his voice chimed with the three men and they finally agreed to accompany the silver clad man, on the assurance that one of the other apparitions would stay and guard the sheep.

Just as they were leaving to make their way down into the town, Aaron shouted, "Wait!"

Afraid that he had yet more explaining to do, Adrian asked him, "What's the matter now?"

"Nothing," answered the shepherd. "It's just that, if we're going to meet the messiah, perhaps we'd better take him something, a gift. I'll grab one of the lambs that's just about ready for market."

"What a thoughtful idea," said Adrian as he turned and led them on down into the town.

* * * * *

Gently, Maikel gave the new-born child into the arms of his mother. Though she had not witnessed an actual birth before, she had imagined that it would take longer and be filled with more pain and anguish than it actually was. Marin's pain was short-lived and the child, a baby boy as predicted, had arrived completely unblemished. In truth, it was Sara, the innkeeper's wife, who had done most of the work and largely directed the entire procedure. Showing little or no interest in either herself or Gaveri, Sara had merely got on with things, reassuring Marin where necessary and asking for their help when needed. Both she and Gaveri had been so intent on the job in hand, they had not even noticed the complete shock that Jespeth had experienced when they appeared as shimmering, silver white apparitions, giving credence, if it had been needed, to what he had previously been asked to take purely on faith. Truly, he had thought, this must be the son of the One God.

Meanwhile, now that the most frenetic part of the activity was over, Sara started to relax, only now looking around at the assembled company and starting to take it all in. What a lovely story this will make, she thought, looking as if for the first time at the two shimmering figures now attending Marin. And thinking that this had to be the strangest birth she had ever attended, she decided then that she would tell this tale to her two young sons, Lucus and Matthias, perhaps as a bedtime story.

Finally, Maikel looked up from her tasks and spoke to Jespeth.

"It is a lot to take in, is it not?" she asked him gently.

"Yes," he answered. "Yes, it is, though in all honesty, if I had any doubts before, I have none now."

"Jespeth," began the other, "it is a heavy responsibility that God has laid upon you. Are you sure that you are ready for it?"

"Well," he replied, incredibly still able to keep his humour, "it seems a bit late to ask me that question., but though we face an uncertain future, both Marin and I will try to live up to what is expected of us. However, I must ask, other than seeing to his immediate needs, what exactly is expected of us?"

"Good question," answered Maikel, "and one which I'm sure the direc… I mean The One, will answer for you in his own time. But for now, well done, and you…"

"Excuse me," said a voice from the stable door.

Everyone turned to observe the speaker who, it transpired, was a tall thin man dressed in fine, colourful robes, obviously a man of some means, who was accompanied by two others, similarly dressed.

"I was about to ask if we were in the right place. Our prophecies tell of a great king who shall be born. The star that we have followed was to be his sign and we have travelled far. We went first to Tevalem to consult your king, Harag, but he told us he knew nothing about this. So, we continued after the star which rests now above this place. Is this the child?"

A voice began in Maikel's head, '*Don't worry, Maikel, they are expected, and they mean no harm to the child or the family. I have the situation under control.*' She knew the voice, of course, and was at once relieved to know that the director was, after all, keeping a close watch on matters.

Realising the solemnity of the situation, Maikel answered, "This is indeed the one who was foretold. Son of the One God and redeemer of his people."

"Then," began the man, "perhaps we will be permitted to acknowledge him? We have brought gifts."

The three gentlemen entered the stable and bowed before the mother and child, placing their gifts on a bale of hay in front of them. While this was going on, Adrian arrived with the men he had brought from the fields. The shepherds were both frightened and embarrassed to find themselves in such elevated company. Seeing the finely dressed men, however, seemed to bolster their courage somewhat and they entered the familiar surroundings of the stable and found themselves touched and deeply moved by the appearance of the small family gathered before them.

"I... I... brought a lamb... for the baby... I thought..." said Aaron, but his voice failed him as he took in the scene.

He brought his eyes back to the newborn before him.

"Is this truly the promised one?" he asked innocently.

"He is," replied Maikel.

"May I ask his name?" he continued.

Then Marin spoke for the first time since she had given birth to the child,

"Empas. He is called Empas," she told him quietly.

* * * * *

The director sat still in his quarters, able to see clearly the scene which was taking place on the planet below. Despite one or two nagging thoughts concerning King Harag and his intentions, he felt quietly pleased that the all-important first stage of the project had come to fruition in much the manner he had envisioned. He was especially struck by the unexpected readiness with which the people below had accepted events way beyond their knowledge and experience, putting them down to 'magic' and 'prophecy' and simply accepting them. Maikel was right, he thought, these people were primitive and easy to manipulate, but nevertheless, unafraid. He must not interfere with them nor treat what he was doing lightly. They deserved better than that.

Well, he reflected, there is not much more to be done now for another ten to fifteen cycles, so perhaps he could afford to relax a little. Once again, he allowed himself a glimpse of the scene taking place below and was touched, just for a moment, by the impact it could have on generations to come. He spoke, telepathically, to Maikel: *'Your work is done, Maikel. Tell Gaveri and Adrian that you should all make your way back to the ship now. Oh, and before you leave, warn those three scientists that they should not go back home via Tevalem as Harag requested, but should travel by a different, and if possible, more circuitous route. I'm sure they will understand. And tell Marin and Jespeth that they should prepare themselves for another journey. They will not be happy about it but tell them it is necessary for their own safety and that of my son, Empas.'*

With that taken care of, he carefully relaxed his watch on the little town.

* * * * *

Harag stirred restlessly in his sleep, the young naked girl by his side forgotten many hours ago. His appetites sated, he had fallen into what he anticipated would be a dreamless sleep. Instead, he was disturbed by a harsh, insistent voice that seemed to be urging him to commit an act which made even him think twice about.

'You must kill them all,' the voice whispered. *'Every child born in and around that town over the last two years must die if you are to keep your throne. You cannot allow any of them to live to become a threat to your kingdom. Act now, Harag of Juhl, before it is too late. Kill them. KILL THEM!'*

With that message still screaming in his mind, the king awoke, sweat streaming from him, panic uppermost in his head. Surely, this was a warning from the gods? A usurper? Born into his kingdom? Yes, of course he must act, but he would need the help of the Thorians. Trembling, he called for the guard outside his door to summon a scribe. He would send a message to the governor, asking for the immediate release of a century of soldiers to his command. When the three scientists returned to tell him where they had been, he would then despatch them, their orders clear and unequivocal. They might not like it, but it was necessary if order was to be maintained. Even if the three did not return, he knew roughly where to look, but a small delay was worth the risk if he could pinpoint the location. He decided to wait just a day or two before sending the soldiers out.

When he had given his instructions to the scribe and sent him on his way, he began to relax a little more. Clearly, the gods favoured him, he decided as he turned back towards the nubile young thing waiting in his bed. Oh yes, he thought, they have certainly favoured me this night.

* * * *

Lucian sat back on his bench, panting a little with the effort he had just expended, but satisfied with the outcome. Having learnt enough about the prophecy from all the individuals whose minds he had invaded over the last cycle, he had also at last begun to sort out who were the main participants in the events that were about to take place. He knew his enemy only by name — the director — but he had worked out the general plan from the prophecy. A leader was to be born or was perhaps already born.

He had found, also, that he was aware when telepathic power similar to his own was being used on a large scale, though he could not invade the targets of that use, nor even locate it accurately. But he surmised, if the director was interested in the birth of a leader, it stood to reason that he would do all in his power to protect that individual at its most vulnerable.

It was purely good fortune when, on one of his probes into the mind of King Harag, he had uncovered the memory of the three astronomer scientists. The king had also had their departure observed, unknown to them, so he knew they were headed north-east, where there were only a few outlying settlements and one town of any size — Bazel. Could that be where the leader would be found? It was all still a little hazy and based on not a little guesswork. The census called for by the emperor had produced such a concentration of people as to make his planning both easier and harder. Easier, because it meant that Bazel would almost certainly be the focus of whatever was coming. Harder, because he could not be sure, given the circumstances, that it was an actual physical birth that was predicted, or the 'birth' of a movement, predicated by the coming together of so much humanity in one place. When he sensed the use of telepathy in that general location, he knew it was time to act.

So, his plan was simple; have all babies born on or around this time exterminated. Extend that to include all births within the last two cycles, just to be safe. The effect would be to eliminate the threat, stop the director's plan in its tracks, and terrorise the local population into continued submission to Thorian rule.

Lucian smiled as he relaxed. Although his physical health was deteriorating, he knew, his mental faculties seemed to be untouched by whatever it was that ailed him. His anticipation of the mayhem and suffering that was about to be inflicted at his command only intensified his feeling of satisfaction. Your move, Director, he thought, and smiled to himself.

* * * * *

A few days after the birth, Marin and Jespeth were woken during the night by another visitation, this time by Maikel accompanied by a person they had not seen before. He introduced himself as Adrian and the message he brought was anything but welcome.

"A detachment of Thorian soldiers is on its way to Bazel," he told them. "The One God has decided that it is not safe for you to stay in this town now that the census is complete. You must leave, now, tonight."

"But where will we go?" asked Jespeth. "We had intended to head back to Wilet and see if our families could help us."

"That is not possible, I'm sorry," said Adrian. "We have to get you as far away from Thorian eyes as we possibly can. I will wait for you on the road leading north-east just outside of the town. Hurry please, we must not be seen."

Adrian left then and Maikel helped the couple gather their few things together. She spent some few moments looking at the baby in the crib and was struck by the way he looked directly at her, as if he knew who she was. This was not possible, of course, she reminded herself as she picked him up and handed him to his mother.

"Are you not coming with us?" Marin asked her.

"Not this time, Marin," Maikel answered. "But you can trust Adrian. He knows the path you must take, and he will ensure you are safe. Now you must go."

"We will not forget you, Maikel," said Jespeth quietly.

"Nor I, you," she answered.

Chapter 6

The boy could see the shove coming but could do nothing about it as he felt himself propelled backwards. His one good leg was not strong enough to save him so, as he collided with the wall, he fell in a heap, his crippled leg beneath him. As he fell, he felt a vicious shooting pain travel up from his ankle to his hip and he cried out in agony. He began to cry, helplessly lost in misery and pain, his tears the only slight relief from the hurt and humiliation he was feeling.

The three other boys in front of him, all older and bigger than he was, laughed and pointed at the leg that was pinned agonisingly beneath their victim, taunting him and daring him to get up and fight back. So full of themselves were they that they did not notice the carpenter's son walking towards them, fury on his face.

"And just how is that funny?" he demanded loudly, barely suppressing his anger.

The reaction was immediate as the laughing stopped and the three bullies turned towards the newcomer, hard, unfeeling expressions on their faces. The tallest, a boy named Saul, clearly saw himself as leader of the little gang and had no hesitation in challenging the lad.

"Go and play with some of your father's wood before you get in over your head, wooden head," he sneered.

Empas stood his ground, emotions working quickly within him. He was torn between his desire to punish these three for the pain and humiliation they had heaped on his little friend, Ben, and the need to simply show them that what they had done was wrong. In the end, it was little Ben himself who provided the answer.

"Don't worry, Emp, I'll just tell my father that I fell. These three just thought they were being clever. It's not worth getting everybody into more trouble," he said, sucking in air to mask his pain.

"What's that supposed to mean, cripple?" demanded Tozel, another of the bullies and Saul's brother.

"He means," said Empas slowly, "that his father is Caspar Mossamed, the wealthy and powerful trader who visits this town from time to time, bringing goods that people — your parents included — wish to buy, and purchasing other items that local people — my father included — have to sell. Mister Mossamed naturally travels with his own caravan guards, you could call them his private army. He is a very nice man, but I have always felt that he lacked a certain forgiveness in his nature. Although Ben has said he will lie to his father just to save you, I have not. So, I'd say you have a choice. Take your chances that Mister Mossamed will be in a very forgiving mood or make some kind of reparation right now."

Empas had always found it easy to speak his mind and to make his point forcefully. Almost always, no sooner was he presented with a situation, than he had summed up all its implications and could present the case for his point of view with ease. As he spoke, the expressions on the faces of the three gradually changed to those of fear and apprehension as the realisation of what they might have got themselves into dawned on them. Empas felt a certain satisfaction as he could almost see the knots forming in pits of stomachs which, only moments before, had been quivering with gleeful animosity.

"Shall we begin by getting him upright to see how bad the additional injury might be?" asked Empas almost nonchalantly.

Suddenly, the stand-off was at an end. The three moved almost as one to lift little Ben away from the wall and the mud into which he had fallen. No words were spoken until they had carried him to the edge of the well in the middle of the market area. There was still some soft grass there and they drew some water for him to drink. The silence was awkward and Empas had still not fully made up his mind about what to do when Saul spoke.

"Look, we're sorry, all right? We've done what we can to help, just don't tell your father."

Empas looked at him and realised that he had achieved nothing. Yes, he had saved Ben from a beating, or worse. But these thugs were not sorry, they were scared. And as soon as the reason for their fear was gone, they would, as likely as not, go and do the same thing again. Empas could see the logic but could not understand the impulse. He shook his head as he turned to them.

"Just go," he told them. "Before I change my mind."

Feeling a little braver now that the immediate crisis was behind him, Tozel decided to challenge this arrogant carpenter's son.

"And just what do you think you can do to us mouthy?" he asked. "You're just one against three of us."

Empas felt fresh stirrings of anger and the power built within him but instead of giving vent to his emotions, he allowed the power to surge as he stared down the confident Tozel.

As the bully continued to marshal his bravery, he suddenly felt a rush of deep sorrow, of a self-loathing so deep he could not hide from it, of hopelessness so profound he felt it would never end and his bravado finally broke, as did that of the other two. They all, as one, turned and walked swiftly away from the scene. Empas continued to stare until they were out of sight and only then did, he seek to control the power that had surged through his mind. He was so deeply engrossed that he did not, at first, hear what Ben said.

"What?" he asked, gradually getting control.

"I said thank you for saving me but was it really necessary to frighten them like that?" answered Ben gently.

"Frighten them?" said Empas. "No, I didn't frighten them, I just made them... I was angry and I wanted to... just a minute, how do you know I did something?"

"I've seen you do it before Emp. You seem to be able to get into people's heads somehow, and not just people, I've watched you with animals. Sheep and cattle calm down when you're nearby. Even that wild rabbit we came across last time I was here, do you remember? It was caught in a snare, wild with panic and pain and struggling so hard it nearly pulled its own leg off. Then you stroked it and spoke to it as I recall. It calmed down almost immediately, enough so that we were able to release it anyway, and then it stopped as it hopped away and turned to look at you, almost as if it was saying thank you. Don't you remember?" Ben continued.

"I don't know what you're talking about Ben," Empas answered trying to find a way to change the subject. "Let's have a look at that ankle. I bet it hurts, doesn't it?"

"Quite a bit, yes, but I don't think anything's broken," agreed Ben.

"Let's have a look anyway," said Empas casually.

Gently he examined Ben's crippled leg, paying particular attention to the ankle — and found, unexpectedly, that he could perceive the structure of the bones and the nature of the surrounding flesh. He could see that the ankle joint was inflamed and that this was the cause of his friend's discomfort. Without thinking, he placed his hand on the ankle and gently massaged the area. Gradually, he saw that the soreness was receding, almost as if he had ordered it to cool down.

"How's that?" he asked only now becoming aware that he had discovered something about himself that he had not known anything about before.

"Pretty good, actually," said Ben. "Thanks a lot."

"Will you be able to walk on it?" enquired the other.

"Oh yes. I've got my stick, so I'll be able to keep my balance," Ben replied, obviously feeling a lot better.

"Come on then," said Empas. "I'll walk home with you, and we'll tell your father what's happened."

"No, Emp, I don't want to do that," said Ben almost too quickly.

"Why ever not?" asked Empas. "They deserve to be punished."

Ben looked at his friend, trying to make up his mind whether to say what he wanted to or not. At last, he decided to reveal what was on his mind,

"Emp," he began, "we've been friends ever since I started accompanying my father on his trips here. And you have always been kind to me, protected me as you did today, and always treated me as an equal, which I'm not, because of this." He pointed to his crippled leg, the physical disability that kept him from joining in with other children at play and ensured that he led a somewhat solitary life.

"Ben, you're just the same as..." Empas began.

"No, let me finish," Ben insisted. "In you, I've found a true companion who seems to understand what it's like to have to live this way. I don't like it, but there's nothing I can do about it — and I don't see the point in either you or I getting angry about it."

"But it's not right," said Empas. "It's so unfair and what those thugs did to you today it..."

"Life isn't fair, Emp," Ben interrupted him again. "But I've found that anger and revenge are not the answers they might seem to be. Yes, they were pretty nasty, but what did they get from it in the end? A passing satisfaction that they were better than a mere cripple? If my father finds out, I don't know what he will do. He's not a tolerant man. You know, I almost pity them. With their attitude, can they ever expect to make a friendship as good as ours? Long ago I vowed to treat other people as I myself want to be treated. Only then can I discover the good in others. With some, it's easy, with others it's harder but I usually find it's worthwhile. The good is in everybody somewhere."

This made Empas pause to think. Though he bore no grudges and had always believed that people had a good side to their nature, he had also believed, as his people's scriptures taught, that evil, wherever and in whatever form it manifested itself, deserved to be punished. Yet here was his little friend, who suffered almost constant abuse and humiliation because of a disability he could not help, telling him that he felt pity for his abusers, not hatred, and he certainly did not seek retribution, or else why would he wish to hide it from his father?

Why? he wondered. Did the bullies and thugs feel true remorse, or did they just go out and do the same nasty and evil things all over again? He was inclined to believe the latter, and if that were the case, who then, he wondered, truly benefited from Ben's attitude? He did not have an answer but decided that the problem was worth the mental effort, so he put it to one side for closer examination another day. One thing was certain however, he thought as they made their way slowly home, he had seen a side of Ben that he had not seen before and he was, he realised, astonished at what he had been shown.

It was a few days later that their conversation and its implications were put to the test.

Empas and Ben had persuaded their respective parents to allow them to venture outside the confines of the village. Ben loved the countryside around here and Empas loved to walk. They took a donkey on which Ben could ride when his leg got tired and talked as they made their way towards a small rise around half a mile away, on top of which was a crown of trees. Empas suggested they make for the rise to sit in the shade of the trees and just enjoy the day.

As they neared the top of the hillock, they heard a loud cry coming from the other side. Hurrying to the top, they raced to the far edge of the trees and looked down to see a scene such as no inhabitant of that country ever wished to see.

A boy lay helpless upon the ground not twenty feet away from where they stood, his face a mask of absolute horror, pain and fear as he stared mesmerised at the enormous snake that was poised over his legs, its hood already spread in anger as it prepared to bite this enemy. Ben recognised him immediately.

"Help me please," the boy cried plaintively. "My leg is trapped."

Sliding down from the donkey's back, Ben grabbed his stick and strode to the scene. Coming up behind the monster he took the stick in both hands and swung it as hard as he could straight at its head. Luckily, his aim was true, and the blow connected with a loud thump, knocking the snake sideways and stunning it for an all-important few seconds. Looking down, Ben saw the boy's crook on the ground. He leaned over and picked it up, looped the crook end around the creature's scaly body and swung the crook for all he was worth away down the hillside, the snake with it.

The creature had had enough. Without pausing, it slithered away into the grass, in search of a fresh resting place and easier prey.

No one moved for a few moments after that, until Ben suddenly sat down on the ground and began to sob with the shock of what he had just done. Empas looked at the scene, replaying the events that had happened so suddenly, and only then did he recognise the boy who lay on the ground, obviously suffering a great deal of pain. It was Saul, the leader of the three bullies who had attacked Ben.

"Is it gone?" he wailed. "Please tell me it's gone. I didn't even know it was there, it just... please say it's gone!" he cried, still terrified at the memory of his ordeal.

"The snake is gone," said Empas. "I think you're safe now."

Recognition seemed to dawn slowly on Saul's face, replacing the terror that he had felt moments before.

"Thank you," he said.

"Don't thank me Saul," said Empas. "Thank him. Ben is the one who saved you."

Calmer now with each moment, Saul turned to look at the sobbing boy on the ground next to him and recognition slowly dawned.

"Wait a minute," he began, "aren't you the cripple my brother and I..."

"He is," interjected Empas. "And he just..."

"No!" said Ben. "Don't say anything, Emp."

Looking now at the boy on the ground, he said, "Yes, I knew who you were. So what?"

"But why would you... Ooooow," he yelled as he tried to move his foot within the crack in the ground where it was stuck. He said nothing more as a jolt of agony ran up his leg.

Sweating profusely now, Saul lay back down as nausea threatened to overwhelm him. Empas moved to examine the foot more closely and was again struck with how clearly, he perceived the nature of the injury. He could see the fracture in the leg bone just below the calf muscle and the ankle joint that was causing the discomfort. He placed his hands over the ankle and began to gently massage the joint. The boy's ankle suddenly spasmed, sending jolts of needle-sharp pain up his leg. This proved too much for the injured Saul. He cried out once more as the blackness threatened to overwhelm him.

Empas continued, sending cooling sensations into the boy's leg, sufficient so that he could finally move the foot and free it from the trap without causing any further pain, although with Saul seeming to drop in and out of consciousness it hardly mattered. He knew, however, that he could not mend the fracture. Empas decided he would tell Saul the truth when he came round more fully.

He realised at once that they had a problem here. Clearly, they needed to get treatment for Saul but if he sent Ben back to the village — a danger in itself for lonely travellers — help would be a long time coming, even if Ben rode the donkey. Perhaps too long for Saul. On the other hand, he could not go as that would mean leaving Ben on his own with at least one and possibly two enemies.

Saul, still groaning with the pain of the fracture, lay down and seemed to lose interest in everything else that was going on around him. Empas motioned Ben to move away from the suffering boy so they could talk without scaring him further. He pointed out the problem as he saw it to Ben, who accepted the situation quite calmly.

"Emp, you must take the donkey and go to my father's lodging. He always has a surgeon who travels with him, in case of injury to either the guards or the animals. Bring them here. I will stay with him and try to make sure nothing else happens," said Ben.

"No," said Empas. "That would leave you here, effectively on your own and in danger if anything else should happen."

"What else is going to happen?" argued Ben. "We'll be perfectly all right here."

"No, I won't leave you here on your own. It would be much safer if you were to go Ben," insisted Empas.

"Listen to me Emp," said Ben urgently. "Perhaps it would be safer, but you will be quicker than I would as I cannot stay on the donkey's back if he gallops so I would only travel at walking pace at best. And besides, I don't know how I know, but I have something I must do here."

Empas considered the argument. He didn't like the idea one bit, but he could see the logic of the argument, but what did Ben mean he had something to do here? As no answer came to him, he finally shrugged, and in an effort to lighten the mood somewhat, he smiled and said to his friend, "Looking at that old beast, I don't think it can gallop even if it wanted to. I've got a better idea. We'll leave the donkey here and I'll run back to fetch your father. You're right, I will be quicker."

It was decided. Ben watched as his friend sprinted away, until he was just a speck, and then turned his attention to the boy next to him. He had stopped groaning, had recovered some of the natural colour in his face and was taking in his surroundings.

"Feeling any better?" asked Ben. "Would you like some water? I'm afraid we brought very little to eat, but what we have you're welcome to," he added as he rummaged in his pack.

"Your friend has gone," remarked Saul breathlessly, still in some pain. But added, "why didn't you go?"

"He went to fetch help," Ben replied. "He'll be much quicker than either of us would," he added lightly.

"He certainly wasn't going to help me the other day," Saul came back.

"Yes, I'm sorry about that. He got a bit angry and… well…"

As if it had hit him for the first time, Saul remembered the incident all too well and also recalled how, despite that, Ben had come to his aid here. *'What made a person do that?'* he wondered.

"You have nothing to be sorry about, Ben," he said. "It's me and my brother who should be saying sorry. You just saved my life, even after what I did to you and — I don't know how to say thank you."

"Well, you just did, and I really appreciate it but there is no need." said Ben.

"Yes, actually, there is a need," answered Saul firmly. "You have shown kindness and consideration to a person who has shown you neither of these things and… I feel ashamed."

"Oh no, please," said Ben quickly, "there's no need. I didn't mean… I only did what anybody would do in the circumstances."

Saul looked at the other boy and saw only sincerity in his innocent face. He could not help himself. Suddenly he came face to face with his own disgraceful behaviour — and realised he did not like what he saw. There was more to this crippled boy than what you could, at first, see, he decided.

"Ben, can we be friends?" he asked seriously.

"I would really like that, Saul," answered the other.

"Empas?" asked Saul after a brief pause.

"Emp? Oh, he's a forgiving sort really and a very good friend to have. You'd like him."

"I think I might," answered Saul. "The question is, will he like me?"

On and on they talked, passing the time and finding many things that they liked about each other and almost laughing about how similar they both were at that moment, neither able to walk more than a few steps without falling over, and so on, cementing, in a short space of time, a friendship that both knew would be real and lasting.

* * * * *

No one would ever know why the monstrous creature did not just continue in the direction it had started to go to escape the enemies it had encountered. But it did not. Slowly, it circled around the little copse of trees and slid its way up the mound until it was once again under the shade of the trees. Gently and silently, it made its way across the small glade to the other side where the two boys sat talking to each other. Slowly now it slid out from the shade and came up immediately behind them, its tongue sniffing the air in front of it. Weaving to and fro, the monster lifted its front end to its full height, spread its hood in the most threatening gesture it could muster, and at last, issued an enormous, loud hiss that startled both of its enemies. Kill, KILL was the only thing on its mind.

Mouth open wide, exposing the two vicious fangs protruding from its upper jaw, it struck downward, suddenly, piercing soft skin and injecting its deadly venom into its tormentor. Again, it drew back to its full height, seeing both of its enemies frozen as if they were statues. It might have struck again, but its venom was spent. So, it reasoned, leave this place, find somewhere to rest and recover its arsenal. The monster moved backwards as easily as it had slid forwards, eyeing its enemies all the time, until it disappeared into the trees, where it turned and finally slithered swiftly away.

No one would ever know why it had happened.

No one — except Lucian, whose manic laughter rang around his prison cell. At last, he exalted. At last, he had found another creature that he could control, and which would do his bidding without question. Not only that, but he could also perceive its surroundings, looking out through its eyes. He could see his enemies! And he knew how to kill them.

* * * * *

"Help me, please. Someone, help me!" Saul's cries rang out across the countryside. "Please, he's dying, somebody HELP!"

Empas heard the calls first and turned to Caspar Mossamed.

"Something is wrong," he cried. "We must hurry."

A few moments later, Empas, the merchant and his surgeon climbed the little hill and arrived at the top. Tying their beasts to the trees they rushed to the other side of the glade where Saul was now sobbing uncontrollably and still crying out for help. The merchant and his doctor both rushed to the side of little Ben, who was lying perfectly still, an unnaturally pale colour now suffusing his face.

Empas moved towards Saul and grabbed him by the shoulders, forcing the boy to look at him.

"Saul, what happened?" he demanded.

"It came back… the snake… it came up behind us and we didn't know it was there until it reared its head and hissed at us. It tried to bite me… but Ben…he… why would he do that? He just flung himself in front of me… why did he do that? Ben… BEN!" he cried out, collapsing into uncontrollable sobbing.

Caspar cradled his son's head, rocking gently backwards and forwards, murmuring softly all the while to his son, while the surgeon worked, trying to remove the poison from the boy's neck, but knowing already that it was too late. Ben had been too weak to start with and the poison had entered his body and quickly spread so that it became impossible to remove it. At last, he sat back on his haunches and puffed out his cheeks in anger and frustration.

"I am sorry, Master Mossamed, I could not save him. He is gone."

The agonised wail that Caspar Mossamed let out on hearing this news would stay in Empas' memory forever. It was the saddest, most forlorn sound he had ever heard. He would also never forget the look of anger and… and what? Hatred? That was what was in Mossamed's eyes. And they were looking directly at him.

He, too, he realised, was taken with a feeling of deep sorrow for a friend he had now lost forever and guilt at having allowed Ben to overcome his instincts about the situation. He knew he should have stayed! He could, perhaps have prevented this. These and many other thoughts passed through his mind relentlessly.

For a while, he just sat, unable to fully comprehend the enormity of the situation. He realised, suddenly, the apparent anomaly here. Saul was clearly deeply upset by what had happened, but what was Ben to him? Perhaps it was just shock or fright at the experience he had just gone through. Yes, he decided, that's what it was.

Meanwhile, the surgeon moved over to examine Saul's leg, soon identifying the fracture and source of the pain the boy was feeling. He sent Empas to his horse to fetch his bag. On his return, the surgeon opened it and took out two wooden splints which he fitted and bound to Saul's leg so as to encourage the bone to heal properly.

By the time he had finished, Saul had calmed down but was looking thoroughly miserable. At last, he looked up and spoke.

"Mr Mossamed, Doctor, I thank you for your help, though I do not deserve it. You must listen to me, please. I treated your son very badly just a few days ago, which I'm sure he didn't tell you about. Despite that, he and Empas came to my rescue here and Ben fought off the snake. We talked and it was only then that I realised what kind of person your son was — one I have never met before. Ben offered me true and undemanding friendship — the first time anybody offered me anything in my life — and I found that I could not help but love and admire him. He died because of me, and I would do anything to change that. You must believe me. If I could have died instead of him, I…"

The admission finally became too much for Saul and he began to sob again. Caspar Mossamed looked at the boy. Despite his grief at losing his precious son, his anger and his frustration, he was moved by Saul's confession. He could see clearly the profound influence that Ben had had on this lad, but his emotions were still too sharp, too acute, for him to be able to think about the implications. At last, he managed a few words.

"We will speak of this again when our hearts are less troubled. For now, let us return."

* * * * *

It was only much later that Empas began to think about the lessons of what had happened. What Ben had done, for a boy who, only a few days earlier, had bullied and humiliated him, was almost beyond comprehension, and yet, with a clarity which surprised him, Ben's words came back to him, '*I vowed I would treat others as I want to be treated. There is something I have to do.*' But to put himself in harm's way for someone he hardly knew and had no reason to like? What was he thinking?

Then there was Saul's confession. Had he really been so deeply affected and changed by Ben? Surely not, and yet the evidence was right there. Saul wasn't lying when he said those things. Somehow, Ben had turned an enemy into a friend and had made a lasting impression on the boy.

And lastly, there was Ben's final act. He was always very quick and perceptive, something Empas admired about him enormously. Could he have taken in the situation so quickly? Could he have known that the snake would surely kill Saul unless he acted? To Empas' surprise, he realised that Ben could, and would, have known these things. So, his final act, the thing he had to do, was to accept death himself in order to save his new-found friend. It was entirely feasible to Empas and in keeping with what he already knew about his crippled friend.

Empas could not shake off his immense sadness at the loss of Ben. He knew that he would always remember him for his strength in adversity, his quick wit, his forgiving nature and his passionate love of all things living. Now, to add to those memories, he also knew that he had learned an important lesson from his little friend, one that he would, he decided, adopt as his own. *Treat everyone as you yourself want to be treated.*

The only thing he could not work out was why Ben's father had looked at him the way he had and had not spoken another word to him since the incident.

He discussed these things with Jespeth, still not fully able to get his head around the events. He also mentioned the strange look the merchant had given him and the fact that he had not spoken to Empas since. As ever, the carpenter, whose skills had been in great demand ever since they had returned from the Bolgish lands, where he had honed them to perfection under Bolgish tuition, took the news calmly, but with due regard to Empas' feelings.

"I'm sure you did all you could, Empas," he said sadly. "And I'm also sure that Caspar Mossamed is presently consumed with grief at the loss of his son. Is it any wonder he looks for someone to blame? It will pass when he has had time to take it all in."

Jespeth noticed, as the lad approached his twelfth birthday, how he had started taking more interest in the people around him, his friends, neighbours, visitors, even the priest at their local temple rather than in the skills which Jespeth was teaching him. In fact, now that he thought about it, he had often seen Empas and the priest in deep discussion, wondering what they could find to talk about so seriously. Listening now to the lad's tale, he was reminded again of how deep the boy's perception had become.

"The world will be a much sadder and poorer place without your friend," he told Empas. "But as to why he did what he did? It would be nice to put it down to common humanity. Unfortunately, such courage is all too uncommon."

"Then that is something I intend to change, Father," Empas replied.

That night, as Jespeth and Marin lay together in their bed, he turned to her and related the story of Ben's sacrifice and its obvious effect on Empas. He told her what he had said to the boy and of his firm reply.

"He means it, Marin. He intends to try to change people's attitudes. I don't know what to say to him or how to begin to guide him."

Jespeth hesitated before he carried on, wrestling with his own indecision.

"Do you think it's time we told him who he is?" He almost blurted the words. Even as he spoke, the enormity of the situation struck him. After all, how would they go about proving that?

* * * * *

The time has come, the director thought to himself. Marin and Jespeth had done everything that he had asked of them and more. They had been loving and tender parents, teaching Empas the difference between right and wrong, and even giving him a practical skill which he may find useful sometime in the future. But not now. Now he was going to try to bring about the next phase of his plan. Empas must be given access to the knowledge of his birthright, and he must be given the choice of which road to follow. He was fairly certain that he knew which road the boy would choose, and he was equally certain that he would not consciously try to influence that decision. The first few meetings with his son, he decided, would be very interesting indeed.

So it was that, a few days later, while Empas was on a solitary walking expedition outside the village, he was approached by a stranger who, at first, he thought must be naked as he could clearly see the shape of his entire body. As he got closer, however, he could see that the stranger was dressed from head to toe in a tight-fitting dark outfit that, strangely, seemed to change colour subtly depending on where the stranger stood.

"Hello, Empas," he said, startling the boy somewhat as he had never met this person before.

Empas stopped in his tracks, unsure of himself and looking around as if he suspected some kind of trap. Seeing nothing untoward, he turned back to the stranger.

"I don't know you, sir, yet you seem to know my name," he said with a calmness he did not feel.

"Don't be afraid, Empas," said the stranger. "My name is Adrian, and I am sent by your father to bring you to him. Will you come?"

"Why would my father send you when he knows perfectly well that I will be back home in a little while?" Empas asked.

"I am not speaking of the father you know, but of your true father, whom you do not," Adrian answered truthfully.

Empas was dumbstruck. His true father? What nonsense was this? Jespeth was his father and Marin was his mother, there could be no question of that — or could there? Just lately, it was true, he had felt himself, somehow, growing away from his parents. Wanting more, becoming more than the simple life they offered him. But he had never questioned his heritage until now.

He studied the stranger — Adrian, had he said? —, and feeling a little braver, he asked, "And where do I have to go to meet my true father?"

"Up," said Adrian.

"Up? Up where?" came back Empas, intrigued now despite himself.

"Up there," answered the man, pointing to the sky.

Empas began to laugh, partly with relief but partly with a new fear in his mind.

"Now I know you are trying to trick me," said the boy, his mood lightening as he realised the stranger was completely mad. He decided to humour him. "Then let's get going," he joked.

"Very well," said Adrian, not quite believing his luck. "Just step into my sled and we'll be off."

Empas could see no — sled — so thought it best to just agree until he could work out what to do next. He took a step towards the stranger — and found that he was, indeed, climbing into some sort of enclosure. But he could see nothing! NOTHING! He wanted to flee but was suddenly frozen with fear. It had been a trap! And he had walked straight into it.

"As I said, don't be frightened. I promise you will be returned to this spot, unharmed in any way., but I must admit, you're going to find the next few minutes pretty strange."

With that, Adrian switched on the anti-gravity unit and the vehicle rose, slowly at first, but gathering pace as it went higher. For the boy's protection, he also switched on the inner opacity so that he could see only the inside of the vehicle, almost eliminating vertigo and all its attendant unpleasantness, whilst the vehicle remained camouflaged on the outside. All they could hear was the light, fairly high-pitched humming of the drive unit which lifted them effortlessly the many miles they had to travel to reach the gigantic ship which was orbiting the planet.

Chapter 7

It had all been too much for Empas. Adrian had made the mistake of switching on the front viewscreen, whereupon the boy had become at first mesmerised and then horror-struck as he watched the ground literally falling away from him. This was followed by the sight of the curve of the planetary globe gradually coming into view and blackness spreading downwards from the top of the screen. Empas became convinced he had been abducted by a sorcerer of some kind and thoughts flashed through his mind of magic, slavery, black monsters, everything a boyish imagination could manage, until finally his mind was overcome, and he passed gratefully into unconsciousness.

* * * * *

"Really, Adrian, that was a fairly basic mistake, letting the boy observe the process of achieving orbit, don't you think?" said Maikel. "What were you thinking of?"

"Obviously, I wasn't thinking all that much," answered Adrian. "I just thought he might enjoy the ride a little more if he could see what was going on. He seemed fairly settled."

"Just shows how wrong you males can be sometimes. I just hope he's not too traumatised. Perhaps you'd better ensure that Doctor Gaveri is on hand when he meets the director."

Empas only caught the very last part of the conversation, as he opened his eyes and beheld perhaps the most beautiful woman he had ever seen, looking down at him with a concerned expression on her face. She was very young, fair skinned with soft rounded facial features that were very easy, especially on the eye of a young, impressionable boy. But it was her manner, the gentle efficiency coupled with genuine concern for him that left the lasting impression. He could not understand the feelings she aroused in him. He could never explain it, but he knew right away that this woman would play an important role in his life.

"Hello," she said. "I'm Maikel. Welcome to our ship."

"A ship?" said Empas. "But there is no water. There is no ground. There is… nothing! Where am I?"

Almost, he began to wail, but his determination not to show weakness won out and he just stared, wide-eyed and frightened, at the vision before him.

"It is not easy to explain," the woman continued. "But it will become clearer once you get used to certain things. Firstly, let me assure you that you have not been captured, abducted or enslaved in any way and you will be taken back home in a little while. We are sorry to have frightened you, but your first visit here was always going to be awkward, so the director thought we had better get it over and done with."

"I don't understand…" said Empas.

"No, of course you don't," continued Maikel. "But if you feel up to it, why don't I show you around some of our home before you meet the director?"

"Thank you… Maikel?" said Empas tentatively.

The next millicycle was spent with Maikel trying to explain what the various places on the ship were for, why the space drive produced a permanent low hum, and in fact, trying to impart the principle of outer space as a concept to a young lad whose only previous experiences included carpentry tools, countryside and people, most of whom, he knew by name and nature. Admittedly, he had always been a thinker and had wondered about the stars, and he had recently discovered certain abilities of his mind that had come as a surprise, but other than what the scriptures of his religion told him, he had no focus and no point of reference to guide him and help him grasp what was happening to him. As a result, Maikel found herself very surprised, and not a little relieved, as she became aware that Empas was quickly overcoming his fear, his disbelief and his total lack of experience and was, in fact, starting to take a healthy and enquiring interest in all that was going on around him.

Far from being afraid, the boy now seemed to be accepting and processing the information being given to him quite readily, eagerly moving from one topic to the next, taking everything in as if he were born to it. *'Which, of course,'* she thought briefly, *'he was.'*

"I navigate the ship from the bridge which is…" she began.

"Where is my father?" asked Empas suddenly.

"What?" asked Maikel, nonplussed for a moment.

"My father," he continued. "Adrian said I was coming to meet my father… my real father."

"Yes, of course, that is the main reason you're here," she stammered. "But I wasn't quite sure…"

A much older man appeared in front of the pair, emerging from a panel in the wall which slid away, revealing what looked to be a comfortable room beyond.

"I think perhaps I might take over from here, Maikel," said the man gently, and with just a few words he had taken complete control of the situation. "Thank you for looking after my son."

"Of course, Director," she said. "It was a pleasure."

The man draped his arm gently across Empas' shoulders, ushering him into the room beyond. The boy did not question this interruption of his tour, nor, strangely, did he feel afraid in any way of this man who, he knew instinctively, would never willingly allow any harm to come to him.

"You are my father," stated Empas flatly.

"That is correct young man," said the other.

"Maikel called you Director," said the boy. "Is that your name?"

"No," answered the man, "it is my title. General Operations Director. Your people on the planet below know me as The One God."

Empas was, understandably, a little outraged. "But The One God is a God. He is omnipotent. You are…"

"It was a deception which I freely admit to," began the director. "Because it was necessary, although I did not instigate it. I merely took advantage of it."

He paused before continuing, as if considering something of great importance. Finally, he reached a decision. "Empas, I have lived for many hundreds of your years and in that time, I have travelled many millions of your miles and encountered many civilisations on many different planets. I have never encountered The One God, nor seen any real evidence of his existence, other than the universe itself, whose existence and purpose — if any — is still, and I suspect, will always be, one of life's great mysteries. The One may, or may not, be 'real'.

Everyone must make up their own mind on that. For me, the universe is the great and overriding reality and we may never know all of its secrets. I have assumed the role of The One not out of any sacrilegious wish to be worshipped or regarded as omnipotent, as you put it, but out of my wish to try to do something that will be the redemption of those people down there and these people up here. Do you understand what I am saying?"

Empas sat in silence for a moment, trying to take in the huge concept he had just been handed. Just about everything he was seeing, and hearing went contrary to the teachings of his parents and the religious leaders of his people. The One — his God — was omnipotent, was everywhere, had created the world and its people, guided and ordered the events of its days. And yet, here was this man who, he was convinced, had no reason to lie to him, and who was telling him that, in all probability, God did not exist. Could that be right? Was it possible? Or was he, perhaps, just misreading the entire situation? At last, he reached a decision.

"I understand what you are saying, sir, but I cannot be sure whether I believe it or not," he answered slowly. "I am sorry if that is not enough."

"On the contrary, young man, it is more than enough, and you have shown me that my faith in you, and in the people, you live with, is not misplaced. There are few, if any, certainties in life. In the end, it may be that faith is all we have. Faith that what we believe to be, is so. And is not that enough in itself? As long as that question remains uppermost in your mind, you will make a good guide and a competent teacher. I am proud that you are my son."

The assertion came as no shock to Empas who, despite his tender years, felt, deep within himself, that he had always known it. His other father, Jespeth, had loved and cared for him, had taught him many of the skills of his own trade, but had always seemed to regard him with a kind of detached awe. Whereas his mother clearly cared for him as deeply as only a real mother could. He did not understand how this situation could be but was prepared to accept that it was.

Father and son now settled into a discussion which covered many basic topics, but which did barely any more than scratch the surface of Empas' inquisitiveness. All too soon, it was time to return him to the planet's surface before anyone started missing him. Before he left, however, the director had a 'gift' which he needed to bestow.

"You have discovered, have you not, an awakening of the powers of your mind?" he asked the boy.

"Yes, I have," he answered keenly. "I can see beneath people's skin, and somehow, I can see the source of their pain. And I can help soothe their discomfort by rubbing the area. Isn't that strange?"

"Actually," answered the director, "it is somewhat unusual, even amongst our people, and you will find that your powers will grow as you yourself become more mature. Do not be afraid of this but explore the possibilities and try to use those abilities to benefit those around you. For now, you will find that you can talk to me whenever you please and wherever you are. You will not need to speak with your mouth, but only with your mind. I will hear you and you will hear me. This does not mean that we are linked all the time, only when and if you wish to communicate.

"Now, you must return. You have much to think about and many things to learn. You may return to the ship at any time you wish if there is something you require that you cannot get down on the ground. Farewell, my son. It has been a pleasure to meet you."

Empas left the room through the sliding panel in the wall and found Maikel approaching from his left. He smiled at her and she returned it, asking, "Did your meeting go well?"

"I think so, thank you," he replied. "It's all still a bit strange, though I think I understand. I need to think about things. Can I go home now please?"

"Of course," said Maikel as she guided him down the corridor towards one of the elevator shafts. "In fact, that's what I have come to tell you. I'm going to take you to the boat deck where Adrian will take you back down to the ground. Will you be all right with that journey?"

"I'm probably going to have to get used to it aren't I?" he said with a hint of a self-conscious smile on his face.

Maikel was struck by Empas' self-assurance and admired the way he had so quickly come to terms with, what must be for him, this outrageous situation. Also, she could not help noticing how tall he was for his age and his rather handsome, though immature, features. '*My goodness*,' she thought, '*whatever am I thinking? This is a twelve-cycle-*

old boy, and I am at least two hundred cycles older than he is.'

On their arrival at the boat deck, Adrian was there to meet them, full of apologies for the previous journey up to the ship. Empas just smiled and said thank you rather shyly, looking around at the various small vehicles stored here — or at least, he assumed they were vehicles despite the fact that he could not see a trace of any wheels anywhere! But then, everything here was strange. He shook his head and decided that he really *did* need to think things through.

"Goodbye, Maikel," he said at last. "Thank you for your kindness. Shall I see you again?" he asked, feeling a little embarrassed.

Oddly, Maikel felt something of his embarrassment. "When you next visit us, I expect I will be here," she answered.

Empas smiled then and stepped cheerfully into Adrian's personal sled, ready for his journey back to normality — if such a thing was ever possible now.

* * * * *

Saul was sitting patiently outside of the lodging house where Caspar Mossamed and his people were staying, as he had done every day since Ben had died. Though he did not fully understand the compulsion he felt, he could not deny the vague feelings of guilt that had troubled him ever since the event. He remembered the grief he had seen on Caspar Mossamed's face, and too, he recalled the thought that had briefly crossed his mind; would anybody weep for me that way when I die?

It was not about self-pity, it was about Ben's innocence and readiness to forgive. Ben had forgiven him completely and unconditionally. What he was finding difficult was how to forgive himself.

Just then, the door of the lodging house behind him opened and one of the servants appeared.

"Mister Mossamed says you are to enter the house," he commanded.

Just as Saul was standing up, Empas walked around the corner. Seeing Saul he came towards him, an enquiring look on his face.

"Hello Saul," he said brightly. "What are you doing here?"

"I am going to see Mister Mossamed," said Saul.

105

"Is that such a good idea, so soon after Ben's death?" asked Empas, taking in the situation right away. "Ben was his only son and who knows what he must be feeling right now."

"I know," answered the boy. "But this is right, and I have never done the right thing before."

Empas could clearly see the enormous change that had come over Saul, and immediately felt a companionship for him that he had not anticipated.

"Would you like me to come with you?" he asked.

"No, but thank you for offering," said Saul. "I am afraid to face him, but I must."

With that, Saul turned away from Empas and entered the house, following after the servant who had called him.

Empas stared after the other and was reminded again of how much change his little crippled friend, Ben, had brought about simply by being who he was. The impact on him was immense and he resolved to learn what lessons he could from these events.

Saul, meanwhile, followed the servant towards the back of the house, through to a central courtyard which was open but cool and shaded due to the high walls surrounding it. Here the servant stopped and indicated Saul should wait upon his master's pleasure. The minutes passed by, and the boy became more and more nervous, wishing now that he had ignored the impulse that had made him wait outside the house, fearful of his imminent punishment, whatever that should prove to be. Only the strength of his resolve kept him there until, finally, Caspar Mossamed appeared upon a balcony above him, dressed in a black, floor-length robe which, Saul could see, was meant to impress both because it was obviously expensive and because it obviously signified that its owner was still in mourning. The boy's stomach dropped, and his heart almost stopped beating with fear. Now that he was here with this man, he thought how foolish he had been to bring it about.

"Sit," the man ordered him, anticipating no defiance. "You claim to have been my son's friend and yet you bullied and humiliated him. Then my son is left alone with you in the wild and now he lies dead in this house while you are alive. Explain."

So, Saul did just that. Hesitantly at first but growing in confidence as his narrative continued. He told of Empas' defence of Ben at the well, of his stumbling upon the snake and how Ben and Empas had heard his cries. How Ben had reacted so swiftly to attack the snake and get rid of it that all of them were caught by surprise. How, during the time Saul and Ben had spent together, Ben had told him he forgave him. At this, Saul stumbled in his narrative, reminded again of how unexpected Ben's declaration had been.

"He just said the words," Saul tried to continue. "I could not understand but as I watched him and listened, I realised that he was totally sincere. I... felt so ashamed, I could not bear to look him in the eye, and I wept. And then his one concern was for me! He did not want me to feel bad, he just seemed to want to wash everything away and start again. I asked if we could be friends and he said... he would like that."

Saul's tears began to flow freely, and for a while he could not continue. Caspar Mossamed sat motionless and did not try to interrupt.

"We talked then, while we were waiting for Empas to return, and we discovered much about each other. We laughed about our mutual incapacities, and we shared our thoughts. But then, the monster appeared behind us, and it reared up. It was looking directly at me, and I knew it had come back to claim me after all," said the boy, recalling vividly the dreadful moment. "It attacked me, just as it was about to before, but Ben was too quick for it, he. He... moved across to shield me from its bite and he..."

Saul stopped finally, looking down at the floor, silent and suddenly at a loss for words. He looked up after a while and addressed his listener.

"Why did he do that, Mister Mossamed? Why?"

As the silence lengthened, Saul noticed a single tear progressing down Mossamed's cheek. The man closed his eyes, clearly feeling the emotional pain all over again and for a long while the two just sat in silence.

"And where was the other one when all this happened?" demanded the merchant.

"I assumed he went to fetch you and your doctor," answered Saul with all sincerity.

"Do you know this for a fact? Or did he just run away leaving my son to face the danger with you?"

Saul was shocked by the questions. In truth he had never even thought about it, being too preoccupied at the time, but in retrospect, perhaps it did seem a little strange that Ben, who could do little if danger did threaten again, had stayed behind and Empas had left. He did not have an answer.

"I don't know, sir," he said truthfully. "I only know that your son saved my life."

"While his so-called friend just ran away and only when he realised what he had done, did he come to my house to call me," added the man vehemently. "He should have stayed with you. Ben should have gone to summon help, is that not so?"

Saul said nothing, only watched as the man seemed to relive the events that had transpired all over again.

"He left my son," Caspar continued. "And I can never forgive him for that. But you, young man, have shown a strength of character and an honesty which is rare. My son called you a friend and so I will honour that friendship. In fact, I have work for you if you are interested."

This last remark drove everything else out of Saul's mind. He had misgivings about the conclusion Caspar Mossamed had come to regarding Empas but decided to ignore them as he became aware that, far from the punishment he had been expecting, this man was offering him a reward, a job and a future. It was his for the asking.

"Thank you very much, sir. I am most certainly interested, and I will serve you in whatever way I can," he said contritely.

"Then it is settled," said the merchant. "You will join my caravan guards and we will see what the future holds."

* * * * *

Over the next few years, Empas went up to the ship on many occasions. He had always been a quick learner, and after that first time, he found that his curiosity and thirst for knowledge quickly overcame his fear at the strangeness of it all. He was able to accept and understand all that he could learn of the Eldoran people and found himself totally in sympathy with their pacifist teachings. He started to realise just how much the building of the discovery ships had meant to them — how these gigantic creations probably represented the pinnacle of their technological achievements. They seemed to him to be combinations of biological and inanimate technologies, taking on a life and even, some might say, an awareness of their own existence. Time spent with Saecra helped him understand just how much the term 'engineering' failed to describe man's relationship with these vessels. More than a vehicle for interstellar travel, the ship became home, provider, comforter and even teacher to its occupants, asking in return only that its working parts be maintained and fed. Some of the crew, only about twenty odd people as far as Empas knew, even went so far as to say there was a telepathic bond between the ship and the director, but this was only ever hearsay.

As his teenage years progressed, so Empas began to recognise and appreciate the enormous divide that existed between these men and women of the future, living in a closed, antiseptic environment, and the people of Rega — the name the inhabitants gave to their own planet — who were but an infant, primitive culture compared with what he saw and learned on the ship. He also gave more thought to his own role in this scenario. Here he was, the only person on or above Rega who could not only exist comfortably in both environments, but also had access to knowledge of the existence of both! What was the purpose of his existence, he wondered? WAS there a purpose to it at all?

At last, his curiosity got the better of him and he asked for an interview with the director.

Empas entered the now familiar office whose door panel carried the inscription General Operations Director — Empas appreciated the irony of that — and saw his father seated in a comfortable chair behind a low table.

"Empas, my son," the old man began. "I haven't seen you in quite a while. How are you progressing with your life and your studies?"

"Very well I think, Father," replied the young man. "Life on Rega passes pretty much as usual, though I am finding it increasingly difficult to make friends. I suppose I should not be too surprised at that, since I feel I have little in common with other people of my age. I find their chatter somewhat inane and knowing what I do of your existence whilst not being able to talk about it, puts me at even more of a distance from them. I am not sure how to handle this, Father."

"Ah, forbidden knowledge," said the director. "It always creates a gulf between those who have it and those who do not. No doubt your peers find you a little strange, perhaps uncommunicative at times? Perhaps they suspect you have something they do not?"

"That is how it seems, yes," answered Empas.

"Hmm," the director nodded. "This is neither easy nor straightforward and no advice that I might offer can really be of much help to you. Tell me, what else have you noticed that seems to set you apart from others, your mental powers, for instance. What is happening there?"

Empas squirmed a little at the directness of the question, obviously unsure of exactly what and how much he should reveal about his developing abilities. Finally, he decided to be completely truthful with his father.

"I am frightened by what I am able to see and do, Father. I can see under the surface of people's bodies, I have a broad working knowledge of how the skeleton functions. This is true with all animals, not just people. I find, now, that I can 'fix' things that have gone wrong by thinking about them. I can mend bones, I can see growths that are destructive and remove them and… I can read minds sometimes. I do not want to intrude into people's thoughts, but sometimes, they seem to hit me, like a high wind. I cannot help but be a party to what they are thinking. I don't know if they are aware of what is happening, all I know is that I am frightened and embarrassed by it."

The director smiled.

"There at least I can help you a little," he said. "The abilities you are developing are collectively called telepathy and they are extremely rare, even among we Eldorans. Before the final annihilation of Eldor, there were still less than a hundred true telepaths among us. It would not surprise me at all if you were the only one on Rega. It is neither good nor bad, right nor wrong that you have these abilities. It simply is. But telepathy left alone, without effort to control or direct it can, eventually, have devastating consequences so I am glad you have told me what is happening.

"The training is neither difficult nor long-winded. It is simply a matter of positive control of your own mind and emotions which will require some effort at first, but which will soon become second nature.

"As we speak, I am beginning to realise that all you are going through, all the knowledge you must keep to yourself, all the training that you need to do will only drive you further and further away from any sort of comfortable relationship with others on Rega in the short term., but I promise you, it will not always be this way. In fact, it must not be this way. You will need to re-establish a full sense of belonging with your people because, only then can they follow you."

"Follow me?" asked Empas. "What do you mean, sir?"

The director wondered, then, if he might have said too much, after all this was still a very young and impressionable man who may or may not be able to grasp the intricacies of what he was about to say. However, he realised he was committed now, so he decided to finish what he had started.

"I mean, Empas, that I foresee a great destiny for you amongst the Regan peoples. Yes, even the Thorians. As a teacher and leader, you must always expect to feel somewhat apart from others, but at the same time you must have an intimate understanding and sympathy with their emotional and intellectual needs as well as their physical ones. That is all I can tell you right now."

Empas sat almost dumbstruck by what the director had said to him. Himself? A leader… teacher? As the director anticipated, he could not fully grasp what was being told to him, but at the same time, enough of it made sense so that he did not immediately dismiss it out of hand as fanciful. But he now certainly had a lot to think about.

"I think we are about finished for now," said the director by way of dismissal. "But talk to young Maikel. I think you will find she may be of some help and comfort to you as you go along. Remember that I am always with you, though I suspect that thought is not always a comfortable one!"

Empas smiled, feeling the warmth and love that the old man always showed him. He left the office and went in search of Maikel, as advised, his head swimming a little with what he had learned.

He found her at her navigation station studying the screens in front of her and decided to just watch her for a while. As he watched he found himself paying more attention to Maikel than to what she was doing. He noticed the way her hair fell gently to her shoulder, the colour of her eyes which were a delicate grey, the pleasing combination of facial features and the gentle curves of the rest of her body. He had experienced these kinds of stirrings before when looking at some Regan girls, but never with quite the same intensity.

Finally, Maikel noticed him standing watching her as she looked up from her station consoles. Unusually, she felt the heat of embarrassment as she flushed under the scrutiny of this unquestionably compelling young man. She shook herself, somewhat in disbelief at her own reaction. Not for the first time, she was forced to reflect on her reaction. What was she thinking? Here she was, nearly two hundred cycles into her life, affected by this — infant — of a mere seventeen or so who was, after all, the son of her leader. That she found him attractive was now undeniable. Whether she could accept that that had any fuller meaning was something altogether different. She shook herself mentally and tried to restore her composure.

"Hello Empas. Is there something I can help you with?" she asked innocently.

"Actually, Maikel, I'm not sure. About anything," he said, stumbling slightly over his words.

"What do you mean?" she asked, concern entering her voice.

"I don't know," Empas began. "It's just something my father said just now. It doesn't make any sense to me. He said I should speak to you, so here I am."

Intrigued, Maikel moved from her station towards him, only then realising how tall he had grown in the last few cycles.

"Perhaps we should find somewhere quiet, and we can talk if you like," she offered.

Without understanding why, Empas was suddenly overwhelmed by self-doubt. It wasn't just what had passed between him and his father. He just felt so uncomfortable, he could not bring himself to say any of the things he had intended to. He gradually became aware that it was this woman who made him feel awkward and reluctant to talk. He did not want to seem like a boy in front of her, yet he recognised his need for her counsel. He tried to consider what was the best thing to do, but his mind was just a jumble of conflicting emotions. No, he decided, now was not the time to talk to her. He could not bring himself to do that.

"No, um, it's all right," he stumbled. "I can see you're busy. Perhaps next time I visit the ship we…I have to go home now. Goodbye, Maikel."

With that he almost ran from the navigation station, back down to the boat deck where Adrian was, fortunately, checking over his personal sled, thus avoiding any further delay in getting him back to Rega.

Chapter 8

Emperor Tyramen sat and considered the document in front of him. It was a report from the Thorian governor of Esteria, a large area of the large eastern continent that the Thorians had conquered and occupied. It covered, amongst other regions, the whole of the lands previously ruled by the Juhl, a strange race that he found difficult to understand. On the one hand, they seemed fairly malleable, as the arrangement with their religious leaders proved. So much of their lives and ways were ruled by their strict adherence to the laws they claimed were given to them by The One God, their great, invincible god — so they claimed! Their high priests were only too willing to go along with the realities of Thorian rule and occupation, in return for the granting of their continuance as religious leaders. Both they, and the Thorians, saw, and made use of, the obvious economic opportunities offered by cooperation. The Thorian emperor allowed them this modicum of power which, by and large, kept the people in line and relatively peaceful, thus allowing the bulk of his army to move on in search of new areas to conquer and enabling him to leave only garrison troops on the ground in Juhl. *'So much for the invincibility of their god,'* he thought. The Juhl had proven to be, apart from the odd incident, quite placid and easy to rule.

At least, it had been that way until now, but as he read on, he realised that these people were capable of offering resistance to his empire. The report contained details, as much as were known, of the latest in a line of terrorist groups that had formed and were currently making quite a nuisance of themselves. As each group arose, they claimed to be led by a 'messiah' of some kind, who invariably turned out to be just another peasant with an inflated ego and a sense of righteous anger. Inevitably, of course, they were captured and put to death, but with each execution, the general population grew more resentful of Thorian rule.

The governor reported that he was keeping a tight rein on matters and that he still had the help of their priesthood, but he requested more troops to bolster the numbers available to garrison the various urban centres in the region and especially the capital, Tevalem. The emperor could not help but be suspicious about this request. He had always regarded Trumius, the current governor, as being a somewhat weak individual, full of self-doubt and indecision, but had thought the posting to Juhl might prove an easy enough challenge for the, otherwise able, politician. Now he saw that, perhaps, he had underestimated these one-god pacifists.

Tyramen was torn between two possible courses of action. He could simply accede to the request and send more troops — although he had to consider the requirements of the army closer to home as the, seemingly never-ending, war against the Bolgs sucked in ever more of his resources. It was said that his father had fought them with the aid of the god, Ares, and victories had been many and swift, but it was now many years since anything had been seen of the god, and since he had organised the successful assassination of his father two years past, he could not ask him if the tales were true, nor could he solicit his advice on how best to fight the Bolgs. He had little time for gods, anyway, having long ago come to the conclusion that his father had been exaggerating and simply trying to prepare the means to have himself declared 'divine'. Gods were just a convenient way of keeping the masses in line as far as Tyramen was concerned. Not that the idea of being 'divine' didn't appeal to him. It could have many advantages and he began to speculate, before forcibly bringing himself back to the matter at hand.

Conversely, he could replace the current governor with somebody perhaps more... motivated to carry out the emperor's wishes as well as bolstering his forces on the ground. Given that the report he had just read was at least two months out of date, he wondered how bad the situation might have become since it was written. Unable to make up his mind immediately, he continued to study the document in his hands, so he did not hear the boy approach him from behind his throne.

The practice dagger was made of wood, but even so it would have caused a very bad, if not fatal, injury had it penetrated Tyramen's chest, even in the hands of a small child. The thought flashed briefly through his mind as he turned and grabbed the boy with both hands, laughing as he did so.

"You have succeeded where so many have failed, my son," Tyramen congratulated the boy. "But let that be a lesson to you. When you ascend to this throne, you will become Emperor Tyrsis the Second. It is then that you must never, NEVER, drop your guard. Not for an instant."

"But you did, Father," answered the boy in all innocence.

The remark made Tyramen stop for a moment before answering his son.

"Yes, yes, I did, didn't I?" he said slowly, finally coming to a decision about the matter before him.

"But I will not be so easy a target for you next time," he chided the boy. "So do not imagine for one moment that I will not have my eye on you always. Because I will."

He smiled then — something he did not do often — as he allowed his pride in his small son to swell. He saw, in the mock assassination attempt, the proud result of years spent coaching his son in the art of survival, and at ten years old, the lad had proved an able pupil. He was already quite proficient with sword and shield — appropriate to his size of course — and had just proved that he had the instincts, if not the skills, of a first-class assassin. This last thought reminded Tyramen yet again that you never knew from which direction, or with which weapon, the attack might come. But eventually, come it would. The smile disappeared from his face then as the reality of what had just occurred struck him.

"Now it is time for you to go, little one," he told his son in as amiable a manner as he could manage. "For your father has much to do. Tell Nazim to attend me, will you?"

"Of course, Father," the boy replied before turning and running to the door of the throne room.

Outside the room, the emperor's personal guard stood to attention as little Tyrsis emerged. The boy ignored him and moved towards the table opposite the door where the emperor's secretary, Nazim, sat. He stood directly in front of the table and said, "My father commands that you attend him, Nazim."

"Of course, Highness," answered the secretary. "I will do so immediately."

He watched the boy skip away before entering his master's throne room. '*Pompous little brat,*' he thought as he moved swiftly to approach the throne from the front and knelt before the emperor.

"You command me, Sire," said the man.

"Yes, Nazim, I have two tasks for you. First, send word to that councillor you were telling me about — Portio Latiedes — that I wish to see him on an urgent matter. The results of that interview will require some paperwork, so you had better attend me as well."

"It is done, Sire," said the man. "And the second thing?"

"Yes," said the emperor, and paused before continuing calmly. "Tell me how my son managed to get into this room, apparently without being noticed by anybody and without one of my personal guards to accompany him?"

Nazim was immediately alert. This question changed the expression on his face to one of fear and apprehension. He had not thought to question the boy's presence, and only now, did he recognise his mistake.

"I cannot imagine, Majesty," he began in a trembling voice. "The guards all have specific orders not to allow anyone to intrude on your privacy. All visitors and supplicants are to present their credentials and request permission to enter your presence, and they must always be accompanied by at least one of your guards."

"AND THAT ORDER INCLUDES EVERYBODY!" exploded the emperor.

After the outburst, the secretary said nothing, fully expecting to be dismissed at the very least for this indiscretion. Or his punishment could be worse! He decided then that *the brat* would pay if he suffered in any way because of his prank. He was surprised, therefore, when the emperor spoke again.

"You are an able secretary, Nazim, and an accomplished spymaster, which makes you very useful. But not indispensable. Do you understand me?"

"Yes, Majesty," replied the man. All business now and ready to do anything to salvage the situation.

"Good. Then you will make it your task to find out who allowed the boy in here and ensure that, whoever is responsible, it will not happen again and that all others in a similar position are made aware of the consequences of failure to carry out my wishes to the letter. Do I make myself clear?"

117

"Yes Majesty," came the reply again.

"Then, that is all, Nazim," said the emperor.

* * * * *

It took Nazim only two hours to establish which of the emperor's personal guards had indeed allowed the emperor's son to enter the throne room through a secret door, known only to himself and the guard responsible. His name was Josias and Nazim had him arrested immediately. Under 'assisted questioning', the man admitted he had a soft spot for the boy and that he thought the lad was simply playing a harmless game of hide and seek. He had not considered that any harm could come to the emperor through his own son.

Nazim arrived back at the throne room in time to see Senator Portio Latiedes just leaving the emperor's presence. Nazim bowed to the senator and offered the usual salutations.

"May I be of service, Senator," he offered as the tall, burly politician was about to brush past him.

"Not unless you have any more influence with the emperor than I have," he returned. "I have just been given the post of Governor of Juhl and the surrounding territories on the Eastern continent, and I am ordered to take three centuries of troops there and restore order quickly. Gods know what I am going to find there. Everyone knows it's the last place on Rega that anyone wants to be. Putting down a few terrorists is not my idea of how to get on in this world."

"Alas, I cannot help you there, Senator. At least, not directly," Nazim answered.

The senator immediately picked up on the unspoken offer, and whilst he would normally have as little to do with the slippery secretary as he could, in these circumstances, he felt it might be worthwhile to listen to what he had to say.

"What do you mean, you sly fox?" asked the senator.

"Oh, nothing melodramatic, my lord," said the other. "Only, it occurs to me that, should you be able to put down these terrorists quickly, you might actually be able to turn this posting to your advantage."

"And how would I go about that?" Latiedes asked, beginning to

118

suspect some subterfuge for which the emperor's secretary was famous.

"Why, through good intelligence from a reliable source," answered the secretary. He continued, "I have been told of a merchant who travels all over those lands. He has no love for the Juhl, ever since his son's death there. It might pay you handsomely to make his acquaintance, Senator. He has a captain of his personal guards who, though Juhl himself, is devoted to the merchant. He is a very capable man in many ways and the merchant relies on him heavily to 'persuade' reluctant buyers and sellers. Hence, the merchant has become very rich and very powerful, but he also has his ear to the ground."

"He sounds like a useful fellow, this merchant. So why has the present governor not made use of him?"

"I do not know, my lord. I can only assume Lord Trumius has his own sources and methods," answered Nazim.

"Huh, it would seem he has precious little of either according to the emperor. What did you say this merchant's name was?" enquired Latiedes.

"I didn't, my lord, but I think it is Mossamed. Caspar Mossamed."

The senator nodded and was about to continue on his way when he stopped and turned back to Nazim. The secretary watched him, clearly unsurprised at his action.

"It has just occurred to me, Nazim, that you have given me some very valuable information here."

"Oh, I simply wish to be of service," began the secretary innocently.

"No, you don't," stated the other. "You never give anything away without wanting something in return, so what is it you want from me?"

"Why, nothing Senator," began Nazim, "except... perhaps..."

"Well, what is it?" demanded the other.

"There are prophecies, among the Juhl and other races over there, that a 'messiah' will come to lead them to some sort of supremacy. Each terrorist leader we have captured has claimed to be their messiah and it is tempting to simply ignore these tales as myths or, at worst, propaganda. But something tells me there is more to it than that. There was the business, almost twenty years ago now, of a so-called miraculous birth of a king of the Juhl. Our puppet, Harag, ordered all the newborn slain to ensure nothing came of it, but rumours persist that, somehow, the child survived. Naturally, the existence of such a person poses a threat to the empire and even to the emperor himself. So, if you should hear anything, I would be most grateful if you could, shall we say, keep me informed?"

"And that is all you want?" asked the senator.

"Of course, my lord," said Nazim. "We both live only to serve the emperor, do we not?"

Although Portio Latiedes did not believe for a moment that the request was as simple or as innocent as the sneaky secretary made out, he could not find anything overtly threatening to his own future well-being in the proposition. He, therefore, agreed to the proposal before leaving the emperor's palace to begin his preparations for departure across the ocean to what he knew would be a new and totally different life. In just over three months' time, he would land on the eastern continent with his own small army and begin the task of cleaning it up for the Thorian Empire.

Meanwhile, the voice inside Nazim's head began again. '*Well done, my little schemer. Soon we shall have proof of the whereabouts of this upstart, and more importantly, we shall be able to do something about him. Or perhaps we may even control him. Now won't the emperor be pleased about that?*'

Nazim smiled to himself as he knocked and entered the emperor's throne room once again.

"Nazim," called the emperor. "Have you completed both the tasks I gave you?"

Nazim knelt before his powerful master.

"Yes, Majesty. The wretch who betrayed you is one, Josias, of the guard. He thought your son was playing a game."

"Did he indeed? Oh dear, it just shows how wrong you can be. It is a shame to lose a guardsman, but they can be replaced quickly. In the meantime, he and all the other guards must be shown that protecting me is no game! Assemble the guard in the private courtyard. He will be executed there so that all can see the consequences of failure to do their duty."

"At once, Majesty," said Nazim.

He rose swiftly and exited the throne room calling, as he did so, for the captain of the emperor's personal guard. He was quite used to these ad hoc executions, and indeed, of late he quite looked forward to them, but he still found time to wonder if the seed he had planted with Portio Latiedes would bear fruit. '*Of course, it will*,' whispered the voice.

* * * * *

Marin sat in her accustomed chair and looked, dumbfounded at her eldest son, Empas. She could hardly bring herself to believe what she had just heard him say. Jespeth, too, was clearly taken aback by Empas' announcement. Finally, she thought she should say something.

"But you cannot just go off, like that, on your own," she began. "Where will you go? Who will look after you and feed you and..." she stopped, unable to continue the tirade, because of the tears that had started. "Jespeth, talk to him, please," she pleaded.

Despite his involvement in this situation, his wife's request caught him somewhat off guard. How do you talk to, or even persuade, your son that he is wrong to want to do a particular thing, when you know, firstly, that he is not your son, and secondly, that this is probably what he was born to do anyway? The two factors added up to a feeling of complete helplessness in this situation. Nevertheless, for Marin's sake, he felt he should try to persuade Empas to change his mind.

"Think of your future, Empas, the business that we have built here, due in no small part to your fantastic command of skills which should have taken years to master. There is certainty and security in this trade and your contribution to carpentry and joinery could be inestimable."

"Jespeth," said Empas gently. "I know that you are both concerned for me, but I cannot help the feeling I have inside me that I must discover who I am. What am I doing here?"

"But you know who you are," answered the carpenter. "You are our son, and you have a future here."

"No, Jespeth. Though I cannot explain it, I just know that I must begin my journey now. I'm sorry, but I have to go. Everyone seems to have plans for me, except me, and I have to sort things out," said Empas, seeming more perplexed and lost with every word.

The statement seemed to knock the wind out of Jespeth's sails completely. He was left speechless in the knowledge that what he had considered secret was probably now known and that, truly, he could wield little or no influence now over this young man who, he divined, clearly had a spectacular future. Marin was destroyed by Empas' revelation. Though he had not said so directly, it was clear he knew that Jespeth was not his real father. She had hoped to reveal the truth in her own time, when she felt he was grown up and mature enough to understand and accept the truth. But even in her misery, she had to admit that her son was a lot more grown up and mature than she gave him credit for. He clearly understood the entire situation — probably more so than she herself did — but nevertheless, she could not help but be worried, as only a mother can be, about the choices her son was about to make. And she could not shake the conviction that she had already known, and had now lost, the happiest years with her son and that, ahead, lay a path ending in disaster.

"The One God says that I am destined to be a leader and that I must get to know my people," Empas continued. "I do not see myself as any kind of leader, but I do need to get to know more about the people of this land. I need to know myself. There are things happening within me, within my mind, that I do not understand, and I'm sorry mother, Jespeth, but I know that you cannot help me with this problem. How can I fulfil my destiny if I just stay here and wait for it to come to me?"

Empas was tempted to continue, to try to explain to these two people who had been his protectors and guides for so many years, but he knew that he could not explain what he did not even understand himself. All he knew was that he had to get away to think, to decide what he must do and where he must go, but the silence lengthened, and with the pause came the knowledge to all three that the matter had been settled. All that remained was the farewells and the sadness of parting. The young man regarded his mother solemnly and realised just how much he loved her. Jespeth too, though in a more distant way. But very dear to him, perhaps more than he had realised before deciding to leave them in this way. Even so, he must leave. He knew that with an unshakeable certainty.

Empas rose from his chair and left the kitchen to go to his own room where he packed his few belongings in a large pouch which he slung from his belt. On his way out, he stopped and looked again into the kitchen, where his parents still sat, dumbfounded.

"I won't forget you both, and I hope you will be able to think well of me. I hope you can understand that I am both sorry to leave and excited and glad about the future, though I do not know where it will lead me. Does that make sense to you? I hope so. Anyway, I will never stop loving you."

He wanted to say more, but the devastation he saw finally became too much. Turning away from his parents, he opened the front door and stepped out into the street and an uncertain future.

* * * * *

The director stood in front of the viewscreen in his office, seeing the curve of Rega below them, noting the cloud patterns forming due to the wind currents generated by the never-ending exchange of heat and moisture between the surface of the planet and the atmosphere surrounding it. The continual process, he knew, but one of many facts of nature which gave the planet its life, its energy, its vibrancy. He had seen many planets, of course, all controlled by the same principles and was amazed once again at how some produced sentient life, some of which stalled early in that process, and some destroyed themselves before they could ever reach that stage.

Once again, he pursued his thoughts. Of those that produced sentient life, virtually all seemed destined for a premature end due to the actions, or inaction, of that same sentient life the planets had nurtured. It didn't seem to matter which type of animal achieved ascendancy, mammalian, reptilian, saurian or whatever, they all struggled to evolve, fought their way to the top of the pile, then managed to destroy their heritage almost before they could appreciate what they had. He considered the irony of it: the very principle that endowed sentient life forms with their ability to survive, tame and eventually overcome their surroundings — the survival of the fittest, the need to dominate — was also the same principle which led to their eventual destruction. He supposed this struggle manifested itself in the militarist actions of all animals seeking supremacy. Yet, he mused, this did not have to be the be all and end all. They could surpass the need to conquer their worlds by force and replace it with peaceable methods of development of their minds, if only they could be shown how. It was this belief, the serendipitous coming together of the solutions to a number of problems, which had led to his actions on Rega below. And Empas was where it all began.

He was interrupted at that point by the knocking at his door. His visitor had often thought about the director's preference that people knock on his door to announce their presence, rather than let the ship's natural systems inform him. Gaveri smiled at the rather quaint, old-fashioned predilection exhibited by his commander.

"Enter," came the call from inside the room and doctor Gaveri stepped over the threshold as the door slid open.

"Well, my friend," said the director. "Have you come to check up on my well-being?"

Not for the first time, Gaveri considered the enormous energy and drive exhibited by this unique man he had accompanied and supported through so many hundreds of cycles and hundreds of different circumstances and locations. They had seen and experienced much of Eldoran history at first hand, and he felt, there was probably not much left in the universe that could surprise either of them.

"Why would I attempt that which I know, all too well, you would dismiss out of hand as mollycoddling?" the doctor answered with sincerity.

"Is that a sample of obverse censure I detect in your voice?" the old man enquired, smiling as they settled into a relaxed familiarity which they had often shared with each other, but with no one else, over their lifetimes.

"No, I am not censuring or scolding you, but I would remind you that you are well overdue for a medical check-up. This past thirty or forty cycles have been a heavy strain, even on your abilities, Director, and I am concerned at your distraction over Empas. It borders on an obsession. I cannot remember when we last spent more than a hundred and fifty cycles in orbit around one planet and I… well, I am concerned, that's all."

Gaveri saw the light of agreement in the director's eyes as he nodded gently, acknowledging his friend's insight.

"You are right, of course, old friend. I cannot stop thinking about him. And I'll admit, I keep an eye on him nearly all the time. But so much is hanging on the future he chooses to make for himself. He grows so quickly, and events are moving. He will be, I think, all that I could have wished for, but he does not seem to relish the role that I foresee for him, and I cannot help but be concerned."

"You have been watching him?" asked the doctor.

"Virtually, non-stop," admitted the director. "Much of his development is as I predicted, but there are so many unknowns and unknowables that I find I dare not ignore him for long."

"Do you intend to intervene?" asked Gaveri.

The director was silent. The question was a broad one, open to interpretation in many ways, but he knew very well what Gaveri was getting at. And he had to admit that the temptation to interfere, to guide, to protect his son from what he saw as misjudgement or ill fortune, was always there. Until now, he had resisted and had every intention of continuing to do so. He had long ago decided that interference in the development of civilisations, beyond the absolute minimum that might be necessary, was not a good thing at all, and to be avoided altogether if possible. In fact, it could be argued, that it was pretty pointless, or even self-defeating, in many ways. Empas was no exception. Though he might observe all that happened to his son, he was determined not to interfere.

Recognising his friend's concern, the old man looked directly at him and replied, "No, I will not intervene, though the direction his future will take hangs in the balance for some time yet. But do not concern yourself, Gaveri, he will be allowed to go his own way. Speaking of which, what news do you have of Lucian?"

"I'm glad you asked, since it was, he, that I came to see you about," answered the doctor. "I fully expected that he would be dead by now, given the evidence of the infection he had which affected his whole body. Evidence from the observation cameras reveal that he still lives, though he does not move much. His body seems completely wasted, yet he is still clinging on. I don't know how he's doing it."

"Hmm. I have my suspicions if that is the case," answered the old man. "He is possessed of considerable telepathic power and there is no telling what influence he may be wielding, or where, without delving into his mind — something I am reluctant to do. Are there any other visible signs that we should be aware of?"

"Not really. As I said, he does not move much. I am concerned in case he should be in pain, though. As a doctor, I find it difficult to allow such a condition to continue untreated, even in one such as Lucian."

"Unfortunately, he brought all this upon himself," said the director sternly. "But I shouldn't worry if I were you, old friend. One of the good things about telepathic power is the ability it grants one to block out pain completely. His entire body could waste away and he wouldn't feel a thing."

"Well, I suppose that's something, though I'm still not happy about the situation," continued the doctor.

"If it makes you feel any better, Doctor, I will undertake to keep an eye on Lucian as well," answered the director. "You never know, it may help to overcome my — obsession — with other events on this world!"

"I'm sure you're right," said Gaveri with a wry smile. "And now I must be getting back to my work, so I will leave you to your ruminations, Director."

"Thank you for your help, and your concern, old friend," said the director as the doctor left the room.

Alone once more, the director considered his friend's words and decided that it might not be such a bad idea to look in on Lucian as he had promised. There was something about that situation that did not feel right, so maybe, he thought, I can find out what it is. For all its power, telepathy was still an imperfect science, and though he knew the extent and limitations of his own ability quite intimately, it was also evident that some surprising aspects of the power could manifest themselves totally without warning. He was also aware that telepathic power could be used just as effectively to destroy as it could to build and heal. Lucian was clearly a prime example of this, and despite the precarious nature of his imprisoned existence, was showing some alarming abilities. Yes, perhaps Gaveri was right to be concerned.

He sat while beginning the process of self-protection and clarity, opening his mind so that he might project a complete image of himself right into Lucian's cell.

The prisoner turned his head so that he could focus on the image forming at the centre of his room.

"Ah, I wondered when you might reappear, old man," he croaked from a throat now unused for many cycles.

"And I wonder just what you are up to, Lucian," answered the image slowly.

"Why, that's simple," Lucian croaked again. "I'm going to upset your plan and stop you from destroying my world."

"Your world, Lucian?" asked the old man. "What makes you think this is your world?"

Lucian then did something else he had not done for many cycles. He smiled.

Chapter 9

No sooner had he left his parent's house, than he was beset with fresh doubt and uncertainty. What had he done? He could not go back — that would achieve nothing and would leave him forever wondering what might have been. But nor had he made any positive plans as to where he should go and what he should do. He just knew he had to get away, from everybody, to give himself a chance to think through what he should do now. His experiences, both here on Rega and on the ship orbiting the planet, had taught him the basic differences between the two realities with which he was forced to live.

On the one hand was the religion-led, primitive and rather superstitious existence enjoyed by the people here who just went about their daily lives, accepting the good with the bad, the hardships and the joys of life, because that was all they knew. On the other was the Eldoran ship and its strange, very long-lived people. Empas had only ever seen around twenty or so people on his visits to the ship, and all looked so young, with the notable exceptions of the director and Doctor Gaveri, yet all, he knew, were at least one hundred and fifty years old and probably more. Even Maikel, for whom he felt more than a little affection, was certain to be into her second century in years, so how could he even contemplate a relationship with such a person?

But this was just one of his many unanswered questions. Of all the people on Rega, only he was aware that there was a reality beyond their daily existence that bordered on the miraculous. What would happen if he were to tell people about the Eldorans, he wondered? Would they accept that other reality, or would they call him a madman, or worse? And there, he decided, was the crux of the dilemma under which he lived. Instinctively, he knew that he could not reveal what he knew to others. That their reactions would be based on fear of the unknown. Yet how could he become accepted; how could he achieve even a fraction of the things he had been told he would if he did not? He had to think this through without any outside pressures from his parents or friends, and especially not from the Eldorans.

Without consciously being aware of it, Empas made his way out of the village where he had spent so many years, and headed in the general direction north-east, which would take him through several other villages like his before ultimately depositing him on the border of Juhl lands. From there he would see the mountain range which ran down roughly the centre of the continent separating Juhl and the other countries this side from what had become almost entirely Bolg lands on the other.

The largely uneventful journey took him almost two months, working a day or two here and there, or helping sick people and animals to pay for lodging and food. In fact, it was his growing power as a healer that became most apparent on his short journey. Somehow, it seemed as if he was able to identify exactly the nature of a fracture or sprain and heal it with little more than a conscious thought. Empas found this ability unsettling, even after all the years he had been aware of it, so he became reluctant to do it too often, but found he could not refuse when faced with the situation. Whilst most people he helped in this way appreciated it and sang his praises, some viewed his ability with suspicion and hostility, despite benefiting from it. He remembered one particular incident when he had been waylaid on the road by a group of men who belonged to one of the resistance groups that had sprung up all over the country.

The terrain was rocky, and the road twisted and turned as it ascended into an area of foothills and canyons where ambush cover was plentiful and lone travellers went at their peril. Empas was so deep in his thoughts that he hadn't taken much notice of where he was. He only became aware of the unnatural silence when it was broken by the sound of a dislodged stone falling down a shallow cliff face. He stopped then and took a look around him, realising almost at once the mistake he had made in coming to this place alone. Apprehensive at first, he soon realised that nothing was likely to happen until he made his next move. He had called out then, not really knowing what to expect, but it seemed a reasonable course of action at the time. He argued that, since he was alone and unarmed, if he could at least see the threat facing him, it might help him find a solution to it.

"Who's there?" Silence. "At least show yourself if you mean to assail me. Or are you only cowards then?" he asked with a bravado he certainly did not feel.

He received no answer to his brave enquiry until two shapes emerged from behind rocks almost immediately in front of him. The tallest one, emerging from the left, seemed to be the leader here, and though he made no move to produce a weapon, Empas knew that the likelihood was not far away.

"You are the healer," he said, more as a statement than as a question.

"I have some small abilities, it is true," answered Empas honestly.

"Then you must come with me," said the man in a way that clearly brooked no argument. Especially when three more men, armed this time with slings and a spear, appeared from behind rocks further up the side of the defile.

"Clearly I must," answered Empas. "But would you mind telling me why?"

"Yes, I would mind. I don't discuss matters with sorcerers. So, if you want to stay alive, just do as you are told and don't ask a lot of stupid questions. Blindfold him," the man commanded one of the others.

Faced with this level of hostility and scepticism, Empas had decided that discretion was probably the correct course here, so he allowed himself to be blindfolded and led to — wherever it was they led him to. Despite the blindfold, his escort made sure he did not stumble and the only way he was aware that they had arrived somewhere other than the path was when cool air enveloped him and his senses told him they were inside a shelter of some kind, probably a cave as he had not been aware of entering through a door. The party came to a halt and the blindfold was finally removed.

It had not taken him long to become accustomed to the low level of light, and as he surveyed the cave he saw a dozen men, all armed and dressed in simple, hunters' clothing. He had noticed that all bore the look of the hunted, rather than the hunters, they clearly perceived themselves to be.

The man who had spoken to him at the ambush pointed to a lone figure lying on a pallet towards the rear of the cave.

"This is why you are here, sorcerer. Heal him, or die," he demanded. "And make no mistake, right now your life is mine to take."

Although Empas was not too worried for his own safety — if they had wanted to kill him, surely, they could have done it by now — he realised that the man who threatened him was deadly serious. But he was more concerned for the figure on the pallet. Saying nothing, he approached the sick man and saw at once that he was burning up with a fever. The cause soon became obvious, firstly from the smell coming from the wound in the shoulder and then, as he removed the rags that were serving as bandages, he saw for himself where the arrow had penetrated. The shaft had been broken off and the head was well embedded in the shoulder, destroying the tissue and gradually depriving the man of life as the sepsis spread.

"I need clean fresh water," he said to no one in particular.

"We already tried that, sorcerer, so don't…"

Empas saw red. This arrogant bandit was not helping at all. He rose and turned on his captor.

"I said clean fresh water — NOW!" he demanded. "For once do as you are asked and stop trying to impress me. Now go!"

The man was taken aback by Empas' outburst but knew that he must not lose control of the situation otherwise he would lose the respect of his men. And they were his men, if the leader died, which he hoped would happen. It was only the obvious loyalty of the men to the leader who now lay on the pallet that had forced him to ambush the healer. So, he continued to glare at Empas as he said, "Samuel, fetch this charlatan some clean fresh water. Let's see if he can do anything with it."

Empas turned back to his patient, saying nothing more. Having assessed the nature of the injury, he was unsure how to proceed exactly. So, breaking his vow to himself, he made silent contact with the director.

'*Father, I need Doctor Gaveri's help here.*'

'*Then you shall have it,*' came the reply. '*I will summon him immediately.*'

'*Thank you. I have a patient with an arrow head buried in his shoulder. Already the wound has turned septic and started to spread. That part, I can handle, but it is the removal of the weapon without causing further damage that I am not familiar with.*'

While the conversation continued, the man, Samuel, delivered the bowl of fresh water, which Empas silently and without apparent action, purified before deciding to use it. Just in case, he thought.

Doctor Gaveri had obviously arrived at the director's office, and having had the situation described to him, told the director how he should instruct Empas.

'Empas, to avoid ripping and damaging the shoulder any further, you will need to push the arrowhead all the way through and pull it out from the back. You will need to drain the wound, of course, but you must also try to ensure that the patient does not lose too much blood. Is that possible?' came the thought instruction.

'Yes, thank you, father, thank you doctor, I think I can manage the situation now,' Empas replied.

'Are you sure? I can send the Security Prefect if you are in trouble.'

'No. I will be fine,' he answered, not totally sure he was correct.

The man lying on the pallet was awake and clearly in extreme pain. He observed Empas and a look of recognition flashed across his face.

"Do I know you?" he asked.

"I don't think so," Empas replied. "I am simply here to help you if I can. In fact, your men insisted on it."

"They are loyal to me, and your reputation is spreading so, here we are," the man said, and then grimaced in pain as the object in his shoulder moved again. When the spasm had passed, he looked at Empas again.

"You look familiar, sorcerer. What is your name?"

"My name is Empas, and I am not a sorcerer. I am simply here trying to help. I can repair your shoulder, but that arrow is going to have to come out first. And I'm afraid that is going to hurt. Since I would rather not be attacked while I'm working, I would appreciate it if you would inform your men of what is going to happen and why," said the young man looking intently at his patient.

The leader studied him for a second before calling to his men, instructing them to stand clear and not to interfere. Loman, the man who had assumed command and brought Empas here said, "Are you sure about this, Andrew? This fool could as easily kill you as heal you and then where would we be? Perhaps it would be better to get rid of him now before he can do any harm."

"Oh, you would love that, wouldn't you, Loman? You think that once I am dead, the men will automatically follow you, don't you?" said

Andrew, gritting his teeth because of the pain. "It takes more than a loud voice and a death wish to lead the fight against the Thorians, so you back off as I have told you and let this man do his work. If I die, only then do you make decisions. Or try to."

Empas was not exactly reassured by this exchange, but decided that he had little alternative anyway, so he decided to proceed.

"Are you ready?" he asked the man.

"About as ready as… Aaaaaaaaaaahhh!" he cried as Empas suddenly shoved the arrowhead right through the shoulder and out the back, next to his collar bone.

Andrew passed out at the sudden shock, so Empas decided to work quickly, while his patient could feel nothing. Using a combination of rudimentary surgical technique and telepathic power, he drained the poison from the wound until the blood ran clean, cleansed it using the purified water then, working from the inside outwards, he repaired the damaged tissue and sealed the wound. Then he sat back and surveyed his work — the perfectly clear shoulder with no sign of the arrow wound, front or back, and he knew, the muscle and tissue within would be as good as new.

The patient was still unmoving as Loman suddenly appeared by Empas' side.

"Let's have a look and see what you've done to him," he demanded, "assuming he's not dead already."

The man looked at the perfectly clean shoulder and saw that his leader was still unconscious. Making one last attempt to wrest control of the situation, he cried, "What trickery is this? What have you done to his body you, necromancer? See, men, this sorcerer has killed our leader with his dark magic tricks. I say he dies, now. Who's with me?"

As the cheer went up from men who did not understand what was really happening here, Andrew's eyes flickered open, and he quickly took in the situation.

"Sorcerer he may be," said the prone figure, "but he certainly knows how to fix a shoulder wound."

The unbroken silence that followed this statement was finally broken by a collective sigh of relief on the part of all of them — all except Loman, who stood facing Empas now, a wicked looking knife in his hand.

"Bewitched!" he cried. "He's bewitched you all. But I won't fall for it."

As he spoke, he took a step towards Empas, who did not flinch. The bandit had raised his knife arm ready to strike but found that he could not do so. In fact, he could not move at all. Suddenly, from off to one side, an arrow flew, perfectly flighted and pierced the man through the heart. He dropped suddenly, dead already before he hit the floor. Empas did not comprehend what had happened at first, but after a second or two, recovered his senses and moved to kneel over Loman. Feeling for any sign of life at all that he could use to build upon, he tried to save the man who had just tried to kill him, but it was useless. He rose, looking around and fastened his eyes on the archer who had fired the arrow.

"He was always looking for trouble anyway," said the man grudgingly, as he lowered his bow.

Empas was horrified at how easily these men could kill others but was equally aware that the arrow would not have been shot if Loman had not tried to kill him. This mixture of horror and gratitude left him momentarily speechless. Finally, he found his voice and addressed the man.

"You did not need to do that. He would not have killed me. But I am grateful that you felt you should try to save my life. I hope The One God can forgive you for the life you have taken."

The man simply shrugged and continued putting his bow away. As if this were a signal, one by one, the gathered men resumed what they had been doing and continued about their business. Empas moved back to Andrew, who was now sitting upright on the pallet and looking a lot healthier.

"Don't bother yourself too much over that one," he said as Empas sat beside him. "He had that coming many times over. He was a cruel, heartless man who never really cared about anyone but himself. I also suspect that he was a thief, but now I'll never know."

"I hear what you say," said Empas. "But I'm afraid I find it difficult to conceive of any reason that is good enough to warrant taking another's life."

"But he was out to kill you, man. Surely that is a good enough reason?" said the leader, clearly astonished at Empas' attitude to the attempted murder.

"No, he would not have killed me," Empas affirmed. "But he was ready to use me as an excuse to challenge you for the leadership of this group. Nevertheless, I am not in a position to judge him for any of these actions or intentions. If I could, I would have saved him, just as I saved you."

Andrew studied the strange young man before him. He was in no doubt that he owed this man his life and he had nearly witnessed his death. Yet the youngster seemed unphased by it all. Again, he found himself wondering why Empas looked so familiar to him.

"Are you sure we've never met before?" he asked.

"I think I might have remembered that," said Empas with a trace of irony.

Andrew then had an inspiration.

"Where were you born?" he asked urgently.

"A town called Bazel, why?" returned the young healer.

Then Andrew sensed there was a conundrum here that required an answer, but it was proving elusive.

"Oh, nothing really," he said nonchalantly. "Strange thing, that. Bazel was where all those babies were put to death years ago. Looking at you, that must've been about the time you were born."

Empas did not pick up on any nuance in the exchange as he became aware that his work here was done, and he should be moving on.

"Well," he said, "you should be all right now, so if you could have your men lead me back to where they found me, I'll continue my journey. I am quite happy to be blindfolded again so that I cannot give away your location."

Well, at least he wouldn't be leading the Thorians to their hideout! Andrew stood and addressed Empas seriously.

"As I said before, you may or may not be a sorcerer, though personally I will not think evil of you whatever or whoever you are. I thank you sincerely for saving my life. I hope to be able to repay you someday."

"You don't owe me anything, Andrew. Let's just agree it was a good thing that I was here when you needed my help. I hope the Thorians won't cause you any further pain."

With that he had left the cave, accompanied by two of the group that had ambushed him, returned to the defile where they had met and left to continue on his way.

*****

He thought now about the reactions he had encountered because of that incident. The mistrust and ridicule he had endured from men who could not conceive the scope of the power that he possessed, and which frightened him more each time he thought about it. Its presence gave him confidence, but also a huge sense of discomfort knowing that he was able to wield it, but not knowing how, and not daring to for fear of the damage that he might do.

These, and other dark thoughts, accompanied Empas all the way on his travels through and beyond the Juhl lands, until he finally found himself at the foot of the mountain range, he had seen all those weeks before. He had reached a moment of decision, but he did not see the point in simply turning round and going back as he still had not found any answers to his questions. Besides, now that he was here, his curiosity took over and demanded that he travel on into those mountains to see what he might discover. The prospect looked bleak indeed but then, what did he have to lose? So, he continued on, aware that he was entering territory that was probably uninhabited and where food and water might well be scarce. *Still*, he thought, *if I really get into trouble, I could ask to go to the ship.* The thought did not bring him all that much comfort, as he had decided that it would be best if he stayed clear of Eldoran influence.

As luck would have it, he need not have worried as there was food, in the form of nuts and berries and other edible plants, water from mountain streams which flowed cool and fresh, filled with snow melt, and the wolves and other wild animals living in the region also seemed uninterested in him. He was unaware that, quite by chance, he had chosen the route taken by Marin and Jespeth when they had fled the wrath of Harag all those years ago and was taken quite by surprise when, entering a low mountain pass, he found that he was not alone.

Standing alone in the middle of the pass was what he took, at first,

136

to be a child, but upon getting a closer look he realised he had made a mistake. This was a full-grown man, judging by the toned, muscular body and the facial features. And yet this man barely reached shoulder height on Empas. He was not fooled by appearances, however, as he recalled seeing people of similar stature from when he was a very young child. And then it fell into place for him. This was a Bolg — a warrior by the looks of it — and he had stumbled into their territory. Not knowing what to expect, Empas did not say anything at first, but just stood and studied the warrior, as he was doing to him. At last, the warrior spoke.

"What is your business here?" he asked.

Empas was surprised that he understood what the man said, but then realised that this was probably also due to his early childhood. He and his parents had spent several years in Bolgish lands before returning home when it was safe. He struggled, at first, to recall the bits of their language he had retained but remembered sufficient to answer the challenge.

"I have no special business here, but I come in peace from Juhl," he answered.

"Travellers here are few. Even fewer are those who travel alone," the warrior said, clearly looking for signs of any hidden companions Empas might have.

"Oh, I am indeed, quite alone," said Empas, "and I intend no trespass upon Bolg lands. I seek only solitude and guidance if it can be found."

Satisfied that there were no others in hiding, the warrior returned his attention to Empas.

"Guidance?" he asked, "What sort of guidance, and how do you know our language?" he asked.

"My parents brought me here from Juhl when I was very young and we lived amongst you for several years," answered Empas truthfully. "But as to what guidance I seek, of that, in truth, I am not altogether sure. I require answers, but I don't even know what the questions are."

The warrior considered this. Clearly there was no way to prove the truth of what Empas had told him, but like all Bolgs, he was endowed with a useful amount of intelligence, and he sensed no ill intent from the other. Just a certain amount of confusion and a kind of honest determination. He decided that Empas may be worth his trust.

"You are not Thorian?" he asked before finally making up his mind about this man.

"No, I am Juhl, and though my country is occupied and ruled by the Thorian military, I have had nothing to do with them."

"That is good," said the warrior. "The Thorians are bad people who kill and steal."

"What all of them?" asked Empas in mock surprise.

"So, it is said," answered the Bolg sagely.

Empas was about to argue the point with the Bolg, but he stopped himself as he realised the futility of the exercise in this situation. Instead, he just nodded slowly, allowing enough doubt to show that the man would be aware.

"If it is truly guidance you seek, you should go to Elder Aortes. He is wise. He may help you."

"Thank you for your trust," said Empas, realising he had just passed some kind of test. "Can you tell me where I will find Elder Aortes?"

"There is a temple, situated quite high in these peaks, though it is not too difficult to reach. At the other end of this pass, the road branches to left and right. You should take the right-hand path. At the Crystal Rock, the path divides again, and again, you should take the right hand. Do not deviate from this path. It will take you to the temple."

"Thank you again," said Empas. "I will seek out Master Aortes. If and when I find him, who shall I say sent me to him?"

"He will know," answered the Bolg, somewhat enigmatically. "He knows us all."

Empas accepted the reply without question, though he did not fully understand it. *'How could a priest who, presumably, lived in a remote temple, know all of the Bolgs?'* With yet another conundrum to conjure with, he continued to the end of the pass, and as directed, took the right-hand path, which began to climb almost immediately.

For many hours he followed the narrow, winding path which led relentlessly upwards until it flattened out and extended into a small, wooded area where he sat to rest. Though the temperature here was considerably lower than it had been at the foot of the mountains, still the sun shone and Empas found a sheltered position on the ground, guarded by the tree trunks, and as tiredness finally overtook him, he slept.

He awoke early the next morning, feeling fresher, even though he shivered a little with the morning's chill. He quietened his hunger, chewing on the nuts he had gathered earlier on his journey and stored in his pouch. Empas decided there was no point in delaying, so he set off almost immediately, following the path which, at the far end of the copse of trees, continued upward again. *'Oh well,'* he thought, *'at least it is consistent.'* The path seemed to wander into the side of the mountain so that, where there had previously been a cliff face on his right and a bottomless drop on his left, now there was also a wall of rock on his left which gradually got taller and taller and the path itself got darker, overshadowed on both sides now by towering rocks.

Later, rounding a bend in the path, he suddenly came upon one of the most stunning objects he had ever seen. Standing almost twice as tall as himself, there in front of him, where the path divided, was a rock which seemed to jut out at an acute angle from the mountainside. Its top was flattened off, giving the appearance of a very small platform which had slipped slightly to an angle. But it was not so much the rock that was spectacular, as the huge crystal which ran all the way up its length and pierced the table-like surface at the top. The crystal was embedded in, but also part of, the massive structure.

Empas stopped to admire this natural phenomenon, caught at once by its beauty and the way it completely dominated all else around it. But it was as he studied the rock that its true nature was revealed. For as he stood in wonder, the sun reached exactly the right position in the sky and its rays struck the crystal, making it sparkle with an intense outpouring of light in all directions. So bright was the reflection that it lit everything around it, banishing the darkness in a dazzling display that, Empas could now clearly discern, must have been seen for several miles all around.

In less than a minute, the display was over as the sun moved on to find, who knew what other, new targets. Empas smiled, thinking himself fortunate not only to have found Crystal Rock without too much trouble, but also to have witnessed its full splendour. It also made him curious. Could it be just a natural structure, perfectly formed out of the otherwise chaotic mass of mountainside jumble? Or was it there for a purpose, carved by some unseen and unknown hand? It was not the first time he had witnessed nature's beauty in his life, but it was a new experience for him to question the origin of its existence. He also wondered what other treasures this journey might reveal to him.

Content now, and strangely uplifted by his experience, he turned to the right-hand path and continued his journey up the mountain. It was another three long, tiring, but otherwise uneventful hours before he came to his destination — the temple.

At first, he doubted that it could be a temple at all, it seemed such a small building and had none of the design features he had expected. No stone columns, no statues, no long flights of steps, no sign of stone-carving at all. In fact, when he first came upon the building, he mistook it for a mountain dweller's cabin, not meant for long-term habitation, but merely a refuge in time of winter storms and the like. On closer examination, he saw that the construction was a lot more substantial than he had thought. The cladding on the walls was certainly wood, but it was cut and mounted with such precision that no chink showed in its surface at all. There was, therefore, no hint of what the building might be constructed of below that level. Then he noticed that there were actually columns, but they too were carved from wood. Four columns, half as tall again as himself, each made from a single tree trunk and intricately carved with abstract designs he had not seen before, all supported the extended part of the pitched roof, forming a small, covered verandah at the front of the building. There was precious little obvious paintwork so the whole building looked quite sombre, as if trying to blend in with its rocky and sparsely wooded surroundings.

What struck Empas most, however, was the atmosphere of peace and tranquillity that seemed to emanate from the simple building, and for a moment, he felt almost as if the building had spoken to him, welcoming him as if it had known he was coming. He shook his head, feeling rather foolish at such thoughts. For all that he was confused and seeking answers about himself, he knew enough to know that buildings do not speak! Intrigued, now, he approached the door which was central in the front wall and under cover of the verandah. When he tried to push it open, it would not move, but yielded easily when he tried to slide it to his right. Interesting, thought Empas, who had seen such doors on the Eldoran ship, but never in his own country.

As he entered the building, he noticed three things. Firstly, there were no windows letting in natural light and the only illumination came from candles placed strategically around the walls. Secondly, he saw that he had been deceived in his first impression of the building's size. Although quite narrow, the temple was very long, running for sixty feet before reaching the far wall. And thirdly, he now knew that the building was most definitely occupied.

At the far end of the room, sitting on a simple cushion on the floor sat a small figure that could have been taken for a child of ten years or so, but was, in fact, a full-grown man of considerably more years. He sat cross-legged, seemingly in repose with his eyes closed, his hands rested in the palms-up position on his ankles, dressed in what looked like a simple toga-like robe which left his arms and lower legs exposed. He was bald and very thin but only his facial features betrayed any sign of age, which could have been anywhere between sixty and a hundred years as far as Empas could tell.

All this left Empas quite speechless, but it was what happened next that really shocked him.

"Welcome, Empas," said the man in a strong clear voice. "I am Aortes. How can I help you?"

Empas was shocked to his core. Not only was the voice incongruous with its owner, but what he had heard could not be.

"H-h-how do you know my name?" he asked incredulously.

The reply came with a chuckle.

"Why, you told me your name yourself! And I have known of your arrival since you spoke to Makoval at the head of the pass."

* * * * *

Some years later, Empas recalled the incident that had accompanied his arrival at the temple with a wry smile. Of course, he had revealed much of himself to Aortes, but the realisation of what had occurred came as a huge shock to him. '*A telepath?*' he had thought, '*But how can this be?*' He was astounded, and to this day, marvelled at how this humble priest could have developed the abilities that he had. He was so shocked that he had forgotten his vow not to contact the director. '*Father, did you know about this?*' he asked.

'*No, I did not,*' came the silent reply. '*But he is interesting, Empas, you should talk to him.*'

Aortes had explained that he was able to speak to most of his people, or certainly those on this continent. Empas had not found that difficult to accept, but that someone else had the power he had thought shared only by his father and himself? That was an entirely different matter. He remembered another conversation they had had a day or two after he arrived.

"Are you also Eldoran, then, Master?" he had asked quite innocently.

"Am I what?" replied the priest unexpectedly. "Who or what is Eldoran?"

Empas had closed off access to his mind ever since the first encounter, so he was not really all that surprised at the question.

"Eldoran is not a who so much as a they," he answered sincerely.

Now it was Aortes' turn to be surprised and somewhat mystified. He thought for a while before answering.

"I perceive that the question is either a test, or you have in your head knowledge that I do not have. You will, perhaps, forgive an old man if I take a while to adjust to this unusual situation," Aortes replied with more than a trace of wry amusement in his voice.

At this point, Empas was eager to put his awareness of the discovery ship and its inhabitants as far away from his conscious thoughts as he could. For some reason he could not explain, he became convinced that this side of his reality was at least part of the cause of his confusion and helplessness. He wondered if this priest might, after all, be able to answer some of his questions.

"Forgive me, Master, it is neither a test, nor is it important. I am simply confused."

The priest considered Empas' words. Clearly there was much more to this young man than met the eye. It was also evident that the youth had at least rudimentary telepathic ability, else how had he been able to close access to his mind so quickly?

"So, what is it that you require of me?" Aortes asked, now serious in his enquiry.

"I am not sure, holy one," Empas replied. "I only know confusion and uncertainty."

"Then," said the priest unhesitatingly, "we will meditate together. And perhaps we shall talk. And perhaps we shall discover things. Do not be afraid, young one, for I have already walked the path that you now follow. It has many twists and turns, and many destinations. We shall try to discover which one is yours. You may ask me many things and I may even be able to answer!"

From the time of that conversation onwards, Empas had discovered an inner peace and security that grew as he learned more and more from the old man. Elder Aortes was something of an enigma, and he was certainly a lot older than the young man had imagined. He had been the spiritual leader of his people since before they first encountered the Thorians. Indeed, it was he who had counselled the building in readiness of bigger ships, able to traverse the wide ocean in case the Thorians ever broke through their formidable defences. Under his guidance, the technical and engineering prowess of the Bolgs had been harnessed in the pursuit, not only of superior weapons of war — primarily defensive — but also of superior machines for agriculture, transport and communication. Builders of canals, bridges, schools of philosophical study and art, the Bolgs nevertheless remained a secretive race, believing that their future lay along a different path from that of the rest of mankind. They were not ignorant of men's ways, but nor, under Aortes, were they anxious to enter the arena of competition for dominance. Thus, they had tried to remain hidden, with some success, obviously, as the Eldoran surveys had completely missed the significance of their culture.

Their religious beliefs centred, not around any gods, but rather the wisdom, knowledge and beliefs imparted to them by their ancestors, who existed on another plane and occasionally spoke to the living. Elder Aortes himself was a product of this philosophical culture, and very early in his life, had decided that his path to peace and serenity lay in the training of his mind and body to function in perfect harmony. Thus, he joined the priesthood and adopted their routines of meditation and simplicity in all things, finding a strength of purpose and a clarity of thought in that simple life that could not have been achieved elsewhere. Though this unassuming man had not sought power of any kind, it soon became apparent that his wisdom was of great benefit to the Bolg nation, and he had found himself the object of a kind of hero worship that he did not desire. The Thorian assault upon their borders gave him both the means and the opportunity to change all that. A man of peace himself, he nevertheless gave his country's leaders sound advice on defensive measures to delay any Thorian advance. These tactics were so successful that the Thorians made no headway at all for many years and may never have done so had it not been for the appearance of a strange warrior that their enemies called Ares. As it became clear that, ultimately, the Bolg lands would eventually be conquered, many rulers, priests, engineers, technicians, artists and philosophers were sent, by their people, to another land across the water where, perhaps, they could start again. The sacrifice made by those who chose not to escape, but to remain and deny the invaders for as long as possible, would never be forgotten by the survivors and founders of the new Bolg nation.

Empas could not fail to draw the parallel between the last act of his little friend, Ben, and the decision by those of the Bolgs who had stayed behind to fight the Thorians. In both instances, men had laid down their lives for the sole benefit of others. For Aortes and the Bolgs who had found their new home, the debt they felt they owed to those who stayed became one of the guiding principles governing their lives. Thus, Empas found himself living in a society that, whilst not blind to the military requirements of security, was nevertheless dedicated to the betterment and preservation of all the members of its society. In this reality, Empas saw what he thought was a glimpse of his own future, and though he grew to love the Bolgs, and especially the old priest who taught him many truths about himself, he knew that, eventually, he would have to return to his own country if he was to fulfil his destiny.

Chapter 10

Nazim was not happy.

For two weeks now he had been having sleepless nights and ever more frantic days due to the growing demands of his majesty, the emperor. Of course, he accepted that, to keep in the emperor's good books, he would occasionally be called upon to perform tasks of a kind and at a rate that might daunt other men, but he had coped with all that to date and still managed to install himself into a comfortable position as official secretary and unofficial spymaster for his liege. Lesser men may have wilted under the pressure, but Nazim had found himself driven by greed and desire for a better life. And so, he had become a very powerful person at the emperor's court, one to be feared and respected if you knew what was good for you.

So, with all these achievements behind him, why did he suddenly feel wary, suspicious, and yes, even a little scared at the way events were playing out? The trouble was, he realised, the voice in his head which, up until now, he had been able to control, and to some extent, block out if he wished. Now, though, it seemed he could not escape its continual presence.

'*What do you want of me?*' he urged silently. '*Have I not delivered all the tasks you have asked me to complete? Have I not brought about all the things you requested? Why then will you not leave me alone?*'

'*Oh, is that what you want my little drudge? To be left alone to sink into a permanent oblivion, a slave of those who would simply ignore you or, worse, would like to grind you into the ground over which they walk to get to the heights of power and influence? Is that what you want?*'

'*Of course not,*' he thought back. '*But I owe my allegiance to the emperor, and I cannot go against his wishes, no matter how much I would like to.*'

'*If you wish to acquire real power then you should owe your allegiance to me. Only I can grant you the means through which you can become your own master., and by the way, I can give you a way to rid yourself of your emperor's annoying offspring. Now doesn't that sound interesting.'*

This last thought made him stop for a moment. It was true that the emperor's son had become a first-class pain to Nazim and seemed to take every opportunity to taunt him in that arrogant, offhand, childish manner so favoured by the progeny of the rich and powerful. And he had vowed many times to have his revenge upon the little brat, so what would be the harm in listening to what the voice had to say? After all, he could always say no, couldn't he?

'What you offer is very interesting, Lord,' he thought. *'But can you tell me a little more about how you might help me bring about this change in my fortunes?'*

'Help you? Why yes, I suppose it would be of help to you, but what I have in mind is far bigger than just you, although you will benefit greatly, of course. But first things first. We need to find something that I lost a long time ago. You must travel west and north across the empire to the place where the disaster happened, and you must find my lost treasure. Then we shall see what happens, shan't we?'

'West and north Lord? But that takes us close to Bolg lands if I am not mistaken. And the further north you go, the more inhospitable the land becomes. It is dangerous, Lord.'

'Yes, yes, I know all that, but that is where the… accident… happened and that is where my treasure is to be found, so that is where you need to go. I can promise you, it will be worth the journey.'

* * * * *

"What is it Nazim?" asked the emperor as the spymaster abased himself politely.

"Majesty, I have been receiving some disturbing reports from my agents operating near the borders of Bolg lands. They say there are rumours of a messiah amongst the Bolgs, a new leader who could challenge even the might of the Thorian empire. They are persistent enough that I feel I should take a personal look at the situation, with your permission, of course."

"A messiah? To the Bolgs? That's the sort of nonsense I would expect from Juhl across the sea, but the Bolgs have never mentioned a messiah before," the emperor challenged.

"I know, Majesty, and that is why I thought I should give the matter my personal attention. If my agents are wrong, or worse, if the network has been infiltrated…"

Nazim left the suggestion hanging in mid-air, knowing that his best chance of obtaining the emperor's permission to travel that far lay in the emperor himself reaching the conclusion that it was necessary. His network of spies had produced much good intelligence on the Bolgs over the years and the emperor knew how important it was to him.

"Isn't there someone else who could go to sort this out? Someone you can trust?"

"Alas no, Majesty. Many in the network are known only to myself and will only communicate with me directly. This needs a thorough investigation."

"Oh, very well then," answered the emperor. "Take a small detachment with you and get back here as soon as you can. Is it likely to be a very dangerous trip?"

"I do not think so, Majesty," said Nazim. "Though I personally may need to enter Bolgish territory, I do not anticipate any immediate threat."

"Good, then you can take my son, Tyrsis, with you. It will be good for him to experience first-hand the sheer size and scope of the empire he will one day rule."

"Is that quite such a good idea, Majesty?" asked the spymaster, fearing for his mission. "After all, speed and secrecy are our best allies on this trip."

"Nonsense, Nazim," roared the other. "Tyrsis will not hold you up, though he may want to do a little hunting on the way, but I will impose on him the importance of your mission and that you are to be the leader of the expedition. How's that?"

"Thank you, Majesty," replied Nazim. "There is wisdom in your words as always."

"That's settled then. I'll let you get on with your preparations."

"Thank you, Majesty," said Nazim, carefully backing out of the emperor's audience chamber.

'There you are, that wasn't so difficult was it,' said the voice. *'Come, my little schemer, we have much planning to do before you leave.'*

* * * * *

Tyrsis the Second may well turn out to be a good, competent, even successful emperor, thought the spymaster sullenly, but right now he was behaving exactly like the arrogant, preening, thoughtless teenage brat that Nazim knew him to be. He cursed his master as yet another two or three days passed by while the emperor's son went hunting the local wildlife — and sometimes the local women — without a thought given to the urgency of the mission they were supposed to be engaged upon.

Meanwhile, Nazim could only pace up and down in his tent, waiting for the brat's return so that he could again try to persuade him that they must not delay any further. Some hope, thought the spymaster.

'Patience, my friend. Your opportunity will come soon, and you must be ready to take it. Then you will be rid of him for all time,' the voice reminded him again.

'I realise that Lord,' answered Nazim in his mind. *'But this journey should have taken only about three months, there and back. Already, five weeks have passed, and this stupid boy has held us up to such an extent that we are still only barely halfway to the Bolg border.'*

'That fact has already played to our advantage my little spymaster,' said the voice. *'Have you not noticed how irritated some of the soldiers have become at being kept from their homes for so long? Soon this will turn to more open hostility, and at that point, you must identify the ringleader for future reference.'*

Quickly picking up on the implications of what he had just been told, Nazim smiled to himself. Perhaps this would all turn out quite well after all!

In truth, it was not just the unwarranted delays that were causing discontent amongst the escort troops. Whenever the prince went hunting, he had a habit of taking enormous risks, not only with his own life, but also with those of the troops he chose to accompany him. Some of the men were themselves seasoned hunters and could see disaster looming from every direction if the prince's actions were not curtailed. Sooner or later, he was going to get himself, or one of them killed. And no one was happy with that thought — except Nazim, who took to hiding his own irritation and actively encouraging the youngster in his rash actions.

After seven weeks, the party reached the border between Thorian and Bolg lands, which ran through the rugged foothills of the mountain range which stretched as far north as anyone knew, although, little, if anything, was actually known of the region further than they could see, except that it was uninhabitable due to the permanent terrible weather conditions.

Just short of the border they made their camp where, Nazim told the party, they could expect to stay for at least a week. "Depending upon how quickly I can conclude my business in the Bolg town just a few miles away, hidden in the foothills. On no account is anybody to take any risks, especially since we have responsibility for the prince's life. I am told there is good hunting this side of the border so, on no account, should any of you stray into enemy territory. Is that understood?"

Having received assurances from the troops, Nazim set off alone across the border, heading towards the town he had mentioned to the troops. However, when he was completely out of sight of the camp, he turned north, towards the foothills, directed all the way by the voice in his head.

'*A little further my friend and our troubles will all be over,*' the voice insisted as Nazim trudged on into the rocky wilderness, filled by tumbled boulders almost as tall as himself. There were so many that he imagined a whole mountainside might have collapsed here to cause so much chaos and devastation.

Soon, though, he noticed a space in amongst the rocks that could only have been cleared on purpose, unless nature had taken to creating almost perfect rock circles. His curiosity piqued, Nazim entered the clearing and looked around, knowing, even without the prompting of the voice, that this was the place he had been seeking.

'*What exactly am I looking for, Lord?*' he asked silently. '*It would help immensely if I knew.*'

'*You will know it when you see it for its composition and nature are things beyond your understanding. Yet you will know how to use it, for I will teach you. For now, all you need to know is that it is small enough to fit into your hand. It knows how to conceal itself, so it will have no colour and its presence will be detected only by careful observation.'*

Given this vague and somewhat frightening description, Nazim searched on, all around the circular clearing, with no success for what seemed like hours with the sun beating down quite mercilessly. Finally, he sat on the ground, willing at last to admit defeat. But the voice had other ideas.

'Giving up, Nazim? No, I do not think so,' threatened the voice.

And with those words echoing through his mind, Nazim found himself falling through an endless void, spinning and cartwheeling so that all sense of balance was lost, his eyes open wide but seeing nothing but whirling and ever-changing shapes, but he knew that he was falling very fast and would soon meet his end in an agonising collision. As panic built within him, he finally opened his mouth to emit a soul searing scream of despair — and he finally stopped, all sense of motion now gone. Nazim looked down to find that he was still sitting on the ground exactly where he had been. He began to sob and inhale deep breaths, almost beginning to laugh as he realised, he was safe — at least for the moment.

The whole episode had lasted but a very short while, yet to the spymaster, it seemed like he had fallen forever. *'What happened?'* he wondered.

'What happened, my friend, is that you thought you might disobey me,' came the voice once more. *'I have shown you the error of that choice, and be assured, I can show you a lot more of the consequences of disobedience, should you so desire. Shall I do so, or shall we continue to search?'*

A thoroughly shaken Nazim had seen enough to know that he was outmanoeuvred here so he slowly rose and resumed searching the area. Fortunately for him, it was not long before he tripped and almost fell over a group of stones, dislodging some of them. As he looked down to steady himself, he noticed a fairly small flattish rock, amongst a pile of others, that was lying with one end raised above the ground, but what held it there at that angle was, apparently nothing. He stopped and studied the rock, walking around it to make sure he had not missed anything. He had not, and yet, there it was with one end suspended above the ground but with nothing to hold it there.

Strange, thought Nazim, not yet quite believing what he was seeing. But the voice of Ares was becoming more and more excited.

'*That is, it!*' screamed the voice. '*Pick it up, Nazim.*'

'*But it is only a rock, Lord,*' answered the man.

'*Not that, fool, the item underneath it.*'

'*I see nothing there, Lord,*' said Nazim.

'*Did I not say it would have no colour? Now you must feel under the rock and take the item that your sense of touch tells you is there, but that your eyes tell you is not.*'

Gingerly, Nazim reached towards the underside of the rock, to what he thought was only air, but which, he was amazed to find, was in fact a smooth, cool item made of some metallic substance, he presumed. The item fitted almost perfectly into his hand. Rectangular in shape, its size was roughly that of a knife's sheath, although much thicker. The top and bottom surfaces were rounded, and the shorter ends were flat. Nazim established all this before he could actually see what he was holding.

'*Feel along the short edges,*' said the voice. '*You will find a small indentation on one of them. Press it gently with your thumb.*'

Nazim did as he was instructed, finding the small indentation with ease. When he pressed it, the object he was holding suddenly appeared in his hand, white, with perfectly regular, unblemished sides and surfaces. He turned the object to study it from all sides and angles, finding only a small hole in the middle of one of the short sides to mark any difference at all to the rest of it.

The object looked innocuous, yet somehow, Nazim knew that he was holding something very powerful and very dangerous. '*A gift from the gods?*' he wondered.

'*No, not exactly a gift, mortal, for I can take it back whenever I choose,*' confirmed the voice. '*However, you have in your hand a weapon such as no man has ever seen before. With it, we are about to change the world. There is only one small problem though.*'

'*What is that, Lord?*' asked Nazim tremulously.

'*It will respond only to my command. To make it work, therefore, you must give me complete control over your mind and body — until we have achieved our goals, after which you can have them back, for I will have no further need for them.'*

'Complete control, Lord? What does that mean? How will I benefit if I am no longer me?'

'Oh, stop worrying, Nazim. You will still be you. And it's not as if it will be permanent. Look, try to imagine, we will both inhabit your mind, I will see what you see, all your senses will be enhanced by the power of my presence. With my help, you will be free of your master and his brat, and my friend, between us we will change the course of history. Once that is done, I will hand you back complete control. It's as simple as that,' said Lucian, excitement building in him as he knew that this was the decisive moment. Once he got control of this mortal, he could solve many of his problems and achieve his ends with comparative ease. But without the man's consent, he could not use the personal phasegun upon which much depended as he had indeed told him the truth — the gun would only respond to his personal command.

But still the man hesitated.

'I am frightened, Lord,' said Nazim, who now began to realise just how much in thrall to this voice in his mind he really was. Was this madness? Was he truly losing his mind? Or did the object he held in his hand really have the power the voice said it had? He would only know if he said yes to the proposition he had been given. But to surrender control of himself to another being? This was too huge to contemplate. And it scared him to death!

As he thought things through, he slowly came to the conclusion that this was, indeed, a step too far. He knew instinctively that, if he said yes to this voice, his life would be changed forever, not necessarily for the better. As self-preservation kicked in, he was ready to give his answer.

"Nazim! Nazim, where are you?" came a voice shouting from not far off which the spymaster recognised all too well. "I wish to hunt, and you must help me prepare. Nazim! Where are you, damned servant?"

'There is your nemesis, fearful one, he has found you, and remember, you are not where you said you would be. It is time to decide. Without me, you are doomed. Decide — now!'

'Yes!' cried the now terrified spymaster. *'Yes, let me be rid of this boy forever!'*

'That,' said the voice, *'will be easy.'*

* * * * *

"I am here, Highness," answered a voice that Tyrsis knew well — that of the hated secretary to his father. He had never liked the man from the moment he had first met him. He knew that, though the secretary had convincing, ingratiating ways and could, apparently, fool his father quite easily, Nazim was, after all, just another servant, and should be treated as such, despite whatever his father said.

"I wish to hunt and none of the guards will carry my equipment. They seem to be afraid for some reason. You must come back and tell them to obey my orders," said the petulant boy.

Startled at first, Nazim began to recover his composure as he listened to the all too familiar whining voice of the prince. Slowly, somewhat to his surprise, the outline of a plan was forming in his mind, and the new companion that he now carried in his head was clearly responsible.

"Highness, the guards are merely concerned for your safety, as am I. In fact, I am somewhat dismayed to find that you have followed me into such dangerous territory. You are far too valuable to the empire to go risking yourself in this way. Your father would definitely not approve. However, let us not dwell on such unsavoury matters. Come, Highness, we should return to the camp together — for it is not safe here — and I shall instruct Optim Rafael to organise a hunt for you before we start our return journey to the capital."

"You have done what you were sent here to do already?" enquired the boy. "That was quick. And you have come quite a distance from where you told us you were going."

"Alas, no, Highness, for the agent I was to meet did not appear, which is why you find me so far from my original destination — I had to look for him. But I have not been successful yet, so I will make alternative arrangements before we return," answered the other more confidently. Inside, Nazim trembled, for it was not he who had spoken to the prince.

'He may suspect that something is not right, but he is only a boy, and besides,' said his companion, 'by tomorrow, it will not matter.'

Prince Tyrsis did not even notice the smile that suddenly played across the other man's face. Had he done so he might, perhaps, have wondered at the subtle change taking place in Nazim's personality. Then again, with the self-absorption of youth, he probably would have ignored it.

* * * * *

As things turned out, the 'event' could not have been easier nor gone more smoothly had Lucian wished it so. Quite naturally, when he had announced the proposed hunting expedition, the grumbles had started again, chiefly with Optim Rafael and his sidekick, Jemora. Though all the men were angry, these two were the loudest, so naturally, he picked them to accompany the prince.

The small party headed north-east, with firm instructions to stay away from the border area. After they had gone, Lucian announced that he was going back into Bolg territory to complete unfinished business but that he should be back by the following day. It was simplicity itself to take a large circular route around to the north and east, well out of sight of anyone else at the camp. In only a couple of hours, he had cut the trail of his quarry, following at a discreet distance until the right opportunity should present itself. This it did when the prince spotted a stag in the open and insisted on taking the beast by himself, from open ground. From a safe distance and in good cover, Lucian could hardly believe his luck as his quarry stepped out from the tall grass and presented a clear target. Luckily, the stag remained unstartled, so the prince took his time loading and drawing his bow. Rafael and Jemora, despite their complaining, knew that the prince was a very good shot and eagerly anticipated the kill. What happened next, however, completely stunned them.

As they watched the lad draw his bow, there was a sudden flash of brilliant white light which seemed to surround and engulf the young royal, who was silhouetted inside the flash but then, an instant later, was gone, along with the light! After no more than three seconds, both men looked at the spot where the prince had been and saw nothing. He had gone, disappeared, as it were, in a puff of smoke. They looked at each other, mouths open in utter astonishment, but said nothing. What could they say when it was just dawning on them that the impossible had actually happened before their eyes? The prince had simply vanished, leaving no trace whatsoever except, strangely, his bow which had remained unscathed, and which now represented the only evidence that he had ever been here at all.

It did not take the two men long to realise that, though they were completely innocent, within a very short space of time, perhaps a day or two, they were both going to be wanted criminals with a death sentence hanging over their heads. Rafael, the more level-headed of the two, decided that, if they were going to flee, they should do so in the only direction that would slow down pursuit, and in fact, might even prevent it altogether. Carefully, covering their tracks as best they could, they set out west for Bolg territory.

Lucian, meanwhile, calmly mounted his horse and retraced his route west and south, returning to the camp the following morning, to be greeted by a situation of panic and disarray, the reason for which was quickly explained to him by the guards who had remained at the camp. The man they took to be Nazim expressed astonishment, then outrage at the turn of events and immediately ordered a thorough search of the area to ascertain what had happened and where the prince might be.

As expected, the men eventually returned with the only evidence they could find — the bow the prince had been using — plus the fact that the two men who had escorted him were nowhere to be found. It took Lucian no time at all to establish in the men's minds the obvious conclusion and to persuade them that the emperor would not hold them all responsible for his son's disappearance.

Lucian was satisfied with the way things were turning out. Inside the head, Nazim screamed in rage, impotence and fear as the full impact of what had happened dawned on him and he realised that, in actual fact, he was a prisoner now in his own body, unable to control action, movement, speech or even the workings of his brain. The voice had taken him over completely.

'*Who are you?*' he cried silently. '*Why have you chosen me as your victim? What have I done to deserve this?*'

On and on he whined, until, at last, Lucian became exasperated.

'*Stop complaining, fool. I have already given you what your limited ambitions required. Now it is my turn to achieve my own ends. Unfortunately for you, it may take some time, but you'll get used to it. Meanwhile, let's consider exactly what we are going to tell the emperor.'*

* * * * *

At first the emperor's anger and grief seemed to know no bounds as he first executed all the soldiers who had gone on the fateful journey, then declared a state funeral for his son — even without a body — followed by a month's mourning for his death. The entire capital city of Prol was virtually closed down for that period with no diplomatic or commercial activity allowed without the express permission of the emperor, which of course, was never given. At the end of the period, many citizens were suffering hunger and privation and sometimes worse and many began grumbling about the treatment they were receiving, but all were now aware, if they had needed reminding, that all power resided with the emperor!

Lucian had talked his way out of trouble by using the testimony of his own soldiers — he had been absent on the mission that the emperor had sent him to perform when the 'event' happened. He had done everything possible to find the body and to bring the murderers to book, but they had escaped, he suspected, into Bolg territory. He had, however, uncovered the highly probable source of the plot to kill the emperor's son. His agents had revealed a cell of Juhl operatives, working from within the Bolg borders, who had clearly persuaded the two Thorian soldiers to kill the prince and then arranged their escape.

"Juhl again!" exploded Tyramen. "Why are they such a constant thorn in my side. Have I not brought them peace, stability, defence, improved roads and communications? What more do they want?"

Inside the secretary's head, a voice cried out '*Freedom*!', but was quickly squashed.

"Nazim, you must go to Juhl, weed out these terrorists and bring me their leaders' heads. I want the one who issued the order to kill my son found and crucified. I will eliminate their troublesome resistance once and for all!"

"Yes, Majesty," answered Lucian. "I will begin preparations at once."

Adrian entered the director's office with a concerned look on his face.

"Trouble, Adrian?" asked the director.

"I'm not sure sir," said the officer. "Our sensors have recorded an unusual energy discharge on the planet. We have not seen anything like it for the past twenty-eight cycles."

"Where did this happen?" enquired the director.

"On the northern continent, towards the north-west corner on the border between land controlled by the Thorians and that controlled by the Bolgs."

"Could it have been lightning, or another form of natural discharge?"

"Very unlikely, sir," said Adrian. "The discharge was steady, controlled, very narrow in bandwidth and directed. In fact, it had all the signatures of one of our own weapons. A hand phasegun unless I miss my guess. But I know that is not possible, so I thought I had better bring it to your attention."

"Has there been any repeat of this event or any sign of the weapon's present location?"

"No, sir, there has been no repeat, and if it is a weapon, it is now in concealed mode because there is no trace of its current location."

"Then let us not jump to any conclusions. There could be any number of explanations, including, of course, the one you have put forward, but until we have back-up evidence, I don't propose to take any precipitate action. Thank you, Adrian. I'm sure it's nothing to worry about, but keep monitoring the planet, just in case you pick up any further signs, in which event, you will, perhaps, keep me informed?"

"Of course, sir."

"That will be all, Adrian."

The director sat in thought for a while before pressing the button to contact the medical centre.

"Gaveri," he said, "we need to talk, old friend. I think Lucian's lost phasegun may have been found."

"I'll be right with you, sir," came the reply.

Chapter 11

Without knowing how he knew, Empas was sure that the time had come for him to leave the peace and serenity he had found in the Bolg lands and under the sure mentoring of the old priest, Aortes. His time here had been a kind of cathartic experience which had given him deeper insight into himself, his powers and his beliefs, and he was reluctant to let go of all that.

He had spent part of his time travelling with the priest, getting to know the Bolgs as a cheerful, peace-loving people. He had healed some of their ills and used the power of his mind to help in mundane tasks. He had discovered their great capacity for laughter and their overriding sense of community and brotherhood, their simple faith in themselves and in their 'priesthood' which was headed by Aortes. In truth, the priests did little more than administer to the poor and the sick amongst them, asking nothing in return. Empas had often wondered why there seemed to be no mystique or wonder surrounding them wherever they went, but in the end, accepted that Bolgish priests simply accepted the love and respect that was given them in abundance.

The examples, firstly of his little friend Ben and then of the gentle Bolgs, had left him with an indelible conviction that peace, harmony and true mental and spiritual advancement were all possible if people would only 'love others as they themselves would be loved'. Some might call the philosophy simplistic and idealistic, nevertheless Empas — idealist though he might be — was convinced that it could be made to work. He had seen it work here! And now, he was sure, was the time to put his ideas into practice.

He had still not resolved the ever-present question of his relationship with his real father — the director and leader of the Eldorans — and he quickly decided that this problem had to be faced as soon as possible. He was not sure what the outcome of such a confrontation might be, but he was quite convinced that further Eldoran interference in the affairs of people on Rega was both unwise and unnecessary and he was determined that his father should be made aware of his point of view.

The director had said that he saw Empas' future as a leader of his people, one around whom they would rally and drive out the invading Thorians, taking back their freedom and self-determination. Empas had never been able to see himself in that light, though he could see how he might aspire to a similar position of influence to that of Aortes here — spiritual guide, healer, advisor and comforter to a people in need of all these and more. By definition, the road to his destiny lay in defining the religious, rather than the military, beliefs and aspirations of his people, the Juhl. But even as he came to this conclusion, he was instinctively aware of the dangers inherent in challenging a firmly established religious doctrine. He would need to convince the priests and church hierarchy if his efforts were to succeed, and that meant he must travel, eventually, to Tevalem.

The mundane, purely physical, aspect of his journey was, in this way, quickly determined. What was not clear was how he might convince people to follow his teaching, which was quite revolutionary by any standard. Perhaps the director might shed some light on how he should proceed. After all, he was vastly more experienced in the subjects of life, religion and philosophy than Empas could ever hope to be, and despite their diverging views on the means, he felt that their ends were still very much the same.

One step at a time, then, thought Empas as he went about his usual morning routine of physical chores, solitary meditation and study prior to his interview with Aortes. This happened most days, and even after all these years, he still looked forward to the exchanges with the sharp mind and great perception which the old man displayed. Not so today, however. Empas felt both sadness and apprehension for he knew their time together was coming to an end.

* * * * *

"So, young Empas, you are troubled. And I think I perceive the reason for your sadness. You have decided to leave us. Is this not so?"

The old man's insight never failed to amaze Empas. Even though, as he reminded himself, Aortes was a powerful telepath, Empas had learned enough about his own power to be able to shield his mind instinctively. So, it was clearly insight rather than telepathy which had led to the old man's statement.

"How do you do that, Master?" he asked boldly.

"Do what, young man?" Aortes replied.

"Manage to perceive other people's intentions and futures so accurately," said Empas.

"It is not difficult to understand the restlessness of youth when one has not only seen it so often, but also experienced it oneself. And besides, we have come to know each other over the years you have spent here. It entails no great leap of perception to sense that a new reality has entered your thoughts, and with it, a determination to effect change where you feel it has become necessary. So, walk with me and tell me how I can be of service to you."

As they walked together, alone into the wooded area surrounding the temple, Empas told the old priest of his thoughts and conclusions concerning the Juhl and their church, their leaders and their relationship with the occupying forces. He told him of his hopes for the future of his people and his vision of their path to peace and enlightenment. He spoke of his wish to bring about a happy, peace-loving nation which might, in turn, hasten the birth of other telepaths and advanced minds which might lead them to a better way of life, and who knows, perhaps even drag the Thorian empire along with it.

Aortes listened with the patience that only age can bring. Though he could see the inherent dangers and pitfalls in Empas' vision of the future, he could not but admire the idealism and determination which had brought the youngster to this point. Strangely, though, he experienced no feelings of happiness or contentment as the young man's plans unfolded. Quite the opposite, in fact. He felt only fear and apprehension at the thought of the road Empas was clearly going to take. He, therefore, tried to consider his words very carefully before he spoke.

"In many respects, then, you wish to emulate the Bolg philosophy of life and superimpose its principles upon the Juhl culture. Am I correct?" asked the old man.

"In essence, yes, Master. Your race have achieved a remarkable level of development and an enviable ability to survive and resist forces which would destroy your culture. Look at how you have defied the Thorians for all these years. Not only that, I sense that, as a race, you have acquired a collective power and awareness that, given enough time, could enable you to take the lead in human development. I see a similar path for my people," Empas replied.

"Then I must make you aware of certain — weaknesses — in your argument. Firstly, though you are correct in your assessment that we have given the Thorian empire much to regret, ultimately, we recognise that we must fail! We are, to all intents and purposes, doomed to extinction because, for all our resistance, all we have really achieved is to strengthen the resolve of our enemies. Already they have nearly wiped out our race on Gauros. It will not take them too long to establish that many of our people escaped to this land — and they already have a presence here. All they have to do is find us. We are still too few to offer much resistance.

"Secondly, your people are already under occupation with none of the technological advantages that we had. You produce few engineers — we have many. I fear you will start your journey from a very weak position.

"And thirdly, you must remember that we Bolgs believe it is our ancestors who help to lead us on the path to enlightenment. That is our 'religion' if you will and such rituals of worship that we have are based firmly on historical fact, whereas the religious belief of the Juhl focuses on a mystical, other-worldly deity, whose existence cannot even be proven or disproved. We believe that only we, ourselves, hold the balance between success and failure, survival or extinction. The Juhl, on the other hand, rely on 'The One' for guidance and protection. Their sacrifices and rituals are all aimed at pleasing, or bribing, a somewhat whimsical God, whose displeasure at some imagined slight could make the difference to their success or failure in almost any endeavour. Do you not see that this mentality effectively passes responsibility for survival from themselves to some other being? And that it is this that presents the main stumbling block to your mission. Simply teaching people to love one another and to seek peace and development within themselves will be confused and complicated by the question, 'Am I doing enough to please God?' Because there will always be those who will attempt to impose answers to that question that run contrary to the basic lesson. The corruption and weakness start there."

At first, Empas was surprised and not a little irritated by what he had just heard, so he thought about the old man's words before he framed his answer. Through the massive jungle of his own emotional response to criticism of his theory, he could see that there was much wisdom in what Aortes said and he took it all on board.

"Is it your advice, then, that I should not embark upon this mission to save my people?" he asked.

Aortes shrugged non-committedly.

"I would not presume to advise you, Empas, for I am but a man and subject to the same tendency to be wrong as any other., and I am sure, there are many other factors in your life which have shaped your determination to do this thing of which I am unaware. I offer only opinions based on my own knowledge and experience. Also, it is my wish that you be kept safe so that you may achieve all of which you are capable. One thing you have already achieved. I, and the rest of my Bolgish brothers and sisters, will go to our fates knowing that we have been blessed because you were amongst us for a while."

The young man did not know how to answer his mentor at this unexpected revelation. He had come here to learn and clarify his mind. That he had achieved anything else came as a complete surprise to him. At last, he felt able to frame a response.

"Master, I am humbled by your words. I can see that I have a long and dangerous road to travel, made more so because I will be distant from your wisdom and from the love of your people. But I see no alternative to my chosen path. I must go where my convictions lead me. As for the Bolgs, I can only hope that your future turns out to be brighter than you fear."

"Our future?" replied the old priest. "I came to the conclusion long ago that the Bolgs can have no future here, amongst the rest of mankind. Our philosophy, our teachings, our entire lifestyle, seems to be as much of an anathema to the other races as would be, say, living under the ocean. And there are now too few of us to make a real difference. I have, therefore, devoted much of my time to the problem of survival for my people and I have advised our rulers of my thoughts on the matter. Should they choose to follow my advice, it is likely that this world will see little, if anything, of the Bolgs in the future. They will stay hidden, and eventually, mankind will forget they ever existed."

Empas was appalled by this revelation. What the old man was saying amounted to the total loss to mankind of the entire knowledge and wisdom acquired by these people. Why?

"Surely, you cannot mean what you say, Master. The Bolgs can offer so much to the rest of mankind. It is unthinkable that all that you are, all you have become, should count for nothing. Should just disappear from the face of Rega. No! This surely cannot happen. The Bolgs are too valuable to lose," he declared with such vehemence, it surprised even him.

"Ah! I see that there is still one lesson that I may teach, or rather remind you of. It is the principle of self-determination. Freedom of choice if you will. You speak of the value of the Bolgs to the rest of the world, yet it is surely our value to ourselves that must enter the equation. We have accepted that we cannot bring about major change in the actions or motivations of our foes, the Thorians, by fighting them. We must, therefore, take away the reason for their enmity," said the old man quietly.

"And what is that reason?" asked the young man.

"Why, it is simply our presence. Our being here and occupying lands that they, or rather their leaders, covet for themselves. So, the Bolgs will disappear, seeking peace and enlightenment away from the tragedy of constant war and the struggle for survival.

"But do not look so concerned, young Empas. For you have taught me that the struggle for enlightenment is also worthwhile pursuing, even in the face of seemingly insurmountable odds. I have, therefore, also decided that, though my people will disappear, I shall not join them. I intend to travel the lands of this world and try to find other peoples who may adopt our philosophies and beliefs. Who knows what may be discovered in this way? I know that my own life will be enriched by whatever I find. I would like to think that mankind may be the seeker of his own salvation, without the need for outside interference."

These final words took Empas by surprise. Did the old priest know of his alien heritage despite his best efforts to hide it? Surely not. And yet, he could not overcome the feeling that Aortes knew more than he was saying. He had to know, one way or the other.

"To what sort of outside interference do you refer, Master?" he asked innocently.

"You know the answer to that far better than I do," answered the priest. "But do not concern yourself. We both seek the same end, though our methods may differ. But I fear yours may be the harder road to take. Go with my blessing, young man. May your message be well received."

Abruptly, Aortes turned to the young man and placed his open hand to his forehead, a position they both held for a few seconds, before the priest slowly began to retrace his steps back towards the temple. Empas realised that there was no more to be said here and began to make his way down from the mountainous land in which he had lived for so many years. He was almost ready to return to his own people. His last conversation with the priest had been, at once, both enlightening and confusing and he knew that he would need time to sift through the many points they had raised. He felt immense sadness at the forthcoming loss of the Bolgs to the world. Yet, Aortes had instilled hope into him by his declared course of action. He knew, with a sense of deep joy and satisfaction, that his would not be the only voice urging mankind to pursue a peaceful path. Maybe one or the other would succeed. Maybe they both would! That was a thought that comforted him as he travelled and convinced him that he had made the right choice. He was ready to face the Juhl, his mission, the Thorians and any other obstacle that might be put in his path. But first, he knew, he must face his father.

As he walked, he sent out a mental call, '*Father, I need to speak to you.*'

* * * * *

The director was both pleased and troubled at his son's arrival on the ship. He sat contemplating the forthcoming meeting, wondering if there was indeed anything to the warning his friend Gaveri had given him just a few minutes ago.

"Director, I fear you may have set in motion events over which even you will have little control. You have, wisely in my opinion, left Empas to his own devices, to make his own decisions and follow his own goals.

164

However, the freedom you have given him may well turn out to be a double-edged sword."

"But what other choice could I have made?" he had asked the doctor. "From the beginning I have determined that I will not interfere in Rega's affairs. That I created him at all was an enormous leap of faith which, nevertheless, I deemed absolutely necessary."

"Yes, and I know why you saw that necessity. So, I do not blame or accuse you," interrupted Gaveri. "But do you not see the danger in what you have started? Empas is, potentially, a powerful telepath, but last time he was here, he had only discovered a fraction of his potential so far. What if his association with the Bolg priest has somehow unleashed more of his potential power and turned him against your plans for him? What if he simply decides that we are irrelevant to his plans, or that he wants to usurp your position, or any of a hundred possibilities?"

The director considered his friend's comments before replying.

"I believe your fears are unfounded, Gaveri. Don't forget that I also have powers beyond those you may have witnessed, though I would always be loath to use them. But I have neither seen nor heard anything that would lead me to suspect my son of wishing us or anyone else harm of any kind. No, my concern is for the future that he sees for himself on Rega. I feel I must try to persuade him that my 'plan' for his future — vague as it was — is a valid way forward towards the goal of peace and enlightenment."

"But that is exactly the point, Director," said Gaveri. "You have just said it, 'the future that he sees for himself of Rega'. That could very easily make us — you — irrelevant in many possible scenarios. Does that not concern you?"

"Of course, it concerns me," answered the director. "But we are, after all, just speculating here. Let us see what Empas has to say before reading into the situation any more than might be there. We can do no more for the moment."

With that, the meeting had ended, but the words they had exchanged left the director wondering what, indeed, his son had to say that was so important. Oh well, he would find out soon enough, but the doubt had been planted at the back of his mind. Had he really been wise to interfere in the planet's affairs, even to the tiny extent that he had? And could he exercise any control over what might happen as a result of that? As with all questions and speculations of that nature, he realised, no answers would be forthcoming until they actually happened. Despite his enormous mental power, even he could not see every eventuality.

His attention was drawn back firmly to the present by the knock on his door.

"Come in Empas. I would imagine, from the urgency of your call, that we have much to discuss."

"Hello again, Father. Yes, there is a lot I have to tell you, and though I have decided on my course of action, I seek your advice before I embark," answered the now grown and bearded Empas.

For a moment, the director almost did not recognise his son, he had changed so much from the gangly youth he had once been.

"Then let us begin our discussion," said the director.

"In truth, sir," said Empas, "I don't know if 'discuss' is the applicable word. I've made up my mind as to my broad future course of action. I must follow my beliefs — and I know what I believe!"

"Do you?" asked the director. "Do you really know what you believe? Because I will tell you now, young man, the older I get, the less I know about what I believe."

With this statement, a kind of pent-up agitation seemed to be released from the old man. Though he tried to maintain equilibrium at all times, especially when dealing with others, he found that, despite himself, his emotional attachment to his son and his dedication to his plan, made him afraid — yes afraid — for a future he could not accurately predict.

"We are both agreed on the desired ends," he suddenly cried. "Why can you not see that my plan carries only a minimal risk, both to yourself and to Rega, and it is within our grasp? Why can you not see that?"

"I can see perfectly well, Father," the young man answered. "And from your point of view the plan has much to commend it. But there are questions you have not answered, consequences you do not appear to have thought about, but which I have thought about a lot, and I consider them to be of prime importance."

"Such as?" enquired the director.

"Such as, the fact that your plan contains a fatal flaw. Setting me up as leader, with future technology that they do not understand, is a sure way to instil resistance in some. This will turn to fear and resentment, a feeling that they are being led against their will. Pretty soon there will be revolution and war — the very thing you are trying to eliminate. How will that smooth the path to peaceful development? Do we — you — really have the right to interfere that much, if at all, in the development of Rega? Can you guarantee that your actions will have a totally positive outcome? No, of course you can't! And I believe you do not have that right. Only God has that!" declared Empas vehemently.

"God?" asked the other. "Since when did the concept of God enter this argument?"

"Since I came to the conclusion that, in all probability, He exists, despite what you say. And consider this, if I am right then He could well have directed your actions in bringing me about. If that is true then, from one very important point of view, you could argue that I am the Son of God. I'm not making any such claim, father, but do you understand what I am saying?"

The director looked at his son, as if seeing him for the first time, and realised just how far things had drifted from his original scenario. And he had to concede that the introduction of Eldoran technology into such a primitive culture could have disastrous effects. Mindful of the conversation he had just had with Gaveri, he thought a little before asking his next question.

"Do you view Eldoran intervention in the Regan culture as — unwarranted?"

"It's not that simple," Empas replied. "My belief — my faith if you will — is tempered by my knowledge of your — our — existence and by a lack of proof of a higher being. I see a paradox between what I am about to preach to these people about God, and what I know to be sitting up here above their heads viewing what is going on and able, in no small measure, to affect what happens to them. I don't know how that will affect my message, but I am convinced that peaceful progression towards developing their telepathic abilities can best be achieved in this way. If I am to lead, it will be by example."

"Lucian will try to stop you," said the other emphatically.

"Lucian? The madman? But I thought you said he was safely imprisoned and unable to cause more harm."

"Doctor Gaveri and I thought that his injuries would kill him long before now. It would seem that, though they have severely affected his physical body and will eventually cause his death, his mind has become more powerful than ever. He is recovering his memory and his telepathic powers are great enough to affect the minds of Regans — and he is aware of you!"

Having revealed this information, the director seemed to shrink, somewhat, back into himself. As if telling Empas of the danger was somehow tantamount to an admission of failure. And indeed, that was how he viewed it. Lucian's continued survival represented a lapse of judgement on his part that could only add to the dangers facing his son. A note of desperation entered the argument.

"We tried everything to rehabilitate him," he continued. "But his madness left him bereft of all reason — he didn't even know who he was or who we were. There seemed no way to punish him for his crime short of executing him — which I could not do. We couldn't predict how long he would last because of his injuries. Gaveri is still not certain that he has answers to all the infections Rega could inflict on us and he had even fewer then. So, we locked him away where we thought he could do no further harm. The enhancement of his telepathic power is an unfortunate and unforeseen side effect."

Empas was shocked. Though he had known about Lucian in a broad sense, he had never before heard the full story.

"I suppose I should at least thank you for letting me know that before I start. Is there nothing that can be done to redeem him?" he asked.

"No. And there is one more slight complication you should be aware of. We never found his personal phasegun."

"His per…?" Empas asked, clearly shocked. "You mean there is a lethal weapon somewhere down on the planet, which can kill at a thought, and which belongs at least five thousand years in their future just waiting for some stranger to come along?"

"Not quite," added the director. "It only responds to a direct command from Lucian himself and since he is locked up there is, we feel, minimal risk. However, we are monitoring the situation."

Empas sat looking at his father. Speechless, he could hardly take in the implications of what he had heard. Not only was he contemplating taking on the Thorian empire as well as the hierarchy of the all-powerful church of his people, but now he discovered that there was probably a very powerful telepath out there who considered it his mission to stop him, possibly even to eliminate him!

It was not that the extra threat troubled him unduly — it was another factor to take into account, but no more. And he was still convinced of the 'rightness' of the task he had set himself. It was the fact that his father had seen fit to conceal the information until now that made him angry.

"Given the significance of that information, father, don't you think it might have been a good idea to bring it to my attention a little earlier than this? What I have to do will be difficult enough without the need to look constantly over my shoulder where, yet another enemy may lurk."

"Perhaps you are right, and we should find a way to curtail Lucian's activities before you become too exposed. Would it not be better to delay the beginning of your mission then?" said the director anxiously.

"No, my message must not be delayed. If I fear my opponents, then I doubt my own conviction. I have no doubt about what I am going to do or when. I know that is not what you want to hear, Father, but it is how I view things and I will proceed accordingly."

With those words, Empas rose and exited the director's office, leaving behind a frustrated and disappointed, but thoughtful, man.

* * * * *

Maikel encountered Empas just after he had left the director's office. She was struck by his appearance — the beard only seemed to enhance his natural beauty in her eyes — as he looked at once worried, determined, angry and sad. From his expression, she was able to surmise that the meeting could not have been a completely friendly one and wondered at the sudden change that seemed to portend in the relationship between father and son.

"Empas, it is so long since we have seen you. How have you been?" she asked him kindly.

Looking up, Empas saw the woman before him and received a jolt to his consciousness he had not encountered before. Though he had said what he felt he had to say to his father, nevertheless he could not shake the feelings of frustration and fear about his decision. Looking at the woman, he did not at first recognise her as a person, but rather as an interruption. But the sound of her voice seemed to clear his vision and he saw, as if for the first time, her slender frame, her light-coloured hair that fell gracefully to encompass a face he could only describe as beautiful. He noticed, again for the first time, her large grey eyes. Catching his breath, he tried to cast aside his thoughts and his anger as he watched her coming towards him.

"Oh, Maikel. Sorry, I didn't see you there," he answered, still distracted by the meeting that had just ended.

The silence between them began to stretch, becoming uncomfortable to both, and she realised that her speculation was probably on the right track.

"You look worried," she said. "Is there anything I can do to help?"

Empas was about to refuse, unwilling to burden anyone else with his problems, especially those concerning his disagreement with his father. He opened his mouth to speak the words, but then changed his mind. Perhaps a fresh viewpoint might bring much needed perspective to his chosen course of action. He needed, he realised, to speak to someone who had no ulterior motive in the advice they might give. Doctor Gaveri had been his intended next destination, but he decided that could wait a little while. Maikel was uninvolved in the course he had chosen. Her primary motivation seemed to be solely to navigate the ship safely to wherever the director wished her to go. She was not so close to him, either, that she could not take a somewhat detached view in this matter. So instead of rejecting her advance, he accepted, as gracefully as he could.

"Can we get some privacy?" he asked. "There is something I would like to discuss with you."

"Of course," Maikel replied. "I have my own quarters. We can talk there if you like."

"Thank you," he said. "I'll follow you then."

Still mystified, Maikel led them down several corridors and levels until she finally reached her quarters. She spoke her password softly and the door slid open to reveal a room that was larger than Empas had expected. Nowhere near as grand as the quarters occupied by his father, nevertheless, it was spacious, comfortable with couches, a low table, work desk, shelving and bed all positioned to give maximum freedom of movement whilst maintaining a certain cosiness that was difficult for him to define.

Empas was unused to such luxury and was a little apprehensive at first, especially when the surface of the couch seemed to give slightly when he sat on it.

"Do you know," he said, partially to cover his awkwardness, "in all the times I have visited the ship, I never realised that the crew's own quarters would be so — soft."

Maikel chuckled. "Of course, it is easy to forget that life on Rega must be quite harsh in comparison to this. I have seen a little of life on the surface, and I have to say, I am glad that my home is here."

The remark served to focus Empas' attention back onto the matter at hand.

"Home. Yes, that is really at the heart of the matter. You see, although I know about Eldor, this ship, my father, your travels and many other things, and although I realise that I am, in a way, a part of all that, nevertheless Rega is my home. It is where I was brought up and its people are of great concern to me. My father expects me to bring about sweeping changes that will alter the direction of mankind's journey to enlightenment by carrying out his 'plan'. And whilst I can see what he wants to achieve, I do not believe it is the best way of going about it, nor is it necessarily in Rega's best interest."

Maikel listened as Empas unfolded his story and revealed the source of his dilemma. As he talked, she realised that Empas was completely driven by his need to improve the lot, not just of the Juhl, but ultimately for the entire race of mankind on Rega. His revolutionary approach to subtly changing the course of its history caught her imagination and she suddenly and unexpectedly found herself in complete sympathy with his cause.

And with that realisation came another thought. A truth that had eluded her until now. Caught up in the terrifying race to escape from Eldor's fate, across many hundreds of cycles, her life had gradually settled to one of unquestioning duty and obedience to the demands of the ship and the crew. Before, she had thought that was enough, but listening to this man, she realised how comparatively shallow and without direction her life had been. Here was a man destined to achieve, no matter what the odds against him., and she realised, she would like to be a part of that.

As he continued, she began to see him in something of a new light. His determination fired her enthusiasm. His calm pragmatism, coupled with his enthusiasm inspired her admiration for him. Despite their vast difference in ages, she felt that nothing would be impossible with this man if she willed it so.

'What is happening to me?' She thought. *'Am I seriously contemplating trying to help Empas? If so, where does that leave my loyalty to the ship and to the director?'*

These and many other similar thoughts passed through her mind as Empas came to the end of his story.

"…So, what do you think?" he asked.

"What?" she answered, momentarily caught off guard. "Oh, I'm sorry. There is an awful lot here that I need to take in, and I must admit that what you are proposing to do scares me a lot."

"It scared me too at first," he said. "But the more I thought about it, the more convinced I became that it can be done. Making people appreciate and become more considerate towards one another is the easy part, until it comes to their perceived enemies and their ingrained prejudices. Loving your neighbour is one thing, but your enemy? Does he really deserve your love and forgiveness? And will he reciprocate? I must admit, the answers seem to be based only on faith. Sometimes, that seems like a very fragile basis on which to build a philosophy.

"And then there is the small matter of the existing church and the challenge to its authority that I am going to represent. In a way, I believe in the same God that they do, though I don't agree with how they go about worshipping Him. It's certainly not going to be easy, but perhaps, like a small pebble that moves and ultimately creates a huge avalanche, I can bring about a beginning that will eventually eradicate war and help man to understand himself, be at peace with who he is and where he is going."

Maikel tried to concentrate solely on the logic of the intellectual argument being presented to her. Instead, she found she could not shift her attention from a growing need inside her to believe in this man. Her emotions threatened to take over from her intellect and she became uncomfortable at the strange thoughts that kept entering her mind.

The tension built and the thoughts kept coming. She knew that it wasn't the intellectual power of the man or the argument that was attracting her. It was him. Here, in this moment, she realised that Empas was for her and she for him. But how could that be? She hardly knew him. How could this be? The same question kept coming back and something akin to panic took over.

All at once, she knew she must get away from this man and think. She needed time to decide.

To decide what? She did not know, except that she had never felt this way before.

"Look, Empas, can we take this up again some other time. I find that I have quite a headache coming on and I can't concentrate properly. I think I'll go and see Doctor Gaveri and I think that, before you leave, you should go to see him too."

Empas was surprised at her outburst but forgot all about the deep discussion he had been into in his concern for Maikel.

"O-of course," he stammered. "I'm sorry to burden you with my problems. Would you like me to come with you?"

"No, that's quite unnecessary, thank you," she answered, somewhat flustered. "Look, there is an unoccupied suite right next door. Why don't you get some rest while I see the doctor and we can talk again later?"

"All right," Empas replied, "if you're sure you're all right."

"Yes, I'm sure it's nothing," said Maikel as she opened the door for them both. "I'm just feeling a little tired that's all. I'll look in on you later."

Maikel showed him how to enter the suite, then left him — in somewhat of a hurry thought Empas to himself. Was it something he had said? He had never encountered such a reaction from any of the Eldorans before. Come to that, he had not had such a reaction from anybody before, he realised. And then, as if for the first time, he began to realise that, actually, he had never before really given much thought at all to the way people reacted to him. '*The woman's sudden nervousness and clear need to escape from his presence — was that really a headache or something else?*' he thought to himself.

As he lay and considered the situation, his thoughts strayed more and more to her physical grace and beauty, her kindness and concern, her willingness to be of help if she could, all matters that had nothing to do with his philosophical arguments, but everything to do with his desire to be with her. Always a loner, Empas sat up as he realised that never before had he felt a need for another person. Aside from Ben, whom he lost many years ago, he had never really found someone he could call a friend. Even Aortes was more a teacher than a friend, and he had never considered the need or desire to be with anyone simply because they were who they were. '*Why was that?*' he wondered. Now though, suddenly, he found that it was not just Maikel's welfare that concerned him. He wanted her near him for no reason other than that he enjoyed her company.

And as suddenly as the revelation had hit him, he realised, sadly, that it could never be. She was Eldoran, hundreds of years older than he was and she navigated a ship that travelled the stars. He had a mission on Rega that would consume all of his time and energy and would lead who knew where. He could not ask anyone to accompany him on such a perilous journey. So, he lay back, saddened by his reflections, but determined that she would not discover how he felt for fear that she might do something stupid — or worse, reject his friendship altogether. That, he thought, was something he could not face.

* * * * *

"Maikel, are you all right?" Gaveri asked

"What? Oh, yes… no… I. Sorry, Doctor, I shouldn't really be here should I. It's just that I couldn't think where else to go."

The doctor could see that the woman was, at the least, distracted about something. In spite of her distress, he decided that patience might be required above all else here, so he opted for pragmatism and mundanity rather than deep inquisition.

"I assume our orbit is still stable. I haven't heard any alarms."

"No," she answered distractedly, then after a pause, "I mean yes, the orbit is stable. The ship really takes care of itself in our current situation. I just monitor it."

"Oh, that's all right then," he added with finality.

The silence grew until it was almost unbearable, almost like an oppression on them both. Finally, Maikel could stand it no longer.

"Doctor, why do I feel like this?" she blurted out.

"Like what?" he replied. "I'm afraid I have no idea what you mean."

"I mean why do I feel worried and anxious about a man I barely know really, and anyway, his destiny clearly lies on the planet whereas mine is to navigate this ship. I… we… I mean the crew have always accepted that our prime concern is the search for a new home. I have never felt any emotional ties to other crew members. It never even occurred to me. So why, now, do I find myself concerned about some man who has totally idealistic and unreachable dreams, and anyway, is directly related to our boss?"

"Ah," answered Gaveri as understanding began to dawn on him, "you've been talking to our young Empas."

"Not so much talking as listening," she replied. "And his arguments make sense to me in a simplistic, idealistic fashion. But that's not the point."

"It isn't?" the doctor enquired gently.

"No," she answered emphatically. "He's going to go back down there and try to change the world, and do you know what? I don't really care whether he does that or not. I'm just frightened for him. I… I don't want to lose him. I have suggested that he come and talk to you, half in the hope that you might be able to persuade him not to go."

Gaveri was somewhat startled to see tears forming in the woman's eyes. He began to appreciate what he was dealing with. Nevertheless, realising he might never get a better opportunity to obtain information on Empas' plans, Gaveri said gently, "Why don't you tell me what he said and let me see if I can help?"

The dam finally broke, and Maikel told him everything she and Empas had talked about. As she did so, Gaveri felt some measure of relief as he concluded that, at least, the man posed no direct threat to the ship or to the director. He began to speculate, though, upon the source of Maikel's distress. In his experience, the Eldorans were rarely, if ever, given to emotional turmoil, having mastered that part of their nature aeons ago. *'Probably due in part to their longevity,'* he mused. Yet here was this relatively young Eldoran woman who was clearly exhibiting strong emotional links to a man. Worse, that man was neither Eldoran nor Regan, but a mixture of both. '*How interesting*,' he thought. '*And where will it lead, I wonder?*'

At last, Maikel finished her tale and Gaveri knew he should try to offer advice of some sort. He also knew instinctively that this was a problem he could not solve. She would have to do that herself. In the comforting knowledge that Empas was not threatening his world in any way, he considered his words as carefully as he could.

"Maikel," he began, "what you are experiencing is something very rare in one of the Eldoran race. That is not to say that it is wrong or seriously troubling from a medical point of view. Just unusual. But no amount of intellectual counselling on my part, or anyone else's for that matter, can truly answer your questions and concerns. Because they have nothing to do with intellect and everything to do with, what I would call, your humanity.

"Put aside, for a moment, whatever future he has planned for himself — and I will no doubt get a better idea of that when I talk to him. The only question you need to ask yourself is: do you want him to be a part of your future? Neither I nor anyone else — except you — is qualified to answer that question.

"The only other point I would make is that, as your fellow crew member, I do not want to see you get hurt in any way and I would be unhappy to think that whatever course of action you might take would run that risk."

Maikel continued to look at the doctor long after he had finished speaking but she said nothing more. She knew he was right. Her life had just undergone a dramatic change. It was how she managed and coped with that change that mattered. Somehow, she knew, that was not going to be all that easy.

Chapter 12

The constant rocking movement of the ship's deck was having an unfortunate effect on the body Lucian occupied, and not for the first time, he cursed the weakness and frailty apparent in the physical make-up of these people.

'*How do you put up with these ridiculous distractions?*' he thought at the other being that occupied this body. '*The sicknesses, the weakness, the knowledge that your insignificant little lives are so short, how do you cope with that?*' he asked for the hundredth time.

'*I cope,*' answered the other miserably, '*because that is simply what life is — or was before I met you.*'

'*Enough of your snivelling,*' answered Lucian, '*you should be grateful I do not simply snuff you out altogether. Now, tell me about this governor I am to meet, this Portio Latiedes.*'

'*If I do, will you give me back my body?*' Nazim asked.

'*You will be granted that favour as and when I deem it so, is that understood?*' Lucian answered shortly.

By this time, Nazim knew it was useless to argue with this alien presence, which was more than just a voice in his head. It completely dominated his whole being. His body reacted to the other's commands, not his and he could find no way to take back control. He could only watch and listen as the other carried forward his plan — whatever that might be. Despondently, he revealed all the information he knew about Portio and why he had arranged to have him sent here.

'*So, by now, he should have built up a substantial network and have a pretty good idea where and who the potential troublemakers are among the Juhl,*' thought Lucian.

'*I suppose so,*' answered Nazim.

'*Let us hope so, my friend. The future of this world depends on it.*'

Just then a wave caught the warship and pushed it against the jetty to which it was, by now, quite securely moored. Although the movement was not great, it was sufficient to upset the equilibrium of those standing on the deck and Lucian stumbled forward suddenly. Grasping the low rail of the side of the ship, he managed to avoid falling over completely, but was not able to control the contents of his stomach which, having been contained thus far, finally made a bid for freedom and emerged with a loud retching sound. The sailors laughed as Lucian, once again, cursed the properties of the body he was in.

Unsteadily, he got to his feet and glared at the men who had laughed at his discomfort. Moving towards the gangplank he began to disembark. As he did so, he turned and spoke to the assembled company.

"I'm sure," he barked angrily, "the emperor will be glad to know how well his representatives are treated on board his ships. You all know how he expresses his gratitude."

With this, he departed the ship and almost audibly sighed with satisfaction as his feet touched firm ground for the first time in over three months. Looking back, he almost smiled as he saw the grim expressions on the sailors' faces.

The ship's captain, having despatched a messenger to the governor's villa as soon as the ship docked, noted the small military escort which arrived just in time to witness Lucian's disembarkation and quickly whisk him onto the chariot which was to transport him to his audience with Portio Latiedes.

'Glad to be rid of that one,' thought the captain, *'something not quite normal there.'*

He pondered that idea for a moment but came up with no plausible explanation for his discomfort, so he pressed on with his duties, barking orders at the crew and ensuring that the soldiers in his charge were all present and correct before they, too, disembarked and headed for the army barracks.

* * * * *

Andrew stood and surveyed the carnage all around him. Though it had been a tough fight — Thorians, for all that he hated them, were damn fine soldiers — he and his band had managed to kill all six of them, including a junior officer, with just two serious injuries to his own men.

The ambush had been carefully planned, as usual, and they had caught the troop on a deserted stretch of road, completely unawares.

Though the soldiers' reactions had been quick, a short sword is no match for a well-aimed arrow fired from deep cover where you cannot even see your attacker. Two of the soldiers had fallen immediately and a third, hamstrung by a shaft that found the right place on his leg, had been rendered useless. The band of fifteen freedom fighters then sprang from cover, attacking the remaining Thorians from all sides at once. It was, to all intents and purposes, a massacre, and one for which the local population would no doubt pay in some measure. But they didn't seem to count that cost. As long as Al Barab — Divine Arrow — kept killing their enemies, they would never betray him to the Thorians, however many hostages they rounded up and killed.

Andrew put that uncomfortable thought from his mind for the moment as he and his men picked clean the Thorian troop of all useful items — not just weapons and armour but there was some money and even a little food too! All in all, a good day's work, thought Andrew. And it was done in the cause of freedom. Surely his people would understand that.

But in his heart, Andrew was no longer certain of that assertion. He looked around once more at the butcher's yard they had created, sorry to have lost two valuable men. Sorry also for the reprisals that would follow and wondering where it would all lead to in the end. With a sad shake of his head, he led his men back into the rocky hills from whence they had come. There was more work to be done. There would always be more work to be done.

* * * * *

Marin looked at her husband thoughtfully.

"Jespeth, you have been sitting staring at that piece of wood for a very long time. Since you can't be holding a conversation with it, I have to ask — what are you doing?"

"Eh!" answered the man, as if just waking up. "Oh, sorry my love. I was just thinking."

"About him?" she asked softly.

179

"Yes," he replied. "I wonder where he is sometimes, and what he is doing. You know if he's all right, what work he's at, that sort of thing."

"I know," she said. "I do the same — often! I wonder whether we might have persuaded him to change his mind. If only we'd tried a little harder, he might still be with us now. But then I think of the strange people who brought him to us. I can still hardly believe I agreed to their request — and I know in my heart that he was meant to do something other than just follow you into carpentry."

"You're right," said Jespeth. "He was always destined for other things, though I have to say that his woodworking skills were excellent, and he learned so quickly, he could have become one of the best."

"Do you remember his little friend, Ben? The son of that rich merchant, Caspar Mossamed. Empas was never quite the same after Ben died. I wonder what made him change?" Marin added.

"I don't know," her husband answered. "Mossamed used to buy a lot of my work but after his son died all that stopped. Rumour has it that he deals with the Thorians in Tevalem now, and only trades goods from the tribes around Juhl. Strange that, especially since he took that other local lad — Saul I think his name was — and trained him. Last I heard, Saul was pretty much like a second son to him, or at least a very close right-hand man.

"Strange how people's fortunes change, isn't it? A man loses his son, I lose a good customer, a local lad finds a career he could never even dream of, and our son's life completely changed. Sometimes I wonder what The One God is playing at, meddling with people's lives."

"That's hardly fair, Jespeth," said Marin sympathetically. "Who are we to question The One's intentions for us. I just wish we had had more warning before Empas left. I do miss him so."

Marin could contain her tears no longer and they flowed freely. Jespeth enclosed his wife within his strong arms — still well-muscled even after all these years — and tried to comfort her.

"Tell you what," he said suddenly, "why don't we make the pilgrimage to Tevalem we've been promising ourselves for I don't know how long? I have a couple of orders that I need to finish up, but that shouldn't take more than a couple of weeks, and we have some savings we could use for the journey. We could visit your cousin, Elspeth, as well.

She lives down that way, doesn't she?"

Hearing his words, Marin thought, not for the first time, how lucky she was to have a man such as Jespeth for a husband. The sad thoughts and emotions of moments ago were gradually lifted as she found herself anticipating a journey that, for most Juhl, was the aspiration of a lifetime. To make the pilgrimage to Tevalem. *'Yes,'* she thought, *'perhaps I might even find some answers there.'*

* * * * *

Lucian was, despite himself, quite impressed by the sight of the villa, in classic Thorian style, that Portio Latiedes occupied, and which acted as both home and his working environment. *'One of the few pleasures he'll enjoy in this forsaken place,'* he thought. *'Still, it will do very nicely as a base of operations. And who knows, perhaps if Latiedes doesn't co-operate fully with my plans, I could arrange to have him removed leaving a quite desirable residence empty and ready for a change of occupancy...'*

These and other similar thoughts ran through Lucian's mind as the chariot drew up to the elaborate portico that served as a front entrance. Although Nazim was, of course, privy to those thoughts, he could do nothing about them, which only added to his misery.

As he ascended the few steps up to the house, Lucian was met by Portio Latiedes himself.

"Hail, envoy Nazim, and welcome to one of the few places in Juhl that can offer you true Thorian hospitality," said Latiedes with an almost believable joviality which, nevertheless, they both knew was completely false.

"How kind of you, Governor Latiedes, to have arranged transport for me from the docks," answered Lucian, already enjoying the duplicity.

"How was your journey and what news have you from the capital?" asked the governor.

"All in good time, my old friend," said Lucian. "Since, in truth, the journey was ghastly and the news from the emperor is not altogether good."

"In which case," said Portio, "it can wait. Let's get you settled in your apartment and refreshed after which we can begin to move things along. I think you will be quite pleased with what we have achieved here."

They continued with small talk until Latiedes had one of his servant's escort Lucian to his quarters which, the secretary noted, were situated in an eastern wing of the villa, some distance from the family quarters and the throne room where the business of the province was conducted.

'Interesting,' thought Lucian, *'your man plays quite an effective defensive game. He is clearly no slouch when it comes to political matters.'*

'Oh, I chose him because of those very qualities,' answered Nazim, forgetting for a moment the anger and fear he felt for the other.

'How very thoughtful of you. Let us hope he lives up to expectations then. He seems pleased with himself, perhaps he is as militarily adept as he is politically,' Lucian mused. *'Maybe something useful will be achieved here after all. Anyway, I hope his larder is well stocked — having dumped the last three meals at least, I must admit I am not comfortable with this feeling which you call hunger.'*

Nazim kept his silence, but wondered what sort of creature this other being could be that he was not familiar with being hungry?

After a wash and change of clothing, Lucian felt somewhat refreshed, though hunger continued to gnaw at his awareness. He found his way through the house until a servant intercepted him and showed him to a sitting room arrayed with couches and tables bearing food within easy reach. Portio Latiedes and his wife, Ameli, were already there waiting for his arrival.

"Ah," he said, "now our guest has joined us, let us refresh ourselves."

The meal progressed in silence until Lucian, hunger abated for a while, decided to get right to business.

"So, my friend, I have news from the capital which is grave in the extreme. The emperor's son has been assassinated," he said dramatically. "And to make matters worse, we are informed that the atrocity was committed by Juhl agents operating from Bolg lands."

This announcement brought a complete halt to the feasting as the news, and its deeper implications, began to sink in. The governor and his wife immediately saw the reason for this visit — and the danger to themselves arising from the spymaster's arrival. In an instant, both realised that they would have to tread very warily when dealing with the representative of the emperor.

"That is tragic news indeed," answered Portio. "And perplexing if true. But my network of informants have given me no indication that the Juhl might be active outside of their own godforsaken country, though they still give us plenty of trouble here."

"And yet," continued Lucian, "my informants insist that it was the work of a Juhl cell. I am surprised that such a big operation, as it must have been, could have completely escaped your notice, Governor. Could it be that your 'network' is not quite as effective as you believe it to be?"

As the conversation continued — and Portio could see where it was leading — he began to sweat a little more. Surely his network of informers could not have missed such a major plan. It did not occur to him to question the validity of the other's assertion. He knew Nazim to be duplicitous, but always efficient and dedicated to the emperor. Reluctantly, he began to imagine the worst aspects of this scenario and his brain moved into overdrive to figure out how to retrieve the situation.

Lucian smiled to himself. His news had had the desired effect and very shortly, he knew, he would achieve situational supremacy which would grant him virtually complete autonomy and total cooperation from the local force in the actions he needed to take. Now all he needed to do was acquaint himself with some detail of rebel actions in this province, identifying leaders, their names and activities. He knew he would recognise the one that he was after, but full knowledge of the province and its quirks was needed if he was to revenge himself on the director's son. '*Oh yes,*' he thought, '*I am not going to lose sight of my objective despite the other interesting possibilities that present themselves here.*' But with luck, solving this province's rebel problems could provide him with a power base that could lead — who knows where?

Nazim also read the signs — and became more and more frightened by their implications.

"So broadly speaking," began Lucian, "what is the current situation regarding civilian unrest in this region?"

And there it was. The question that Portio had been expecting — and preparing for — but now equally dreaded in the light of the other's insinuations.

"Overall," he said, "the civilian population give us little trouble. The military have seen to that. We have a number of outposts at key locations right across the country, from which light patrols can quickly and easily emerge to quell any potential trouble. Bands of zealots and terrorists still spring up, of course, and every leader still claims to be the messiah, but we have reduced their numbers dramatically. One major band of zealots has moved out of Juhl into neighbouring Asyr and conducts its operations from there. Fortunately, they present no real military threat right now, but until the army can be brought back up to offensive readiness, we are unable to invade Asyr. So, we cannot wipe them out — yet, but we are keeping an eye on them."

Portio paused, as if to gather his breath, but in reality, it was to gather his thoughts and shape his next words as carefully as possible, not knowing how his guest might react.

"There really remains only one major thorn in our side. We are keeping a lid on the problem, but I must confess, it is a problem.

"There is a terrorist leader they call Al Barab — the translation of the term is Divine Arrow — who has a habit of popping up where the military least expect him, catching them unawares. He kills without mercy, confiscates all useful armour and weaponry from his victims, and promptly disappears again before we can ever get a trace on him."

"Perhaps this leader really is the messiah that the Juhl have been waiting for?" suggested Lucian.

"No, envoy Nazim, that is just the point. Al Barab does not claim that title. In fact, he does not claim anything at all, he simply kills Thorian soldiers. It is the people who have given him their loyalty and who refuse to betray his whereabouts. We have tried taking and killing hostages to no avail. We have tried more subtle methods — we do have an effective network of spies out there — but no one will admit to knowing anything of his whereabouts. I have even consulted the Juhl high priests and reminded them of the emperor's benevolence in tolerating their activities, but they also are either too frightened of the populace or genuinely do not know anything themselves. I have given orders that no patrol in future should consist of less than twelve men. This has stopped the attacks on patrols, but now soldiers are becoming wary of leaving their barracks during off-time for fear of being robbed, or worse, when leaving local taverns and such. This, of course, affects the amount of grass roots information we are collecting, as well as the morale of the men."

Lucian pondered the information he had just been given. Clearly this Al Barab was a menace who had to be stopped at any cost. But was he the director's son? Equally clearly, he grudgingly conceded that the governor had taken all the right and necessary steps to try to contain and control the situation and could not immediately see a way to turn the situation to his advantage.

"How did this leader get the title people have bestowed upon him?" he asked slowly.

"Information is sketchy and based largely on rumour, but the legend persists that he was pierced just above the heart by a Thorian arrow which lodged in his flesh. He apparently pushed the arrow all the way through his body and out beside his shoulder blade with his own hand. The shock killed him, but he was attended by a wizard who brought him back from the dead and healed him to full health. As a result, it is said that he has magical, or divine, protection and cannot be killed by any weapon known to man."

The governor paused to allow the implications of what he had just told the envoy to sink in, hoping that he would perceive at least some of the problems the legend presented. The longer the terrorist threat from this leader persisted, the more the legend would grow and could quickly lead to revolt and insurrection. He fully expected the envoy to demand that he redouble his efforts to find this man and bring him to Thorian justice. But he was completely taken aback by Lucian's next comment.

"Resurrected by a wizard, you say?" asked Lucian. "Do the Juhl really have wizards, and does this mystic have a name?"

"Not that we have been able to discover," replied a somewhat disquieted governor. "In fact, the whole subject of wizards and magic, or miracles if you prefer, has not arisen at all until now. The Juhl are strangely addicted to their religious beliefs. Their 'wizards' seem to be limited to the priesthood and we have firm control of them."

"Hmm," said Lucian after some time, "this seems to be quite a complex situation. You are right to bring it to my attention. Both this Al Barab and his wizard must be found and until we do, there is no way to discover how much of the 'legend' is based on truth or how much on pure speculation. There is no doubt in my mind, however, that this problem goes beyond simple military or even political considerations."

"My thoughts exactly," echoed the governor.

"I am not just talking about terrorism my friend," stated Lucian, "Oh no, this is much bigger than crushing a terrorist. If allowed to get out of hand, this scenario could easily lead to general resistance, and ultimately, popular revolt. It is possible the wizard could be even more dangerous than the man he is said to have brought back from the dead. Anyone who can do that is someone we either need on our side, or we need to eliminate him altogether. But first, we must catch the man who can name him."

"Indeed," answered Portio. "And I believe I may have an answer to that problem. Or at least, I will have as soon as my prime agent arrives back in Tevalem. You recall the rumour you told me, before I left Prol, about the merchant? He is a very wealthy trader from Damas in Asyr. He has a captain — quite ruthless by reputation — who is Juhl by birth but Asyr by adoption. Hence, he is not only able to move freely in all areas, but his captain knows the Juhl intimately and thus gathers information that others cannot."

"Is there not a danger of conflict of interest here?" asked Lucian.

"Oh, rest assured, this man has no love for the Juhl! It is said that the merchant's son died saving the life of a Juhl boy — the one he later adopted as his captain — and that another Juhl youth ran away when he could have saved the son's life. Very tragic, and it left the man with a burning hatred that has never cooled."

"So, the vague rumours were true then? An interesting tale," said Lucian. "And it would seem to justify your faith in your network of informers. When are we likely to see this merchant again?"

"He is due back in Tevalem in just a few weeks," said the governor.

"Thank you for your illuminating insight, Governor. I shall give this matter a great deal of thought, and I look forward to meeting your merchant. What is his name, by the way?"

"Caspar Mossamed," answered Portio.

"Well, as I said, I look forward to meeting him. And then, you and I shall plan the total elimination of the Juhl terrorist threat to our glorious Emperor."

"To the emperor," replied Portio, raising his goblet.

"Yes, quite," answered Lucian.

* * * * *

In fact, it was another three weeks before the merchant and his caravan arrived in Tevalem, during which time Lucian took the opportunity to get to know the city and to observe both the manner and the effectiveness of Thorian rule over the country. Despite himself, he was quite impressed. The military presence in the city was low key, its effectiveness well supplemented by the actions of the Juhl high priesthood, whose loyalty had been bought years before. Consequently, there was little unrest in the city, and bit by bit, the populace were learning to live with Thorian authority.

As he travelled further afield, however, it became apparent that the same story was not true of the population outside the city. Here, there was resentment, fear and anger. In truth it was no more than he had expected, but it was sobering to experience the intensity of their hatred for himself.

Overall, his observations did not raise any concerns, but his conversation with Latiedes on the night of his arrival very much roused his interest. Was this wizard, or Al Barab, or both, possibly connected with his enemy in some way? Was the story of magical happenings real or just a product of the fevered imaginations and desperate hopes of the Juhl? One way or another, Lucian knew, he had to meet both of these people and get to know who, or what, he was dealing with. Recruit them or eliminate them, that was Lucian's simple choice.

But neither solution would be achieved by simply sitting around waiting for it to come to him. He knew instinctively that only he could solve this problem.

'*Perhaps I can help,*' whispered a faint voice whose presence Lucian had almost forgotten about.

'*And just how would you do that from your position of power,*' he asked?

'*Well, it is clear that, sooner or later, you mean to go after the wizard. If you go looking as we do now, neither of us will last five minutes. Some hero, or worse, will come upon a lone Thorian, probably in the night, and slit our throat just for the thrill of it,*' said Nazim.

'*I know the risks, fool,*' answered Lucian. *So, what is your solution?*'

'*When in the land of the Juhl, it is best to look like a Juhl,*' said Nazim smugly. '*And I have a lot of experience not only in looking like someone else, but also in not getting noticed.'*

Lucian considered the situation before replying. *'Perhaps you are going to be of some use after all,'* he said before turning back towards the capital.

'Of course, I am,' said Nazim irritably. *'But we must lay the groundwork carefully and make our exit as unobtrusively as possible. The fewer the people who know of your journey, the better.'*

The inner conversation continued unabated long after Lucian arrived back at Latiedes' house.

That evening, Portio Latiedes introduced Lucian to the merchant, Caspar Mossamed, and they explained to him how they needed his help in discovering the whereabouts, both of Al Barab, and of the suspected wizard.

"My captain, Saul, and my men will do all in their power to assist you, Governor," said Mossamed. "I agree that this problem must be nipped in the bud. The Juhl do not need much proof, nor much of an excuse, to get behind anyone who comes along who might be their accursed messiah.

"But their courage is fleeting when faced with the right odds. I am confident we can find the solution between us. It seems clear to me that we must lay some sort of trap to capture this Al Barab and bring him in alive. What do we know about where he was last in action against your soldiers?"

"It is quite a distance from Tevalem — more than eighty miles — but he seems to be able to inhabit the wilder regions of Juhl with very little recourse to visiting villages or towns — and when he does, the local population always hide him and protect him. Anyway, because of this there is no way to tell where he might be now or where he is going," answered Portio.

"Then perhaps we should provide him with a reason to 'be' somewhere at a time of our choosing so that we may become, shall we say, more closely acquainted with his future plans and perhaps acquire some knowledge of his wizard friend," said Caspar.

This suggestion brought smiles to all the assembled faces and planning for the termination of Al Barab's career continued well into the night.

Chapter 13

Jespeth's plane was in mid-stroke when he suddenly stopped. The effect was to leave a sliver of wood still attached to the piece he was working on, the curling flake hanging in the air, unmoving but still accusing, as if to drive home the guilty feeling he should have had that he had just spoiled a perfectly good table leg. Not that it meant he would have to start all over again — the stroke could be completed after all —, but in his mind, the piece would never be as perfectly worked as he required of himself. He would always see the notch left by the incomplete stroke and he knew he would never be satisfied that he had done his best.

But doing his best at his craft was secondary in his thoughts at that moment as he realised, he had not fulfilled his promise to Marin that they would make the pilgrimage to Tevalem. Almost a year had passed, and he had done nothing further to ease her concerns, especially those about their son, Empas. She had not brought up the matter again since they made the decision, of course, but now that he thought about it, he recognised the sadness and longing in her eyes and her general demeanour. He was immediately struck by a greater feeling of guilt and something else — a sense of urgency perhaps? — though he could not quite identify it. Of one thing he was sure, however, he had to make things up to his wife. They had to make this trip.

Marin was scraping the skins off vegetables when her husband entered the kitchen.

"Marin, I am so sorry. Can you forgive me?" asked a plaintive voice that she knew so well.

Smiling, she answered, "Yes, of course, but what for this time?"

"Tevalem!" he declared. "I promised you we would make the pilgrimage to Tevalem, and I have done nothing about it for nearly twelve months."

Marin stopped smiling as she recalled the endless days of disappointment, thinking that her husband had just been humouring her to help her through a melancholy period. Certainly, she had felt a little hurt, a little patronised, but she could not bring herself to blame Jespeth for not wanting to embark on what would be a big upheaval in their lives. So, she had tried to put the matter to the back of her mind, something to be discussed when and if the right time presented itself.

Slowly, she turned towards him, almost afraid to embrace the moment for fear of more disappointment.

"We must leave," said Jespeth. "Tomorrow. No excuses. No unfinished business. We will go to Tevalem. We will make the pilgrimage. And we may even find our son."

She scanned his features, his unusually nervous disposition, and could not help wondering what had caused this sudden surge of decisiveness.

"Of course, I agree," Marin said, unable to disguise the perplexity caused by his outburst. "But do you mind if I ask what has brought about this — abrupt — decision?"

"Truthfully, I've only just thought about it again after all this time," replied her husband. "But there is something else as well. I can't explain why or how, but I know that we have to do it now, or we will be too late."

"Too late? For what?" she asked

"That's just it. I don't know!" he declared in an exasperated tone. "But I trust my feelings in this. We have to go now."

Marin had no difficulty at all accepting the situation. She just felt grateful that her prayers had been answered. Slowly she rose and embraced her husband and he responded in kind.

"Then I had better go and pack!"

* * * * *

Empas realised he was not displeased with the progress he had made in spreading his message throughout Juhl towns and villages. True, he had not been received well everywhere, especially where the local rabbi held a strong position of leadership and respect, but many had listened to his teachings and he could read their thoughtful expressions as they went away from the meetings wondering — at last — why an omnipotent God should be so unforgiving, should require constant 'sacrifice' from his servants, should deny so many aspects of the life that He created to his followers. The list of 'dos and don'ts' offered by the church seemed endless, and to Empas, almost pointless once you strayed any distance from the basic, self-evident, tenets of right and wrong as given to the prophet in the basic laws.

He had also generated quite a reputation among the populace so that now, wherever he went, there was generally a small crowd of people eager to hear what he had to say. There were also as many people, it seemed, in need of his services as a healer, although he realised that the use of his healing power was far more draining of his energy than teaching and the numbers probably seemed greater as a result. He smiled ruefully, now thankful for the impulse that had made him agree to let Doctor Gaveri perform the long procedure that gave him the M-BEATS implant, though at the time he had been dubious of its value.

"But I can heal people using only the power of my mind, Doctor," he had argued. "What makes you think this technology is necessary for me?"

"Ah, but you are mistaken, young Empas, for it can be of enormous help to you. M-BEATS — or, to give it its full name, Micro-BioElectronic Examination and Treatment System — marks the summit of medical advance in our culture. Because it is surgically implanted into the practitioner, the whole, complex system becomes an integrated part of your being. It acts instinctively, using the brain's phenomenal computing speed and power, to provide almost instant analysis of any foreign bodies in the patient's system, abnormalities of blood flow, pressure, temperature and composition, irregularities of organ and gland functions, the list of goodies is almost endless. The nett result, however, is that, by the simple act of laying on of hands to the patient, you will know within seconds what is fundamentally wrong with him or her.

"Then the really clever part of the system begins to manufacture and administer the correct medicines, antibiotics or other additives and administer them, literally, through the tips of your fingers, because they are manufactured and function at the molecular level, passing easily through the skin. Neither practitioner nor patient feels anything other than the effects of the treatment. To a primitive culture, such as the one below on the planet, the process will, of course, seem miraculous.

However, the real point here is that M-BEATS will enable you to treat diseases and conditions far beyond those which you can at the moment using simply your telepathic powers."

"But I still don't understand why you should feel it necessary. I have not really explored the limits of my telepathy. What makes you think it would be inadequate?"

"You are missing the point, Empas. Undoubtedly, your telepathic powers would be up to the task of healing, but you do not have the necessary medical knowledge or background to identify and administer treatment for all the various bacterial and viral infections you will encounter. M-BEATS has its own inbuilt artificial intelligence and medical library. As I have researched the many thousands of bacterial and viral organisms associated with this planet, so I have added that knowledge to the AI. That knowledge is perfectly valid when dealing with beings native to Rega even though I still have not been able to fathom the devastating effects of many of the organisms on Eldorans. It knows what to do even when you don't! And because you have both Regan and Eldoran blood in you, I suspect you are quite capable of handling such infections without harm. Eventually, of course, you will pick up a lot of this information and store it where you can consciously call on it. Presumably, your telepathic power would take over from there. In the meantime, Eldoran technology can achieve the end you desire, and no one need ever know about it."

One of his main concerns had been about the effect of introducing Eldoran technology into this society and culture, reasoning that it could only slow the necessary intellectual and cultural development of the people, making them dependent upon 'machines' rather than themselves. But in his own case, he could see that he was already regarded as a 'miracle worker' in their eyes so the invisible technology which he now possessed would make no difference. The doctor's argument proved superior to his resistance, so he had undergone the procedure, which had been relatively quick and quite painless. Even now, so soon after the surgery, most visible signs had disappeared.

The more he thought about it, the more obvious it became that it had been the right decision. M-BEATS saved him an enormous amount of both mental and physical energy and its efficacy was such that his reputation as a healer had begun to spread far and wide. The case of cardiac arrest he had encountered a few days ago had been a typical case in point. Restarting the heart had been simple, of course, though the man had been clinically dead for a while. What his telepathy could not do, because he did not have the knowledge, was to repair the slight deterioration in organ and brain function and bring the heart problem — which had caused the arrest in the first place — back under control. M-BEATS had done all that, and in the process, he had absorbed a good deal of information about the working of the human body.

He was pleased with the outcome for the man — Lazarus by name — but the fallout among the people who witnessed the act and told their friends and families, who in turn told theirs, and so on, was enormous. Not to mention the fact that Lazarus himself was constantly berating anyone who would listen, telling them that Empas had raised him from the dead! Suddenly, he was no mere healer or magician, but a miracle worker to those kindly disposed toward him. Others began to call him a necromancer. It was soon common knowledge that this teacher was able to conquer death itself. What else could he not achieve? The process was, he realised, something over which he had no control. His abilities, even the words he spoke, would, he knew now, be blown up out of all proportion the more times they were reported in conversation. And he also realised that the polarisation of opinions would become more extreme.

This worried Empas somewhat, but he knew that it could not be reversed so he turned his attention to finding ways to make his inflated reputation work to the advantage of his message — which had not changed, though, of necessity he had had to include concepts such as their God to help them understand what he was trying to get them to do. And while some were persuaded by his words, understanding that they need only follow his simple instructions to lead better and more productive lives, others were put off and remained tied to their traditional religious upbringing, partly because what they heard seemed complicated and even far-fetched.

He had also acquired a small group of followers who went everywhere with him, and indeed, took on some of the 'management' tasks associated with a travelling ministry. Though their reasons for joining him may have been varied, all were agreed that here was a teacher with a real message that could change mankind. Some even thought he might rid them of the Thorians and found it a little confusing when his message seemed to imply that they should treat the foreign invaders as 'brothers'. But understanding came only gradually sometimes, and Empas was aware that, though his followers, his 'disciples', were loyal to him, they were, also, only human and subject to the same fears and limitations as anyone else. So, he spent some time with them alone, trying to clarify his teachings.

He was troubled, somewhat, by a development brought about by one such conversation where one of his followers had asked, "Master, are you truly the son of God?"

Though surprised by the sheer magnitude of the question, Empas could not lie, but neither could he explain in full exactly who he was — they simply would not have understood nor believed him. Instead, he decided to take a more oblique approach.

"We are all of us sons of God in many respects, for without Him none of this would be possible," he had answered, and continued. "My father's kingdom is in heaven, and he desires that one day, we will all join him. But the way to the kingdom is plain. Simply believe in me and follow my example."

Even as he finished speaking, he knew he had failed to make things any clearer. Quite the opposite, in fact. But Empas could not have foreseen the ultimate consequences of that conversation.

* * * * *

Al Barab was feeling apprehensive, though he could not have explained why. This was just another raid, albeit one which promised to yield him money and resources which would last them a long time. In fact, it was the size of the prospective booty which had made the ambush so attractive, though he thought it unusual that such a large amount of tax levy should be travelling so relatively unprotected as this was. Still, though he had suspected a trap, his scouts could find no hidden cohorts of soldiers in the vicinity. All they had seen was a trader's caravan, itself quite well guarded, but travelling some way ahead of the tiny military unit accompanying the tax wagons.

Anticipating no trouble from the commercial caravan, he had set up the ambush and had his men now in position, awaiting only his command. It was perfect. And yet he felt a concern which would not go away.

As the small convoy rounded the corner and entered the narrow defile he had chosen for the attack, he judged his moment. At his yell, the hills on both sides of the defile filled with bodies and arrows began to fly.

But instead of panic and confusion, the attack was met by a series of short sharp commands as the wagons turned laterally on the road, effectively blocking it, and the escorting soldiers quickly took cover behind them. Andrew did not view this as a problem, though their quick reactions had surprised him, but he and his men made their way down the hillsides and approached the defenders, convinced that, seeing how outnumbered they were, they would run before death overtook them.

Andrew halted his men short of the defence, his growing concern now threatening his own cohesive thinking. But he ploughed on.

"Will you surrender without a fight then?" he called.

"No, but you might," came a reply from behind his position.

He turned to see, behind and all around his rear, the mounted guards who had been accompanying the trader's caravan, all with bows and arrows carefully trained on him and his men. It had been a trap, and like a fool, he had fallen for it.

"Fire!" came the command and before he or any of his men could react, the arrows each found their marks. Ten of his men fell immediately, to be followed by another six as the second volley was loosed.

Andrew could see all too clearly that they were indeed trapped, and unless he acted quickly, every one of them, would soon be dead. "Drop your weapons," he cried. "It's over."

The leader of the mounted guards eased his horse towards the bandits and stopped in front of Andrew.

"My name is Saul," he said. "And you must be the infamous Al Barab. Though I am not pleased to meet you, I know a group of people who, I am sure, will be."

Andrew only stared at this rather arrogant young soldier who was certainly no Thorian. In fact, everything about him screamed Juhl.

"Traitor!" he spat, with as much contempt as he could summon.

The man only smiled. "He's all yours Septim," he shouted to the officer commanding the now assembled Thorian soldiers, who were immediately instructed to capture and bind the remaining few attackers. Al Barab was securely tied by his hands to the rear of one of the wagons. It was going to be a long walk to Tevalem.

* * * * *

News of Al Barab's capture travelled fast, bringing with it fresh despair. The people saw their one hope of resistance of salvation perhaps, dragged in chains towards Tevalem and the judgement of the Thorian overlord. And their hopes sank.

But there was also news of another 'messiah'. One who spoke of peace and brotherhood, of a forgiving God and the kingdom of heaven and a strange new power to every man. Desperate now for any ray of light in the long darkness of foreign occupation and oppression, more people began to gather to hear Empas preach wherever he travelled. His disciples found themselves working harder and harder at managing the sheer numbers. Generally, he would find a raised position somewhere and the crowd would gather around him, and he would simply begin to speak. He found that he seemed to have a natural gift for holding people's attention. Sometimes they might ask questions, always seeking the reassurance that there was something better than the lives they had to live. Helped by the fact that he truly believed that, if people could learn to love one another, they would find their lives improved, his answers seemed to hold out hope where there was otherwise nothing but fear.

One of his disciples, Simeon, happened to mention to his brother, Andreas, that strangely, whatever amount of food they had managed to scrounge from the local supporters, it always seemed to be enough to go round everybody. Nobody was left hungry, and they began to believe that Empas was, somehow, causing the phenomenon. There was no other explanation surely! How else could such meagre amounts feed so many?

The speculation and the number of unanswered questions just grew and grew, but Empas seemed totally unaware of any of it. He was simply glad that so many people were willing to give his message a chance.

Although he knew that many would fall by the wayside, he also knew that some would be genuinely converted to his point of view. To him, it mattered only that as many as possible should be given the opportunity to make their choice between his god or that of the Juhl priests.

* * * * *

By the time Al Barab and his captors had reached Tevalem, Empas' reputation as the true 'messiah' was becoming well and truly established. Portio and Lucian sat on low thrones in the judgement room and watched silently as their prisoner was brought before them. Two guards dragged him into the room and shoved him roughly to the floor. Andrew was exhausted, not just from the long, forced march he had endured, but from the beatings he had also suffered from the guards. He had not been tortured as yet, but every nerve in his body seemed to be creating pain. Every muscle ached and he had not even the energy to stand and face his enemy.

Whatever fate awaited him, he thought, it could not bring any more misery than that which he was feeling at that moment.

"So," began Portio grandly, "we meet, at last, Al Barab, great hero and divine hope of the Juhl. I have anticipated this moment for a very long time. Your reputation has grown enormously amongst our soldiers, and if only half of what they report is true, then you must have led them a merry chase indeed over these past few years. Some of our finest have walked in fear of you and your men and we are constantly told, in no uncertain terms, that we cannot kill you. You are divine, immortal, unafraid of death as it has no power over you and that, therefore, we should cut our losses — stop while we are ahead — go back to where we came from and leave you in peace. Or face the wrath of you, your God and his wizard!

"And yet, here you are. From what I can see, just another jumped-up hero, lying flat on your face on the floor of my judgement room. I see no signs of immortality here. No earth-shaking threat of divine vengeance. No, Al Barab, I sense your fate is entirely in my hands. You will find that Thorian justice is swift and unyielding in the face of terrorism and insurrection. But our legal system is also part of the reason

197

we are accepted by the peoples we conquer. Every accused is given the opportunity to state their case or plead their innocence or whatever else they care to say. That is taken into account before judgement is passed. Don't you find that fair? Even you, a known terrorist, caught in the act, shall be able to state your case and I shall consider it. Have you anything at all to say before I pass judgement upon you?"

Andrew was only half aware of what the Thorian had been saying. He was long since resigned to his execution and despair had accompanied him ever since his capture. His only real regret was that he could not have taken even more of these scum with him. Hero? Immortal? He had never claimed any of those things, so where was this man getting all that from? Ah well, if it had given them a bit of a fright, then it was all well and good.

Immortal? Despite the pain and exhaustion, Andrew was intrigued. His curiosity seemed to lend him strength as he struggled to, first, sit and then stand up in front of this two-man tribunal. Slowly, he observed both of the men before him. He could see the power and arrogance in the governor's whole demeanour and presumed it was he who had spoken, and virtually, condemned him. But when he looked at the other seated in front of him, he was puzzled for he could read — nothing — and suddenly, he felt an ice-cold certainty that here was an enemy that he could never hope to defeat.

Again, despair threatened to overwhelm him before he recalled something else the governor had said. Something about a wizard? Yet he could not remember ever having dealings with magicians or anyone else of...? Unless he was referring to Empas and their fortunate meeting in the cave where he had lain injured? Yes, of course, that was it. The story of his recovery had been broadcast, gaining somewhat with repetition. Empas! It had been many years since he had thought about the boy. But even then, there had been something about him that had made Andrew believe that he was worth saving. He had always believed that Empas truly could work miracles given the chance. It seemed that the population believed that he already had.

Andrew smiled, recalling the incident clearly. So, they were aware of the healer? And they clearly did not have Empas. So, were they afraid of him? In their arrogance and position of power, probably not, but

Andrew could not resist the urge to plant a seed. Maybe he could not defeat this enemy, but perhaps Empas could.

"You have captured someone you perceive to be a deadly threat to your authority. Whether I can be killed or not remains to be seen. I will not bother arguing with the likes of you because, no matter how you try to ease your consciences, there is no justification for taking away people's freedom to choose who shall rule them. There will be others, many others, just like me, who will continue to fight you to the bitter end. And there is already one who can beat you. I know his power for I have seen it — and you should be very afraid. I will not reveal his name, but I tell you this; you will know him when he comes and his coming will rock the entire Thorian empire. So do your worst, puppet. And prepare to face your own destiny."

The blow came from behind Andrew and was hard enough to make him lose consciousness. As he fell, the guard who had struck him said viciously, "No one speaks to the governor that way, heathen."

Portio surveyed the scene, somewhat surprised that the prisoner had not begged for his life. Even more taken aback that he had had the nerve to threaten him —, and indeed, the whole empire! Who was this man, and more importantly, who was this 'other' in whom he placed such faith? He turned to face Lucian.

"I share your concerns, Governor," said Lucian, without waiting for the other to speak. "And I think I begin to see a little of what makes these Juhl the way they are. Their hope springs eternal and they are convinced of their ultimate infallibility. I do not think we will force this one to give up the name of the wizard we seek, but neither do I think we should simply wait for him to appear. I have an idea how I might seek out and get close to this 'messiah', but I will need to immerse myself in a complete disguise. We must, therefore, establish a code whereby the military will recognise who I am, and when I call for their assistance, they will come to my aid. Let us adjourn and make plans."

Lucian was overjoyed at all he had heard. Surely this 'wizard' — whom he now knew to be Empas — had to be the one he was seeking. If he could find and deal with him, it would be the summit of all he had worked for these many long years. He could deal a devastating blow to his nemesis, destroying and ruining all he had tried to achieve and at the same time, put the planet's development back on its correct course. Yes! All he had to do was use the forces available wisely and the result was foregone.

Though he could do nothing about what was happening, Nazim was, despite himself, intrigued at the reaction of the being controlling his body. Why was the Juhl's messiah so important to his captor? He also realised that the other seemed unaware, or totally unconcerned, that he, Nazim, was still capable of cohesive thought and he began to wonder what else he might be capable of if he put his mind to it. *'Take it slowly though,'* he thought. *'We don't want to get his attention.'*

Pleased at the start he had just made, Nazim settled into a new routine of speculative thoughts, determined to find a way to reclaim his body if he could.

Rising from his throne, Portio said, "Guard, find a suitable hole for this prisoner while I deliberate on his fate."

Slowly, the governor and the emperor's envoy made their way from the throne room. Andrew half regained consciousness and was dragged from the room, to take up residence in quarters where he would rarely see even the light of day.

* * * * *

"Enter," the steady voice called in response to Maikel's gentle knock. The door slid noiselessly to one side, and she crossed into the private quarters of the director feeling slightly — and strangely — nervous at the unusual summons that had brought her here.

"Sit down here, Maikel," said the director, "where we can have a little private conversation."

The woman sat, a little stiffly, as she was unused to being summoned to a private meeting in this way. But that was not the reason for her nervousness. She wondered if Doctor Gaveri had broken her confidences about Empas and whether that had been the reason for the call. After long hours of deliberation, she was now convinced that she had to try to help Empas in whatever way she could, but she was also aware that her decision might well be seen as a sign of betrayal to the man who had led them countless distances across galaxies unknown to this time and place.

If he knew of her decision, this could well be some kind of reckoning.

The director decided to try to put her at ease right from the start.

"Before you ask, no, Gaveri has not spoken to me about you or Empas, so please do not condemn him. Also, I want you not to be too concerned about the doubts and fears you are now experiencing, due to your feelings for my son. I do not see your involvement as a betrayal or negation of your loyalty to me. In fact, I am glad he has found someone so capable to champion his cause.

"Though I do not agree with the path he has chosen, I do see that it has merits and I promised not only him, but myself, that I would not interfere further in what goes on down on Rega. I am about to break that promise if you will agree to help me."

"Director," she began, "I cannot deny that my feelings for Empas are very strong — I believe that I love him — but my first loyalty has always been to you and this ship. That these facts could force me to make a choice frightens me beyond belief. If there is any way I can avoid that, I will willingly take it."

"Good! Though no such choice will be necessary," added the director kindly. "However, we are about to embark, you and I, on a little subterfuge and I need you to keep my involvement in it to yourself. If my son ever thought that I was 'interfering' again, there is no telling what might happen.

"I want you to go down to Rega, disguise yourself and work your way into his group of followers. Get as close to him as you can. I'll leave it to you whether you reveal yourself to him or not. I can see no harm in his knowing that you have followed him, but he must not know that I sent you. We can manufacture and supply all the physical accessories you will need to disguise yourself and we can even alter your general appearance if you feel it necessary. I will ask Doctor Gaveri to implant one of Saecra's communication devices for you. You can switch it on and off so your privacy is assured but I would like you to keep me informed of anything that might mean trouble for him."

"Trouble?" she asked. "Do you foresee something, sir?"

"Almost certainly," stated the man. "Though I cannot tell how serious things might get at this stage. That is why I want you there so that, should he need it, our help can be given with the minimum delay. Despite our differences, he is my son and I care what happens to him. Will you do this for me, Maikel?"

"Certainly, Director," she answered without hesitation, feeling only joy that she would see her beloved Empas again — and that with the director's full approval!

"Good," he said. "That's settled then. And now I suggest you go and see the Doctor and make your arrangements. I'll leave the detailed planning of your quest to you. Only remember that you mustn't risk revealing anything of our presence to anyone other than Empas. That really could cause trouble!

"Much depends on you Maikel. I wish you success."

After she had gone, the director sat and allowed many thoughts to drift through his mind. There were now so many variables in the equation that even his intellect could not accurately assess how all of them might interact. Not to mention the intervention of fate, that uncontrollable, unpredictable process whereby men succeed or fail, live or die. He knew only that all the pieces were now on the board of the enormous game that was being played out in this sector of the galaxy. Would his strategy be successful? Did he truly know who his opponents were and how they might play this game? So many variables. He had already considered many different outcomes of the current scenario. Which one would be valid, or was there one he had not even thought of?

'Time,' he thought. *'Everything will happen in its own time.'*

Chapter 14

Sitting round the campfire they had built on the shallow beach which bordered part of the inland sea — the only one in Juhl — Simeon's thoughts began to wander. He could still not quite believe that he and his brother, Andreas, had just left their jobs as fishermen simply because the master had told them to. But that is exactly what happened. He came along, said he had a job for them to do and they had immediately followed him, leaving behind their entire livelihoods, their only source of income!

Why? Whatever had possessed them, he thought? And yet, when he considered what they had found and experienced accompanying this strange man on his mission, he began to perceive how much their lives and their outlooks had changed for the better. He felt more fulfilled, more committed somehow to a life which, he knew, could never more include chucking a net over the side of a boat!

Simeon felt so sure that he had told the master that he would follow him wherever he led them, and he meant it too. But strangely, the man he so admired just turned to him and said, "Simeon, you are a rock, and I could build my church on and around you. Pedor I shall call you — my foundation, my rock! You mean so much more to me than you could ever know, and yet, I wonder if you yet have the strength to truly follow wherever I lead. You will probably deny all knowledge of me should the occasion arise."

Simeon could not remember having felt both proud and humiliated at the same time before in his life. How could the master possibly believe such an outrageous thing? He could never desert or betray the master. Determined to prove him wrong, over the months, he had worked harder and harder at his tasks, more or less assuming command of the little band of followers, taking care of the many things that needed doing to enable Him to carry out his mission with as little concern for detail as possible. He became if anything, even more dedicated to his master's calling, and made himself indispensable.

But now, as he stared into the flames, the doubts started to creep back into his mind. Was he really so indispensable? If so, why had the master gone off without telling him where he was going? Just what did he mean when he as much as accused him of betrayal? Where was all this leading to anyway? After all, it wasn't as if the master was preaching revolution or stirring up any kind of insurrection, was it?

As he thought more about it, Simeon began to realise why he had so readily given up everything to be with this man. It was the marvellous feeling of peace that came from practising love towards his fellow man. Yes, even the Thorians, for whom he had previously held nothing but hatred and suspicion. Now, he could put even them into perspective. He felt sure he could turn the 'enemy' to a friend if he ever got the chance. And it was all down to the master. What might the future not hold if He could persuade the leaders of the Juhl church to see his point of view?

Turning to his brother who was sitting beside him as usual, Simeon asked, "Does anyone know where the master has gone or how long he'll be gone for?"

At his question, the low hubbub of conversation stopped as all within hearing considered the question.

"He didn't tell me anything," answered Andreas. "Does anyone else know where he is?"

There was a general negative murmur before individual conversations started up again and Simeon was left looking at his brother, slightly perplexed now as no one seemed to know where Empas was at that moment. Although there had been no overt threats to his safety, Simeon could not shift a growing feeling of unease that his master might, at that moment, be in danger, and he, Simeon, was in no position to do anything about it. But since that, evidently, was the case and because, presumably, the master had intended it this way, was there really any point in worrying?

The afternoon wore on and it would soon be evening. The first signs of approaching darkness were appearing as Simeon, once more, turned his attentions to the flames in front of him.

* * * * *

204

Empas had been walking for so long, he had completely lost track of time. Vaguely aware that he had been heading steadily upwards, he looked around him as he reached the top of the foothill he had been unwittingly climbing.

The view could only be described as stunning as he looked out from his vantage point. Situated near the northern border of Juhl, the hilltop offered a breathtaking vista reaching literally miles out across open, rolling countryside. Interestingly, from this point, he could see into two of the lands bordering Juhl territory, and in the far distance off to his right, he could even see the line of the mountains where he had spent so many happy years among the Bolgs.

For the moment he was content just to take it all in, wallowing in pleasant memories and allowing himself an exquisite oneness with creation. The beauty of the panoramic vision before him almost threatened to overwhelm the senses and he knew that, as the sun went down in the west, he would perceive even more wonders. It was just so comforting to be able to forget, for the moment, his work and his responsibilities and all those who depended upon him, and to just enjoy this little miracle in silence.

"You could rule all this," said a voice suddenly.

Momentarily startled, Empas whipped around and saw, not many yards away from him, a man wearing a Thorian-style travelling tunic, but unusually if he was Thorian, no weapon nor armour. None that were visible anyway.

"You are wondering how I could creep up on you and get so close without your noticing," continued the man. "Well, it really isn't that difficult. After all, you were so deeply engrossed in your own thoughts, it wouldn't surprise me if ten soldiers in full gear and on horseback had been able to catch up to you. You really should be more careful."

Now over the initial shock of seeing the man where he had thought he was entirely alone, Empas began to study both the situation and the man. As he looked more closely, he realised that, actually, he could see right through him, even though his outline and features were quite clearly defined. An image then? Was it real at all, or just a figment of his imagination?

"I am real enough," said the man, "though not quite in the way you might imagine."

Clearly there was little or no immediate threat here, otherwise the Thorian would have brought the soldiers he mentioned with him. So, what could bring one lone soldier, bureaucrat, politician, or whatever, to this place at this time if it were not to simply talk with him? Was he really Thorian? There were so many questions, and as yet, no answers. And yet another question belatedly sprang to his mind; how did the stranger know what he had been thinking?

Not that he was overly concerned, but he was becoming increasingly intrigued as to what this stranger wanted with him. Almost without thinking, he directed his telepathy to the other's mind — and was immediately met with a block. So, he did not welcome any mental intrusion, and obviously had power to prevent it, at least partially. He withdrew straight away as he became vaguely aware that this was indeed no ordinary Thorian. And at that point, he threw up his own mental defences, only then realising that the man had, as he had begun to suspect, also been gently probing into his mind.

"You must forgive the intrusion, but as you are now aware, you are not the only one here with telepathic ability, and that fact alone should, at least, get me a fair hearing, would you not agree?" the stranger added, with increasing assurance.

Now that the words had been spoken, realisation began to dawn on Empas. A fair hearing? This person had a case to state and had obviously gone to some trouble to ensure that he could speak uninterrupted. So, who was he? The possibilities must be limited. One of his father's officers from the ship perhaps? '*Possible, but unlikely,*' he thought. The director had given his word that he would not intervene any further. No, there was another factor at play here and Empas struggled to identify it. Then it clicked into place. For some reason, he was becoming almost sure that he was facing and actually speaking to the one his father had warned him about. Lucian! His father's arch-enemy.

But not yet his enemy as far as he knew. He had never met Lucian before — and had never really expected to do so — but his father had warned him that the renegade Eldoran was, indeed, still alive and active in some way. '*Obviously very active,*' thought Empas.

Satisfied that his mental defences were proof against the probings of this being, his confidence started to return, and he sat down, inviting the man facing him to do the same. '*Let him speak his piece,*' he thought, '*then I'll know just what it is I am facing.*'

Instead of sitting, however, the man still stood and studied Empas. '*Definitely a mental projection, then,*' thought Empas. Truthfully, Lucian was somewhat surprised and a little unnerved by Empas' reaction to his challenge. He had expected a little more fear and trepidation, not this self-assured, calm reaction. However, knowing that he was both physically and mentally safe, he decided to proceed.

"You are at a threshold, young Empas. Oh yes, I know your name. In fact, I know all about you. Who you really are, who your father really is and what your mission is on this planet? Putting all the clues together took a little longer than I would have wished, but I have finally got the whole picture. I must say the director seems to have trained you well, but he has set you on the wrong path. I am here to try to save you from your father's folly. Did you know that the disagreement between your father and me was simply about ways and means? And that he forced me to adopt the methods I did to achieve the ultimate end? The irony being that the 'end' is the one thing we can all agree on. But only I, apparently, could see that you have to let nature take its course and use that process to achieve the result. And for that your father unjustly condemned me.

"The way of nature in general, and of mankind in particular, is that the best and fittest, through aggressive striving for dominance, will, in the end, acquire it. My way of moving this race more quickly along the road of progression and dominance is to use that principle, take leadership and control and introduce technology which is, perhaps, thousands of years in advance of what they have now to those individuals who can wield it. By doing this, they, and we, can be much better prepared for what will undoubtedly face them and us in the longer-term future. That is the road to their salvation, their redemption if you like, and it is the only one that will work. The director has chosen to ignore that, and in his arrogance, believes that he alone can control the destiny of worlds such as this one. Surely you cannot subscribe to such folly and self-deceit.

"Before you answer, consider this as well. There is more to this situation than just natural selection. Add into the equation the powers of telepathy that we can bring, and you have a sure way to create a future for this species that, under our guidance and control, can be brighter than ever you can imagine. Think of it, Empas, all these lands that you see before you, and more, can all be yours if you follow my lead and help me bring it about. Can you not see that it is our duty, our responsibility? These people will worship us as gods, and we will give them their future long before they might otherwise earn or deserve it. There will be no danger of them wiping themselves out because we will prevent it by our mental dominance. Believe me, I have thought about this for a long time, and I can see no problem that we cannot overcome.

"Face it, Empas. Your father could not be more wrong about them or about me, nor could he have done me a greater injustice. But that is another matter which will undoubtedly be settled later. You, above all people, must see that you cannot bring about cultural, physical and mental progress by peaceful means with these species. The laws of nature won't let you. Follow me and success is virtually guaranteed. Both Eldorans and Regans would reap enormous benefits. What do you say?"

Empas continued to stare at the image. The argument he had just heard had been delivered with passion and — yes — sincerity by this creature he saw before him. He also perceived anger, hatred and a desire for vengeance so strong that it permeated and tainted all the other arguments. But was there truth in what he heard? Was Lucian's 'plan' for mankind's future so very different from the one his father had designed? If you weighed one approach against the other, which came out better or more profoundly beneficial to the Regans?

His thoughts moved around his head and his mind actually began to clear as he realised that having heard Lucian's argument, he now had both sides of the debate fully laid before him. He had now actually reached the point that he previously only thought he had at his last discussion with his father. His decision to take a third path seemed, more than ever, to make total sense to him — and Lucian seemed, fortunately, unaware of it. Setting aside, for the moment, the question of whether God actually existed or not, what was clearly most important to Empas was man's right to exercise his free will. In that context, God was irrelevant. And so, he argued, were both Lucian and his father. They were representatives of another species, albeit one that had already obtained enlightenment, longevity and enormous technical power, but they did not belong on Rega! And though he could not yet see his own destiny clearly, he now felt he had all the information he needed to make some important decisions about his message and his efforts to bring mankind to a better future. That was what counted.

Certainty brought release of all the tension he had felt as he marshalled his resolve and determined to face down Lucian.

"Having heard your words, I now know why my father considers you so dangerous, Lucian. You speak of benefits to the Regans, of making them better able to face a future which does, of course, hold many dangers as you say. But no future possibility is as deadly, poisonous or humiliating as the awful reality you would present to them should you succeed in carrying out your plan. Instead of creatures who would determine their own future, you would create slaves and cannon fodder for an intergalactic war which you are determined to fight solely on your terms. You do not offer them a better way. You offer them only a way which suits you. You are not concerned with their dominance, but your own and the fact that millions of Regan lives would be spent achieving that seems to mean nothing to you. At least my father seeks to save them from that! Your lies and half-truths contain nothing that I can see would be of benefit to the Regans, only to you."

"A pretty speech, young man, and I find your concern for these primitives touching, if somewhat misguided. But I have galactic history and nature on my side, and they tell me that without my help, these people are doomed. Why, I probably have the power to bring that doom about right now if I want to. But I am merciful, and in my own way, I do care what happens to them. You have obviously inherited your father's arrogance, but not, I think, his power and you would do well to consider your options carefully before you speak again. You think you can oppose nature, oppose me?"

"Well, well," said Empas, "having tried persuasion and failed, you now offer me veiled threats? Oh, Lucian, I expected so much more of you."

At this jibe, Lucian's patience exploded. "You expect more? Well, don't let me disappoint you!"

And with that he immediately began a mental attack on his opponent with such ferocity that Empas was, at first, physically flattened against the ground. He felt the agonising pain in his head as wave after wave of pure mental energy, reinforced with venomous hatred, assaulted his senses. Momentarily stunned, he could do nothing but defend by instinct, unable even to move. He could feel the blood beginning to seep from his nose, his eyes and his ears as the pressure continued to build and the thoughts tumbled in his head, no longer bearing any resemblance to logic or rationality, and it seemed there was nothing he could do about it.

As panic threatened to take over completely, from somewhere came the image of the Bolg priest, Aortes. His kindly, peaceful features began to take shape in his consciousness. Through the pain, the old man seemed to whisper to him, '*You have the strength, you have the power, you need only add the resolve.*' With these words Empas found, deep within himself, the discipline which the suddenness of the attack had sought to destroy. His mental wall suddenly snapped into place, whole and sturdy, and the attack immediately lost its penetration and its momentum. The young man even found the time to examine the force of the attack, at once understanding its nature and its power source. He did not need to retaliate aggressively. Instead, he simply turned the mental force back in upon itself and redirected it to Lucian.

Now it was Lucian's turn to feel the deadly effects of his own power. Fortunately for him, the rebuff had been directed at the image which he was maintaining from many miles away. Nevertheless, the mental link necessary to do that acted like a conduit as the energy travelled through it back to the body that lay at rest in the Thorian governor's residence. Lucian suddenly sat bolt upright and uttered a cry of pure agony that reverberated throughout the mansion.

Nazim, too, could feel the agonising explosion as the energy spread through his body. But displacement had its compensations, he discovered. And something else. He felt, just for a moment, the total grip which Lucian had over him had slipped. The alien was struggling to maintain control. Nazim only had time to contemplate, briefly, the nature of a force that could do this to his invader before it again spoke to him.

'*Don't get excited, my little slave, I am still in control here. My enemy has shown he has more power than I gave him credit for. I will not make such a mistake again. We have merely begun the conflict and he thinks he has already defeated me. This is clearly not the case, but I will have to change tactics. He is young and determined, but his arrogance will ultimately work against him. What cannot be achieved by frontal assault can sometimes be brought about by subterfuge.'*

Nazim heard the bravado in the alien voice, but he thought he also detected just a trace of something else — fear.

'You speak of subterfuge, my lord? How, in what way?'

'Patience, little servant, patience. Having discovered where he is, who he is, what he looks like and somewhat of his plans, I now need to get close to him and then — we will see what transpires. To do this, I will need those unmatched skills at disguise which you spoke of.'

'As what do you wish to disguise yourself, Master?'

'As a Juhl, of course—'

Just then the door to Lucian's apartment flew open and two soldiers rushed in.

"We heard you cry out, Envoy. Are you all right? Is there an intruder?" said the senior of the two.

"I am fine," said Lucian. "It was just a bad dream. There is no intruder, as you can see. Thank you for your prompt arrival, but you may tell the governor that there is no cause for alarm, and I will see him at our evening meal. That will be all."

* * * * *

Empas sat with his back against a boulder breathing heavily just in order to get some precious air into his lungs. His strength was almost spent, and at that moment, he felt like he could have done little else. He contemplated how close he had come to defeat in the encounter in which he had just taken part. Nothing in his entire experience had prepared him for such fierce and determined hatred, such raw mental power, directed solely against him for the purpose of destruction. The very concept was totally alien to him. And he was not at all comfortable with the thought that, almost certainly, he would have to face this adversary again. *'He is determined to be my enemy then. How many more do I need?'*

Gradually, his breathing eased, and the M-BEATS began its process of healing, this time directing its energy to its host. The sensation of pain and the horror of the assault slowly began to recede from his mind. He did not know where the power or the ability to turn Lucian's weapon back on itself had come from, but he felt that, at least he had not compromised his principles by attacking his assailant but had simply defended himself as effectively as possible. Instinct? Possibly. Survival of the fittest? Now that was another story altogether.

For the moment, he gave himself over to contemplation of the so-called natural law of domination. Undoubtedly, all species were born with the instinct, which could not be denied, and he could see clearly how and why it formed the basis of Lucian's argument. But what, he thought, of intellect? Of self-awareness? Of free will?

These were attributes which, Empas was convinced, both Lucian, and to some extent, his father, had failed to fully take into account in hatching their plans. These precious qualities must be nurtured and protected above all else. The only way he could see he might achieve that was to neutralise the law of domination and replace it with one of true brotherhood, mutual respect and peace. But then, what of Lucian? Could he, Empas, learn to 'love' even this enemy who seemed dedicated now only to his destruction? If he could not, how did that impact upon his principles? Was it his destiny to defeat Lucian or to bring him back into the fold of brotherhood?

And the point of it all? Ah, there was the great unknown. He hoped that the word he spread would lead Regans to an Eldoran-like state of being, more quickly than might otherwise be possible., but he finally conceded, he could not be sure of that. And in any case, it was very unlikely he would be around to see it, even if he had inherited some of his father's longevity.

Was he to lead them to this brighter future, like some divine general, marshalling his armies in the cause of peace? The irony of this thought did not escape him! Or was there a different way to achieve the goal?

He did not even bother to pursue the question of whether he was, indeed, 'sent' to do any or all of these things, or whether he was simply a self-appointed, possibly deluded, prophet crying in the wilderness. He was too tired, and growing weary of all the philosophising, he closed his eyes for a few moments and rested.

He knew only that many more questions had been raised that day than answers supplied. Time and events would undoubtedly reveal more of his destiny.

* * * * *

The hours seemed to have flown by as Simeon looked up and realised that evening was here already. The sky darkened, tinged by a radiant red glow as the sun set in the west. No wind blew and the evening was soft and warm. The waves of the inland sea lapped gently against the shoreline. For a moment he wallowed in the almost sensuous feelings that the sight gave him, before turning his attention to more practical matters.

"Is there anything to eat?" he asked. "And has anyone seen or heard from the master yet?"

As if by magic, just as he spoke these words, Empas appeared, walking slowly down the beach towards the little encampment. Simeon rose and went forward to meet him.

"Master, I am so glad to see you. We have been concerned for you. None of us knew where you were, and we were becoming more worried."

"Pedor," answered Empas brightly, "ever and always concerned for my welfare. I hope I have not caused you too much alarm. Come, my friend, let us sit by your glorious fire and talk. I have made some decisions and I would like to discuss them with you all."

"Of course, Master," said Simeon. "But should we not first find something to eat?"

"Has anyone brought provisions to the gathering?" asked Empas.

Without exception, all in the little company answered negatively.

"Then, my friends, we shall do without food for tonight. There are other things that will sustain us, I am sure."

Though Simeon and the others groaned inwardly at this news, they all settled and grouped around Empas so that they could hear him speak.

"My friends, my brothers, I have decided that it is time to take my message where it will have the most impact and where it will be heard by the most people. I must begin to make a much bigger sound," declared Empas with a determination they had not heard in him before.

"This decision has led me to an inevitable conclusion — I need to go to Tevalem now, rather than later," he continued. "And though I do not ask you to come with me — for there is undoubtedly danger ahead — yet I would welcome your company on the road should you decide to do so. The choice is yours. You do not need to go. But I must."

As Empas had anticipated, his announcement was met with a stunned silence as each of his followers took in the news and began to discern what it might mean for their immediate and longer-term futures. Then, a slow, but growing murmur began, as each asked questions of themselves, each other, and of him. But he gave them no answers, for he knew there were none to give really. This would all boil down to a question of faith.

It was one thing to be part of a band of harmless prophets, teaching and preaching to the inhabitants of the rural wilderness of Juhl, even including the few small towns they had visited. It was quite another to go marching toward the very capital of their country, where they would probably be perceived as a real threat. Where the occupying Thorian forces would be in great evidence, not to mention the chief priests and heads of their own national church whose power they were set to challenge. Putting their heads into the lion's mouth? Though they had been told that they would do so eventually, it still needed some thinking about.

Empas let the many conversations continue for some time, giving no assurances to queries about their intentions, nor any comfort which he felt would be false in the circumstances. As the evening wore on and his followers continued talking and arguing, he felt weariness stealing over him again. As he felt he had nothing more to add right now, he lay down and slept.

Early the next morning, as he awoke, he looked around him and saw that his loyal band of followers had been reduced to eleven in number. Sufficient, he felt, for all the organisational needs his continued crusade might entail. He knew that, as they passed through the numerous small towns and villages still lying between them and Tevalem, they would attract larger and larger crowds as the message went before them, but he was confident that these eleven would handle each situation as it occurred.

That news of his approach would get through to the capital long before he physically arrived, he had no doubt. His encounter with Lucian the day before served to remind him that he would also be faced by others who would be determined to stop him, one way or another. He was not unduly perturbed by this thought, though he knew he would have to work out how to handle each confrontation as it occurred. Unused to thinking in antagonistic terms, and unwilling really to do so now, Empas felt a little unsure exactly how he should approach the problem of opposition. There was no strategy he could devise, and his only weapon would be the truth and authenticity of his message.

'So be it, he thought. *If I truly believe in what I am doing, then that 'weapon' must be enough. Though, it would obviously do no harm if I were to learn a little more about politics and dealing with authority as well?'*

He gathered his followers to him and addressed them with a cheerfulness he was not sure they all shared.

"Well, my friends, because you are still here, I believe we are all determined to go to Tevalem. Many miles still lie between us, and our destination and I am sure I will need all the support you feel able to give me. Thank you for your faith in my leadership. I trust I shall prove worthy of it. Let us begin."

Chapter 15

Maikel took great care in concealing her sled in a small cave, high on the hillside a few miles outside Tevalem, all the while checking that she was totally unobserved. It was unlikely that she would have been, the cave being on the side of the hill facing away from the road, but she did not take any chances. She covered the small entrance carefully with a few large stones and bushes, but she was still not satisfied with the result.

"Director, can you hear me?" she said into the wrist implant.

"Yes Maikel, I can. Is there a problem?"

"Not really sir, except that I am a little concerned about my efforts to conceal the sled. Is it possible to erect some sort of illusion of solidity here just in case any curious wanderer might happen by?"

"I have your location, Maikel. Do not concern yourself with this any further. I will send somebody to take care of it," answered the director, "You are not that close to Tevalem, you know. Is there nowhere suitable within easier and quicker access?"

"Not that I can find, Director," said Maikel. "But I will keep looking and if I find somewhere more suitable, I will move it. In that event, I will, of course, contact you again."

"That's fine. Do that. One more thing, Maikel," added the man. "Now that the communication link has been established, you will find that it will work on the level of thought alone. You need only project your thoughts to me through it and I will hear you. That is why you have the ability to turn it on or off."

As the full meaning of the director's words sank in, Maikel managed a quiet, "Thank you sir," before she switched off the little device. She could only imagine how the old man had felt when he told Saecra to include the on-off switch. He must be desperate to know exactly what was happening, but he had respected her privacy, and by inclusion, that of his son. Again, she experienced new feelings of respect for the director's guidance. Even when it came to the fate of his own son, he respected his, and her, freedom of choice.

Relieved that her arrival had gone unnoticed, she checked her clothing. Although her enviro, worn beneath her Regan attire, made things a little more uncomfortable for her, she knew she must keep it on as much of the time as possible. The immuno-nanos that Gaveri had given her would only protect against some of the Regan bacterial and viral life forms, not all. Should she get a cut, a wound or injury of any sort, it could be extremely dangerous to her very existence. She had long ago decided that this was a risk she was willing to take for Empas' sake. She only hoped that she would not need to put herself into a situation where the possibility was tested.

Maikel had already decided on the name she would use on the planet. Over the years, talking to Empas, she had picked up many of the fine nuances of Juhl language that would enable her to pass as Juhl herself and she was confident in her ability to blend in. The name she had chosen for herself was Marin Madane — Marin 'the faithful' — a name she felt sure Empas would connect with, even if he did fail to recognise her in her Juhl disguise.

With many thoughts going through her mind, she decided to make her way to the nearest village on the road heading east away from Tevalem. She knew that Empas and his followers were moving towards Tevalem on that same road, so they were sure to pass through the village, possibly stopping to preach or, at the very least to rest and eat. It was there that she would join them.

The village she came to was actually more the size of a small town with a few recognisable streets, shops, evidence of craftsmen of all types and a central square — an area around a large well which was kept clear except for market days. The town had two inns and Marin decided to enter the less seedy looking of the two to seek lodging and supplies. Her nervousness increased as she passed through the door and surveyed the large common room. Fortunately, there were only a few patrons, who, nevertheless, cast suspicious glances in her direction.

'A woman alone in an inn? What's going on? Not the most usual turn of events,' was the general direction the patrons' thoughts took. Maikel immediately recognised her mistake and a momentary panic threatened her, but despite this, she decided to brazen it out, so she boldly approached the man she thought was the tavern keeper.

"Excuse me," she said, in perfect, clearly upper-class tones, "can I get a meal and a room here?"

Whilst speaking, she produced, from her purse, a small silver coin — enough to feed and house quite a few guests in this humble place for more than a few days. Seeing the coin, the man she had addressed, who was indeed the tavern keeper, turned out to be quite helpful, faced as he was with this unusual situation. Pocketing the coin, his expression immediately became one of extreme helpfulness.

"Yes, of course, madam, I still have a private room available. I'm sure you can understand that, with the Blessed Passing nearly upon us, we are somewhat busier than usual with travellers — pilgrims mostly, on their way to Tevalem. Would you happen to be one of them?" he asked quietly.

"As it happens, I am on my way to Tevalem," she answered. "But I am expecting some friends to join me before proceeding any further."

"Oh damn!" said the man with evident concern. "I hope there are not too many of them. I only have one room left now. Still, I expect we'll cope. I will have my daughter show you your room, and unless you prefer to eat here, I will have your meal sent up to you."

When Maikel had left the common room, the tavern keeper turned to the assembled company.

"All right, you lot. Haven't any of you seen a real lady before? And just so there's no misunderstandings, the rooms — especially hers — are off limits. I want no aggravation, just because she's travelling on her own. I don't know why, and I don't want to know. I suggest you all adopt the same attitude. Clear?"

At this admonition from the landlord there was a general murmuring, but no detectable malice, so he disappeared to organise a meal for his new guest.

Maikel surveyed the small, but tidy, room that was to be her refuge, at least until Empas showed up. It would do, she decided, somewhat surprised at herself for not experiencing more of a culture shock at her new surroundings. *'Ah well,'* she thought, *'perhaps I've been subconsciously preparing myself for this all along.'* She turned to the landlord's daughter.

"What's your name?" she asked politely.

"Rachel, ma'am," the girl answered shyly.

"I'm Marin. Would I be right in thinking that we girls should stick together in this town?" Maikel said with a wink that was unmistakably conspiratorial.

"Oh, it's all right really, ma'am. The locals are fairly harmless, and we don't see too much of the Thorian military here, despite being so close to the Tevalem garrison. But I wouldn't test the situation too much, if you know what I mean," said Rachel with a little more confidence.

"Thanks for the advice, Rachel. May I ask what is wrong with your foot?" asked Maikel kindly.

"N-nothing, ma'am. At least, it's not injured or anything. I just — it's always been like this since I was born. It makes me walk funny, but it don't hurt at all. Only trouble is, young men don't go for girls who are lame, so I'm stuck 'ere with my dad. I wish, sometimes, it wasn't this way, but I suppose you can't have everything can you?"

The girl raised her hand to her mouth and gasped, amazed at herself for opening up like that to a complete stranger, albeit a woman who seemed kind enough.

"I'm so sorry, ma'am," she almost cried. "I didn't mean to burden you with my troubles. Please forgive me."

"Think no more of it," Maikel answered. "There is nothing to forgive. You have my sympathy for your affliction, though. It must be terribly hard to bear sometimes. But don't give up. I have a friend who, I think, would be more than interested in trying to help you. Especially after you have been so kind to a woman alone in a strange place. Don't say anything to anybody, let it be our little secret and we will see what happens."

Rachel smiled, then — something she did rarely — and knew that this woman, who at first, she had thought a bit haughty, was actually very approachable. Far from wanting nothing to do with her because of her clubbed foot — most people's usual reaction — she had offered comfort and possibly help. She made up her mind then that no harm would come to this lady while she was under her father's roof if she had anything to do with it!

"Thank you kindly, ma'am," she said. "I'll go and fetch your meal."

From that first meeting, Maikel took Rachel under her wing. It was obvious she was going to be here for a few days, so she saw no harm in getting to know the girl a lot better, enjoying her company and the relative safety in numbers. The kindness she showed to the girl did not go unnoticed by her father, the tavern keeper either and he, too, became more than casually interested in Maikel's welfare.

In fact, the only uncomfortable moment Maikel had while waiting for Empas was when one of the local clergy — a faris, or clerk to the rabbi — walked into the tavern and started enquiring after the 'strange woman' who had suddenly shown up in the town.

"Forgive me, rabbi," said the tavern keeper. "But what is the church's interest in the lady?"

Just as the faris was about to answer, Maikel descended the last stair to the common room, having heard the man's enquiry.

"Can I help you, rabbi?" she enquired confidently.

"Ah, yes," answered the man hesitantly. "Madam — Madane? — is that correct?"

"It certainly is," said Maikel. "What can I do for you?" she asked again.

"Well, the chief rabbi is somewhat anxious to meet you. It's not often that we get such a fine visitor from — where did you say you were from?" he asked.

"I didn't, actually," answered Maikel with a confidence she did not feel. "But since you ask, my family are originally from Tevalem, though I have spent many years now amongst the folk who live in the mountains, on the eastern border of Juhl. I am waiting for some friends to arrive before travelling on, but please tell the chief rabbi that I would be happy to meet him if he wishes to spare a few minutes of his valuable time to talk with a humble citizen."

"I will certainly pass your comments on to his reverence," said the somewhat flustered faris.

Clearly, he had expected his presence to induce more — respect — in those not of the clergy. Instead, he found himself floundering and fast losing confidence faced by this woman who was clearly not cowed by his arrival, nor concerned at the prospect of a meeting with his boss.

"Good day to you all," he said as he backed towards the door and left hurriedly.

"Be careful, ma'am," said the tavern keeper. "The local clergy are not to be trusted. They carry out the functions of the church, all right, but they also take a more than healthy interest in the pilgrims who are on their way to Tevalem, if you get my meaning. More than a few have left here with far less worldly goods to get them to the capital after a talk with the chief rabbi. And he never seems to go short of good food and fine clothing."

"Thanks for your help and advice," said Maikel. "I wonder what the chief rabbi thinks he has in store for me?"

As events turned out, the meeting never took place, but shortly after the encounter, the same faris was seen leaving the town, on the road to Tevalem, evidently in a hurry.

The following day, Maikel was woken by a repeated knocking on the door of her room. At her command 'enter', the door was almost flung open as Rachel burst into the room, clearly agitated about something.

"Rachel, what brings you here so early in the day?" she asked.

"He is coming!" said the girl excitedly. "The master, the messiah, he is coming to our village."

"Oh," said Maikel, feeling a flutter of excitement herself. "Well, perhaps we should go and see him then. Go down and tell your father we are going out. I will join you in a little while."

"Yes, ma'am — I mean Marin — oh, isn't it exciting? They say he is the son of God, and he will be the next king of the Juhl. And he's actually coming here. I wish I could get to meet him, but he probably won't even notice someone like me. All the same, it will be brilliant to see him, won't it?"

"Yes, Rachel, it will," answered Maikel calmly. "Now leave me so that I may get myself ready to see the messiah."

And Maikel did feel strangely calm now that the moment had almost arrived when she would see her beloved Empas once more. Though she wondered, wryly, what his reaction might be to her presence on his world and among his people. '*Oh well,*' she thought. '*Only one way to find out!*'

As they exited the inn, they could see that a number of people were all shuffling towards the eastern entrance to the town and they could already hear a noise, far off as yet that signalled a sizeable crowd coming into the square from the east. The two women joined the movement towards the noise, which grew louder as they walked further east. At last, rounding a corner, they saw the cause of the commotion as they were approached by an imposing figure dressed in white, who was followed by maybe fifty or sixty people, men and women of all ages, all, it seemed, speaking at once. The town's inhabitants slowed to a stop to allow this crowd access. The man in the white robe strode boldly towards the well at the centre of the square.

"Would somebody be kind enough to draw some water so that our thirsts may be quenched?" he asked politely, looking round at the assembled townsfolk.

"Here, Master, let me draw the water. We have been expecting you," answered a woman's voice that Empas thought he vaguely recognised.

He looked again and saw the woman, with her back to him, move towards the well and begin to draw some water from it. Intrigued, he watched as she withdrew a bucket filled with water. She turned and offered him a ladle dipped in the liquid, which he took from her and slaked his thirst.

"Thank you, lady," he said. "But don't I know you from somewhere?"

"I hope so, Lord," she answered. "For we met in Bazel a while ago."

Empas was puzzled then for he knew he had not been to Bazel since well before he left his parents' house in Wilet. And Maikel's disguise was so cunning that all he saw was a Juhl lady, obviously high born, with an accent he did not recognise and to whom, naturally, he could not put a name.

"I don't understand, lady, I…"

"I am Marin Madane, Lord. If you recall, we last spoke in… more elevated surroundings?"

The name and the coded reference to where they had met penetrated his mind at last as realisation dawned.

"Of course, Marin, now I remember well our discussion. You have travelled far. But for what purpose I wonder?" he said quietly.

"To see you, of course," Maikel replied, deciding that complete honesty would serve her better here than attempted deceit. "And may I introduce my friend, Rachel. She and her father run the inn across the square where I am staying and where, I'm sure we can arrange lodging for you."

Fortunately, the general level of many conversations going on all at once had masked their conversation from all but the closest to them. However, Simeon and one or two of the other followers had picked up on some of it.

"Master," said Simeon with a hint of suspicion in his voice. "I did not know you had more friends, and in high places if I am not mistaken."

"Be at peace, Pedor," retorted Empas. "For this lady and I are old acquaintances, and she holds to our beliefs with a passion that will match even your own, my friend."

He then turned his attention to Rachel, who had been standing quietly, wide-eyed at the natural friendliness of this man they called the messiah.

"Rachel, please accept my thanks to you and your father. If you can find room in your inn for myself and eleven others for a night or two, we would be most grateful."

Rachel just stared. This man had spoken to her! He had actually spoken to her! For a moment she did not even move., but at a slight nudge from Maikel, she seemed to gather her wits again.

"I... I'm so sorry, sir, I mean, Master. I did not... yes, of course, my father will find room for you all. I will go and tell him you're here," she blurted, embarrassed and flustered. He had used her name!

She turned and limped off hurriedly towards the inn to arrange for the accommodation. Empas noticed the limp and turned to Maikel questioningly.

"She was born with the affliction, poor thing. It seems to have affected her whole outlook on life. She has no reason to feel anything but sadness, yet she manages to live through each day without complaint and the locals all accept her — albeit they would not allow their sons to marry her."

At this revelation, Empas' eyes softened, and he said to Maikel, "I can see that we have quite a situation here — and an awful lot to talk about, Marin Madane."

Simeon and the rest of his followers went amongst the crowd, telling them that the master would teach the following day, but now he must have rest. The people slowly began to break up into smaller groups. Some of the pilgrims who had accompanied them into the town decided to travel on through the rest of the day towards Tevalem. Others found places to sit, eat and drink and make their own decisions later. The disciples followed Empas towards the inn. No one seemed to notice the lone figure who continued to sit on the edge of the well.

Lucian decided that his best option, for the moment, was to wait and watch. He had picked up quite a bit of gossip from the crowd about the messiah and his wonderful powers of healing. Much of it, he thought, was probably exaggerated, but he was definitely interested to see what Empas might do with the lame girl. '*This is going to prove interesting if nothing else,*' he thought.

When Rachel's father heard that he was expected to find room for another twelve visitors, he almost despaired.

"Just where do you suppose we're going to accommodate them?" he asked in a plaintive tone, clearly annoyed as the situation seemed out of control.

"I... I'm sorry father," Rachel stammered. "I didn't stop to think. I just knew that he had to stay here.

"He is wonderful, father," she exclaimed. "He spoke kindly to me, and I felt... I don't know... at peace somehow. Oh please, let them stay."

Her father looked at his daughter with sadness and sympathy. Rarely had he seen her so happily agitated, and he would be grateful to this stranger if only for that. Further to which, this man was obviously one of the 'friends' the lady Marin had been waiting for. But he still did not know where he was going to put them all.

Just as he was pondering his dilemma, the small group who had been occupying his dormitory room entered the bar.

"Sorry to depart so suddenly, innkeeper, but we have to move on today. Word has reached us that we are required in Damas, so we'll settle up now if we may. Pity, too, because now we'll miss the entertainment offered by the new arrivals."

The tavern keeper could not believe his luck! Now he could fit everyone in — at a squeeze, granted, but at least they would all be sheltered. He thanked God for the intervention, a thing he, and almost everyone else in his trade, did very rarely indeed.

A few minutes after the group had left, Empas, Maikel and the rest of his followers entered the tavern. The rest of the day and the evening seemed to speed by as they all rested and enjoyed the food and service provided by Rachel and her father. While they were eating and talking, Rachel unsteadily approached the table where Empas and Maikel were sharing a quiet moment. As she got close, her foot slipped from under her and she went down with a cry of pain to the consternation of all those assembled.

Empas leapt up from the table and knelt to pick the girl up off the floor. Turning to her father, he said, "Have you somewhere private where we can take her. I would like to have a look at that foot."

"Please do not bother yourself, sir," said her father. "I will look after her."

Empas looked him straight in the eye and answered, not unkindly, "You have already done all you can for her. Now it is my turn."

Realising that he was dealing with a power he had not come across before, the man bowed his head and nodded slowly. He led Empas to her private room away from the inn's common room where Empas laid her gently on her bed and sat on the side of it facing the girl.

"I... I'm so sorry, sir, I don't know what happened, it just gave way. I don't want to be any trouble," she said unsteadily, trying to control her pain.

"Rachel," said Empas gently. "I can help. Just let me see your foot."

He turned, and despite her protests, removed her sandal to reveal a small foot, misshapen and turned in upon itself, which was now starting to bruise. He could see that it was causing the girl great pain, and drawing upon his telepathic insight, lifted the limb with one hand. With the other he began to move the entire foot outwards towards a more normal position.

Rachel could feel nothing, but she was sobbing uncontrollably at her complete loss of dignity. Her obvious distress made little difference to Empas, who was concentrating hard in an effort to reshape the necessary bones and set them to a normal position. It was working, but it was taking time and effort. Maikel entered the room and sat on the other side of the bed. Taking Rachel's hand she whispered gently, "Don't be upset Rachel, didn't I tell you he would want to help you?"

"Oh, Marin, I..." she cried softly.

"Hush now," said the woman, "just let him work and stop worrying yourself."

The father had stood at the foot of the bed and seen all that transpired. With wonder in his eyes, he saw his daughter's foot change shape and position. Her whole leg straightened, and a natural colour returned to her skin. Finally, Empas laid the foot back down on the cover and stood, extending his hand to the girl.

"Come, Rachel," he said gently. "It is time for you to show us your true beauty."

Taking a last look at her friend, Marin, Rachel tentatively moved her legs to drop over the side of the bed. Taking Empas' hand, she stood and looked at his face where she saw only kindness and concern. Responding to his smile, she looked down at her feet and wriggled her toes — all of them.

Then she looked at her father and walked slowly towards him, as normally as any other person would. Tearfully, she fell into her father's arms, and he hugged her tightly. Lifting his face towards Empas, he mouthed 'Thank you' and resumed hugging his daughter.

"Time for us to retire Mai… Marin," said the young man quietly.

Much later that evening, Maikel could still hear the commotion going on in the inn's common room downstairs. Though it was the first time she had actually witnessed it, she could well understand how a 'miracle' such as the one Empas had performed on the girl would affect the local population so wildly. Despite her knowledge that he had used telepathy and advanced Eldoran technology, even she had been impressed and she smiled at the pleasant memory of it all! She heard the knock on her door that she had more than half expected.

"Come in Empas," she said, confident that it could only be him as, in fact, it was.

The door opened and he entered, closing and locking it behind him. Turning to Maikel he said simply, "We should talk."

"Yes," she answered.

"Not that I am not pleased to see you, Maikel, but why did you come?" he started in straight away.

She decided to be equally forthright and candid.

"I came because I want to be with you. I know that is probably not what you want to hear but please just listen to what I have to say. When we spoke, when you were last on the ship, I realised that, not only did I agree with your point of view, but I also began to feel something more, something I could not explain. Doctor Gaveri told me of our Eldoran physiology, how we rarely feel emotions, and explained that, though it was unusual, it was not unheard of.

"Empas, I am feeling these emotions that I do not fully understand. And I need to know where I stand. When I am beside you, I am happy in a way I cannot explain. I did not know just how true that was until I saw you walking down the road towards me and when you came through that door just now.

"I don't want to distract you from your mission, which I know is all important to you. But I want to be near you all the time. Please tell me you understand."

Empas was momentarily stunned at this admission from the woman that he, too, had felt emotionally attached to for some time., but thinking that she was totally out of his reach, he had tried to close her out of his mind and concentrate totally on his cause. Now, as he took in her words, he realised that what he had thought impossible was actually being put before him, and the woman he had previously decided that he desired above all others, was here for him.

When he first came into her room, he had been prepared to have a talk with her and send her back, fearing that this was another attempt to influence him with, what he had come to think of as, the Eldoran point of view. Now, hearing her frank revelation, he became much less sure of himself, and as he continued to look at her, he remembered again the feelings he had experienced when he last saw her on the ship. This had nothing to do with his mission, but apparently, everything to do with just the two of them.

He became aware of a feeling akin to light-headedness. A feeling of resolution, as his concerns for his mission, his followers, in fact everyone and everything else, melted slowly away. He became aware that this was a moment for which he had waited a long time.

"Maikel, I…" he began, stumbling over his words for the first time. "We… What are you saying? Are you sure you truly feel something for me?"

"I am sure," she replied as she moved to embrace him, turning her face towards his and offering her lips to be kissed.

There was a pause as he considered what was happening. Then, all Empas' doubts disappeared in that moment, and he brought his lips to hers as they kissed long and hard for the first time. Both felt their passions start to rise and their bodies to respond to each other. Empas pulled away from her slightly as doubt threatened to return. Maikel only sighed and said softly, "I love you and I want to be with you."

At that, the doubts receded altogether and Empas gave himself over to the physical warmth and passion that was already threatening to overtake them.

"Take off your enviro," he told her softly, passion turning his voice gravelly and deep.

"But it is my only protection," she whispered in return.

"No," he replied. "I am your protection. Take it off."

Realising that they had gone beyond a point of no return, she moved away from him and removed not only her Regan clothes, but then the one piece, skin hugging enviro-protective that she had not previously dared to take off since landing on the planet. Shyly, she stood naked before him as he surveyed her perfectly shaped body.

Consumed by the feelings the woman aroused in him, Empas swiftly removed his own clothes and led her to the bed where they fell gently together, kissing each other and revelling in the warm embrace that began to reveal all the contours of their naked bodies. Slowly they explored each other, senses sharpening with each new moment of discovery. Then their motions became swifter and more agitated as basic animal instinct took over. Their first union, as he entered and penetrated her most secret place, was like an explosion of feelings and sensations for Maikel. Not in her wildest dreams had she anticipated the feeling of sheer joy she experienced as she surrendered completely to this man who was now, at last, becoming a part of her.

Empas, too, felt an ecstatic joy as his physical needs finally found their fulfilment in the womb of this beautiful woman. He cried out softly at his final release, eliciting a similar cry of ecstasy from her, and revelled in her complete surrender to his passion. Peace descended on them both at the culmination of their first coupling and they rested, still physically locked together until, at last, their senses started to cool. Then Empas lifted himself gently off her and they laid side by side, trying to take in the full meaning of what they had just done.

For a while, neither of them moved, each lost in their own thoughts and feelings and unwilling to shatter the peace that had descended on them. Eventually, however, Empas turned his face to her and whispered gently, "And I love you too."

At that, Maikel kissed him again and their physical reactions began to take over once more. Their lovemaking was sometimes wild, and at others, slow and sensual, but always totally fulfilling. They were totally unaware of time passing until at last, they fell apart, both panting heavily with the physical exertion they had indulged in. Finally, Maikel rested her head on Empas' shoulder and fell into a contented sleep such as she had never had before.

Empas opened his eyes suddenly, knowing that he must have slept, though he could not tell for how long. As he listened, he could hear no noises coming from the common room below, so he guessed it must be quite late. He turned his face towards that of the woman sleeping on his shoulder, smiling gently as he recalled the sheer joy of their activities together. He could not recall ever having felt that way before, but then, he had never been with a woman before. It was not just that, though. Somehow, he knew that he and Maikel had been meant for each other and that, now they had joined, nothing and no one could tear them apart. It was, as far as he was concerned, a simple basic law of the universe.

He started suddenly as that thought sparked another train of deliberation. Though Eldorans had no rules or traditions regarding relationships between men and women, all peoples on Rega, as far as he knew, certainly did. And his own people, the Juhl, were stricter about it than any other race that he knew. Logically, he could see no reason why such traditions should be honoured to the point of fanaticism — but neither could he deny the strength and depth of feeling that the breaking of those traditions would elicit.

The poor, the oppressed, the hungry, these people had little that they could hold onto except their dignity and their pride. Traditions such as marriage helped to reinforce that pride. That the church had ruthlessly turned that necessity into a 'commandment' that gave it yet more power and helped ensure that the oppressed remained that way through fear of reprisal, was another matter. The fact was, the people from whom Empas drew his main support, and to whom he gave his utmost efforts, would undoubtedly condemn him as a 'sinner' if they knew about his newborn relationship with Maikel. That they might also attempt to stone both of them to death did not really concern him. What did matter was that he must be seen to be free of all 'sin', otherwise his message became as frail as leaves on the wind.

He became more exasperated as he contemplated the awkwardness of this new situation, and the unnecessary complications that the Regans' ignorance and superstitious beliefs imposed on his message. From the preacher of simple global brotherhood through love, he had become a messiah, a saviour, a king, sent by an improbable God to redeem them, not only from occupation by the Thorians, but from sin itself! What would they expect of him next, he wondered?

He needed to think this through, so he turned again towards his lover and whispered, "Maikel. Maikel, wake up. We have to talk."

The woman stirred and smiled as she woke from a refreshing sleep.

"What is it, my love?" she asked, sensing the urgency of his call.

"We need to sort out a few things — and we have to discuss our future actions. Our lives may depend on it."

"I know we have reached a new stage in our relationship, but is there any need to hurry? After all, we are only just getting to know each other."

"No, it's not that," Empas replied. "And whatever happens, I know that our love for each other will grow. It's more practical I'm afraid."

Empas quickly explained the situation as he saw it regarding his public life on Rega. Maikel took in all the information she was being given and considered for a moment before adding her comments. Actually, she realised, the situation potentially made her mission for the director easier to carry out if their relationship remained secret. Though she hated the thought of hiding anything from Empas, she had given her word to the director, and she could not break it. The more she thought about it, the more sense it all made.

"Empas, my love, my lord," she began. "I cannot tell you all of the things I am feeling right now. I can't explain the happiness I feel. And you must never doubt that I love you with all my heart, but as I said last night, I did not come here to disrupt or interfere with your mission. If that means our relationship must be secret, then so be it. Just tell me one thing, my love."

"What is it?" he replied.

"Do you feel guilty or ashamed of what we have done?"

"How could you ever think that?" he answered, astonished at the question. "I am only th…"

"Hush," she said. "If you feel no guilt or shame, then you truly are still 'free of sin' aren't you? And as long as we are the only ones who know about this relationship, you can continue to preach your message with a clear conscience. I, meanwhile, will continue to be Marin Madane, the faithful follower of her lord and saviour. Your other followers will just have to get used to the fact that I am a woman!"

Empas immediately saw the logic in her analysis and was once more amazed at the insight she showed when dealing with matters concerning humans. Though he had the power to teach them new ways, she had the insight to deal with their current ones.

"I'll go back to my room now, then," he said, reluctantly nodding and acknowledging the sense in her words.

Chapter 16

Even Nazim was sickened by what he had witnessed that day.

He realised again that the entity that was controlling his whole being was irretrievably evil. It seemed to have little purpose other than the predatory one of seeking out and destroying this man everyone was calling the messiah. And it did not care one iota about the damage it caused to those who stood in its way or might be useful in achieving its ends. There seemed to be no limit to the lies and treachery it would employ to reach its goal. He recalled the whole episode slowly to be sure he had not missed anything.

The day following the healing of the tavern keeper's daughter, Empas had gathered his usual crowd of locals, well-wishers and pilgrims on their way to Tevalem and eager for his message. He had preached for a while and then declared that they were bound for Tevalem and any who wished to travel with them were welcome. It was plain that the company would travel only as far as the remaining town between here and Tevalem that day and that he might do the same there as he had done here. Stop overnight, declare his message to any who would listen — as usual, attracting the biggest crowd from the ranks of the poor and the oppressed — and then move on towards the capital.

Lucian had seen no immediate opportunity, so after the crowd had left, he made his way to the tavern where Empas had stayed and sat alone considering his next move. After a while, father and daughter entered the common room, clearly in the middle of a discussion that threatened to become heated.

"But I must go, Papa," the girl said. "After what he did for me, I cannot just forget him. I owe him a debt I can never repay."

"Now don't be silly, Rachel," the man replied. "I already told you, he asked for nothing and sought only your welfare. I, too, feel grateful to him, but that doesn't make it right to up sticks and simply follow after the man. He would agree that was foolish. Besides, I will not let you

232

travel on the road to Tevalem alone and there is no one I can ask to go with you. So, my answer is still no — let that be an end to it."

The girl had glared at her father in frustration. Lucian, however, had been watching and listening to the conversation and an answer to his problem seemed to come to him all at once. In fact, if he did this right, he might complete the destruction of his enemy's plans and of his son at the same time.

He shuffled over towards the pair who had stopped arguing to observe him.

"Pardon me," he said politely and as gently as he could. "I could not help overhearing your conversation and I wonder if I might be of service. It is a wonderful thing the master did for your daughter, sir, and I can understand why she would wish to be near him. We all feel the same. I and his other followers. I had one or two things to see to here before leaving to catch up to the rest so, as you can see, I am still here, but bound for wherever the master leads us. I would never dream of going against a father's wishes for his daughter, but if she is determined to follow him, I would be happy to act as her escort and protector on the road. It is not that far, and we might even catch them up before they stop at the next town."

Rachel immediately turned on her father, "You see, Papa?" she cried. "God has even provided me with an escort so that I may be with his son. Please say I can go."

Her father looked from one to the other, perplexed at the unwelcome turn events were taking.

"I don't recall seeing you amongst his followers," he said to the stranger, "so who are you?"

"I am... Jud Descar," said Lucian, thinking quickly. "And the reason you didn't see me is because it is my task to give comfort and guidance to those who wish to follow Him but find themselves confused and needful of reassurance. This often means I am busy when the others are not, but I do not mind if it is helpful to our mission."

The smile Lucian displayed, and his general disposition seemed just enough to sway the father. After all, it was not that far to the next town — a couple of hours or more — and if she had an escort, well...

Reluctantly, the tavern keeper said, "Very well, I will trust you and place my daughter under your protection. Please see that she reaches him safely. If any harm should come to her, especially now, I would never forgive myself."

Lucian nodded his assent and turned to Rachel. "You should bring some extra clothing with you and a little in the way of sustenance for us both would be most welcome."

Not long after that, the two of them had left the tavern and taken the road towards Tevalem. The journey had seemed quite swift, although it was late afternoon when they arrived on the outskirts of the little town. Rachel was obviously very tired and was limping slightly, despite her newly healed leg. She had not had to walk any long distance ever, so she was unused to such exercise.

Lucian said to her, "My dear, you are clearly in some discomfort. Why don't you sit in the shade for a little, while I go on into the town and find out where the master is staying. After you've rested, if you feel up to it, you can make your way in to the square. It is not far to go I'm sure, and I don't think any harm will come to you this close to civilisation, do you?"

Gratefully, Rachel agreed and sat beneath a tree in a small grove which effectively hid her from the road. Glad to rest her now badly aching leg, she settled in the gentle shade, happy that she would soon meet the master again.

Later, after she had slept for a while, she rose, and finding that her leg had stopped aching completely, she was able to walk, though it was now getting dark, and evening was drawing on. However, she knew she should follow Jud's instructions and make for the centre of town where she would be safe.

Lucian had observed her progress from his hiding place, into the backstreets of what was the worst part of the town, and into the trap he had set for her with three of the local ruffians. Had watched as they soundlessly abducted her, carrying her via dark alleys to the shack they called home. Callously observed the three of them having their way with her, as he had promised them, they would, and as they had been paid to do. Contentedly, he wandered away to carry out the next part of his plan, which involved a visit to the local chief rabbi.

The following morning, Lucian walked into the common room of the inn where Empas and his followers were staying, noticing that the woman Empas had met two days ago was still there. He was now about to carry out the most daring and dangerous part of his plan.

He walked straight up to Empas and said, "Master, I think there is a problem and I fear for the safety of one of our number."

Not recognising the man, Empas replied, "We seem to be having more of those just lately, but I'm sure we can handle one more. Who are you, by the way?"

"Forgive me, lord, I am Jud Descar and I have been travelling with you on your road for some time, though I did not like to impose upon your time. I have seen the light of your message and I am eager to serve you if that is possible. I accompanied a young girl, who said she knew you, to this place. I left her safely hidden outside the town yesterday, while I came in search of your whereabouts. Alas, I was set upon by thieves and beaten up. Luckily, I had nothing worth stealing and they decided not to kill me, but I was badly hurt and unable to continue my search. I must have slept then, but when I woke, I returned to the place where I left her, but she was gone, and I do not know where she is. Did I do wrong, Master? If so, please forgive me but I am afraid for her."

Empas took in the man's story and asked after his injuries, though he was slightly curious as to why he had not simply brought the girl with him into town. Lucian/Jud insisted that he was all right but kept pressing the urgency of his search for the girl. Empas turned to his followers.

"Pedor, Andreas, Thomas, all of you, please go out into the town and see if you can find any trace of the girl this man brought here. Marin, would you also look. I have a feeling you might locate her where others may not. Jud, you must be exhausted by now. Stay here and rest a while. We will try to find your runaway."

A little while later, the woman — Marin — had returned full of urgency and concern.

"Empas, you must come quickly, I have found her, and she is a little way off the central square, surrounded by angry men. It is Rachel."

"Rachel? But what is she…?"

"Later, Master, they are about to stone her!" cried Maikel as she turned and ran off towards the edge of the square.

The small mob had Rachel cornered in a conveniently quiet plaza, away from the main frequented areas. Empas was, nevertheless, surprised that more onlookers had not been attracted to the spot by the commotion the men were causing. He saw that there were five men in all surrounding her and that a rabbi was standing close, observing the scene. All five were shouting at once, calling her whore, witch, adulterer and demanding her death by stoning. The girl looked terrified, cringing against the wall as her eyes darted everywhere, desperately seeking some help.

Empas immediately took in the urgency of the situation, and uncharacteristically, barged through the men towards the girl.

"What is going on here!" he demanded loudly.

The cacophony ceased but was followed by a lone man's voice. "She is a witch and an adulterer and must be put to death as the law demands."

Empas could hardly believe what he was hearing but was, by now, angry enough not to trouble himself with internal debate.

"And who says this is so?" he demanded again.

"I do," answered the same man, "I am happily married with a family. She has been following me for days and so far, I had managed to avoid her, but last night, she came upon me as I was walking home. She bewitched me and my two friends and made us all slaves to her wicked desires. We were forced to… do things with her that no loving husband and father should. She so beguiled us and slated her wicked desires that we were exhausted and fell asleep. When we awoke, she was gone, so I went immediately to the rabbi here to confess my sin. He said we should find her, so that justice could be done."

On hearing this, Empas knew that the men were lying. He turned to the terrified girl.

"Rachel," he said softly.

"Master," she sobbed, trying to catch her breath, her desperation growing worse. "I did nothing, they… raped… me."

No one else had heard the exchange. Empas was outraged and he turned back towards the men, focusing on the rabbi who was standing off to one side.

"You believe all this rabbi?" he asked.

"I have no reason to disbelieve," the priest intoned in return. "I have known this man for many years. He is an upright citizen, and to my knowledge, faithful to his wife and family. If he has been bewitched by this — woman — then she must be put to death by stoning. It is the penalty demanded by the law."

"And is it the law that the accused has no right of reply? Is it the law that a priest of the church should collude in an act of murder?" Empas asked vehemently.

Without waiting for a reply from the priest who shifted uncomfortably, he turned to the man who had spoken.

"You say she has been following you for days?" he said.

"Yes," answered the man, confident that his lie would hold.

Empas then stared straight at the man and his two companions. "It is strange then, is it not, how this girl could have been enticing you for days, as you claim, and yet, only yesterday, she was still helping out in her father's tavern many miles from here. How, I wonder, could she manage to be in two places at once? Also, doesn't the law state that the accused should be given a chance to defend herself? Why then are you all so anxious to deny her that right?"

Silence then ensued as the assembled men who, moments before had been yelling for blood, now began to consider the situation in a new light. They began to look sheepishly at each other. The rabbi surreptitiously backed away from the crowd and turned to hurry home. As Empas held their eyes, all three men could see that their subterfuge was starting to fall apart. What had seemed an easy — and pleasurable — scam was turning out to be something entirely different.

Empas did not need to use his telepathic ability to know that he had these brigands exactly where he wanted them. In truth, he wanted to punish them for what they had undoubtedly done to Rachel. THAT, he knew, was the duty of the law. But administering rough justice was not in his nature, nor his remit. Nevertheless, his thoughts began tumbling. Before he became lost in his own musings, he decided to accuse and test these men.

"The one of you that is without fault here or at any other time in his life, should cast the first stone," he said emphatically.

Each man recognised the challenge in that statement, and each declined the invitation, though not with good grace. They had already been paid for their night's work and this man could prove nothing, they thought, so they quickly shuffled away, glad to have got away with such a rich reward.

Lucian had observed all of this from behind a building on the corner. When the crowd had all dispersed, he decided to play his last card and came hurrying around the corner.

"Rachel, at last I have found you," he said breathlessly. "Where did you get to?"

The girl, still terrified at her ordeal, could not answer him but only shrank even closer to Empas. She seemed about to speak when he hurriedly continued.

"Oh, never mind, I'm sorry to have been so long coming back for you but I was waylaid by three men and my injuries delayed me for a while. Master, thank God, you found her,"

Empas only turned to Rachel, and putting his arm around her, led her gently back to the inn where they were staying. There he ensured that she was given something to eat and drink and she was taken to his room, where she could rest for a while. The followers — disciples they now called themselves — drifted back in, having been unsuccessful in their various searches. Empas called them all to him and explained what had happened, introducing Jud Descar as their new companion at the same time.

"Pedor, Andreas, I would like you to accompany Rachel back to her home if you will. We shall be here for tonight anyway so you should be back in time to get some sleep if you set a good pace."

"Of course, Master," said Simeon. "But will she go with us? I would be surprised if she ever trusts a man again!"

"I will go with them," said Maikel suddenly. "She may not trust you, Simeon, but she does trust me. We are friends. And besides, I think I can explain things to her father a little better than you."

"Are you sure about this?" asked Empas doubtfully.

"Yes, lord, I am," she answered as their eyes — and their wills — met.

Not at all happy at being separated from Maikel even for a short while, Empas nevertheless agreed to the suggestion, emphasising to Simeon and his brother that they should watch and protect the women with their lives.

Entering his room, Empas moved to the bed upon which the girl was now lying, staring at the blank wall. He could see clearly the pain and the utter hopelessness within her due to her ordeal and he knew he must help her again if she were to survive this trauma. He sat on the side of the bed and took her hand gently.

"Rachel," he said again. "I am honoured that you should wish to be with me, and I cannot tell you what your dedication has done for me. But you have been brutally wounded and I need to heal that wound. Do you understand?"

Slowly she turned her tear-streaked face towards him. Seeing the gentleness and concern mirrored in his eyes, she nodded, and gradually, she knew a little peace at last as, without her knowledge, Empas gently probed her mind, and bit by bit, drove away the awful memory of what she had been through, replacing it with an entirely fictitious, but gentle, story of her visit. Then he laid his hands upon hers and commanded the M-BEATS to investigate the contents of her womb. His analysis found nothing to concern him as she was not pregnant. Satisfied, he told her to rest for a little while before starting back to her father's house.

"But I wish to serve you, lord," she said.

"And so, you shall," Empas replied. "But you can serve me best by looking after your father, spreading my message of love and brotherhood to all in your village, and by eventually making some lucky man very happy to share your life."

"Lord, you will embarrass me," she replied shyly.

At that, they both laughed. She rose from the bed and accompanied Empas down again to the common room. Rachel immediately ran to Maikel and hugged her, gathering up her few things which Lucian had thoughtfully brought in for her.

Empas took Maikel and the two brothers aside and said to them, "She will have no memory of her ordeal so you should not bother to mention anything to her father. Just get her safely home."

They left shortly after to take the girl home.

Lucian sat in the common room contemplating all that had happened. Though things had not worked out exactly as planned, he was pleased with the overall result. After all, his disguise had fooled Empas, and far from being found out, he had now become accepted as one of the 'disciples'. The rabbi would undoubtedly send word to the high priests in Tevalem, warning them of Empas' approach and of his apparent power over people. Oh yes, they would be much better prepared for his arrival and that would suit his purpose admirably.

He sensed that events were, at last, beginning to move inexorably towards a conclusion that he was confident he would be able to predict and control. He would see his adversary defeated after all. A comforting thought, he mused.

Nazim was indeed, sickened.

Empas, meanwhile, retired to his room. He had much to think about and he could do so far better in privacy. The events of the last few days had proved most unsettling, and on more than one occasion, had caused him to question his own approach to his mission. Not the least concern was confirmation, beyond all doubt, that he had made enemies along his way. He knew instinctively that the rabbi in this town, whatever else he may be guilty of, had been at least partly complicit in the events of that morning. He would not have been surprised if the whole thing had been arranged just to test him, as indeed, in a way, it had. Though he had not given in to his desire for revenge, nevertheless, he had experienced the emotion and knew its power. Further to which, he had challenged the church and the law publicly. That both had been found wanting was no real comfort. He knew now that he had taken on a mighty task indeed.

He still felt horrified that an innocent girl had been used, abused and very nearly murdered in order to entrap him. *'What else are these people capable of?'* he thought, not really wishing to examine the many possible answers to that question.

Then there was the dilemma of Jud Descar, now his twelfth disciple. He was definitely suspicious of the man, and he could not shift the feeling of unease which accompanied his account of how he found them. There was nothing that he could pinpoint. Jud's story was plausible enough, and Rachel had not countered it in any way — though she had not really been in any condition to think straight. So, he was left with a large doubt in his mind about Jud Descar. Yet, strangely, he was also convinced that letting him join the group had been the right thing to do. It was an odd thought, considering his suspicions about the man.

And inevitably, his thoughts kept coming back to the problem which lay at the core of the matter. How could he play an adversarial role in this deadly game of politics and power, and yet still maintain his integrity as a teacher and practitioner of peace and love? He did not know, but he was convinced that he must, somehow.

Where was Maikel now that he needed her so badly?

As if in direct answer to his question, there was a knock at his door. At his invitation to enter, both Simeon and Maikel came in.

"We saw the girl safely home," said Simeon. "Her father was distressed at first when he saw her accompanied by two strangers, but then he recognised us. She seemed glad to be home and did not speak of her experiences, so we saw no reason to mention anything."

"Thank you Pedor," answered Empas. "I hope Rachel will find the peace and happiness she seeks. And now, if you will forgive me, I need to speak with Marin further about the girl. Find the others, including Jud Descar. Make sure that he is involved with everything that needs to be done."

"Is that wise, Master?" asked Simeon. "After all, we do not really know him and his arrival was somewhat unique, don't you think?"

"Don't worry yourself, Pedor. Jud Descar has an important role to play in our mission. Go now, make preparations and then rest for tomorrow."

When Simeon had left, Maikel came straight into his arms and they kissed hungrily, each knowing the urgency of their bodies' demands for each other. Again, they made love well into the night until both were physically exhausted.

Afterwards, as they lay contentedly together, Maikel turned towards her lover and asked the question which had been on her mind.

"What did you do to Rachel?"

Calmly, as if he had been expecting the query, Empas answered, "Nothing, if by that you mean, did I affect her physically. But she had been badly traumatised. It was so bad that she was on the brink of shock and could, at any moment, have lapsed into deep trauma, perhaps even coma. I could not let that happen, so I wiped clean the memory of the experience and replaced it with a gentle, fun, but believable alternative.

I determined that she was not impregnated by any of the men so there will be no repercussions. Does that answer your question, my love?"

"But Empas, you vowed that you would never invade another's mind. I can understand what forced you to make this exception, but what other rules and vows will you break before you are finished?" she asked seriously.

Empas looked at her and decided that the discussion was needed, so he arose and dressed while Maikel did the same before, they sat down to face each other.

"Maikel," he asked. "Do you love me? Do you trust me?"

"Of course, with all my heart, is the answer to both questions. Although these feelings are new to me, I am as sure of them as if I was born with them," she answered. "But what has that to do with my question."

"It matters because I sense that things are going to become a lot more difficult and dangerous in the near future and all of us will be tested to some degree. I have chosen a path whose terminus I did not foresee when I started. Even if I had, I like to think I would still have chosen this. But now, at this moment, I realise that it is no game we are playing. It is the ultimate fate of mankind on this planet that will be won or lost depending on what happens when we reach Tevalem. And I know that I need you there beside me for as long as possible, no matter what happens. So, knowing that you love me and trust me, as I do you, makes a big difference and I can answer your question now.

"I don't know how many 'rules' I might be forced to change or break. Naively, I suppose, I had thought that I might win over those in power through the strength of my argument in debate. Now I see that open and fair debate is the one thing that they cannot allow to happen. They, it would seem, have already made me their enemy, so I suppose they must be mine, even though I wish only to teach them the ways of peace and brotherhood. I suspect that Jud Descar may be an agent of those enemies, though what role he has to play is not clear to me."

"Empas, you are frightening me," Maikel said urgently. "If you suspect this man, why have you let him join the disciples?"

"Because now I can keep an eye on him," answered Empas easily. "You see, already I begin to think like a tactician — which I am not —

and I find that I must consider a more adversarial role in this, though the prospect horrifies me."

"Oh, my love," cried Maikel. "No matter what dangers you face, I will always be with you, you know that."

She wrestled with her conscience as she took in the meaning of his words, knowing she had but to switch on a little device which would allow her to access both help and advice from above, but knowing also that to do so would betray Empas' trust in her. She could not bring herself to do such a thing to the one man she did, or would ever, love. So instead, she just clung to him as if her very life depended upon it. She, too, had never imagined that her task would prove to be so involved or so difficult, and though she had no way to see the future, a dreadful, cold premonition of forthcoming disaster settled in her stomach and would not move.

Chapter 17

Caiaphas was uneasy. Reports had been coming in regularly regarding Empas' progress towards the capital, including details of his teachings, the many 'miraculous' healings he had performed along the way, and the occasions on which he had repeatedly challenged the authority of the church. This last consideration was the one which bothered him the most. Clearly this people's messiah could not be persuaded or bought off very easily, if at all, unlike all the others who had come along since he had been in power. Equally, it was unthinkable that he could allow his own authority, and that of the church, to be openly questioned. He was the voice of God, and His will was carried out only through himself. That, he was determined, was not going to change, especially at the behest of some upstart calling himself a messiah!

The chief priest had never been entirely convinced of the coming of the Messiah to the Juhl anyway, and his long standing 'arrangement' with the Thorian governor of the region was proving to be far too lucrative to allow anything so potentially menacing as a 'Son of God' to threaten it. No, an answer had to be found. There must be some way to put an end to Empas' progress and his naive theories about 'loving your enemies' and 'treating everyone as you would want to be treated'. What nonsense! Whilst, in theory, these ideas held their attractions, in the end they amounted to little more than romantic notions meant to convince pathetic, helpless peasants that they mattered. As if!

Caiaphas had never been in any way socially minded. As far as he was concerned, the whole purpose of being in this world was to make and take as much from it as possible. If you succeeded, your life had meaning, and you had a degree of comfort denied to others. If you failed, well, obviously, you were not good enough. God looked after those who took care of themselves. And besides, hadn't he managed to keep the occupying forces from committing some of the worst atrocities upon his population? That alone ought to be worth their thanks. If only they knew how much it cost him personally, every year, to keep the Thorians relatively quiet and the garrison in place whilst the Juhl basically got on with governing themselves — within occupation law limits of course — the thought sent a shudder up his spine.

And now he found himself summoned, like any commoner, into the presence of the high and mighty governor. He knew what the meeting would be about, of course, and he also knew that, as yet, he had no answers that would satisfy the authorities. He would just have to bluff his way through this encounter, he thought uncomfortably, and hope that a solution would present itself before things started to get out of hand.

There was one positive note. Empas was obviously coming to Tevalem, so it would be relatively easy to keep an eye on him and his activities directly once he was here and you never knew when opportunities might present themselves. Even so, there was a potential downside. If Empas managed to get the Tevalem 'mob' on his side, there could be trouble, civil unrest leading, perhaps, to a Thorian crackdown and a curtailment of his activities.

There was no denying, he was facing a very uncomfortable scenario. Caiaphas walked on.

* * * * *

"Your eminence, how good to see you again," gushed the governor, "Please come through to my private study."

"It was good of you to spare me the time Governor Portio," said Caiaphas, observing his part in the charade of politeness, which was maintained, at least in public, between them.

The two men made their way through the mansion to a central courtyard which had, as its main feature, a bubbling water feature framed by small, elegant palms and desert flowers, lovingly cared for by servants who dare not let them die! Both sat on a single bench in the relatively cool shade offered by the high-domed roof.

"So, my friend," began Portio, "how go things with the church?"

"Satisfactory, Governor, with one exception that I know is of concern to us both," replied the priest, deciding to cut straight to the point of the meeting.

"Ah yes, the messiah!" intoned the governor. "A most unfortunate turn of events, wouldn't you say?"

"Bah! We both know that he is no messiah. He is just like all the others who come in from the wilderness claiming to be sent from God. We try our best to deliver them all to you when we can. It is, after all, in our joint interest to preserve the status quo. And we will find a way to take this one off the streets."

"Maybe, but there sits your problem," said Portio. "Though he could be called a rabble-rouser, according to our information, he doesn't actually do anything wrong. He incites no violence — quite the opposite in fact. He preaches only peace and brotherly love. Why, some of our own soldiers have been quite seduced by his words. I assume he has broken none of your Juhl laws either?"

"None," answered the priest. "He observes the sabbath and tells people to just live their lives, pay their taxes and love each other. He does not blaspheme nor indulge in any wantonness, although he does spend a lot of time with beggars, tavern folk and general low life. It's pathetic really that so many are prepared to listen to him. There is no fire or fight with him, though he does seem to delight in publicly debating religious philosophy with the local clergy. The rabble, of course, love it when he does so. We are not universally loved by our people, Governor, though they do respect us while we hold power. That is how we are able to keep them in line, making things somewhat easier for you and your military I might add."

"Yes, yes, I am well aware how important your efforts are in that regard. And I personally, have no complaints about our arrangement, but should this man continue to cause trouble, I can see it possibly having, shall we say, an adverse effect on your hold over your people. This would, of course, change things. And we wouldn't want that, would we?" the governor added pointedly.

"Is there nothing you can do to help?" asked the priest.

"We are already doing what we can," replied Portio. "We have a reliable agent in place who feeds us a lot of information. But this is, in all respects, a Juhl problem, and therefore, regrettably, I must decline to offer any further Thorian involvement until absolutely necessary. However, you have my full support for any action you might be forced to take — within the law of course."

"Then you will, in effect, stand idly by while this threat grows daily? You know we have no military strength of our own, and if it comes to it, there is no law other than Thorian law whereby we can have him put to death. You must become involved," the priest said heatedly.

"Enough!" shouted Portio, "You press me too hard, priest. I shall allocate ten of my men to act as Temple guards. They will be directly under your command. Do not ask me to do more. He is your problem, Caiaphas. Get rid of him!"

The chief priest of the Juhl temple, stood and bowed slightly, without further comment before turning to leave, making his way back through the mansion. The governor continued to sit and stare at the man's back as he left. He found the priest very irritating in many ways, though he could not deny that the arrangement the man had offered was proving very economically worthwhile. In return for relative inaction by the Thorian troops, the Juhl church paid him a very generous fee. What they did to their own people was no concern of his, though he was constantly receiving complaints from the public about harsh taxes and tithes to the temple. But he simply referred them back to their own bureaucracy who, it seemed, continued to fleece them for as much as they could despite their complaints.

The puppet king, Harag, that the Thorians had imposed, had shown himself to be a big nothing really in the order of things. Although theoretically the ruler of the Juhl people, nobody paid him any attention and he spent his time feasting and fornicating in the privacy of his palace, oblivious to the machinations of the true Juhl authorities — the high priests. He represented yet another layer of bureaucracy, however and Portio could not deny that this had proved useful at times.

All the same, this messiah was becoming a nuisance and the emperor's envoy, Nazim, seemed to be playing a dangerous game though, if he were honest, should anything happen to Nazim, Portio would not be displeased. He had never liked the man and he still felt very uncomfortable around him, despite their distance from the empire's capital. But Nazim was a problem for another day. He wondered just how the Juhl were going to handle this affair. If nothing else, it should prove interesting.

When Caiaphas returned to the temple, he ascended the steps to the entrance slowly, noting that the trade in temple sacrifices, money changing and souvenir sales to the regular supply of pilgrims waiting to be fleeced, was proceeding healthily. None of the traders were happy about the prices they paid to the church for their pitches, nor the percentage tithes they were forced to pay, but all smiled and nodded to the chief priest as he passed by before resuming their raucous activities. None of them complained loudly or within earshot of any of the clergy. Despite the kickbacks, there was no such thing as a poor trader in the temple at Tevalem.

The chief priest entered the temple and went straight to his office where he sat and exhaled loudly. *'Damn you Latiedes!'* he thought. Meetings with him were never easy but this one had been a disaster. He had hoped to persuade the Thorian to take a hand in stopping the progress of the upstart, perhaps even arrest him and get him out of sight. That way, the priests could have publicly blamed the occupation forces and be seen to sympathise with the many followers that this man was gathering to his teaching. But that was clearly impossible. Portio had outmanoeuvred him there and all he had got was ten Thorian soldiers with which to stop Empas. Which, in fact, he thought, should be enough in purely practical terms. But politically, he still had to find a way to get hold of this man, call for his execution and get the mob to agree with him. Anything short of that risked losing control of the populace.

Of course, Caspar Mossamed's small army, led by their captain, Saul, were also doing a reasonable job breaking up meetings of the 'faithful', applying some force where necessary and generally discouraging those who might want to convert to this new faith. But even he could not really help in this situation. Now that he had reached the capital, Empas seemed to be followed and protected by ever swelling crowds. They could not simply arrest him in front of all those people without risking starting a riot. And that would be disastrous. The governor would be forced to take extreme action and almost certainly, everyone — including the church — would get caught up in it. No, whatever he did, Caiaphas knew, he would have to do as covertly as possible. But how?

As he sat thinking, one of the faris knocked on his door to announce

248

the arrival of a messenger from the rabbi at Asper, the town just a few miles up the eastern road from Tevalem. He was ushered in to the chief priest's presence and told to give his report, which included details of the failed attempt by the rabbi to get Empas to openly disobey the law. Instead, he had turned the tables and caused the rabbi some considerable embarrassment, to the apparent delight of the crowd that followed him.

"Does the crowd always support him in this way?" asked Caiaphas.

"Oh yes, your eminence," replied the faris messenger. "They are always eager to proclaim him as their saviour, Messiah, Son of God. Some even call him the next king of Juhl, and he does nothing to halt their enthusiasm."

"Great!" yelled the chief priest. "That's all we need. They are calling him king, so now we'll have Harag and his crew as well as the Thorians to worry about! This is all getting well and truly out of hand."

"There is one other thing, Eminence," offered the messenger.

"What!" demanded Caiaphas.

"Well, the Thorian spy told the rabbi not to worry and that he had a plan which would put paid to this menace for good."

"What spy?" asked the priest.

"The Thorian. He says he now has first-hand information on the man's whereabouts and his plans once he gets to Tevalem. He said he would contact both you and the governor once he has arrived here in the city."

"A Thorian? How is he getting this information and how reliable is it?"

"I have not been told any details," Answered the messenger. "But apparently, he is disguised as a Juhl and might well have become one of his followers — part of the small group that call themselves disciples."

Caiaphas sat back on his rather plain, but extremely comfortable, throne. Resting his elbows on the armrests, he brought his extended hands together in a pyramid and brought the tip to his lips. After a few moments, he leaned forward again and addressed the messenger.

"That is... interesting. Unless there is anything else, thank you for your report and you may go. Please inform the rabbi of our gratitude and assure him of our continued support."

Once the messenger had left, the priest resumed his thoughtful posture and found that his mood had lightened considerably. '*Perhaps the situation is not quite as bleak as I had imagined,*' he thought to himself. '*Now we know a lot more than we did before. So, they call him King? That won't go down too well with Portio.*' And as he continued to contemplate events, the embryo of a plan began to form in his mind. With the feast of the Blessed Passing coming up they might just be able to manipulate events sufficiently — if they acted quickly!

For the first time that day, a smile formed on Caiaphas' lips.

* * * * *

Jespeth and Marin had entered the great city of Tevalem through the gate in its eastern wall. Though both were of the direct line of kings of the past, neither of them had visited the capital before. Like all tourists, they had been amazed and eager to absorb all of the city's sights and grandeur, so they had delayed going to the temple to offer their sacrifice so that they could do some sightseeing. And besides, they had thought it would be nice to fulfil their pilgrimage on the day of the Blessed Passing. It would top off this once in a lifetime trip beautifully.

Doing the rounds, they had picked up on the main topic of conversation on everyone's lips — the approach of the man they called the messiah. Through snippets of information gathered here and there, they understood that he was a miracle worker, healing the sick through a touch of his hand, making the blind see again by simply touching their eyes, even raising the dead by all accounts! He spoke of love for each other, of the coming of the Kingdom of God, of man's ultimate conquest even of death itself. All they had to do was believe in him and their sins would be forgiven, God would love them and take them all into His Kingdom. There would be no need for sacrifices because He was a God of love and forgiveness. Some even dared to whisper that the messiah would release them from the bondage of Thorian occupation and rule! His arrival was expected any day now and it seemed as if the whole city was intending to go and greet him.

Jespeth viewed much of this information with a slightly sceptical eye. He knew how rumours easily became inflated with the passage of time and repetition. Even so, he could not deny that he was intrigued.

Marin had not said much about it. But she had her own ideas on what the truth was. Her mind kept wandering back to a little stable, thirty-three years ago, where she had given birth to a baby boy who, she knew, was not entirely what he seemed. She had always believed that her son was destined for great things — hadn't the old man said so when he thanked her? And she was fast becoming convinced that he — if indeed this strange messiah was him — was about to do something amazing that would change the world forever.

"Jespeth," she asked her husband, "everyone keeps talking about the messiah, but what is his name?"

"I don't know," answered Jespeth truthfully. "But he is definitely causing a stir. I'll ask someone."

As luck would have it, he didn't have to look far to find an appropriate source of information. A faris was attempting to hurry by at that moment but was being constantly held up by the gathering crowds.

"Excuse me, your reverence," began Jespeth. "We keep hearing about the messiah coming to Tevalem and we would like to greet him, but we do not even know his name. You wouldn't happen to know that would you?"

"If you want my advice," said the faris, "you will steer well clear of him. He brings only trouble and disturbance. Just look at this unruly crowd. How do you think the Thorians are going to react to this? So, if you don't want to get arrested and charged with insurrection, stay away. Go and make your sacrifice at the temple and then go home."

"But you haven't answered my question," Jespeth protested.

"His name is Empas, but you don't want to know any more than that, believe me."

Marin gave a gasp and clutched at her heart. Alarmed, Jespeth took her arm and led her to a nearby low wall where she could sit for a moment.

"Marin, my love, it isn't necessarily him. It could be anybody. It doesn't take much doing to simply adopt a name. Don't be upset, and please, don't get your hopes up. We will go and check it out but I'm sure it will just prove to be another zealot masquerading as a saviour."

"No, Jespeth," the woman answered. "It is him. I know it is. I think I've known ever since we started hearing the rumours about healing and miracles. My son always cared greatly about people right from when he was very young. Don't you remember his little friend, Ben? Look at what he tried to do for him."

Although her statement had pricked him, Jespeth had long ago come to terms with the fact that Empas was not his son. He, too, was aware that they had been chosen for a very unusual task by some very strange people and he had gladly agreed to go along with it for her sake. He did not blame Marin in any way for the peculiar relationship there had been between father and firstborn and he had tried to do his best for Empas always. He could not help regarding Empas as his son, however, and her denial of his involvement hurt just a little. As ever, though, his love for his wife overcame all other obstacles.

"We will go and greet him along with all these others," he told her kindly. "Though I'm beginning to think that there are so many heading the same way, we'll be lucky to get even a sight of the man, let alone get near enough to identify him. Don't worry, Marin. We will see him."

Marin nodded and smiled at her husband. Feeling a little better for his kind words, she rose and allowed him to lead her through the city's streets towards the eastern gate.

* * * * *

The director found that, unusually, he was quite 'moved' by the depth of emotion which bound Marin and Jespeth together. He had promised that he would watch over them and he had done so faithfully ever since Marin had agreed to carry his son. It was simple coincidence that he had 'listened in' to their conversation in the city, seeking only to assure himself of their safety. Now, however, his thoughts moved towards consideration of the emotional effect Empas seemed to have on all those with whom he came into contact. Even he found it hard not to feel pride in what his son was achieving with just the simple message he carried. He was sure that Empas had not considered what a tremendous power base he would build amongst the ordinary people of Juhl when he first started his ministry., but according to Maikel's reports, he was beginning to appreciate that, against the many enemies he was slowly but surely making, he would need 'weapons' of a sort. He had flatly refused Eldoran technology, but perhaps, thought the director, the people themselves might become his most potent defence.

He was also sure, now, that the enmity his son had generated amongst the various powers that be, was being orchestrated, at least in part, by Lucian. Once again, he bitterly regretted his vow not to interfere in matters below, for it meant he could not use his telepathic power to seek out the man, and perhaps, help to remove one of the most dangerous elements facing his son. No, he must rely on Empas' judgement and on the accuracy of the reports he got from Maikel.

With that thought, he focussed on the content of her latest report concerning the incident with the young girl at Asper. Maikel had voiced her suspicions regarding the new disciple, Jud Descar, but could present no solid evidence to justify her fears. It was just a feeling she and Empas shared about the man. The director decided to include Descar in his list of people to watch carefully, but he was comforted that Empas had his doubts about him. This was a good sign. Clearly his son was no longer the naive evangelist that he had been when he started out. He could only hope that Empas' awareness of possible threats would be enough.

The gentle knock on his door interrupted his reverie. At his invitation to enter, the door slid back to reveal Doctor Gaveri, Saecra, and Adrian who had taken over the job of security.

"Gentlemen, thank you for being so prompt," he said in welcome, inviting them to sit.

"I intend this meeting to be brief, so let us not waste time on preliminaries," began the old man. "Our immediate problem is to fill the seat of navigator of the ship since, temporarily or permanently, Maikel has seen fit to vacate the post and travel down to the planet, I presume so that she can be with Empas."

Though this was not news to the doctor, he pretended to be as shocked as the other two at the director's revelation.

"She has deserted us. Are you sure, sir?" queried Saecra.

"No, I am not sure," answered the director. "But I have to assume that may well be the case. Though the ship is perfectly capable of taking us wherever we want to go by itself, still it, like all other lifeforms, gets used to the nearness and companionship of other beings, and I am concerned that, should we decide to move on in the near future, it should continue to feel the comfort of a human presence at the helm."

"Of course, Director," continued Saecra. "And on that score, I am sure young Suren will be up to the task. Maikel has been training her for some years and she seems quite competent. But that, surely, is not our main concern. If Maikel has gone down to the planet, it raises many important questions, not the least of which is, can she survive indefinitely? Will her presence in any way upset the balance of life down there? We all know the dreadful consequences the last time someone deserted the ship."

"Yes, Engineer, thank you for reminding us of the danger," said the director. "Though I do not see any immediate cause for concern on that score just now. I would like to see what happens over the next few days before we start to worry about unknowables like that. For myself, I am convinced her visit will be temporary, I just want to cover all eventualities."

"Would you like me to go down and keep an eye on her, Director?" asked Adrian, keen not to play down the matter that had been raised.

"Thank you also, Adrian, but again I do not think we should overreact to this situation. However, it could do no harm for you and a security team to hold yourselves in readiness should the need arise," said the old man reassuringly. "Now, is there any other business that I should be aware of?"

The others all shook their heads and answered in the negative.

"Then, gentlemen, I won't keep you from your duties."

Gaveri was the last to head towards the door. He was stopped when the director said, "Oh, Doctor, may I speak to you a moment?"

When the others had left, Doctor Gaveri turned to the old man and said, jokingly, "Sir, I do believe you are becoming more devious by the day, and you are enjoying it! I think this planet has had a bad influence on you."

The two men chuckled as only two old friends can.

"Gaveri, how do you always seem to know what I am up to?" asked the director pleasantly.

"Oh, it's quite easy. You had Saecra make a communications device for a fictitious patient. When he asked me how said patient was doing, I knew something was going on. I told him what he wanted to hear, of course. Then, when Maikel left the ship and no one raised an alarm, or even an eyebrow, I put two and two together and surmised that you were scheming, once again."

At this point, the doctor's face took on a different, more serious expression.

"Seriously, old friend, are you sure you are doing the right thing? It's a precarious game you are playing, and I have to say, I find it a bit uncomfortable that you are playing with that girl's life."

The director was tempted to come clean in light of his friend's veiled accusation. He opened his mouth prepared to present all the plans and arguments that had brought them to this point. Inside, he desperately wanted to confide in somebody and Gaveri would have been his ideal choice. But still something stopped him. Events had not yet run their full course, and until they had, the burden was his and his alone. Maikel was still so young and naive herself in many ways, and at this thought, the director smiled.

"I remember when she and most of the others first came aboard this ship. Mere children, all of them — except you, myself, Saecra and Lucian — and I have watched them all grow and become more mature over the many years we have spent travelling the galaxy. They all mean a great deal to me, and yes, I am taking a risk with Maikel's life. But I promise you, she is fully aware of all the possibilities we can foresee. In fact, if you recall, it was you who revealed to me how she felt about Empas and the budding relationship between them. This made her the prime candidate for what I needed her to do. All the same, I would not have asked it of her if I thought it would put her in great danger.

"In truth, I grow more concerned for them both with every day that passes, but she can reach me immediately if she needs to and I must hold to my vow to my son not to interfere."

"Just be sure to let me know if I can help," said the doctor softly.

He could see the lack of assurance in the director's face and thought he could perceive the reason for it, but he held his own counsel, deciding that there would be a better time and place where everything would be revealed. With a nod, he left the room to return to his own quarters.

* * * * *

Again, Caiaphas was interrupted by a knock on his door.

"Yes!" shouted the exasperated chief priest. "Who is it and what do you want?"

"Forgive the intrusion, your eminence," said the faris hesitantly, 'but we, that is, the high faris, thought you should be informed immediately."

"Well?"

"Oh… um… there is a man. We thought at first that he was another beggar or a pilgrim unhappy with his treatment by the sacrifice sellers. But it turns out that he is, or says he is, one of 'them'," said the faris, a certain smugness returning to his voice.

"What are you talking about, man?" yelled Caiaphas.

"The man who has come here asking to see you, your eminence," answered the faris quickly, realising his mistake. "He claims to be one of the messiah's disciples and he says he has information for you alone."

At this Caiaphas' temper began to cool a little as he swiftly surmised that this might well be the 'spy' that had been mentioned previously.

"Very well," he said coolly. "You may have him shown in here but have one of the temple guards standing by."

'You can never be too careful,' thought Caiaphas.

A little while later, a Juhl peasant, dressed in plain garb and looking decidedly travel stained, the priest thought, was shown into his office and told to stand quietly until spoken to. As the door was being closed, Caiaphas saw a guard taking up his station outside.

Feeling a little more relaxed — Caiaphas had never been particularly good, or comfortable, with the peasantry — he looked up from the illusory work he was doing at his desk and studied the man.

"You asked to see me, something about information? This had better be worthwhile or you could find yourself in trouble," said Caiaphas making the threat as plain as he could.

The man facing him did not tremble or quake as he had thought. Instead, he looked directly at the priest before saying, "Is that the way you normally address a Thorian?"

Despite the shock he felt at this reply, the priest managed to keep any hint of failing confidence out of his voice.

"If you are a Thorian, why are you dressed like a Juhl? And just who are you anyway?" he asked with only slightly less authority.

"The name you will know me by is Jud Descar. As to why I am dressed like a Juhl, I should have thought that would be obvious," said the stranger.

"So, you are the fox Portio has set amongst the hens," replied Caiaphas.

"That's right," said Lucian. "The governor wishes the matter of the Messiah to be handled by you exclusively as far as possible, so I am here to give you your instructions."

The chief priest coughed and spluttered a bit at this last statement. He was tempted to call the guard and teach this insolent one a most unpleasant lesson. But something in the man's look warned him to tread carefully.

"And just what, exactly, are my 'instructions'?" he asked carefully.

"Now that we are here in the capital, the man will be mostly surrounded by adoring crowds, and he will undoubtedly preach at least one or two sermons while he is here. You are to avoid confronting him in those situations at all costs. He is far too clever when it comes to debating theology. He knows his scriptures. Even when he is not followed by crowds, there is still the matter of his disciples, now we are twelve in number, and we are almost always by his side. There is also the woman who accompanies him. She seldom leaves him — I suspect they are lovers, but I have no proof of that.

"However, there are times when he says he needs to be alone to think, or communicate with God, or whatever. When that event occurs, and I am sure it will, I will know in advance, and I will bring you word of where he will be and when. I assume your guards will follow your orders implicitly?"

"Of course," affirmed Caiaphas.

"When I tell you, you must act quickly and arrest him. Your men can fend off the disciples easily enough. I will take care of the woman. Once you have him, secure him inside the temple and try him, or whatever it is you mean to do. But ensure that you have a valid accusation and evidence to back it up before you bring him to Portio Latiedes," concluded the spy.

Realising that this was the plan he had been searching for, Caiaphas' mind had raced ahead and already he had hatched an addition of his own that would, he felt, satisfy all parties.

"I'm sure we can provide the governor with a most compelling reason to execute him," said the priest.

Reaching beneath his robe, he pulled out a small pouch and tossed it towards the spy.

"What is this?" asked Lucian.

"Oh, just a little something to cover your expenses and to show our appreciation," said Caiaphas nonchalantly. "I'm sure Portio does not pay you anywhere near enough for your services."

Lucian hefted the small pouch and considered throwing it right back at the pretentious priest he saw before him. But he thought better of it. After all, there was the small matter of the danger of discovery and the discomfort he was suffering — if only to his feet after all that walking! So, he just smiled crookedly and tucked the money inside his own robe.

"You will hear from me soon," he said as he turned to leave the office.

After the spy had gone, Caiaphas decided to pay a call on the governor to check on the authenticity of the man's claims — although he was already pretty well convinced — and to bring him up to date on the situation, since it was unlikely that the spy would go directly to the governor's mansion! He looked forward to seeing Portio's reaction to this unscheduled meeting and felt very sure that he would enjoy this conference much more than he had the last.

* * * * *

"Your eminence," said the governor, somewhat flustered at the unexpected arrival of his guest. "What a pleasure to see you again so soon."

Without speaking further, they passed into the inner part of the house again, finding the privacy they needed.

"Well priest," began Portio, "have you come with good news this time?"

"I received a visit from a man today. Called himself Jud Descar and claimed to be one of the messiah's disciples. Does that name mean anything to you?"

"Indeed, it does," confirmed the governor. "He is a most capable fellow, though not exactly my choice of table companion, if you understand what I mean."

"I do indeed," replied the priest. "But then, we can't always choose those with whom we have to work, can we."

"Caiaphas, I have no time for your word games. What do you want to discuss with me?"

The chief priest told Portio of the plan that his spy had devised and knew that it met with his approval as the governor nodded enthusiastically. When he had concluded, Portio looked at him and asked pointedly, "I assume you will be able to bring him before me with a suitable charge and evidence to support it? Because I can see another problem arising. Don't forget, it is your Feast of the Blessed Passing in a few days, and by tradition, I have to release one prisoner to the demand of the crowd. What happens if they demand that I release him?"

"Oh, I am ahead of you there," answered the priest with barely suppressed glee. "Don't worry about the mob, I think we can guarantee that they will demand the release of Al Barab, to which, of course, you can readily agree since you have not yet pronounced final judgement upon him, have you?"

"No, I have not," said the governor. "But he is an extremely dangerous criminal, and I would be reluctant to let him go after all the trouble I went to capture him."

"Would you rather have this 'messiah' on the loose? Worse still, would you rather risk he and Al Barab being out there, together? Because it could easily happen if we lose control of the situation."

"Hmm, I see your point, priest. Very well, we seem to be in agreement. I look forward to meeting this messiah of yours. It promises to be quite interesting," said the governor, rising to announce that the meeting was over.

Just as Caiaphas was turning to leave, Portio addressed him once more.

"Oh, by the way, Caiaphas, assuming everything goes according to plan, I don't suppose you could also manage to do me a small favour, could you?"

The priest was intrigued as he replied, "Of course, my friend, you know you have only to ask."

"It's just a small matter of course, but if something — 'untoward' — were to happen to Jud Descar, you have my assurance that we would be most understanding of the circumstances."

"By 'untoward', am I to understand that such an event might even be fatal?"

"Oh, Gods forbid the very thought, but we both know how accidents can so easily happen."

Both men looked at each other, complete accord between them firmly established. Nothing more needed to be said and Caiaphas was, at last, quite happy when he left the governor's mansion.

Chapter 18

Lucian exited the city at the eastern gate to find that, even before he entered, Empas had gathered quite a large crowd around him and was leading them towards a nearby hill which was covered in olive trees. He recognised the other disciples going about their duties and saw that the woman, Marin, was still right by his side. Now that he came to think about it, she hardly ever left him. Women were not generally accorded so much attention in this country. So, was there something between them? Now there was an intriguing thought. Would this 'blameless' messiah dare to flout the laws of his church and his country because of this woman?

As he speculated further on the nature of their relationship, he found that he was looking hard at her. Something about the woman's demeanour, the way she moved. Strange that he had not noticed before, but there was definitely something familiar about her that went back a lot further than their apparent first meeting in Asper. What was it? He couldn't quite pin it down. '*Never mind,*' he thought, '*it will no doubt come to me in time.*'

The man made his way through the crowd, smiling and encouraging people and taking up his role as an appointed disciple. Like the others he made sure that people were seated and comfortable, answered any questions that he could and made sure the master's message would be heard by as many as possible.

Once the crowd were assembled and the master began to preach, Lucian lost interest in the proceedings, going over in his mind the somewhat complicated plan that had been forced on him due to the governor's wish that Empas' destruction be seen to be clearly decided by the Juhl themselves, thus absolving the Thorian Empire of any responsibility in the affair other than that of carrying out the wishes of its subject people. '*Clever move by the governor,*' thought Lucian. '*I must remember that when it comes to the time of reckoning. Never underestimate your opponent!*'

Then his thoughts drifted back to the vexing problem of the woman Marin. He looked for her, expecting her to be, as usual, right beside the master. But she was not there. Where had she disappeared to? Then he remembered. Once Empas began teaching, she would generally go into the town or village to arrange food and lodging for them all. He assumed she had gone on that errand now. Such devotion in one so young — and such innocent features. But he was sure he had seen that face before. The eyes were quite unmistakeable. They reminded him of… Maikel! That was her name. That was the woman he had known. He started to recall a conversation… a long time ago.

'I'm sure I could have thought of some way to satisfy your needs.' The words jumped around in his mind and he recalled that she had more or less offered herself to him. What was it she had said? Something about, what was in it for her if she offered her services? The little whore! He had, in the end, rejected her, he recalled, now here she was consorting with the son of his arch enemy. *'Won't she be surprised when she finds out who Jud Descar really is,'* he thought ruefully.

Slowly, he dragged his attention back to the sermon Empas was giving, his thoughts growing ever more bitter towards this misguided offspring of a foolish old man. He focussed his attention for long enough to comprehend the simple prayer to 'God' that he was teaching them. A total waste of time, of course, but he could not deny the basic poetry and timbre of the phrases he used. *'Such a waste,'* he thought, *'the man could have been a great leader if only he had listened to me!'*

His reverie was interrupted when he saw the woman, he was now convinced was Maikel returning from the city. Studying her more closely, he began to feel something that he had not felt for many long years. Physical desire! It was an odd feeling when felt through someone else's body, though not in any way unpleasant. In fact, he thought, it might be interesting to take on this body permanently, if nothing better could be found. It offered many possibilities!

'Nooooooo!' screamed Nazim silently.

At last, the sermon was over, and the crowd began to disperse, some to their homes, some to other parts of the city to find lodgings. Many remained, however, to sing and dance and celebrate their new-found belief in the messiah and his soul-warming message. They clearly worshipped him and wanted to elevate him to his rightful position above them. Finding no other way to show their devotion, they hired an ass from a local stable and insisted Empas ride it into the city to celebrate his coming. Everyone seemed to be going wild, throwing palm fronds in front of the ass as it, and its passenger, made their sedate way into the city, followed by Maikel and the disciples, smiling their approval at this obvious show of acceptance of their master and his message. Lucian joined the disciples, now determined to discover who Marin really was. If she was Maikel in disguise, then all sorts of possibilities presented themselves in his imagination. *'Who knows,'* he thought, *'I might even persuade her to join me this time.'*

Maikel had chosen an inn on the edge of the temple district. She knew that Empas intended to go to the temple the following day, so she had chosen the place carefully. Gradually the crowd diminished, their enthusiasm spent for the moment, and Empas, Marin and the disciples were able to enter the inn. Some welcome rest beckoned them all. They knew that the next few days would be busy ones.

Empas seemed unphased by the exhaustion he must surely have been feeling, deciding to try to talk to all of the patrons he found in the common room of the inn. Maikel told him she would retire to her room, and he nodded absently as he continued his rounds. She ascended the stairs and went straight to her room where she laid down for a few minutes to recover.

No one seemed to notice as Lucian also took the stairs a few minutes later, first checking to ensure that Empas was busy and likely to be so for quite a while. Quietly he made his way along the short corridor, listening at each door until he heard the distinctive rustle of clothing being removed. Sure, that this was the woman's room, he knocked gently, smiling as he heard the response.

"Come in, Empas."

Quickly he opened the door, stepped into the room and closed the door behind him. He turned to survey the woman before him who stood clad only in her Eldoran enviro-protective.

"So, I was right," he said. "Hello, Maikel — it's been a long time."

"Jud? What are you talking about?" she replied anxiously, sudden fear making her voice tremble. "My name is Marin as you well know."

"Maikel, don't try to pretend. We both know that Marin Madane is a total fiction, whereas Maikel, the Eldoran, is standing right before me."

Maikel was confused, and something in his voice made her feel just a little bit frightened. She had not met this man before their encounter in Asper, just a few days ago, so how could he know who she really was? Then, as if for the first time, she realised she was only wearing her enviro. A slow chill of fear ran up her spine as she became even more confused.

"You have clearly mistaken me for a lady you must have known in another place and time, Jud. But now, as you can see, I am quite busy so, if you would just leave, I will forget all about this intrusion."

"Nice try Maikel, but I'm afraid your bluster won't work. I know you, but of course, you don't recognise me. How could you when I am occupying a completely different body to the one you once knew?"

The woman's brow furrowed as she tried to make sense of what this man was saying. Occupying another body? That was impossible, unless, of course, you were a telep... Oh no! It couldn't be. It couldn't possibly be him?

The look of sheer horror that crossed over her face told Lucian what he needed to know. Unfortunately, persuasion was out of the question with her. Which left only force — or death.

"You don't seem glad to see me again after all these years. And yet I well remember when you couldn't wait to offer me 'your services'. Well, here I am and here you are. Why don't we see exactly what you are offering underneath that enviro?" said Lucian with obvious intent.

Maikel felt the panic rising within her. She had never thought she would be facing Lucian again, but she was, and she was alone with no help at hand. Desperately she looked around, but her eyes refused to focus. Her breathing quickened as she came dangerously near to hyperventilation. She began to cry.

"Lucian, if you feel anything for me, please leave me alone. I cannot betray Empas. Please don't make me."

"Ah, but that is the point, isn't it?" he said ominously, advancing towards her. "You will betray him because I command it. You will not resist me. You are not capable."

Lucian then tried something he had not done before. While still maintaining control of the body he was in, he exerted his mind to invade

Maikel. Gradually, he could feel her resistance to his invasion weakening as he forced her hands to begin removing the enviro-protective that enclosed her. She was still in panic as she saw, as if from a distance, her own hands obeying a will that was not her own. In sheer desperation, she uttered a loud cry, which seemed to affect Lucian's concentration enough for him to stop the pressure on her mind.

He pulled back and found that he was panting, physically weaker than before. At once he realised that he would need more time before he could successfully carry out a challenge such as this.

"Very well," he said coldly. "If you will not submit to me, then I'm afraid you leave me no choice."

Lucian's hand moved under his robe. She gasped, terrified as she recognised the slim rectangular shaped metal weapon that he now held in his hand. Maikel backed up against the wall and closed her eyes, knowing at last that she had failed and was about to die!

"LUCIAN, STOP!" commanded the voice from the doorway.

Quickly Lucian spun on his heel, extending his arm and bringing the phasegun up to point directly at Empas' chest.

"This is where it ends," spat Lucian, now completely consumed by his anger.

But instead of depressing the button on the gun that would end his foe's existence, he found he could not move his thumb. Nor could he even exert his will to force the gun to obey him. In fact, he was struggling to maintain any kind of control at all as Empas focussed all of his embryonic telepathic ability on him. Slowly, he began to regain control, enough to begin concentrating all his effort on making his thumb move towards the weapon's trigger point. The thumb began to move. Empas increased the mental pressure, stopping it once more. Lucian redoubled his energy input, every pore of the alien body now sweating with exertion.

The thumb began to move again, and Lucian smiled as he knew he was going to win.

"Goodbye, Empas," he said and began to laugh.

"BEGONE MONSTER!" came back a command which Lucian found he could no longer resist. His laughter died and with a gagging noise, he watched as the phasegun disintegrated in his hand. Looking up, he focussed on his enemy's eyes, now ice cold and piercing every fibre of his consciousness with a pain that just grew and grew. But he also saw pain on that face too so, with a despairing mental thrust he returned to the attack…

Too late, he realised that was exactly the opening Empas had been waiting for. A shaft of white hot, searing pain shot through his very existence as he lost hold of Nazim's body and of his very consciousness. A loud despairing cry was heard as he was finally forced to leave the physical body he had occupied for so long. Nazim dropped to the floor, out cold. Empas, too, staggered back and fell over a stool, finally ending up flat on the floor, barely conscious.

Maikel had watched terror-stricken as the battle unfolded and did not, at first, dare to move when both men dropped to the floor. Her breathing still quick and shallow, she went, first, to her lover, kneeling and lifting his head gently off the floor.

"Empas, are you all right?" she demanded. "Please, speak to me, tell me you are all right."

The silence continued. There was no sign of life from the man in her arms and she began to weep, fearing the worst. He had saved her life but sacrificed his own. She could not get past that thought and so she simply wept on, uncontrollably.

She only stopped crying when she heard a stirring behind her. Turning, she saw the man she knew as Jud Descar raising his torso on his arms, shaking his head groggily and moaning. Gradually, he regained a little of his senses and looked at Maikel.

"Is he dead?" he asked unsteadily.

"I think so," she answered dully. Then she seemed to gather her wits. Turning to him she spat, "And you have killed him!"

"No, not me," he replied. "I am not — Lucian? Is that what you called him? No, he is gone and for that, your friend has my sincere thanks. Let us get him up off the floor at least. I will help you."

Together, they lifted Empas and laid him on the bed. As they did so, a gentle groan escaped from his lips, and he began to breath visibly. Soon, he opened his eyes, focussing on individual objects as he surveyed them. Still, he did not speak.

"Empas, you are alive!" Maikel cried as she cradled his head in her arms.

"Yes. I am. Though I am not sure how," he answered haltingly. "Is Lucian…?"

"Gone," answered the man standing behind Maikel.

Empas focussed on the man.

"How can that be when you are still here?" he asked.

"It is a long story and I fear you will not welcome hearing all of it. Perhaps it is sufficient to say that your enemy had had control of my mind and body for a very long time — since before I left the Thorian capital. Thanks to your efforts, he has left me, and I am forced to admit that you have probably — no definitely — saved my life. I am no longer this Lucian that you speak of, but neither, in all honesty, am I Jud Descar. I am Nazim, secretary and spymaster to my emperor, who sent me here to put an end to you. He sees you as yet another terrorist threat, perhaps the greatest yet to his authority. I am supposed to be your executioner.

"Yet now that I have met you, watched and heard you, I realise that you are a man who teaches only peace, not insurrection., and I owe you, my life. This puts me in a very difficult position. One that I must resolve as best I can."

Nazim paused, obviously wrestling with his conscience, before he eventually continued.

"You have saved my life, and so I owe it to you to say that Lucian, the Thorian governor and your own chief priest, Caiaphas, have laid a trap by which they mean to arrest you. You have already been betrayed and there is nothing I can do about it. In all truth, even without Lucian, I would probably have tried to do the same. It is why I was sent. But I see in you a new philosophy, a different way of looking at life, a… hope for all men, that I have not seen before. If only things were different… I cannot help you further because you are still my enemy. The governor received news recently that our armies have finally overrun the whole of the Bolgish nation. I cannot, therefore, in the end, betray my emperor and still hope to live. There is no longer anywhere for me to hide."

Nazim hung his head, unable to look at either Empas or Maikel. In the silence that followed, Empas took in all that the man had said and found that, even knowing what he now knew, he could not hate nor even blame him. He was simply doing what he had been told to do.

"Nazim, I am glad that I saved your life, and I forgive you for what you must do. Most likely your emperor will never know what a loyal servant he has in you. Thank you for the warning. It is likely we will not meet again, but I wish you well, whatever your destiny."

"Thank you, Master," said Nazim as he made his way unsteadily to the door. As he reached it, he turned and asked innocently, "What is an Eldoran anyway?"

"That, too, is a long story," answered Empas. "Perhaps it would be best if you just forgot about that altogether."

"You are probably right," said Nazim, opening the door and leaving the room quietly.

Once the spy had left, Maikel found a clean piece of cloth, soaked it in water from the basin and began to wash Empas' face with it. For a while he laid back and enjoyed the simple luxury of being fussed over by the woman he loved.

As the evening drew on and became night-time, inevitably they came together as lovers. For Maikel, their lovemaking had an urgency she had not felt before. She thought she had lost him and still recalled the utter devastation she had felt. She did not think she could stand to lose him again, so she clung to him as if her very life depended upon it.

During the night, while his lover slept soundly, Empas rose and thought about the information Nazim had given him. So, a trap was already set for him. Clearly, though he knew that his enemies would probably stop at nothing, he had underestimated the speed with which they would make their move. Forewarned was, however, forearmed and he pondered what it must have cost Nazim to tell him about their plans. He could not imagine the dilemma Nazim must have been in. But speculation on that matter was probably pointless. What was clear was that, suspecting what was about to happen, he found himself at a moment of decision.

Should he withdraw from the city? Marshal his resources? Continue teaching and get more of the population on his side before tackling the church and the Thorians? Would that be seen as a sign of weakness or, worse still, a betrayal of the very principles he was preaching? If that was so, what was the alternative? Should he risk arrest and tackle the church head on? Would logic and reason carry him through such an ordeal? And if not, would his telepathic power come to his aid? So how was he supposed to handle the situation?

Reluctantly, he came to the conclusion that walking into the trap was probably the right thing to do, though the prospect scared him a little. Methodically, he worked through the many possibilities this course of action presented. And found he did not relish any of them! At best, he felt, they would not listen and would continue to work against him with all the power and might they could bring to bear. At worst? He preferred not to think about that yet. But he knew that he must think it through, if only because it was what his father would have done.

Try as he might, however, he could not predict the future, even though its course hung on what he decided to do right now.

Later, when Maikel awoke, he decided not to confide in her all the conclusions he had drawn. Instead, he spoke vaguely about some of the consequences of his future actions, hoping he had managed to hide from her what, to him, was becoming more obvious with each passing hour. His actual options were very limited, and he now found himself somewhat at the mercy of events as they would unfold.

For her part, Maikel went along with the charade, though she knew he wasn't telling her everything. Nevertheless, she could read between his words and instinctively knew that they were now in a very frightening place. After the shocks she had suffered over the past few hours, she felt very vulnerable and much in need of help and advice.

After Empas left her to return to his own room, she sat on the edge of her bed to compose herself. Though she did not really want to do it, she desperately needed someone to talk to. Taking her left wrist in her right hand, she gently depressed a tiny switch on the implant.

"*Director, are you there?*" she thought.

* * * * *

Though he would never admit it, the director had rarely felt so relieved as when he finally received the call from Maikel. The relief, however, turned to something more ominous as she recounted the events of the last few days. The news of Empas' battle with Lucian had been especially vexing. She had almost cried again when she told him how she had thought Empas dead from the fight. Though concerned for his son's

269

safety, hearing her reactions made the director fix on a truth that had finally become clear to him. Empas and Maikel were lovers in every sense of the word. A new excitement took hold of him, and he barely heard the last part of what she was telling him.

'Maikel,' he thought, '*are you both all right?*'

'*Oh, yes, sir,*' she replied. '*Empas seems like his old self again and I was not in any great danger I think once he had come to my rescue.*'

'*Do you need any immediate assistance at this time?*'

'*I don't think so, Director.*'

'*You don't think so? What does that mean Maikel?*'

'*Well,*' she began, '*he has attempted to explain the situation to me in general terms, but I sense that he is holding something back and I don't know what it is.*'

'*Would it help if I spoke to him?*' asked the director.

'*With respect sir, no, it would not. Whatever he is planning to do, he is determined not to give you the opportunity to interfere, as he puts it, any further. I'm sorry Director.*'

'*That's all right, Maikel,*' answered the old man. '*I understand. But if I cannot help him, I can surely help you. What of your own safety? Are you secure and if, as you suspect, events turn violent, is your escape route clear?*'

'*My sled is hidden not far from the city, and should I need help, I'm sure the disciples would volunteer gladly, though I will not risk revealing anything they should not know. Speaking of which, unfortunately, the man Nazim witnessed the battle between Empas and Lucian, heard Lucian utter the word Eldoran, and of course, was aware of the phasegun before Empas disintegrated it. I wonder whether this might turn into a problem.*'

'*Hmmm,*' thought the director, '*it's possible, of course, but I think we will be all right. After all, who would he tell that might believe him? And he has no proof of anything. Even so, I will keep an eye on him. Is there anything else you wish to tell me, Maikel?*'

She thought about the question for a moment, debating with herself whether to confess to the director that she and Empas were in love and had a physical relationship. But in the end, she decided that it could wait for a better moment.

'No sir, I have nothing else right now, but I will contact you if things change. Thank you, Director.'

'Thank me? For what?' asked the man.

'Simply for being there, sir,' she said as she switched off the device.

The director summoned Doctor Gaveri to him shortly after he had finished his conversation with Maikel. While he waited for the doctor to arrive, he began to speculate on the latest turn of events. He could not pretend that he was happy to know that his son was preparing to walk into a very dangerous situation with his eyes wide open. This was not at all how he had foreseen events shaping up and he was, if truth be known, becoming increasingly concerned that his plan for the people of the planet was falling apart, not to mention the probable danger to Empas. On the other hand, it was now obvious to him that Empas and Maikel had found each other, and she had chosen to stay by his side, supporting him. That much, at least, was a comfort.

But what exactly did the Juhl priests, and the Thorian governor have planned for Empas? Were they simply out to stop him? Or to kill him? This last thought, unappealing as it was, must nevertheless be faced, he knew. The people on the planet were barbaric, superstitious and very backward when it came to technology. They were also aggressive, politically astute, and when it came to inflicting pain and death, very efficient! If, indeed, they planned to kill Empas, how could he stop them without interfering? Could he break his oath, even for the sake of his own son? Especially when it was he who had specifically asked him not to interfere.

Gaveri's arrival put a temporary stop to his grim speculation as the director told his friend of all that had happened on the planet.

"So, the flash of energy that we picked up on our scanner some hours ago must have been the battle between Empas and Lucian," said Gaveri.

"It would seem that way, old friend," said the director. "But Empas beat him emphatically, forcing him to leave the body he had occupied. I have checked on him and Lucian is definitely back inside his own body. I suspect my son has inflicted a deeper injury on him than either could have guessed. Let us hope that it is enough to keep him in his own body until he eventually dies."

"Who knows," answered the doctor. "But my gut tells me that he has more mischief to bring about yet before he is finished."

"I fear he may have already caused more trouble than I had thought possible," said the director solemnly, and he went on to tell the doctor what he knew of Empas' plans and of the trap laid for him by the priests and the Thorians.

The doctor took a while to consider his response to the director's revelation.

"You suspected it might come to this all along, didn't you," he said pointedly. "And yet you still allowed events to proceed unchecked."

"I don't really see what else I could have done," answered the director defensively.

"Don't you?" said the doctor, beginning to get a bit heated.

Before he said any more, he stopped to consider what might be achieved by getting into an argument with his boss — old friend or not! Would 'I told you so's' really achieve anything at this stage, except possibly to make a father feel even worse than he did now? No, he decided, they would not, so he calmed himself down, determined to take as pragmatic a view as he could, and if possible, to inject a little optimism into the situation.

"Whatever they might think they can do to him, let's not forget that he is now a telepath of not inconsiderable power, and he is aware of that. So, I think to write him off at this stage would be to do him a gross injustice and cause you a lot of unnecessary pain and anxiety."

The old man sighed.

"Thank you, Gaveri, you remind me yet again what a blessing it is to have someone who will listen. I know that you think I have — miscalculated — in this entire affair, and you may well be right. Even I have begun to have doubts about the wisdom of starting it all in the first place. But I have always seen what I believe to be a bigger picture. Though it may turn out to be extremely painful, I am hopeful that it will all end successfully."

"From what you have told me, would I be right in assuming that events are accelerating on the planet?" asked the doctor.

"It certainly looks that way," answered the director.

"Then we don't have too long to wait for our answers, do we?" said Gaveri.

Chapter 19

The morning following Empas' confrontation with Lucian, he awoke feeling strangely tired and irritable. Unsure that it was wise to appear like this, he stayed a bit later in his room than he would normally have done. He used the time on his own to meditate on recent events. His thoughts seemed to continue from where he had left off the previous night.

Nazim said he had already been betrayed, presumably by Lucian himself, but he still had no clear indication of what form the betrayal would take. He knew only that the Juhl chief priest and his council were eager to bring him before them. But to what end? Of what could they accuse him, he wondered? And what power did they have, in the end, to stop him from doing what he was doing — peaceably telling people that they should love one another. The crowds of people that he was growing used to attracting all shouted his praises and claimed they were now true believers. Of course, he was not so naive as to believe that all of them were suddenly converted from the cloying clutches of the Juhl religion to his own faith in the brotherhood of mankind. But there were surely a few more each time that he preached. Their numbers were growing as surely and steadily as an olive tree.

What then did the priests plan to do? Capture him? Certainly. Try him? Probably. Convict him? Execute him? Was that what they planned? If so, how would they go about it? Of what could they possibly accuse him?

They would have to bring forward witnesses at any trial — bought no doubt — but nevertheless, willing to testify against him. If they were already bought and paid for, then the accusations could amount to anything, and the witnesses would bear them out. How could he defend against that? The weapons he had with which to fight this battle seemed weak and ineffectual. And fight he must, he realised.

His faithful crowd of followers would not be expecting any sort of confrontation with the church, certainly not this soon. How many might he lose when they realised, they must strive to protect their new-found faith? Amongst the poor, the weak and the downtrodden, the human spirit is all too easily broken by the sheer muscle power of authority. He could see no reason to suppose it might be any different with his people. And he could not blame them. The right of might and wealth had been established for too long. The rules were all set by the rich and powerful — amongst whom he counted the priests — and they would prevail over any small-scale passive resistance. Besides, did he really want to inflict that sort of pain and defeat on people who, in all innocence, were only following his instructions?

No, not only could he not count on the crowd, but he also realised that he did not really want them to risk coming to his defence, so where did that leave him, and how equipped?

He could change their minds, of course. His telepathic powers could be relied upon to force his accusers to tell the truth, even to admit that they had no basis on which to pursue their allegations. There were sure to be quite a number of people lined up against him. Could they all be made to relent? By a single attack from his now very powerful mind, could he make it all go away?

But if he did — and he was sure that he could — what then?

He staggered a little as the awful realisation finally dawned on him, that if he used his mind on his accusers, he would simply be affirming the very thing he was fighting against — that might, is right! Might of a different kind, to be sure. They were much weaker than he in this respect and he would be forcing them to do something they did not believe in. That would make him as guilty as they!

That revelation led to another — he could not involve his friends and followers in any if this. They would be in enough danger after he was gone. He could not be responsible for risking their lives in what was still his problem. And what about Maikel? He certainly couldn't risk her life, although she did, at least, have a ready escape route in case of trouble.

Empas felt close to despair. If he could not use any weapon that he had, and he must stand alone, how could he defend himself? How could he be sure that the seeds he had been planting all this time would have a chance to grow, become fruitful and multiply?

With a heavy heart, he finally left his room and went down to join his disciples in the common room.

* * * * *

Simeon approached Empas as he descended into the common room.

"Ah, there you are, Master," he said brightly. "We were wondering whether to disturb you or not."

"That won't be necessary, Pedor," said Empas with a not altogether convincing smile. "I am here, as you can see, and we must be on our way soon. I intend to visit the temple today and pay homage to God at the altar. After, we will relax for a while and then we will eat. Finally, I would like to visit the gardens of Gessam where I hope to find peace and communication with a higher authority. That is the plan so, my friends, I hope you can find a little rest from your toil for today at least."

The disciples all murmured their enthusiastic agreement at this pronouncement. The thought of a whole day without trying to control a crowd brought them a great feeling of relief.

Despite his outward appearance of light-heartedness, Empas was aware of something that the others were not. There was no sign of Jud Descar among the disciples, and no one had mentioned his absence. But Empas knew that he could not be far away. And in all probability, he had just given him all the information he needed to complete his task. So be it, he thought.

Had he known what Empas was thinking, Nazim would have agreed with his conclusion. He now had all he needed to carry out Lucian's plan. He was well hidden beside a window, and he had heard everything clearly. Carefully he moved away from the inn and began to make his way towards the temple. He became plagued with doubt. Though he knew he had to do this, did he really want to? The man had given him back his life. For all he knew, Empas had destroyed the being who had taken him over. Nazim owed him everything. For the hundredth time, he asked himself what he was doing. Wasn't there some way he could walk away from it all? Empas did not deserve this. He was a good man. '*And I am about to bring about his downfall, or something even worse,*' he thought.

The idea made him suddenly choke as a feeling of self-loathing stole over him. But raw fear meant he could not bring himself to betray the

Thorian emperor. He sobbed uncontrollably as the sad reality of his impossible situation became more evident with each step that he took. '*If people back in Thoria could see me now,*' he thought. '*What delight there would be.*' The once proud, devious and all-powerful spymaster, who had the ear of the emperor, reduced to this snivelling wreck and all as a result of his own ambition! The self-pitying thought made the irony of the situation clearer and awakened some deep-rooted impulse within him. Perhaps it was self-preservation that forced him to keep walking towards his destiny, and as he did so, he decided, for good or ill, to face up to whatever the consequences of his actions might be.

Nazim finally reached the temple itself, and working his way round the outside, entered by a seldom used, and thankfully, deserted rear entrance. He quickly strode towards where he knew the chief priest's office to be, and only then did he encounter any guards.

Though the soldiers did not recognise him, they had been told the password that he gave them, so they were prepared to let him in.

"A word of warning though," said one of the guards. "The priests are in conference at this time so they may not welcome your intrusion."

"They will see me," answered Nazim, sure that his news would be welcomed and feeling the bile start to rise in his throat.

The knock on the office door was immediately followed by its opening.

"Get out, can't you see we're busy!" shouted Caiaphas.

All the assembled priests and scribes turned in Nazim's direction.

"I am sorry to intrude — Eminence — but I am sure you will want to hear the news that I bring. And I would remind you, again, that I am a Thorian citizen," answered the spy robustly.

"Oh, it's you… Jud Descar is it, or have you changed your name again?" said the chief priest.

The others stood and watched as the exchange took place, unsure who was superior here. The silence deepened as the two men glared at each other for a few moments. Caiaphas with disdain for someone he considered inferior to himself. Nazim with pure hatred for the man partly responsible for what he was about to do.

"You said you have news?" began the chief priest questioningly.

"Yes. The opportunity you seek will occur this evening. The man,

Empas, intends to visit the Gardens of Gessam. It is a popular tourist spot, though at that time it will be deserted. He seeks solitude, though he may be accompanied by his close followers. At some point, however, you will undoubtedly find him alone and unguarded, and you can arrest him. But you will need to get him away quickly before his disciples can raise a fuss."

Caiaphas managed to conceal his delight as the last piece of his plan fell into place. He could not help imagining the look on Portio's face when he delivered this messiah to him all trussed up, tried and convicted. But before that, he had one more piece of business to attend to.

"This is indeed welcome news. You have served your master well. However, we must have a positive identification. After all, to a soldier, one Juhl looks very much like another. Since you know him so well, who would be better to identify him than you? You can accompany the guards, and at the right time, go up to him and greet him with the usual kiss. By this, the soldiers will know who to arrest and they can also protect you from his supporters. An extremely workable arrangement I feel. Would you not agree, gentlemen?" said the priest to the assembled company.

Nazim looked around the room with pure hatred and disgust permeating his every breath as the priests and scribes started congratulating each other and laughing as if the deed were already accomplished. Finally, he brought his attention back to Caiaphas. He realised he had been backed into a corner even he could not get out of.

"Very well," he began. "I shall do as you ask. You will get your man, much good may it do you!"

He spat the last words, and as he did so, reached under his robe and produced the pouch the Chief Priest had given him. It spilled open as he tossed it onto the floor in front of the man he now detested, and its contents rolled all over the place.

"The price of your treachery towards one of your own!" he shouted. "I will not take it. I'm sure you will find a good use for it. So, take it back — and be damned!"

With that, Nazim turned on his heel and marched towards the door. Before he reached it, however, he heard Caiaphas shout "Guards!"

Two soldiers appeared in the doorway as it opened.

"Yes, Eminence?" said the senior.

"See to the comfort of our guest. There will be a task for you this evening and he will be accompanying you. We wouldn't want him to get lost, would we?"

"No, Eminence," replied the soldier.

With a final glance at the chief priest, Nazim exited the room, flanked by the two soldiers.

* * * * *

Empas, Maikel and the disciples left the inn and started making their way towards the temple. Though it was not far, they decided to take their time and enjoy the sights and sounds of the city which none of them had visited before. In this area, most of the foot traffic was heading towards the temple itself so there was little chance of missing their way. People coming away from the temple were not so numerous, possibly because the fast-approaching feast of the Blessed Passing was persuading them to stay on in the city for another day or two.

Gradually, they became aware of the sounds of the city, getting louder, it seemed, the closer they got to the temple. Empas began to grow concerned. Surely the Thorian military couldn't be creating trouble within the temple grounds? That would be totally out of keeping with their usual hands-off policy. Typically, he thought that he might be able to help calm things down, so he quickened his steps slightly and headed directly towards the temple.

They turned the corner of a building and finally saw what was causing all the noise. This was no military intervention, nor a riot of any sort. It was a market place, the entire forecourt area covered in stalls, with merchants selling all variety of goods. And it was bustling with trade. They made their way through the chaotic rows towards the steps of the temple, where they saw an even more unexpected and unpleasant sight. On the very steps themselves, right up to the door leading into the hallowed place, there were traders selling sacrifices of all kinds, from small chickens upwards to lambs and goats, merchants selling souvenirs and money changers, dealing in what they called 'temple-sheks'.

Apparently, you were highly unlikely to get the 'ear' of God, or even to be able to enter the temple, if you did not have a 'suitable' sacrifice to offer. And you could only buy these special sacrifices using 'temple-sheks'. Studying what was going on, Empas noticed that the exchange rate between normal currency and temple-sheks was such that the price of even a small sacrifice became incredibly high, immediately robbing most pilgrims of whatever meagre resources they might have brought with them.

He saw how the money changers and sacrifice sellers wooed and beguiled their customers, smooth tongued as any self-respecting street trader would expect to be. But he was appalled when he saw and heard various low ranking faris and scribes actually justifying and excusing the daylight robbery which was being played out before their eyes every minute, encouraging poor pilgrims to give up their last dregs of money in the hope that they might achieve a short spell at the altar where they could talk to God.

His manner became more austere, and his temper began to rise as he moved slowly amongst the tables and stalls. He saw an older couple approach a money changer's table and listened to the line he began to spin them about the exchange rate. When he heard the woman query the amount, he was momentarily taken aback. Surely it couldn't be…

"Mother, is that you?" he asked.

The woman turned, and the man accompanying her, and he immediately recognised them both.

"Mother! Jespeth!" he exclaimed. "I never expected to see you here. This is so good!"

The money changer, annoyed at the prospect of losing a valuable sale, looked up and addressed Empas.

"Yes, very touching, I'm sure, but may I remind you that your parents won't be able to get into the temple without a sacrifice and they can only buy a sac…" was as far as he got before Empas finally exploded with fury.

"Can only buy a sacrifice using this so-called currency that you are using to rob people every minute of every day, yes I know," he rejoined heatedly. "And how do you live with your conscience knowing that what you are doing is against the law and every precept of honesty and piety there is?"

"THIS IS SUPPOSED TO BE A HOLY PLACE," he shouted,

looking around at the astonished traders. "How dare you turn it into a den of thievery and hypocrisy? HOW DARE YOU!"

With that tirade, and for the first time in his adult life, he lost his temper. He began attacking the tables and stalls, turning them over, spilling money and goods all over the steps. Astonished traders and pilgrims alike backed away from his fury as he strode through the assembly, upsetting as many pitches as he could find.

The disciples began to grow apprehensive at this show of force. They were suddenly making a lot of noise, right in the centre of the seat of power in Juhl — and it could only have bad repercussions. Simeon and Andreas noticed a pair of faris and a guard moving through the crowd towards Empas. Swiftly they moved to his side and grabbed at his arm.

"Master, we have to leave!" they urged. "You have attracted some unwelcome attention."

As if on cue, the faris with their guard arrived.

"What is the meaning of this?" demanded one of the faris importantly.

Empas wheeled on him, tearing his arm from Simeon's grasp. His temper seemed to cool, but his fury did not.

"You," he pointed at the clergy, "are making a mockery of what should be a sacred shrine, available to all. Your false pompous outrage means nothing to me. You are a disgusting example of the corruption that seems to fill this so-called church. Get this filth removed from these sacred steps, or answer to God for your crimes!"

The faris were astonished at this verbal attack. Never had they encountered such insolence, especially here at the temple. They watched dumbstruck as Empas reluctantly allowed his followers to drag him away from the scene of wreckage and confusion, gradually becoming swallowed up in the crowds who, murmuring in astonishment at the scene that had just played out before them, once more began to go about their business.

After the incident, the street traders and money changers began to pick up their wrecked tables and stalls, embarrassment evident on their faces, quickly trying to reclaim spilled resources so that their losses would be minimal. One or two of them thought about complaining to the priests at this interruption and demanding more protection than they received at the moment.

Marin and Jespeth left the scene soon after Empas' departure, no longer certain that they were doing the right thing by being there. Marin felt both pride and fear at the commanding person that her son had become and wished to speak to him more than anything else. Jespeth sensed the importance of the meeting of the two of them and led his wife along the path that Empas and the retreating disciples had taken as best he could. Eventually, they found themselves at the inn where Empas was staying. Opening the door, they saw immediately that their son's group were all here. And there was a woman that Marin thought she recognised, but she could not be sure.

The reunion between mother, stepfather and son was an emotional one which, amongst other things, had a calming effect on Empas, enabling him once more to relate pragmatically to the realities surrounding his life, his mission and his actions. He told them of his mission and expressed his beliefs in the hope that they would understand why he had said and done all those things at the temple.

It needed little persuasion for Marin and Jespeth to wholeheartedly embrace their son's teaching and to come to the conclusion that he would indeed cause a mighty revolution in the world given the chance to do so. They were so enthusiastic that they decided to stay on in Tevalem for a few more days to be near their son.

Maikel arranged for a room to be found at their inn for them and paid the expenses from her plentiful supply of currency. As she was showing them to their room later, Marin turned to her and whispered, "Please look after my son as you once looked after me."

Maikel smiled and nodded, pleased that Marin had remembered her after all these years, and grateful that she had kept her own counsel on the matter. This was, indeed, she mused, a woman of exceptional strength and character and she deserved to see her son succeed.

Entering Empas' room, Maikel sat on the bed and looked at her lover.

He seemed almost unnaturally peaceful, as if the morning's events had somehow removed some major doubt or worry from his mind. She could be mistaken, of course, but she thought she knew him well enough to read him quite accurately.

"What I saw going on was outrageous. An offence to the God they

profess to worship. And yet, they steadfastly refuse to recognise the…
evil… in what they allow to go on. It's as if they don't want to pay any
attention to anything but their own welfare," said Empas quietly and with
an air of resignation.

"Well," she said at last. "It looks as if you have got their attention
now!"

* * * * *

Caiaphas left his office hurriedly, having caught the back end of the
disturbance that was going on outside on the steps. He saw the two faris
and their guard entering, looking rather shaken and confused as he
approached.

"What is going on?" he demanded. "What just happened?"

"Oh, it was nothing very much, Eminence," said one of the faris.
"Some maniac came to the steps demanding that we send all the traders
away. Said they were defiling the holy place as he called it. He caused a
little bit of trouble, but we sent him away."

Sensing that this was probably nothing like what actually happened,
the chief priest asked, "And did this maniac have a name?"

"Not that we heard, Eminence," said the other faris hurriedly. "One
of his henchmen called him 'Master' but that was all we heard."

Caiaphas turned suddenly, his features blackening as he lifted his
eyes skywards, rolled his head and exploded with rage.

"Why am I surrounded by fools? Did you not realise that this man,
who is known as the master, is the very one we are trying to arrest? We
could have had him, and all his followers here and now had it not been
for your stumbling total mishandling of the situation."

"We are sorry, Eminence, we did not rea…"

"As indeed you should be!" shouted the priest. "It's lucky for you I
am a benevolent man, or you could already be looking for a new career
outside the church."

The chief priest continued to the front of the temple and stood
surveying the scene before him. Gradually, the stalls and tables were
being put back in place and business was resuming. Once again, he
realised how badly he wanted this man off the streets and out of his way.

He was still fuming at the lost opportunity due to his own people's incompetence but gradually he managed to regain control of himself. '*Still*,' he thought, '*if all goes according to plan, by tonight the nuisance will be safely in custody and well on his way to extinction.*' The idea gave him a feeling of deep satisfaction.

* * * * *

That evening, Empas, the disciples, Maikel, Jespeth and Marin arrived in the large upper room, which Maikel had organised, to find a long table laden with simple fare — bread, fruit, cheese and wine as Empas had requested. Additionally, there was a large bowl and pitcher containing water on a table set to the side.

It did not take long for all assembled there to realise that something special was planned for the evening. Some of the disciples thought that, given Empas' outburst earlier in the day at the temple, he was going to announce how he finally planned to take on the leadership of the established church. Some were brimming with optimism, while others, Simeon included, were not so sure. Maikel felt a sense of dread at what might be coming. Empas' strange moods of introspection over the last few weeks had taught her that his mission was turning out to be more complex than even he had imagined, that no strategy would be simple, and every plan would be risky. Marin, too, could feel the inevitability of something ominous and very frightening approaching, though she could not have been any more explicit than that. Jespeth, ever the practical man, had inspected the furniture and found it adequate if not great. He did not share the others' sense of doom and was quite happy for the moment just to know that his wife was reunited with her son. That made her happy, therefore, he was happy too.

Once they had all sat down to begin the meal, Empas asked for their indulgence before proceeding.

"May I start by reminding you all of my mission. It is, simply, the betterment of man through peace, true brotherhood and love. I believe with all my heart that this is a better — and quicker — route to salvation and redemption than eternal warfare and struggling for power. I know that my heavenly father, whom we know as God, sees this as the way to

283

eternal life for mankind and He has entrusted me, his son, to show you the way. In fact, it goes even further than that, because I AM the way. You need only to believe in me and follow my example to achieve that everlasting peace.

"That is not to imply that I am in some way superior. I am not and have no wish to be. I simply have, what you might call, a head start on most. My role as master is to serve, in every respect."

As he said this, he took the pitcher and poured water into the bowl. Then, moving to each person in turn, he knelt and washed their feet. Though the symbolism of the act was not lost on the company, still some objected. But Empas stopped their objections by saying, "As I do this for you, so I will expect you to do it for others."

When he had finished the task, he sat once more at the table and paused before continuing.

"When I started, some three years ago, I did not think I would find enemies as implacable as those I have encountered here. And it has vexed me to discover a way in which I can 'fight' those enemies when the whole point of my existence has been to abolish fighting. This is the dilemma I have faced over the past few weeks. I can now tell you that I know how it can and must be done. I have an important task before me, and in all probability, I must leave you soon and ask others — namely you — to continue the work I have started. Don't think I'm deserting you because that is not the case. But you will find your own depth of faith and belief tested in the days and weeks to come. I cannot tell you more because the future is still uncertain., but as I said earlier, believe in me. It's all I ask of you."

At this a general raising of many voices was heard. All expressing their confusion and anguish at the prospect facing them. Continue the mission without the master? Surely that was not an option. Of course, we believe in him, why else would we be here? Only Maikel and Marin sat quietly, both lost in their own misery and sense of impending loss which Empas' words had prompted. Neither understood the details of what Empas was talking about, but both knew it would be something final and irrevocable.

"Be at peace, my friends," he continued when the noise died down. "The fact is that I have already been betrayed and the time is now right for me to face my accusers. Nothing we can say or do will change that. So, hear me out, please."

He took the large flat loaf of bread and passed a piece to each person, then he took the flagon of wine and poured some into each goblet. Then he returned to his seat.

"If you're concerned because I might not be here to guide you then, each time you eat bread and drink wine, think of them as my body, and my blood. If you do, I'll be with you. So now, eat, drink and then we'll go to the Gardens of Gessam. I'm told they are a spectacular sight by moonlight."

As the menfolk continued the meal, Empas rose and took Maikel by the arm and led her outside the room. She had been silent up until now but was determined to say what she was feeling. Before she could start, however, Empas spoke to her.

"Maikel, you must listen to me and believe what I say. I love you more than I ever knew it was possible to love, but you already know that. And we both know that, unless I can complete my mission, my whole life has been pointless. To do that, however, I now realise that I have to begin taking a few risks. It is the only way I can defeat them. Do you see that?"

"Yes, I do," she answered, close to tears. "I knew you had reached some sort of decision, but until now it has all seemed... I don't know... unreal somehow. It was almost like a game that you could never lose. You would create enough support, send the Juhl church packing and that would be that. But it's not going to be that easy, is it?"

"No, it isn't," he said slowly. "These are primitive people and I have tried to balance their religious and superstitious beliefs with the simple truth by which I have lived and taught. Somehow, they can't overcome their fear of upsetting their God. Unfortunately, they see me as a messiah, a redeemer, I am even called the Son of God, and apparently, I am here to save them from what they perceive as 'sin' — basically anything which displeases Him. Put simply, what pleases God is good, anything else is sin and punishable by death. But I have taught them to regard Him as a loving and forgiving being, interested only in their welfare. I don't know how it has happened, but I have, apparently, become a 'gift' from God, without sin myself, but here to take away theirs. However, you look at it, it boils down to establishing a new philosophy amongst those who will hear. But the old teachings must be challenged, and the corruption exposed. That is clear — and I am the only one who can do that."

"I understand what you're saying," Maikel replied, sobbing now despite her resolve. "But I still don't want you to put yourself in danger. Why must you take them on alone? Has it not occurred to you that you could die?"

"Of course, it has occurred to me," he said hurriedly. "But don't forget one thing. I am a telepath. And it's certain they haven't encountered one of those before!"

Maikel was still unconvinced, and try as she might, she could not shake the feeling of impending doom. "Is there no other way?" she asked meekly.

Empas did not answer her, only looked at her with real sadness and resolve in his eyes. Maikel cried then, not wishing to hold back the tears. She knew in her heart that he had spoken the truth, but the truth was too awful for her to bear right now, so she excused herself, kissing him softly before leaving and returning to her room.

Empas watched her go with deep regret. There were so many things he wanted to tell her, important things that only they could care about. None of them would be said now. Sadness descended upon him as he realised how much he already missed her.

He went back into the room, and assuming a smile he did not really feel, announced that they should make their way to Gessam.

Chapter 20

In all his years of experience as a spy, bureaucrat and servant to a cruel, demanding emperor, Nazim had never felt so frightened or alone as he did at this moment. Prevented from going to the governor's house to report his success, he had instead to play out his role as a Juhl to the end, he realised. In the high priest he had found someone who could best him when it came to intrigue, and he had no illusions that his position was anything other than precarious at this moment.

As he waited for Empas to appear, he looked around at the group of temple guards who had been sent to carry out the arrest and saw only grim determination in the faces of men who did not question orders, only carried them out. Somehow, he knew, he was unlikely to find any allies amongst this lot! So, what were his options?

The only idea he had been able to come up with so far, was to carry out the betrayal as planned and then, assuming there would be some confusion and confrontation between the rest of the disciples and the guards, make his escape while no one was looking, get to the governor's mansion as fast as possible, get rid of his disguise and make his way back to Thoria. As a plan, it was not without its risks, but it beat being escorted to the Juhl temple to face the chief priest again. An event, he was now sure — if he was any judge of character — he would not live long enough to regret!

No, he needed to be on his mettle and take advantage of any opportunity as and when it presented itself. As his thoughts continued to wander, he considered whether he truly believed in what he was doing. It came as a revelation to him that he had never really thought of it before. He did what he did. It wasn't a question of belief, only of survival.

But this man, Empas. Here was someone he could not fathom. The man knew he would have betrayed him, even if Lucian had not already done so, and yet he had forgiven him! *'How do you work that out?'* he thought. Regrets? Strangely enough, now that he thought about it, he did regret what he was doing in one way. But what choice did he have? Once again, his thoughts turned to the emperor's vengeance if — no when — he caught Nazim, should he betray the Thorian cause, and he almost froze in fear. No, he decided, he could not afford regrets. It came down, again, to survival.

A rustling sound interrupted his troubled thoughts, and he brought his mind back to the job in hand. From his hiding place, he could see Empas and his band approaching. The man turned to his followers and said something he could not hear. Then they stopped and sat, leaning against the trees, as Empas continued a little further along the path, coming ever closer to the trap that had been laid for him.

* * * * *

Feeling a little irritated that his followers did not seem able to stay awake, all thoughts of protecting him or joining him in contemplation driven from their minds, apparently, by the sweet smells coming from the trees and flowers in the garden, Empas moved away from them a little so that he could immerse himself fully into the upcoming conversation. He sat on the ground, making his body as comfortable as he could, before sending out a mental call which, strangely, he found more difficult than usual.

'*Father,*' he thought, '*are you there?*'

'*I am here,*' came the reply, '*but your thoughts are barely reaching me. What is wrong?*'

'*I don't know,*' Empas replied, '*I am finding this hard to do, but I have no idea why.*'

'*Do not worry,*' said the director. '*I will strengthen the mental pathway between us so that you may use less effort. Is that easier?*'

'*Much better. Thank you. Father, we must talk. You have kept your word and not interfered in my life and for that I am grateful. But events are now happening very quickly, and I would appreciate your advice.*'

'*Of course, I will help if I can. But don't bother with preliminaries. I already know much about what is happening. And before you ask, Maikel told me.*'

'*So, you have been interfering after all...*'

'No, I have not. Nor has Maikel betrayed you in any way. She loves you and she is frightened for you. In desperation she informed me about what has taken place over the last few days and your incomprehensible decision to confront the Priests. You do realise, I hope, that you are walking into a trap?'

'Of course, I realise it, but it is the only way...'

'No! I cannot believe that we have come this far along, only to see you throw away your chance of success at the very point when you could achieve everything we planned. You have already exposed the Church's corruption, you have sufficient numbers of followers to overthrow them, what could stop you now?'

'Overthrowing them now is not the answer. Father, you do not know these people as I do. The situation has become complicated. My message to them has become mixed in with their traditional religious beliefs. They believe that I can save them from sin and death, and this is now intimately bound up with my message of brotherhood and love for each other. And the strange thing is, in one way, I can save them. I can give them an example to follow. If I confront them now, I can make them question their own actions so deeply that they will be confused and unable to stop the advance of my message. Even after I'm gone, my disciples will continue the mission. Its power will only grow and become enhanced by time and distance. Eventually, as their civilisation advances, they may come to accept the 'peaceful alternative'.'

'So that is your plan? It's a fine vision you have, Empas, and I follow your logic, but it entails great risk, and in the end, your message could simply be forgotten. Buried under years of war and hatred. Had you thought of that?'

'Yes, sir, I have. And it is the very reason why I have to go to such extreme lengths. You remember my old Bolg teacher and friend, Aortes? He was a naturally occurring telepath and led his people by example, which largely accounts for why the Bolgs are so gentle and caring. But even he, and they, could not survive the onslaught of all-out war. Why? Because their religion has no mystique. It is founded on the reality of ancestors — with all their faults and frailties. They therefore saw no dilemma in accepting the reality, and consequences, of the war that assailed them. There is no faith involved, as such. But faith and hope *form the basis of the Juhl religion. By doing what I plan to do, I give them a stronger hope, a deeper faith.'*

There was a pause in the conversation as each one took stock of the arguments flowing back and forth, totally unheard by anyone else. Finally, the director spoke to his son.

'Empas, I suspect that you are not telling me everything, but I will not invade your privacy. However, you cannot know the depth of heartache that you are causing me. I had not foreseen this situation in all my plans, and I must confess, I don't really know how to handle it. I only hope that you do, since you are clearly determined to go ahead with your plan, despite the knowledge that you may be risking your life for nothing. As a father, I am only just becoming aware of the burden of emotion that comes with parenthood and how easy it is to be wounded by someone else's actions. I don't know how I can possibly help or advise you in this situation.'

'You have already helped, Father, simply by listening. I suppose I just wanted you to know that I don't feel that I am risking my life. I have telepathy and they will be unprepared for it. I believe with all my heart that, if the seeds I have planted can grow, then your aim of accelerated advancement will be achieved without the untold cost in human lives involved in the alternative. If you feel I have let you down by not following your plan, then I am truly sorry and ask your forgiveness. Believe me, if I could see another way, I would take it. But I cannot, so I must follow my conscience. Goodbye Father. Try not to think badly of me.'

With those words, Empas broke the mental connection to the director, convinced now that his decision was the right one and that he was right not to tell anyone — even his father. But there was one thing still bothering him. He could not help feeling a little concerned that he had not had the power to control the mental link from his end and he wondered what it might mean. He stood up and made his way back towards the disciples. That was the moment when his world changed completely.

* * * * *

The old man sat and stared into the distance. Unusually for him, his mind was in turmoil, and he could not seem to focus on any one thought. There was no pattern, or shape, nor even a clear definition of anything he saw in his mind. Only perpetual motion, uncertainty, chaos and confusion. It was a totally new experience for one so used to exercising complete control over everything for so many years. There was also, he realised, pain and sadness. A deep heartache that he had not felt since he had watched Eldor become consumed by a tragic, uncaring, natural event, the vision still sharp in his mind even after all these years.

He had watched the complete annihilation of a whole civilisation that was, as far as he knew, unique in the entire universe. Yet not even that had affected him as deeply as the conversation he had just had with his son. He saw his plan, his dream, and more importantly, his son, all heading for disaster and there was nothing he could do about it.

Intervene? He could, but he would certainly still lose his son because he would be breaking his promise, and he could not guarantee that it would help in the end. Stand by and do nothing? The thought was anathema to him. What then? Was there a way to salvage the situation? He was certain Empas was keeping something important from him. But because of his promise, he could not probe his son's mind to find out what it was.

After a while he became calmer and more relaxed. As had always been the way with this most ancient of Eldoran telepaths, he finally managed to put the doubt and fear, pain and emotion to the back of his mind. Clear of conflicting interests, he bent his will towards finding a solution. He could no longer just sit and wonder. He had to do something.

"Ship," he commanded. "Give me a refresher course on the religious beliefs and traditions of the Juhl people on Rega. The same for the Thorians and get me everything we know about a race called the Bolgs and a priest they call Aortes."

Unseen and unheard by any of the crew, massive bio-electronic circuitry bounded into action as the requests the living machine had been given were processed and the information given to its master and companion.

Taking in the enormous amount of information offered by the ship was no problem at all for the director, and by the time he issued his next instruction, he was already well into his revision.

"Doctor Gaveri," he said to the communicator. "Do you have a few moments you could spare me in my quarters?"

He returned to his studies, confident in the fact that, by the time the doctor arrived, he would be as informed as he would ever be about life on the planet below. He decided the time had finally come for him to confess all to his old friend. Perhaps another mind on the problem might help to come up with a solution. At this stage, anything was worth a try.

* * * * *

The man had risen from the ground and began walking back to his companions. Nazim knew the right moment had come.

"Follow me," he said to the troops as he moved out from his cover. "Master," he cried. "Wait, please, I have something important to show you."

Empas turned towards the voice and saw Nazim, flanked by a troop of Thorian soldiers, moving hastily toward him. '*So, this is it*,' he thought and was surprised to note that he felt almost relieved that the moment of his betrayal was now here. There would be no more manoeuvring, no more half-truths to his friends, his lover and his family. Here was the point of no return. Was he truly ready? He had to be. His own fate, and that of mankind, depended on it.

"Jud Descar, I have missed you," he said to the spy.

Nazim went straight up to him and kissed him on both cheeks. No sooner had he done so, than the soldiers moved in and grabbed him, intent on getting him away as swiftly as possible.

Before they could do so, however, the disciples came running up to them, the three that were armed drawing their swords, intent on rescuing the master. Seeing that they would come to blows with the soldiers, Empas cried out.

"Hold! Do not strike in anger. That is not what I have taught you. Put away your weapons!"

The disciples were, understandably, bewildered by his command and stood staring at the scene before them. The soldiers, seeing their chance, hurried off with Empas in their midst, making no attempt to escape.

Nazim, too, followed the group through back streets and alleys until they were well away from Gessam.

When they were sure they were no longer being followed, the leader of the troop turned to Nazim and said, "Come, spy, the chief priest has a special message for you."

With well drilled efficiency, he and another, tall, well-built guard, each grabbed an arm and forced Nazim down a convenient side alley. The rest of the group continued with their prize to the rear entrance of the temple.

Despite himself, Empas was impressed with the speed and professionalism with which the abduction had been carried out.

* * * * *

The three temple guards were feeling surprised and not a little aggrieved as they looked at their beaten and bleeding prisoner, now prone on the floor of his cell. He was quite a big man, capable of looking after himself they reckoned, yet he had not even tried to protect himself when they began the beating, they had been commanded to give him. Neither had he given any indication that he was in pain, though he must have been. The three of them were trained to inflict it in expert fashion.

Now, at the end of their 'session', they found little satisfaction in the job they had done. Still, orders were orders, and he was supposed to be able to stand up, so that the trial could proceed. Pouring a half-filled bucket of cold water over his head, they brought him round, lifted him up and half-dragged him to the council room, the part of the temple that few except the high priests and those accused of criminal acts would ever see.

Empas was placed in the middle of the room, facing a series of tables arranged in a line, behind which sat a group of priests dressed in ceremonial black robes. The chair in the centre sat empty for the moment and the room was unnaturally quiet.

Feeling the effects of his treatment, Empas struggled, at first, to focus on exactly what was happening. However, the longer he stood, the more he regained his strength and a level of calmness and concentration as the M-BEATS embedded in him did its work repairing damaged tissue and anaesthetising the main sources of pain. By the time, a door at the side of the room opened to allow a man, also dressed in black robes, to enter, Empas was feeling much more like himself, though by no means fully recovered.

He studied the man, whom he took to be the chief priest, as he strode to take up his position in the central chair. There was a scowl which seemed etched into the man's facial features. Empas did not believe it was there simply for his benefit, though he could not imagine what level of unhappiness could cause such an expression. The look did make him realise that here was an adversary that he should in no way under-estimate.

The silence stretched on until the chief priest finally looked up from the scroll he had apparently been studying and looked directly at Empas.

"Do you know why you are here, Empas of Galle?" the priest intoned

Empas said nothing as it seemed pointless at this stage.

Caiaphas waited only a short while for the answer which, he knew, would not be forthcoming, before he continued.

"You are accused of heresy and blasphemy against the Church and the Juhl people, and you are here to answer for your crimes."

Still Empas did not speak, which seemed to cause a little consternation among the supporting cast of High Priests. '*Good,*' he thought. '*A little confusion at this stage can do no harm.*'

"Let us hear from the first witness," droned Caiaphas, determined to shake the man before him one way or another.

The priests produced witness after witness who made various claims about what Empas had said and done. Each had been carefully primed to make their accusations clear and precise. Their testimonies covered many incidents, mostly fictitious, and the so-called evidence mounted up as, one by one, they accused him of everything from claiming to be the son of God, deriding the church and its clergy, abusing the sabbath and disobeying just about all of the commandments handed down by God apart from 'you must not kill'.

Despite the weight of accusation, they were able to bring to bear, still Caiaphas was unsettled and unsure of the outcome, until one witness, he could not recall his name, gave him exactly what he wanted.

"He proclaimed himself king — said he had a kingdom waiting for him greater than any other," said the man who, in truth, had gone well beyond what he had been prompted to say.

"Are you sure of this?" asked Caiaphas, hardly able to contain his glee. The words had been said and entered into the court records. He wondered if the accused could wriggle out of that one.

"Empas of Galle, do you truly believe yourself to be a king? You are a Juhl, and therefore, we must presume that the kingdom you speak of is Juhl itself. Are you, then, King of the Juhl? If so, where is your proof?"

Empas thought back to the many times he had spoken of the kingdom of heaven, using euphemism to illustrate what he wanted mankind to achieve without resorting to what might be proved, in the end, to be falsehood. So, the witness had, at least, been to one of his gatherings. He felt sad that he had not been able to convince this one. But he realised that the moment had come when he had to speak in his own defence.

"You know as well as I do, that the accusations brought against me in this court have no legitimacy and no basis in fact. It is simply your power base that is under threat, which is why you have, yourselves, committed crimes for which you will answer to God. As for the ludicrous suggestion that I might be a king? Remember, those are your words, not mine. I have nothing more to say to you."

Deciding to dispense with all pretence at formality, Caiaphas stood from his seat and spoke directly to Empas.

"But I have something to say to you!" he snarled. "You think you can come to this place and accuse us? Accuse me? You think you can threaten me with your 'holy, free of sin' reputation? How would it be received, do you think, if your followers knew what you and your woman got up to in private?

"Know this, Empas of Galle, you know nothing of the power I wield. But soon, you will. Take him away!" he commanded the guards who had been standing silent during the proceedings.

At this, Empas was utterly shocked, and he knew he was facing an enemy, perhaps even more dangerous than Lucian. He could not miss the direct threat to Maikel that had been made and he immediately feared for her safety. She was someone he was definitely not prepared to risk. So perhaps Caiaphas was Lucian in another disguise? The thought had not occurred to him before, but now that it had, he had to know. He put out his mind towards the priest — but found that he could not find a way into his head! He was not being blocked, of that he was certain, as he would have felt the reverse pressure. No, it was simply that he did not have the power to penetrate this ordinary human mind. What was going on? he wondered with dismay, as the guards moved to forcefully escort him from the chamber.

He still had no answer to his question as they pushed him back into his holding cell.

* * * * *

The director was stunned at the travesty he had just watched being played out on the screen before him. The Juhl priests had made little effort to hide the fact that the charges they brought against Empas had been nothing more than trumped up fiction. He was proud of the response that his son had given them and fully expected him to use his telepathic power to end this confrontation. Yet he had not! The moment had passed and Empas had been taken away, back to a cold cell.

'Why did he not use his power?' the old man asked himself, over and over. He turned to his friend with a questioning attitude.

"I don't know," answered Gaveri before the question was even asked. "I have no experience in trying to work out how or why telepathy works so I can't help you. Is it possible he chose not to use it?"

"I don't think so," said the director. "It looked to me as if he tried to use it but failed! But how could that be? You either have telepathy or you don't."

Gaveri thought for a moment.

"I may not know about telepathy, but I do know a bit about the human body, and it was clear to me that Empas had been pretty badly beaten before he appeared in that chamber. Now, it is possible that the injuries inflicted on his body, despite M-BEATS, could somehow have affected his telepathic power, shutting it down or, at least, weakening it substantially until he regains full health?

"Also consider this, Director. His battle with Lucian a few days ago obviously cost him a great deal of mental energy. Isn't it possible that

296

this, too, could have had a draining effect on him? Lucian was, after all, a very powerful telepath himself."

The director's thoughts raced, and he found himself remembering a day, many uncounted years ago, when he had convinced a whole fleet of warmongering aliens that his people did not even exist. Though the act had been a straightforward one, he recalled that he had felt drained and empty for days afterwards. Could it be that both he and his son had explored the limits of their own powers?

On the one hand, he hoped this was so. On the other, he was suddenly reminded that, in the end, they were all mortal — and vulnerable!

* * * * *

Caiaphas turned to the assembled priests, determined that he was not going to let this opportunity slip through his hands.

"We must act quickly," he said to the assembly. "Issue instructions to every faris and scribe to mobilise every contact they have. I want a howling mob gathered before the gates of the governor's mansion by tomorrow, midday. We can convict him of heresy and blasphemy, but only a Thorian decree can convict him of high treason."

"But we have no proof of that at all, Eminence," interjected Parminius, one of his closest associates. "And he has flatly denied it."

"Has he Parminius? I don't remember that. Does anyone else recall him denying the accusation?" he asked smoothly, the implication in his voice quite plain.

No, no, of course not, not at all, came back the replies from all — including the outspoken Parminius.

"Then we are agreed, gentlemen. Regrettably, we have a madman who claims he is King of the Juhl on our hands. He must be taken before the governor to be tried for treason. Unfortunately, under Thorian law, which is punishable by death!"

As Caiaphas was leaving the chamber, he was intercepted by one of the guards who had arrested Empas and then taken Nazim.

"Did you carry out my orders?" asked the chief priest quietly.

"It will look like suicide," answered the other. "He did not offer much resistance."

With a nod and a smile, Caiaphas dismissed him and carried on about his business

* * * * *

Empas sat disconsolately on the floor of his cell, still wondering why he had not been able to penetrate the chief priest's mind. He was so taken up by this vexing question, that the full implications of what had transpired in the chamber had not really occurred to him at all. Now that he had time to think about things, however, the true extent of the trouble he was in was becoming clearer. And his fear for Maikel had not diminished either. Alone and in the hands of enemies who would stop at nothing to destroy him, he knew now, beyond any doubt, that they meant to kill him one way or another. And whether he had ever truly intended to use his power to stop them or not, was now moot. His power seemed to have deserted him!

As his conclusions sank in, he became more philosophical. There were things he had left undone — or were there? Perhaps he had already done as much as he could do in the flesh. Wasn't it possible that his mission, and the message carried by his disciples, would become more powerful still with his death? The converted faithful saw him as a man without sin, sent from God to save them from their own sin. His thoughts drifted back to his childhood friend, Ben, who had given his life to save a boy who had only despised him. All at once, Empas recognised the powerful symbolism in his own death, for followers and foes alike. He would lay down his life for them all, just as Ben had done. The logic seemed perfect. All he had to do now was to face his impending doom with as much dignity as he could. As he reached this conclusion, all fear and doubt concerning his lost telepathic power seemed to melt away. His one regret was that he would not be with his beloved Maikel ever again.

These were his last thoughts before guards came and forced him to his feet. Without preliminary, he was marched from his cell by a squad of soldiers, out of the temple and along the alleyways which made up the short distance between the temple and the governor's mansion. But he was not taken into the house. Instead, he was thrown into another cell, part of the barracks that housed the Thorian governor's guards. There, a fresh group of soldiers laid into him, just to remind him that he was at the mercy of Thorian justice now.

* * * * *

Despite the best efforts of the soldiers at the behest of the priests, the arrest and abduction of Empas had not gone entirely unnoticed amongst the citizens of Tevalem. Even that late at night, there were still some people about in the streets. And it was amazing how quickly news travelled, even at that hour. Several times, as they made their way sadly back to the inn, the disciples had been accosted and questioned by passers-by, some of whom vaguely recognised them as followers of the arrested man.

Troubled by fears for his own safety and that of his friends, Simeon had been forced to deny that he even knew him several times. It was early morning before he thought back to what the master had told him so long ago. And he wondered, '*How could he have known?*'

Maikel knew, without being told, that something terrible had happened as soon as the disciples returned. Her apprehension rose further as they recounted the events to her, reaching terror proportions when they told how he had been led away by the guards, but they did not know where they had taken him.

Her instinct told her that something had gone wrong and that Empas was now in the hands of the very people he should have stayed away from. She felt sick and knew she had to get away from the crowd in the common room to somewhere more private. She left the building through a rear entrance that took her to a small courtyard where she promptly threw up. After a while she stopped retching as the nausea receded. She sat on a bench which had been thoughtfully placed there and tried to gather her thoughts.

Where was he? What was going to happen to him? How could she reach him? Could she effect a rescue? All these questions demanded answers which, she realised, she did not have. For the second time in just the space of a few hours, she began to cry.

Chapter 21

Andrew had got used to the confines of his cell. In the time he had been here he had counted every stone, felt every contour, snaffled every beetle and other insect that dared to invade his new domain and generally made himself acquainted with every aspect of what he took to be the sum total of his life before the Thorians took that away from him. A prospect he did not relish at all!

The rattling of keys and the sound of the lock on his door turning wakened him from his doleful meditation. The door swung ajar, and the form of a man was pushed through it. The new arrival stumbled, and unable to maintain his balance, fell to the floor almost at Andrew's feet.

"Some company for you, Barab! Since you're both messiahs, I'm sure you can work out how to escape now that there are two divine heads instead of one."

The door slammed shut and the sounds of laughter gradually receded, leaving the two occupants of the cell in gloomy silence. Neither man moved for quite a while, Andrew because he was assessing the new situation, Empas because he found he was incapable of movement after the pummelling he had suffered. Eventually, though, the M-BEATS did its job and he felt well enough to move a little, giving out little groans when he found parts of his body that still gave him pain.

Andrew had not seen his companion's face, but he knew it must be bruised and misshapen by now unless the guards had decided to ease up on their victim — a most unlikely event! He crawled forward and tried to help the other man to sit up and make his way to a wall for support. He cringed as he saw that the other's face was as bad as he had imagined.

"How many did you manage to get before they caught you?" he asked casually.

"None," came the surprisingly firm reply.

"None? What kind of partisan fighter are you to get captured before you can even strike?"

"I am not a partisan. I never was," said Empas getting a first look at his new cell mate. "But I recall helping one who had an arrow in his shoulder a few years ago."

The statement sent a jolt of recognition through Andrew that he had never anticipated.

"Empas? Is it really you? The last time we parted, you were on your way to the mountains. What possessed you to come back to this worthless land?"

"I can't give you a simple answer to that question. It's very complicated," said Empas, his strength now returning.

Andrew noticed that the bruising on his face was also reducing, sufficient anyway for him to fully recognise the man who had saved his life all those years ago.

"But you are just a healer," he blurted. "Albeit a very good one with a power I call magical. Why have the Thorians brought you here and in this condition? You must have upset somebody pretty powerful!"

"It wasn't the Thorians, it was our own high priests who had me arrested," answered Empas. "I was teaching people things they did not want them to know."

For the next hour or so, since there seemed to be little else to do, they sat and discussed matters, telling each other their individual stories and swapping backgrounds. Andrew had just related how and why he first joined the partisans.

"So, wait a minute," interjected Empas. "You left your family because your sister became pregnant before marriage, and you didn't really give her much chance to explain, did you?"

"That's right!" said the other. "I couldn't believe my own sister would try to cover her shame and deceit. I wanted no part of it, so I walked away"

"Your sister," said Empas slowly. "Her name wouldn't happen to be Marin, would it?"

"That's right," said Andrew. "But how…"

"And she wasn't betrothed to a man called Jespeth, was she?"

"How could you know that?" asked Andrew, becoming confused.

"Andrew, I have something to tell you which you are going to find hard to believe. But if I'm not mistaken, it could alter your opinion of

301

your wonderful sister forever," said Empas mysteriously.

"Why would I do that?" asked the other, only beginning to suspect what was coming.

"Firstly, let me ask you something. Have you heard the tale's people are telling, of a messiah who is reputed to be the Son of God?"

"Of course, I have — I even threatened the Thorians with his arrival. With all the rumours of acts of healing and even resurrection, I suspected it might be you," said Andrew with a chuckle.

"And do you believe those rumours might be true?" asked Empas again.

"If they are, then either he is a powerful wizard, like you, or he must be the Son of God."

Andrew stopped and considered for a moment before he continued, "You know, I believe they could well be true."

"I'm glad," said Empas. "Because I happen to know that some of those rumours, at least, are true. I am the one they call the Son of God. I also happen to be Marin's firstborn son, and I can tell you that she was never unfaithful to Jespeth. In fact, he was aware of her mission and complicit in the whole scheme."

Andrew was dumbfounded at the revelation. She wasn't unfaithful? And yet, she became pregnant! How could that be? The things this man was telling him were simply impossible.

"Listen," said Empas at last. "You believe my powers of healing to be magical, right?"

The other man simply nodded.

"Well, I must ask you to take it on faith that they are, and they aren't. At the moment, for example, my 'powers' seem to be non-existent, which is partly why I am in this mess! But that's not so important right now. The other thing I must ask you to take on faith is your sister's fidelity. She and Jespeth suffered much so that I could be born and brought up in this land. I would count it a personal favour if, should you ever get out of here, you would find them both and be reconciled with your family. You have served your people as you saw fit. But it is time for peace, love and brotherhood now. That is why I am here. It's why I was sent. To help bring that about. It would be a comfort to me to know that you and your family were a part of it."

Still stunned by this devastating revelation, Andrew could only continue to nod in acknowledgement of Empas' words. He knew in his heart of hearts that the man spoke the truth, or certainly the truth as he saw it. Yet it went against all that he knew, all that he was, to believe that his sister had borne a child whose father could only have been God. Could he really put his faith in what he was being told? Or was it stretching credibility too far? He couldn't bring himself to decide right now.

Instead, he looked at his companion, and his grim humour returning to the surface, he said, "You can't honestly believe that either of us is going to get out of here alive, can you?"

"Right now," said Empas seriously. "You're not the only one who doesn't know what to believe! But I must confess that I have a feeling they're going to let you go."

These were the last words Empas spoke before the cell door was again thrown open. Two burly guards entered and grabbed him unceremoniously, ushering him roughly out through the door which was slammed shut to leave Andrew alone to sit and ponder on all that he had heard.

* * * * *

Marin found Maikel sitting in the little courtyard, looking shaken and pale. She came to the girl — for that was how she saw her — and put a comforting arm around her shoulder.

"Are you all right, child?" she asked calmly. "Did the atmosphere and the noise become too much for you?"

"Yes, thank you, Marin, I'm fine, I just needed some air," Maikel told her gratefully.

"Strange, isn't it," said Marin, "that I should be calling you 'child'. Yet how many more lifetimes than I, have you already lived, and still, to me, you look like a young woman."

Maikel smiled at the companionable remark.

"I am puzzled, though," continued Marin. "You were there for me when Empas was born and here you are, unchanged thirty odd years later. I take it, then, you are an angel?"

Maikel was taken aback at the insight shown by the woman. She would need to tread carefully, she knew, or else she might find herself revealing something that she shouldn't.

"I am a servant of God, yes," she said. "I am called Maikel. On Rega, though, I am known as Marin Madane, a name I chose in your honour actually."

"I am truly honoured, Maikel," said Marin humbly. "But indulge me further please. Do I not understand correctly that you love my son, as a young woman loves a young man?"

"That is also true," answered Maikel. "Though I had hoped to hide it."

She continued after a short silence. "Marin, it is not good that the world should be aware that we walk amongst them. It is not God's way to reveal such things."

Marin took her by the shoulders and turned her so that they would be face to face.

"I have obeyed God's will," she said seriously. "Who am I to question his way?"

A companionable silence grew between them. They shared knowledge that went beyond what two women might normally share. And although Maikel was certain she had not given anything away, she was also sure that Marin had perceived far more from their conversation than was actually said.

"Will my Empas grow older at the same rate as you, or as one of us?" Marin asked out of the blue.

"I honestly do not know," replied Maikel, startled somewhat by the question. She realised she had not really given the matter much thought. "Why do you ask?"

"A woman should think of these things when she is in love with a man," the woman answered sagely.

Turning then, Maikel suddenly threw her arms around Marin and hugged her tightly, as if she might draw strength from the physical contact. Moments later, she pulled away slightly and looked directly at the older woman.

"Marin," she began. "You have always been my hero since you decided you would carry the son of God. You risked everything to give birth to this unique man. And I promised myself, when I helped you deliver him in that awful stable, that I would look after both of you. I felt strong enough to do that. Such arrogance on my part! What have I managed to do so far? Certainly, nothing for you and falling in love with your son has shown me all the frailties a Regan woman is burdened with. Such a thing is not expected of... an angel. I was not prepared for the impact such an emotion would have on me. My love is in desperate trouble, I know it in my heart, and all I can do is sit here and weep. I don't know what the will of God is in this. All I know is that I have never felt so helpless."

She turned away from Marin as she finished speaking and the tears welled up in her eyes yet again.

The older woman stiffened and patted her shoulder gently.

"Perhaps that is not all," she said. "We women, and angels, must find our own ways to help our menfolk — while they themselves run around like headless chickens most of the time!"

They both laughed at Marin's observation and Maikel felt a surge of comfort and support she had not expected.

"Come my girl," said Marin sharply. "It is time you and I found out what is happening around here."

With that they both rose and made their way quietly and unnoticed by the men through the inn's common room and out into the street. Intent on making their way to the temple, they noticed that groups of people, men mostly, seemed to be moving steadily in another direction, towards the governor's mansion. Though they were concerned to find out what had happened to Empas, they were also curious to see what was drawing such a crowd of people together. There was also the suspicion in Maikel's mind that this could have something to do with Empas' disappearance.

They followed in the footsteps of several groups and became aware of a growing rumble of noise coming directly from the mansion up ahead. Gradually, they started to pick up bits of conversations as they proceeded.

"Said he was a king..."

"Walked all over our sacred traditions..."

"If he broke the law then..."

"They say he's committed treason..."

"...don't want trouble from the Thorians..."

"…claims to be a wizard…"

Though the two women wondered, at first, who they were talking about, their fears grew that they might already know. As they drew nearer to the gates of the mansion, the noise generated by so many people grew louder and louder. Maikel and Marin pulled away from the throng slightly so that they wouldn't be in danger of getting crushed against a wall but remained near enough to see and hear what was happening.

They had been there about an hour when the general noise level suddenly increased, and the voices turned to shouting — mostly obscenities — at something happening on the steps of the mansion. They looked — only to find their worst fears confirmed. There on the top step stood the Thorian governor, Portio Latiedes. In front of him was a row of six guards armed with spears and in front of them were two grimy and dishevelled prisoners. One could barely stand up, so badly had he been flogged and beaten. They both recognised him immediately. Marin also knew the other man.

"Behold, citizens of Tevalem," the governor shouted. "I bring you a gift."

The crowd cheered and then quietened so that they could hear what the man had to say.

"It is our tradition on the day of your feast of the Blessed Passing to release to you one prisoner," he continued. "And this day shall be no exception. Indeed, I offer you a special favour, for each of these two is known to you as a messiah. So, you shall have at least one back. And he shall be free of all charges, provided he behaves himself."

There was a muted cheer from the crowd at this announcement.

"But which shall you have, for there can only be one. Will it be the man known as Al Barab or he who is called Empas of Galle?" enquired the governor grandly.

To no one's surprise, except the two women and a few other sympathisers, the enthusiastic cry went up.

"Al Barab. Al Barab. Al Barab."

Maikel and Marin were both horrified as they listened to the howling mob, baying for the release of a terrorist, while their beloved Empas stood forlorn and convicted — but of what?

Finally, the chanting eased, and the governor's voice could be heard again.

"Very well, you have chosen. Release Al Barab," he cried ceremoniously.

The cheers went up as Andrew was released and allowed to walk out of the gate, looking very bewildered it had to be said. He had certainly not expected this. He accepted the congratulations, pats on the back and thumps of the shoulder offered by various members of the assembly with an air of unreality as he walked away. Not really knowing why he looked in that particular direction, he lifted his eyes and spotted Marin, his sister, standing next to another younger woman, both looking terrified.

He walked over to them and stood close as the crowd seemed to forget he was there.

"Marin…" he began

"Hello Andrew," said Marin. "It has been a long time."

"Yes," he answered lamely, "Look, we have things we must discuss. We must…"

He was interrupted as the governor continued to address the crowd.

"But what of this other?" he cried. "It is said that he is the Son of God."

"No! Not true! He lies!"

These and many more denials were shouted back as the mood of the crowd turned derisive and ugly.

"I must tell you that I have… interviewed him… and I find no fault, except the matter of the claim to be King of the Juhl. What do you say?"

The baying and calling became a cacophony. He is not our king! We have no king, we have an emperor! Long live the emperor! It was clear that the crowd would have nothing to do with the claims.

Then, as if on cue, the governor made one last appeal.

"What shall I do with him then?"

Crucify him! Crucify him! Crucify him! Crucify him! The separate calls seemed to quickly coagulate into a chant which grew in intensity as the crowd whipped themselves into a frenzy at the prospect of an execution!

The governor stood for a moment surveying the baying mob assembled before him, both pleased and appalled that such a final judgement had been so easy to extract from the very people whose approval he needed. No blame could be attached to Thoria, and as a symbol, he ordered a basin of water and a towel to be brought to him. He washed his hands of responsibility for what was about to happen. Slowly, he turned away, and as he passed inside, noticed the chief priest standing and observing the proceedings with obvious satisfaction.

"That would appear to be that, then priest," said Latiedes. "We shall carry out the execution, but it is your people who demanded it. Do not forget that."

"Of course not, Governor," said Caiaphas smoothly, "And may I also remind you that the matter of the spy has also been attended to. Apparently, he committed suicide. Such a tragic end for a fine Thorian citizen."

The governor stopped momentarily and looked hard at the man before him. '*Life would be so much simpler without men like this*,' he thought to himself.

Out loud, he said, "It would seem that we have both got what we desired this day. When this is over, let us hope that peace will return to this… interesting… country."

Empas was led away while the mob was still baying for his blood, his fate now sealed. He had been beaten again and flogged earlier that morning, part of the standard Thorian routine for softening up prisoners — especially political ones. His body was a mass of pain, even despite the fact that M-BEATS was working harder than ever to try to keep up with his injuries.

Despite his discomfort, he still recalled the confrontation with the governor. He had been manhandled into the chamber that served as a court and thrown to the floor in front of the governor's throne, already weak from the constant beatings he had suffered over the past twelve hours. Unable, for the moment, to do anything else, he simply laid there catching his breath. He had expected unfair treatment, to be sure, but not outright thuggery! *Was this, then, the true nature of his enemy?*

After a few more minutes, the governor had entered, went straight to the throne and occupied it, managing to look surprised to see the broken man before him.

"And who is this?" he asked of no one in particular.

"Empas of Galle, Lord. Says he's the king of the Juhl, apparently."

"Oh dear, that IS serious, isn't it?" the governor said jokingly. "Anything else?"

"Well, the priesthood has accused him of blasphemy and heresy, sir."

"Hmm," said Latiedes. "We all know how much the priests value truth, honesty and piety, don't we?"

General laughter.

"And what have you to say to these charges, Empas of Galle?"

Empas had somehow found the strength to stand and face the Thorian — an act which itself aroused surprise in those present. Few could achieve such a thing after a Thorian 'softening'.

"I answer to a higher, more powerful authority than you or the priesthood. So, I have nothing to say to them or you that will alter anything. What will happen, will happen."

This had obviously taken the governor by surprise and Empas thought he had detected a glimmer of something in the Thorian's face. *'Not fear, no. Respect? Could it be?'*

"Of course, we take the charges of blasphemy and so on with a pinch of salt but claiming to be king — that is treason I'm afraid, and punishable by execution. What do you say to that?"

"That if I have a kingdom, then it is far beyond the reach or understanding of anyone here. A king? Those are the words they used. I didn't!"

"You intrigue me, Empas of Galle. Whilst I do not have time to debate politics or theology with you, I find myself persuaded of your integrity and your self-conviction. All the same, you clearly do not understand all that is at stake here. Whilst there is no proof of your guilt, still I cannot let you go. I'm sorry, but as you said, what will happen, will happen."

And with that, the 'trial' was over. Empas had found himself taken once again from the courtroom. That was all he recalled clearly. Now, sitting alone in his cell, he knew finally what was coming. And honestly, he could not deny that, subconsciously perhaps, he had planned it this way, and he reflected, in many ways it could not have gone better. There were enough witnesses at every stage to verify that his trial had been a travesty, his conviction simply a political convenience. When they executed him, they would be killing an innocent man and his reputation, and his message would be intact! Far better this way than to fight back, possibly costing many lives that he considered to be innocent.

The pain was easing all the time as M-BEATS began to achieve supremacy over the injuries inflicted on him. He reflected wryly on how grateful he was for the technology he had once so vehemently rejected, and how effective it was at its job! With any luck at all, he would be back to reasonable health before they killed him!

* * * * *

Andrew grabbed Marin by the hand and put his other arm out to include the other woman.

"Quickly," he said. "I must get you away from here. I recognise some of these men and they are not amongst the most honest or reliable of people I have ever known. The mood is turning ugly, so let's go while we still have a chance."

Maikel was still paralysed with fear and horror at what she had just witnessed. She could hardly believe that her worst fears had been realised, all within the space of a few hours. Still reeling, she allowed herself to be led away by Andrew until they were some distance from the crowd.

Without speaking, he led them down streets and alleys that neither woman recognised. They were sure that they were being taken well beyond the confines of both the Thorian's mansion and the temple district. Finally, they arrived at a row of flat-fronted, two-storey dwellings which appeared to be unoccupied at the moment. Choosing the first door, Andrew opened it without knocking and bundled the women inside.

The place was furnished and in obvious use, but no one was home currently.

"This house belongs to a friend. We will be safe here for a while," said Andrew as he searched cupboards for food, drink and utensils.

Stopping in mid-search, Andrew bowed his head and seemed to come to a decision. He turned back towards his sister, came and knelt before her chair and took her hand in his.

"Marin, the man they have condemned," he began haltingly. "He said he is your son."

"That is true," answered his sister, tears beginning to well up in her eyes.

"He also said that you were not unfaithful to Jespeth before you wed. That you had borne him as some sort of 'mission'."

"That is also true. He is the son of God. My companion can confirm this."

Andrew looked at Maikel, who was still in shock and staring at the door. She had not heard anything.

"Can you?" he asked gently.

"What?" asked Maikel as her attention was dragged back to the present. She too, Andrew noticed, was crying.

"Does my sister speak the truth?" he asked again.

Maikel studied Andrew before making up her mind whether to answer or not. The only way to settle this matter between brother and sister was to verify what Marin claimed. Again, she found herself on dangerous ground. Before she could speak, however, Marin came to her aid.

"She is an angel of God," said the woman. "And she does not lie."

"Empas' father is certainly not of this world," she affirmed. "Nor, for that matter, am I. Marin did not have any carnal relations with anyone before she married Jespeth. She agreed to the pregnancy because God asked it of her. She is indeed a very brave and special lady, and you are lucky to have her as a sister."

"I do not understand," said Andrew, bewildered despite half expecting to hear what he had heard.

"No," continued Maikel. "I don't suppose you do. Nor should you concern yourself with understanding, but simply accept the fact in good faith. Empas was sent into this world. He is your salvation. He is the one thing standing between mankind and total destruction — and your people are about to put him to death!"

Maikel almost screamed the last at him, and finally, the dam broke. She collapsed against Marin weeping uncontrollably. Marin simply put an arm around her and looked hard at her brother.

"She could prove all of this to you, but we must not ask it of her. She is a servant of God and though we cannot understand the nature of angels, it is plain she has been through enough already and we both have yet more evil to face. Please Andrew, help us if you can. If not, simply let us go and we will bother you no more."

"It's you who don't understand now," he replied. "I know how special Empas is. He once saved my life and now, it would seem, the only way I can repay him is by honouring his request. Marin, I was wrong to leave the family and I ask your forgiveness.

"I need no persuading, though I confess it is the strangest thing I have known. Empas asked me to be reconciled with you, and if you agree, we will be reconciled. He also asked me to look after you. Again, I agree wholeheartedly. But how do I give comfort and support to an angel of God? Yet I can see I must try, so I offer my services, such as they are."

"Maikel," said the woman. "Her name is Maikel, and we both accept with thanks."

* * * * *

News of the impending execution spread like wildfire throughout the city, and it took hardly any time at all for the tidings to reach the disciples. Despondently, they all sat around in the common room of the inn, no one saying anything, each lost in his own thoughts. It would be fair to say that all of them felt a measure of guilt at their inability to prevent the abduction of their beloved master. And there was bewilderment too as they remembered him telling them to put away their swords. In the cold light of day, they would not dare to challenge fully armed Thorian guards, but at the time, it had seemed a perfectly reasonable thing to do.

Simeon was particularly disturbed. Stung by his confirmation of the prediction made by the master, he was ashamed of himself for being so weak. For allowing panic to overcome his true convictions. And they were true, he realised. He had always seen the sense in the master's message of love and brotherhood, though he did not fully understand how it might achieve His ends. Yet, He had been adamant that his way was the only way and Simeon agreed.

He was still frightened and apprehensive about what was going to happen to the master, but the more he thought about it, the clearer came the realisation that Empas had probably planned it this way. He knew, almost certainly, he was going to die. And suddenly, Simeon knew that he could, and would, use that sacrifice to preach the same message that

He had.

"Look friends," he said to the others suddenly. "We are all feeling frightened and confused right now. Anyone could be forgiven for getting up from his chair and walking out through that door away from all this. I would be the last to point a finger of accusation. But let me say this. It is my belief that He would want us to stay together because he has created what may well be the perfect opportunity for us to carry out his instructions and spread the message he brought. At least consider this: all the attention of the Thorians and the priests is concentrated on Him. These must be the enemies He spoke of, and he knew them. Would he have gone to them if He was not confident, He could beat them? It may be that He intends to beat them by his death, somehow, and we must try to understand that., but what is important is what we do following all this. For myself, I will watch and follow the events closely and try to understand what He intended. Let us also ask for guidance from God. He will surely have something to say about the sacrifice of his Son."

As he finished speaking, Marin walked back through the door of the inn. The disciples turned to look at her as she went straight to her husband. Without a word, she took his hand and he smiled as she led him back out through the door into the street.

"Marin and Jespeth must have much to talk about," suggested Andreas. "By the way, does anybody know where Marin Madane is?"

"I think I saw her leave with Marin earlier, but I haven't seen her return," said Simeon.

This is getting confusing, thought Andreas, although he did not follow that train of thought. Instead, he looked back towards his companions.

"Yes, it's definitely time we talked to God."

Marin and Jespeth joined Andrew and Maikel a couple of streets away from the inn and they all made their way back to the house Andrew had supplied.

The atmosphere of sadness and despair had not dissipated, though now Andrew brought a measure of security to them as he recounted his conversation with Empas in the prison cell. He also explained in detail how he had originally encountered Empas at the mountain hideout, and how he had saved Andrew's life.

"So that is where he went after he left us," offered Jespeth. "His mother and I often speculated on that. I wonder where he went after he left you?"

"I last saw him heading in the direction of the eastern mountains, far away from Juhl," said Andrew.

"I wonder what he found there?" asked Marin.

"He found peace and guidance from a totally unexpected source," explained Maikel. "He needed to make his mind up what he was going to do. He found a sense of purpose and he also found the friendship of an equal. I think that's why he stayed there for so long."

Chapter 22

The time had passed quickly. The physical agonies inflicted upon him, firstly by the priesthood and then by the Thorians, had paled somewhat when compared to the humiliation and verbal abuse he had received from the inhabitants of Tevalem.

Forced to walk through the streets, a condemned man, carrying the crossbar of his own instrument of execution, he had hoped that he might encounter some, at least, of his remaining supporters. But he heard nothing except the taunts and jeers of the crowd who had, apparently, condemned him. He had stumbled badly on some steps, not far from the hill where he was headed, and the soldiers had roped in a burly stranger to carry the burden the rest of the way. This was just as well, since Empas himself could hardly, at that point, have continued to carry it.

Yet even in his weakened condition, and through the pain that racked his entire body, he had been able to contemplate the nature of their reaction of hatred and abuse. Whilst it was true, no doubt, that the mob outside the governor's mansion had been bought, heart and soul, by the Juhl priests, even they, surely, could not purchase the opinions of every citizen of Tevalem? '*But then, if you disappoint people, they will easily become disenamoured of the message you sought to give them,*' he mused. Their disappointment would have led to confusion and rage, a need for a measure of retribution. This was why, presumably, they had all turned against him. So, he had found himself completely alone, without support, and apparently even robbed of his telepathic talent. Whether that was permanent or just temporary he did not know. It hardly mattered now!

As a joke, the soldiers had plaited a mock crown out of the thin branches of a thorn bush and placed it on his head. The thorns had cut in so deeply, it became difficult to think because of the pain they caused. Strangely, with all the other sources of agony he was suffering, the nails they had driven into his wrists and ankles had hardly had any further effect, though he felt himself growing weaker with every minute that went by due to blood loss and exhaustion.

Was it just minutes? Or was it hours? He had no way to know. Despite M-BEATS' best efforts, he was losing cohesion and delirium was becoming his normal state. Periods of stability and recognition were becoming fewer and shorter.

During one such episode, he surprised himself by his ability to muster enough telepathic power to speak to the director.

'Father, this is what I planned, though I find I am afraid, now, of the possible consequences. Forgive them — they can't know what they're really doing. Don't forget me!'

The telepathic message sent, his strength seemed to fail him. He could feel himself sinking further and further into an abyss of blackness. Then nothing.

* * * * *

The director had watched it all on the screen the ship had generated specifically for the purpose. Gaveri sat beside him, also horrified at what he was seeing. He had watched the director's reactions change from silent, apparently impartial observation, to agonised outright protest at the outrage taking place beneath them. Neither had been able to believe that Empas would actually allow himself to be put to death, especially in this cruel, barbaric way., and truthfully, the director had always had some remaining doubts concerning the logic of Empas' argument concerning his own death. He had died to save them all from sin. Would it be enough to start a theological and psychological revolution?

His speculations stopped when Empas contacted him, and his self-control finally broke when he realised his son had lost consciousness again so he could not hear the director's reply. So, prevented from offering silent words of comfort to his dying son, and against his very nature, he found his emotions boiling and he experienced real hatred and a desire for vengeance such as he had not felt in a very long time.

His immense power gathered itself and concentrating on the natural forces that he knew how to control, he caused a huge storm cloud to gather over the city below. It darkened the entire place and people began to look to the sky fearfully. When the storm had gathered enough pace, the winds began to blow with a fierce intensity that simply grew and grew. Thunder erupted in everyone's ears and lightning exploded in front of them. The rain fell in such torrents that people began to fear they might drown in the flash floods cascading through some of the streets. Everyone ran for cover, knowing at last that God was very displeased at what was going on.

The director cried out with the intensity of his own feelings.

"They should all die! They're not worth saving! They want a vengeful God. I'll give them a vengeful God! How dare they kill my son!" he shouted and choked on his own words as the tears of anger started to flow.

As if to accentuate his anguish, a huge rumble was heard all throughout Juhl and the land itself began to shake violently. Had anyone been looking, they would have seen a huge shifting of the mountains to the east of the country and their outline contour seen against the morning sky would be changed forever. A new peak appeared amongst the other established mountain tops. This one was different from the others in that there was a rock standing proud at its summit. The rock had an enormous crystalline structure running right through it.

Gaveri was also becoming agitated at the actions taking place and he realised that things might well get out of hand very quickly. He had never seen the director like this before! In desperation, he tried to think of anything he could do to help. Even as he began, though, he thought, *'How do you contain the grief of an all-powerful father who could easily destroy everything below if he chose to do so? And who is to say he is not entitled?'*

Then he played the card he knew he had to play.

"Director!" he shouted. "I think we can save him. Listen to me, we can save him!"

The doctor's words finally penetrated the director's consciousness, and he turned his attention to his old friend. Although no longer driven by his anger, the storm continued to rage below, but at least it would get no worse provided he could divert his frustration.

"How can we save him, Gaveri? He is all but dead. I am about to lose my only son and all hope goes with him," he sobbed as the futility of his actions seemed to hit him all at once.

Gaveri chose his next words very carefully. He had long prepared for this eventuality. He had researched for many hours the nature of Regan physiology and he was reasonably sure of his ground.

"Yes, he will die. But I believe we can bring him back."

"Bring him back from the dead?" queried the director. "How could that be?"

Though his tone was accusatory, the director was clearly intrigued. And the doctor thought he detected a trace of hope in the voice.

"Well, I know it's never been tried, but that's only because, by the time we Eldorans reach the moment of death, there is never any question of wishing to live on. We are so long lived anyway that it is almost a welcome visitor. However, there is a will to live amongst other peoples, particularly the Regans, that makes their approach to mortality vastly different. They will fight to hang onto, or to regain, life with everything they have. I suspect Empas will do the same, and he has an advantage over others. He has M-BEATS!"

The director listened with growing eagerness as Gaveri explained that M-BEATS, by its nature, was both an integral and a separate part of the practitioner. He believed that it would continue to function for quite a long while after the organs of the body, including the brain, had shut down. So, despite the fact that Empas was clinically dead, provided they were able to reach him in time, he could be brought back to life, unimpaired and unaffected by the experience.

"What length of time are we talking about?" asked the director.

"In my estimation, we need to act within twenty-four hours of the last breath to ensure complete recovery," replied the doctor. He did not bother to mention that after that time, the chances of bringing Empas back at all were reduced to almost zero.

The old man considered what he had just heard. Anger and frustration began to give way to hope and with it, a degree of rational thought. Empas died to save the people of Rega. But what if he didn't stay dead? What would they read into that? Slowly a smile spread across the director's face, and he sat up straighter in his chair.

"Wait a minute," he whispered. "If you are right, Gaveri, then I do believe we can add a dimension to Empas' predictions that he could not have even considered. If I'm right, he will end up sending the world such a powerful message that they won't be able to ignore it!"

"I'm mainly concerned with getting you your son back, but tell me anyway," said Gaveri.

"He was convinced that, by his death, people would believe that he had saved them from sin. That he had died in their place, and they would follow his teaching because of it. Powerful, but still, I have always believed, a bit tenuous, incomplete if you like. But what if they believe he has conquered death itself? Which he may well do if your theory is correct.

"People will be a lot more inclined to follow a teaching that says, 'Believe in me for I have conquered death, therefore, you too shall have everlasting life'. It appeals directly to their own need to hang onto life. A message that powerful could have no limits. It could, literally, change the viewpoint of all the peoples on Rega eventually.

"But that's only part of it as we both know. Bring my son back to me, Gaveri, for our sakes as well as for theirs."

"I'll go and prepare everything," said the doctor. "But you will need to contact Maikel. She needs to ensure that we can get Empas' body away from public view so that I can do my work. I will have to go down to the planet to perform the operation."

"Of course," said the director. "I'll speak to her. Thank you again, old friend."

"Don't thank me yet," said the doctor. "We still have a lot to do and there are no guarantees!"

* * * * *

Marin, Maikel, Jespeth and Andrew had stood at the foot of the cross where Empas hung, hardly able to believe their own eyes. The disciples had also approached halfway up the hill to watch the tragedy unfolding before them. Each with his own thoughts. In some instances, hope was replaced by a sense of loss, but mostly, anger and frustration gave way, ultimately, to utter despair. Had all they worked for come to an end at this lonely, gruesome place?

As usual, Simeon provided the strength and solace they needed as he reminded them how this had all come about and how the master had planned it all along. He choked trying to keep his own emotions in check, but he was more than ever determined that the master's message would not be lost now, not after all that He had sacrificed.

Marin and Jespeth just continued to look at their son, silently pleading that he come down from that thing and tell them it hadn't happened. And when that didn't work, they prayed to God that he might be spared from this fate.

Maikel was numb. She found she could no longer think straight. She just stared up at the man who had come to dominate her life in so many ways and who was now taken from her in such a violent and — final — manner. All her hopes disappeared as she watched his life leaking away before her eyes. Though the wind blew, the thunder crashed, and the rain poured down, still she stood and looked up at the devastation until she could no longer bear it and she fell to her knees, heartbroken. Looking down, now, only at the wet ground beneath her, she knew with certainty that this would be the end of her too. She no longer wanted to carry on, as there was no future she could imagine that would be tolerable without him. Her misery was beyond all measure.

Something stirred within her as she became aware of a voice, she recognised calling to her. Only after a moment did she realise that the voice was in her mind.

'Director? Is that you?' she asked silently.

'Yes,' came an excited reply, *'Maikel, I have to talk to you.'*

All at once she felt angry at this intrusion upon her personal grief, not to mention the violation, no matter how mild, of her mind.

'I am sorry sir, but I do not wish to talk to you, or anyone, right now. Please leave my mind.'

The director, realised his mistake as soon as she began, and he immediately voiced his remorse and sorrow.

'I'm sorry, Maikel, I know how you must be feeling. I love him too, you know.'

The sympathy offered made her regret her outburst and her misery deepened still further. She could think of nothing to say, even to the director.

'Believe it or not, I bring good news. Gaveri believes we can bring him back and he is preparing to come down to Rega to do it.'

Maikel could not take it in. *Bring him back? From the dead? Surely not.* Yet even as she thought it, a new hope stirred within her. Was it possible?

'*Maikel, it sounds far-fetched, and I know none of this has been easy for you, but we need you to ensure that Empas' body is moved as soon as possible to a private place where Gaveri can work in complete secrecy. Can you do that?*'

'*I will try, sir,*' she replied, still reeling with confusion, not daring to assume any confidence, even to herself.

'*Have faith, my dear. We will not give up on him now!*' the voice concluded with a strength and urgency she could not ignore.

She stood up and looked at her companions. With the rain coming down so hard, none of them could tell whether it was tears or fresh water from above that was streaming down their faces.

"We need to claim his body and lay it to rest as quickly as possible somewhere it will not be disturbed," said Maikel looking at each in turn. "It is the right thing to do. We cannot deny him a measure of dignity, even in death. So, we cannot leave him there."

"Agreed," said Marin. "But we are far from our homes, and we own no land here. Where will we find such a tomb."

They all looked at Andrew, then, as their one remaining hope.

"I know a man," he said slowly. "He may be willing to help."

* * * * *

Portio Latiedes had never ever been scared by weather in general and storms in particular, even as a young child. He recalled his mother running into his room on one occasion when a particularly nasty storm was taking place, as they often did across all of Gauros and particularly in the Thorian capital. She was, naturally, concerned that he should not be frightened, and she wanted to calm his fears and comfort him. But he did not need any of that. When she arrived, he was sitting quite calmly watching the lightning and listening to the thunder rattling away. Not that he found them attractive particularly, but storms had never held fear for him. He remembered he had turned to his mother and asked why she was there.

"To comfort you until the storm is past," she had answered.

While he had quite liked his parents, he had found their somewhat overbearing concern for his welfare a bit hard to take even at his age and it did not get any easier as the years went by. In the end, they had parted company when he joined the Thorian military, and he couldn't recall seeing much of either of his parents after that. Always something of a loner, Latiedes had learned to rely on his own resources and had climbed to political prominence through a series of bold military achievements and astute manoeuvrings amongst his political rivals. The only fly in his ointment had been Nazim, the hated spymaster who had undoubtedly persuaded the emperor to give him this godforsaken job, in this awful land.

The news that Nazim was dead had lightened his mood considerably and he had begun to consider how he might accomplish a return to the Capital and to his emperor's side. Surely his handling of the Juhl messiah affair would fetch him some not inconsiderable credit in court? Perhaps he could expect a recall sometime soon, who knew?

An extremely loud clap of thunder, sounding as if it started in the room itself, shook him suddenly from his reverie. It was followed by forked lightning which seemed to reach right into the room, almost as if it was searching for him. It struck the floor not many feet away from where he was sitting, splitting the neatly arranged tiles into a jumbled mass and throwing them in all directions. He jumped with sudden panic and fear, something, he acknowledged, he was feeling for the first time in his life. *'Was that lightning really coming after me?'* he thought wildly. It had certainly looked that way.

As the moments passed and the event was not repeated, he gradually regained an air of calm and wondered, in passing, if any of his own children had been frightened by the storm. Or had the storm gone after them too? He decided to check, just in case.

"Gods, I really hate this country!" he declared as he left the courtroom and made his way to his private dwelling quarters.

The full extent of the casualties caused by the extraordinary storm would probably never be known. But there were a few notable exceptions. No fewer than three Thorian guards had been struck directly by lightning, all of them killed. The head of a notorious and large family, who had been particularly thick with one or two of the temple priests, was seen to burst into flame by one of his wives. His charred remains could barely be recognised. A number of citizens had actually been drowned as flash floods raced through the streets. Most noteworthy, though, was the sudden death of the chief priest of the temple, one Caiaphas by name. It seemed he died of a heart attack when a thunderclap exploded right over the temple. This was followed by a fork of lightning which seemed to aim straight for the temple, severely damaging the roof and causing the collapse of two of the columns that supported the front portico. The resulting chunks of masonry, large and small, were scattered all over the front steps. It took several days to clear up the mess. The man had apparently been standing almost immediately beneath the portico when it collapsed.

* * * * *

An hour or two after the storm finally subsided, Portio was relaxing with his wife when there was a knock on the door. On hearing the command to enter, an officer of the guard opened the door and announced that a man and a woman had turned up at the gate asking to speak to the governor.

"And why would I want to speak to them at all?" enquired Portio.

"Your pardon, Lord. I would not have bothered you, except that they say they are the parents of the man we executed earlier today. They say they need to speak to you urgently about him."

Despite himself, the governor was interested. He hadn't even known that the man had parents — and he had certainly not expected them to be in the city! *'How odd,'* he thought. *'Oh well, it can't do any harm to speak to them briefly.'*

"Show them to my private office. Since they are here, I may as well see them."

Jespeth and Marin were kept waiting in the governor's office for a further twenty minutes before he finally made an appearance. He walked straight in and sat at his table. He studied the couple before him. Just an ordinary man and his wife judging from appearances. He decided to cut the meeting as short as possible by intimidating them.

"You claim to be the parents of Empas of Galle, the criminal who has just been executed?"

"We are his parents, Lord, but he wasn't a criminal," said Jespeth respectfully.

"Not a criminal? Of course, he was. Tried and convicted — by your own people I might add. All I did was execute him as the law demands," retorted Portio. "Now, kindly tell me why you are here and why I should not have you arrested immediately."

"We mean no offence or harm, Lord. But we would ask if you might allow us to bury him instead of just leaving him where he is. It is our custom and we would count it a boon."

Portio had not been expecting this at all. In truth, he had found no guilt in the man, and he could find no guile in these two. Only, he suspected, a deep sense of loss. Not given to softness or pity, however, he considered for a while before giving his answer. He admitted to himself that there could be political mileage in allowing the burial to go ahead. On the other hand, if the body was taken away out of sight, what was to prevent an imposter from appearing on the scene? If he looked sufficiently like the deceased, he could claim to have arisen and the problem could start all over again.

No, if he allowed this request, there must be safeguards.

"I am not an unreasonable man, but if I allow this burial, you must accept that the tomb will be sealed, and I will post guards outside it to ensure that no one disturbs the body. Provided you agree to that, I grant my permission to take him down from the cross and remove him for burial," he said, not unkindly.

"Thank you, Lord," said Jespeth. "May God bless you for your kindness."

"I think that is unlikely. Go in peace and claim your son."

Jepeth and Marin left the governor's residence, happy that they had done their part by securing the governor's agreement to the burial. Now they had to hope that Andrew had been successful in securing the tomb in which he might actually be buried.

They returned to the secure house where they found Andrew and Maikel waiting for them. Maikel was particularly relieved when they told her they could bury Empas. Giving the excuse that she needed some air, she left the others and went into the small courtyard at the rear of the house where she immediately contacted the director.

Having established the place of burial and that they would be fetching the body within the hour, she switched of the wrist communicator and returned to the others. She smiled shyly as she entered the room, nodding her assent when asked if she was feeling better.

"I shall be much better," she said, "once we have rescued him from that awful place and buried him with the respect and dignity that he deserves."

"Then let's go and get it done," said Andrew firmly.

* * * * *

The tomb was cool and dry, and as luck would have it, situated not too far away from the execution site. Andrew and Jespeth had carried the body on a narrow pallet, refusing the help of the two Thorian guards who had been sent to oversee the process. Marin and Maikel had walked slowly beside the pallet, completing the burial party.

They laid the body gently on a slab of rock which was conveniently flat and began to bathe it, ensuring that all the blood was removed before anointing him with a preservative oil and dressing him in a white shroud. Maikel noticed that the injuries he had suffered, including a stab wound in his side, were actually healing up! This was something of a mystery to her as she was unaware of the implant in Empas' body, and she had never studied medicine anyway. Putting the matter aside for the moment, she decided not to mention it to any of the others. Instead, together with Marin, she finished the process of cleaning and preparing the body.

Satisfied at last that their beloved Empas could rest in peace and dignity, they trooped out from the small tomb into the daylight, where they were met by a Thorian officer, a septim, who had brought with him a squad of six soldiers to join the two guards.

"Is the body laid to rest?" he asked bluntly.

"Yes, sir," replied Jespeth, clearly distressed by the whole business.

The officer ushered the group to one side, out of earshot of his soldiers.

"Look," he said softly. "Just so that you know, we are not all tyrants.

I actually heard him speak and what he said made sense to me. As far as I'm concerned, he was no criminal and I think the Thorian empire will live to rue what we have done over the last few days."

"That is kind of you, sir," said Marin. "It is good to meet a believer in what he was trying to do."

"Yes, well," said the septim, slightly embarrassed "If I could have my way, I would allow you access to the tomb, but I have been ordered to seal it up and set a guard. You have my assurance, though, that his peace will not be disturbed and no Thorian, or Juhl, will defile this tomb in any way. It's the least I can do."

"Thank you again, sir," said Marin. "May God bless you for your kindness."

The officer didn't seem to know what else to say, so he turned on his heel and began issuing orders to his men. They searched around the site, which looked as if it might, at one time, have been part of a quarry working. Eventually they found a suitably large boulder which it took all eight men to move. They rolled it into position in front of the tomb's opening, then added mud around the edges, effectively sealing it tight and ensuring that nothing would be entering that tomb.

Finally, the septim detailed two of his men to stand the first guard watch. They would be relieved in six hours by two others. The tomb was to be guarded in this way, twenty-four hours a day, permanently until the order was countermanded. With a final nod to the four mourners, the man marched the rest of his squad away back to their barracks.

Maikel was the last of the four companions to leave the tomb, having first spoken to the director so that he could pinpoint the location on his screen.

Later that night, after the watch had been changed, a two-man sled glided silently, and invisibly, to the ground. Two men, totally encased in transparent enviro-protectives, exited the craft and carefully approached the tomb. The two guards stood immobile, eyes staring fixedly outwards, held in a kind of stasis by the director, which would allow the other two to work. This they did, methodically melting the mud seal all around the boulder which fronted the entrance, before fixing the two anti-grav units to the rock which would make it almost weightless. Easing the boulder aside, they entered the tomb.

Adrian moved the rock back in place, just in case any snooper did drop by, while Doctor Gaveri set up his equipment. Using only his headlight for illumination, the doctor began the operation. First using only his hands, he laid them on the body's torso and allowed his M-BEATS to perform their examination. A few moments later, Adrian heard him give a soft yelp of delight as he discovered that Empas' own nano system was still working and there was a good chance of resurrection.

Immediately, the doctor released his treatment nanos which flooded into the body, boosting the work of healing already being done. Mostly it was a case of keeping the bloodstream clear of clots. Next, he placed one of his tiny stimulators over the heart where it began gently massaging and stimulating the muscles back into action. At the same time, it activated the muscles controlling the lungs so that they began to take in small amounts of air. After a while, he was satisfied that he could move on to the next stage, which was to use another similar stimulator on the brain. Again, it began its work, gently encouraging and spreading the electrical pulses which formed the vital connections between all the billions of cells which gave a body consciousness, and it could be argued, all of the functions which constituted sentient life. Three hours later, he sat back and removed the artificial stimulators. Empas' body was now fully functional again and he was well on the way to regaining consciousness.

"It looks like we've been successful. Now we must let M-BEATS complete the process," said the doctor. "We can safely leave him now. I'll put him in a semi-comatose state until we return in forty-eight hours, by which time I hope to have him up and about. Let's go, Adrian."

The two exited the little tomb and resealed the entrance and it was not until the sled was high up in the atmosphere that the director released the two guards, who would find that their shift had passed, uneventfully, and a lot more quickly than they expected.

* * * * *

In the early hours of the following morning, Saul mounted his horse and marshalled his elite unit of caravan guards, ready to escort and guard the latest of Caspar Mossamed's caravans to head from Tevalem to Damas.

It was quite a long journey, but the road was well travelled and there was little rough country between here and there, so he expected to make good time — completing the journey in eight to ten days at the most, he estimated.

He did not intend to make any detours this time, to beat up or scatter empasists, as they called themselves. With the death of their messiah, which he had stayed in Tevalem to witness, he thought the cult would soon die out of its own accord. All the same, he was ready to act if any of them got in his way at any point.

He had grown quite wealthy carrying out Mossamed's orders to disrupt any of the cult's meetings and to threaten, where applicable, dire consequences if they did not change their ways. On some occasions, he had been ordered to resort to violence to break up meetings, cracking a few heads together to make his point. These had been especially profitable for him.

He knew, of course, that ultimately, all the orders had come from the temple. The priesthood of his own church wanted the cult to be put down but were unwilling to be seen doing it. Saul wasn't entirely comfortable with that state of affairs, but he argued, Caspar Mossamed was his employer — more like a father figure really — and he was duty-bound to obey his orders. If the priesthood had bought him off, who was he to question it.

The caravan moved off at a steady pace.

Chapter 23

It was less than two days later that Doctor Gaveri was able to report to the director that the operation to resurrect Empas had been completely successful. Their presence had not been compromised in any way, and Empas himself looked and sounded very much as he always had. The assertion was further borne out not long after when the director found himself being called from the planet.

'Father, thank you and thank Doctor Gaveri for me. I am fully recovered thanks to his efforts. But I must ask, why have you done this?' asked the young man.

'Son, I will explain everything when I see you.'

'Oh, I intend coming back to the ship. In fact, as I'm sure you knew, I will have to return to you permanently. Once they know that I am alive, the Thorians will have to come looking for me. While I can protect myself, and probably my immediate helpers as long as they are near me, I won't be able to protect the hundreds, or possibly thousands of followers who will undoubtedly get caught up in the empire's campaign to eliminate me. That means I must leave here as soon as possible. The problem is how to do it and avoid repercussions for my believers. As far as I can see, my work here is just about done, and there is little I can add that will make any difference now, though I do have one or two bits of unfinished business. And I have a personal reason for wanting to get them done as soon as possible,' added Empas.

'You mean Maikel, of course. Yes, it's time she returned to us. We don't want to push the risk of her becoming infected with something we can't cure.'

'Father, I love her, and since I am alive, I would like to be with her. However, the longer we stay here, the higher the risk to her from the Thorians.'

'I agree entirely,' replied the old man. *'Complete your tasks, then, Empas, but try not to put yourselves in too much danger.'*

'You can be sure I won't,' said Empas, ending the conversation at that point.

The director could barely contain his joy.

* * * * *

The two women made their way carefully through the cool meadow that constituted the graveyard which adjoined what used to be a quarry. Gingerly, they avoided stepping on graves, detouring where necessary. Eventually they approached the small cave that had become Empas' tomb. They were taken aback, however, when they saw that the boulder was no longer blocking the entrance way, neither were there any guards about. Only the officer they had spoken to when they buried Empas was there, sitting on the ground looking very perplexed.

Marin was the first to react, running past the Thorian and into the cave. She looked around but could see no trace of the body of her son, nor of any of the things they had left in the tomb. Thinking that the Thorians must have removed him, she ran back outside and knelt in front of the officer.

"Sir, please tell me what has happened here. Where have they taken my son?" she wailed, feeling her grief return all over again.

"No, lady, don't weep. Thorians have not done this. I came up here to check on my guards this morning and found them asleep at their posts. I dismissed them immediately, but then I took a look around. As you can see, the stone had been rolled away and there was no body inside the tomb! I am as worried as you are. This could mean my head!" asserted the septim unhappily.

Marin did not know what to say. She looked around her wildly as if she might spot Empas hiding somewhere, but she saw nothing.

Maikel was only surprised to find Empas gone — she had expected to see him alive but had not anticipated this. She too looked around to see if she could spot him, but she only saw a gardener tending to one of the graves. Looking for information, she approached him from behind.

"Excuse me," she began, "but do you happen to know where they've taken the body of the man who was buried in the tomb yonder?"

"They' haven't taken him anywhere, Maikel," he said as he slowly turned towards her, "I'm still here, though I never expected to be. I must admit, I'm glad to be alive again."

"Marin!" she called. "Marin, come quickly. It's him. Empas. He's alive!"

Marin answered her call and came running towards the pair. Empas opened his arms and encompassed both of the women in a loving embrace. They both began weeping with joy to be reunited once again.

The Thorian officer couldn't believe what he was seeing. Rising from the ground, he too approached the man they called messiah. Nervously, he reached out to touch Empas and found him solid enough. He looked at his wrists and saw the puncture marks where the nails had been driven in.

"I'm afraid I will always carry those scars," said Empas softly. "But septim, I see that my being here is causing you some concern."

"You can say that again," said the man. "It's bad enough that your body is no longer in the tomb — but if I return and tell them you're alive! In all honesty, Master, I cannot imagine my head still attached to my body by tonight."

"I see your difficulty," said Empas thoughtfully. "I am so sorry to have put you in this situation. Is there anything I can do to help?"

"My name is Boran. Pray for me, Master. I have to report back to my superiors and when I do, there will be hell to pay. And as likely as not, that's where I shall end up."

"You call me, Master. Are you a believer then?" he asked.

"Ever since I heard you preach. You showed me a glimpse of what might be possible without war, and though I was raised to fight for the empire, I knew that your way was the right one. I regard myself as a loyal Thorian. I just wish we could find some other way to relate to the rest of the world," answered the septim sincerely.

"Boran," said Empas. "I have an idea which might save your life and be of great service to mankind — including the empire — at the same time. The choice must be yours to make, of course, but if you choose this path, you will always have my gratitude."

"What can I possibly do, Lord," replied Boran. "When the governor learns that you have been seen, he will not believe it, but he cannot afford to risk letting anyone else believe it either. He will hunt you and all your supporters down. He cannot let political subtlety get in the way of military efficiency any more. The army will be ruthless, I know this from experience."

"You are quite right, of course," said Empas calmly. "But if the Thorian response can be 'managed', I believe we may be able to avoid the carnage that you foresee. It is all a matter of timing. The problem is… there will be some risk to yourself involved."

"If I thought I could help, I would gladly accept that risk, Lord," answered the Thorian earnestly.

"Then listen to what I propose," said Empas and proceeded to explain what he wanted the officer to do. The plan was simple, but as he had said, there was some risk to Boran as they could not predict exactly how the governor would react to the news of Empas' resurrection.

At last, Boran fully understood the measure of the risk he was being asked to take, and though the prospect scared him, still he was determined to carry out his task.

"I will do as you ask, Master," he declared. "But I worry for you and the disciples should anything go wrong."

"That is my problem," said Empas. "Don't let it be of any concern to you. Just carry out your task to the best of your ability. And Boran — I want you to know that you would be welcomed by any of my followers, should you wish to change your life. If you ever need assistance, look for the man they once called Al Barab. He is no longer a partisan, but he will know how to help you escape the Thorian military. No matter what happens, I tell you that hell is not where you will end up. God will find a place for you."

With that, the Thorian officer left.

"Mother," said Empas, turning to her. "I am truly glad to see you and I will come with you to greet Jespeth and Andrew. But I must warn you that, though I have returned, I cannot stay. To do so would be to put you and everyone else in danger. I have one or two things to do and then I must leave you."

Marin nodded her agreement, sad at the thought of losing him again, but glad of this opportunity, no matter how brief, to be with him. '*It's God's will*,' she thought. '*What will happen, will happen.*'

Jespeth and Andrew were equally dumbfounded when Empas

walked through the door of the house they were still occupying. Jespeth soon adjusted to the fact, taking comfort in the fact that his beloved wife had her son back, even if only temporarily. His down-to-earth acceptance of the evidence before his eyes was sufficient to lighten the mood considerably, while Andrew was clearly mystified at everything that was going on.

Empas took him to one side.

"My friend, thank you for following my advice. Have you ever seen your sister look more radiant?" he asked.

"Honestly, no I don't think I have, even when she was a girl," Andrew replied.

"And it is at least in part because you have come back to her," Empas explained. "And she and Jespeth will need your strength and support in the future because you and they have a long journey ahead. I have one or two tasks to complete, but I must leave you soon. I won't allow Thorian vengeance to fall upon any of you, but as long as I am here, there is that danger. I ask you to accept the responsibility I place on your shoulders."

Andrew still did not fully understand, though he knew all about Thorian vengeance! However, he had taken so many things on faith just lately concerning this man and his family, what was one more to add to the list?

"You have my word, Empas. My fighting days are over. Perhaps there is something in what you teach. Who knows? But I will devote myself to them."

"And I have a further boon to ask of you," continued Empas. "There is a Thorian septim, named Boran who may need your help. Should he seek you out, please, look after him as you would me."

"You ask much, Empas. Yet, I trust you so, again, you have my word on it."

"Thank you, Andrew. And now we must all leave quickly, but before we do I need to speak to Maikel."

Andrew and the others began clearing the house of all trace of their presence while Empas and Maikel retired to the courtyard.

"This wasn't part of my plan," he told her.

"I know," she replied. "The director arranged it all. So, he has, once again, imposed his will on events. I'm so sorry, Empas."

"Don't be," he replied. "Whilst my father has 'imposed his will' as you put it, I still carried out what I had intended to do. In any case, I begin to see perhaps why he did it and I admit that the course of events may be immeasurably helped by what he has done.

"My only regret is that you and I will not be able to stay on this beautiful planet. That may not be a huge problem for you, but I have spent my entire life here. It is home and I shall miss it."

"Then we must find somewhere to make a new home," said Maikel. "There must be any number of places in the universe where we can bring up our family in peace and happiness."

Empas could only stare at her, dumbfounded for a while.

"What do you mean, are you pregnant?" he asked, raising his voice in excitement.

"I think so," she answered with a smile. "Though I haven't consulted Doctor Gaveri about it."

"A child?" he said incredulously. "For us?"

They both began to laugh as they fell into each other's arms, tears of joy starting in each of their eyes. At last, they parted and looked at each other lovingly.

"Now control yourself and keep your voice down," she admonished him. "This is one secret we must keep to ourselves until we are back aboard the ship."

"Yes," he said, still hardly able to believe what she had just told him.

Together, they went back inside the house. Empas was, naturally, feeling very excited. For now, he had another, far more personal, reason to ensure that the next couple of days went according to plan.

"If we are all ready," he said, "we must leave. Andrew, lead the way."

* * * * *

When Boran returned to the barracks, he immediately had the two guards who had been on station at the tomb arrested and held for questioning, then he ordered his men to get ready for active operations. He also sent a small squad back up to the tomb with instructions to search it and the surrounding area for any trace or clue as to what had happened.

With these things done, he steeled himself for what he thought would be the biggest test of the day, perhaps of his life! He was not particularly good with people. The military life had not asked that he try to be, so he was not used to having to lie or explain things to anybody. He was especially apprehensive since, he surmised, the governor probably told and listened to lies all the time and would, therefore, be likely to recognise them easily.

'*Oh well,*' he thought. '*I promised the master I would try, so here goes.*'

With that, he checked that his uniform was in perfect order and marched straight up to the governor's office door and knocked.

*****

The interview did not go as badly as he had thought, even though there were one or two moments when he caught the governor studying him carefully, as if trying to make up his mind about something. The worst part came at the end of the conversation.

"…And you're sure there was no sign of him or any of his supporters at the tomb?"

"Yes, Excellency. There was only a gardener talking to a woman. She was asking if he knew where her son was. He said he didn't know."

"Can you describe this woman or the gardener?" asked the governor.

"Not really, Excellency. They were both Juhl, and I'm afraid they all look alike to me."

Boran had hesitated only for a second, but it may have been enough. The governor was pacing up and down while interrogating him, but suddenly he stopped and came up to the soldier and looked him in the eyes steadily. Boran managed, somehow, to keep looking straight ahead, not betraying any sign of fear nor any other emotion.

Finally, the governor backed away and resumed a position behind his desk.

"Very well, septim," he began. "Carry on with your search and when that is complete, mobilise the garrison, I want squads out searching this entire city and I want this man, if it is him, and his followers all in custody before the day is out, is that understood?"

"Yes, Excellency."

"And septim," said the governor. "If I ever find that someone has tried to — mislead me — in any way, I generally manage to make them regret their decision sooner or later. Do I make myself clear?"

"Yes Excellency," replied the officer. "I shall ensure that all interrogations are carried out rigorously."

"Yes, of course," answered the governor, knowing full well that the man had understood precisely what he was telling him. Deception and half-truth were his stock-in-trade. It would take someone cleverer than this soldier to lie successfully to Portio Latiedes. He had no proof that the man had tried to lie to him, but he would keep an eye on him in the future. It never hurt to be prepared.

"You are dismissed. Go about your duties."

Closing the office door, Boran turned and marched out, back towards the barracks. His heart was still thumping when he entered his own small room. With any luck at all, he thought, the worst was over for him. He had bought as much time as he could for Empas and his group. He could only influence events in small ways now, sending squads to areas of the city where he knew the fugitives would not be, that sort of thing. He only hoped it would be enough.

Then he started to think about his own destiny. Hadn't the governor issued a veiled threat to him at the end of their interview? He would, perhaps, be wise to start thinking about his own future. With his new-found belief and dedication to the master's cause, could he really stay with the Thorian army for much longer? Perhaps an answer would present itself before he found himself in deep trouble. He could only hope so.

* * * * *

The disciples had already left the inn and made their way out of the city by the east gate by the time the tomb was found empty, so they were blissfully unaware of all the fuss that was taking place behind them in Tevalem. They made their way quite noisily along the road away from the city, back towards Asper where, they had decided, they would make their final decision on how to proceed now that the master was gone.

Some, led by Simeon and Andreas, were for continuing the work the master had started, even with all the danger that might involve. They felt they were ready to face the risks involved so that his message would not be lost but would spread farther and wider and would gain strength and momentum with each person they managed to convert.

Others were not so keen, fearing a huge Thorian backlash to any new religion, no matter how peaceful, that they might see as a threat. Especially one arising from a man they had put to death. He would be seen as a martyr, a powerful symbol that could rally people to the cause. A glorious vision in one sense, but also one that was fraught with danger. Fear and discretion were beginning to appeal to their better judgement.

The arguments continued back and forth all the way down the road. But they were all arguments about principle, not about the practicalities of how they should proceed from here. That, they decided, could wait until they had reached the village safely and were able to take stock.

Thomas had been expressing his doubts on the matter for some time, but like the others, he had seen and felt the wrath of God when they put His son to death, so even he had not been able to decide, finally, what he wanted to do with himself.

And so, it went on as the distance between them and the capital lengthened. Had they but known, leaving the city was the wisest thing they had done collectively up to that point.

* * * * *

Andrew led his little group steadily through the streets of Tevalem, always keeping to the less frequently used alleys. Sooner than they would have liked, however, they began seeing more and more soldiers, patrolling the streets, visiting house to house and interrogating anyone they thought was acting suspiciously. The hunt was certainly on for them, and Andrew began to wonder if, with all this activity, he could actually get them out of the city.

Empas tried to reassure him.

"Just get us to the eastern gate," he said after a particularly close shave where they had only just managed to avoid discovery.

"But that will be quite heavily guarded!" argued Andrew.

"And because of it, that's where they will least expect us to try to escape," answered Empas.

Andrew was still doubtful, but reluctantly agreed to take them there and changed his course, heading for the gate which they reached in just a few more minutes.

There was a whole squad of Thorian guards at the gate, four checking everyone coming in to the city. No one was being allowed to leave and there was a small queue of people waiting to exit which would only get steadily longer.

"There, you see," said Andrew. "It's pretty hopeless. We should try another way."

"Give me a moment," said Empas with authority, "and I will get us through."

'Father,' he urged. 'Can you help us here?'

'Of course,' came the response. 'You shield your people, I will take care of the guards.'

With that, Empas knew exactly what he was going to do,

"Stay very close to me," he told them. "We're going through that gate now."

"Are you mad?" asked Andrew agitated.

"Trust me once more, Andrew," said Empas calmly.

"If you say so," he answered, not at all convinced.

With that, Empas led the little group directly towards the gate. Calmly they passed through, careful not to brush or touch anybody coming the other way and certainly steering well clear of the guards, all of whom ignored them completely as if they were not even there. It was only when they were well away from the city and could no longer be seen from the walls that anybody even dared to breathe properly. Looking back, years later, Andrew could still hardly believe that he had been a part of one of Empas' last miracles, perhaps the last, on Rega.

Meanwhile, Empas took Maikel to one side of the road while the others walked on.

"Maikel, where have you hidden your sled?" he asked urgently.

"In a cave not far from here as it happens," she replied. "Why do you ask?"

"Because I need to be at a place a long way from here quickly and I think the sled is my only chance of getting there," he said. "Will it take two?"

"Oh yes," she answered. "Quite comfortably, and before you ask, the answer is yes we can travel transparently."

"Good," said Empas. "That's settled then. Show me the way, my love."

Empas caught up to the other group and announced that he and Maikel had to make a detour which may take a little time. "Go on to Asper," he told them, "And catch up with the disciples there. When you leave, you must take the east road and head directly for your home. I will meet you on the road."

Looking a little puzzled, nevertheless, Andrew, Jespeth and Marin agreed, although Marin clung to him for a moment before, reluctantly, she turned and walked on. Empas and Maikel left the road immediately and were soon out of sight. It took them less than half an hour to find and uncover the entrance to the cave where Maikel had placed the sled. There it was, still in its hiding place. Maikel was, of course, an experienced pilot so she soon had the sled ready for action.

"Where are we going?" she asked

"East," said Empas. "Until we cut the Damas Road."

Chapter 24

It happened at dawn on the third day out from Tevalem. The caravan had made very good time and was now on the Damas Road, well ahead of schedule. Just before sunrise, Saul decided to ride up to the crest of one of the neighbouring hills to enjoy the spectacle of the world revealed as the crimson orb rose above the horizon. It was not far away from the road, within shouting distance at least, and besides, he didn't think there would be any danger at this point.

He sat quietly as the sun began to rise, but then sat up and stared at the scene before him. The dark outlines of the distant mountains were spread before him, and they should have looked familiar. Except that now they didn't! They had changed and there was now an odd looking peak nestled in amongst all the others. It seemed to come to a sharp point not far below some of the higher peaks, which had also shifted slightly. He sat looking at this in wonder, not quite believing his eyes, as the sun continued on its daily journey. His sense of wonder and grandeur increased with every moment that passed. Then, all at once, angles were confirmed, temperatures at the right level, the air was clear of dust and debris. Light from the sun shone directly onto the huge crystal embedded in the stone atop the peak and was reflected in a single beam that reached out, unopposed and unscattered, covering the miles in between it and the unsuspecting watcher in less than a second. That was all it took to burn out his eyes and rob him of his sight completely.

Saul cried out in pain and confusion, falling from his horse as he did so, slightly injuring his arm as he fell. He cried out again as the agony of the searing heat and light pierced his brain, but this time, someone heard him. Fortunately, one of the guards was also up and about that early. Hearing his master's distressed call, he made for the hilltop and found Saul writhing about on the ground, clearly in great pain.

"Master, what is wrong?" asked the guard tremulously.

"I am blinded, I am blind!" screamed the man on the ground.

"I will get help," said the guard.

It did not take them long to carry their captain back to his tent, where they laid him down, still sobbing with the extreme pain that he was suffering. The guards milled about outside the tent for a little while, trying to decide what they should do. There was a village on the road, not far ahead. Should they take him there and hope that they had a doctor or someone who might care for him? And what about the rest of the caravan? They couldn't hold it up for long without costing their employer a lot of money. Indecision ruled and their captain's pain did not get any easier.

They stopped and stared at the stranger, who seemed to come from nowhere, and calmly walked into the camp. He walked confidently up to the group of guards and said without preamble, "I am looking for Saul. He is in need of me."

One swarthy guard with black hair and dark features pointed at the tent and said, "He is in there, sahib, but he cannot see you."

"Oh, is he busy then?" asked the stranger.

"No," said the guard. "I mean he cannot see you, or anything at all. He has been blinded and we don't know how. Do you know of a doctor who could attend him?"

"I believe I can help," said the man.

"And who are you that we should trust you with the welfare of our captain?"

"Just tell him that Empas is here."

Saul was just about able to bear the pain and sit up to receive his visitor as the swarthy guard announced him and ushered Empas into the tent.

He went and sat quietly on a stool placed at the side of the makeshift bed. He recognised Saul immediately, though he had changed in appearance a little over the years, but he still recalled the childhood bully whose life had been saved by a crippled little boy. As he looked at the injured man, however, Empas realised that, far from bearing him any ill will, he felt quite the opposite. He could sense that, deep within this man, there was an honesty and strength unusual to find. And something else. Knowledge of a debt he could never repay. No, it was more than that.

"Hello Saul," said Empas at last. "It's been a long time. I'm sorry to see you like this, though. What happened?"

Saul related the events of the morning to him, strangely finding a measure of comfort talking to this man. Eventually, though, curiosity got the better of him.

"Empas, if you truly are he, why and how are you here?" he asked. "You died a matter of only days ago. And if you, are he, you will know also that I have spent a lot of my life trying to destroy your work."

"Why, I would have thought, was quite obvious," replied Empas. "But as to how, well let's just say it's God's will that I am here. And though you have spent a lot of time persecuting my followers, you do so at the behest of a man who, we both know, cannot get past the grief of losing a much-loved son. But you are quite right, I did die days ago, and now I am risen from the dead. And now you're wondering if I truly am the Empas that you remember."

He stopped then and considered what he would say before continuing.

"Do you remember the incident with the snake? When Ben saved your life?"

Saul knew then that Empas was who he said he was. Nobody else knew of the incident, and few knew that he had been taken in by Ben's father, but he was still curious as to where the conversation was going.

"I don't remember much after I was bitten," he admitted. "I was in and out of delirium much of the time."

"But do you remember Ben and I arguing over who should stay and look after you?" asked Empas. "Ben won that argument through sheer force of logic, or so I thought at the time. Now, I'm convinced that he knew what he was going to do even before it happened. He foresaw the effect his actions would have on both of our lives, and he knew he was going to die. Yet he stayed. Why do you suppose he did that?"

"I don't know," answered Saul honestly. "But your words have made me remember the event a bit more clearly and you're right, you did try to persuade him to go home. His father has blamed you for his death all these years, but you were not responsible."

"And neither were you, Saul," said Empas, sensing that it was guilt that drove this man as much as anything.

"Ben taught us both a lesson. There can be no greater love than that

342

of the man willing to lay down his life for his friends. We both owe him a great deal, don't you agree?"

Saul sat silently, unable to weep because of his damaged eyes, but feeling the grief of the memories, nonetheless. He found that he had to agree with everything Empas was telling him.

"I have been so wrong for so many years," he admitted unhappily. "How can I ever make amends?"

"Easily," said Empas. "Instead of pursuing and persecuting my people, join them. Lead them! Since I cannot be here myself in the flesh, I will rely on those I know I can trust. Spread my message far and wide. Take it to distant lands that you now know so well, so that others will follow where you will lead them."

Saul was a bit disoriented by the sudden turn of the conversation. He soon realised the truth of what Empas was saying. Of course, he couldn't be here. The whole Thorian empire would be looking for him soon and would show no mercy if they knew he lived, either to him or to his followers. But to take his message and spread it far and wide? How could Empas ask it of him, his enemy? Yet, even as he had that thought, he knew it was no longer true and that he could truly make amends, to Empas and to Ben, if he carried out his wishes.

But was he ready? Suddenly he knew the answer to that question.

"Master, don't you usually baptise your followers in some way?" he asked humbly.

Empas smiled as he leaned forward towards him.

"Sometimes," he agreed. "But it's really not necessary. However, I think in your case a baptism of sorts would be a good idea. I baptise you and call you Paul — friend — and soon the world will know that for a fact."

As he said this, Empas laid his hands over the other man's eyes. When he took them away only minutes later, he said, "Look at me, Paul."

Paul opened his eyes and discovered with joy that he could see again!

"God bless you, Empas, I never thought I would see again! I will do as you have asked me."

"I have to go now," said Empas. "When you return from Damas, if you think it wise or necessary, try to get Ben's father to let go of his grief. This may be difficult, so I leave it to your discretion, but then you should

343

go to Galle and seek out Simeon and his brother, Andreas, two of my staunchest followers. I named Simeon, Pedor. You will agree with me that he's a rock, on which you can both build my church. Goodbye Paul, I wish you well."

With that, Empas rose and left the tent. He went to the swarthy soldier and told him, "Your captain will be hungry, see that he is fed right away."

And so, he left the camp, finding the sled and his beloved Maikel waiting exactly where he had left them,

"How did it go?" she asked him as they rose into the air, unseen by anybody or anything.

"Much better than I had expected," he answered. "And now I must go and say my farewells to the disciples."

* * * * *

Andreas couldn't believe his eyes. One minute he had been looking at the road ahead and seen that it was deserted, empty as far ahead as the eye could see, the next minute, there he was, standing in the middle of the road right in front of them.

"Simeon, can you see what I see?" he asked his brother nervously.

"What?" said Simeon, and then he gasped as he saw his master standing in the middle of the road.

"But this cannot be," he mumbled. "They crucified him."

As if he had heard what the man said, Empas smiled and said, "And I am here, risen from the dead."

At that, the disciples all began shouting and talking all at once, the shock and relief clearly mirrored in all their faces. Simeon approached and spoke to him directly.

"Forgive us, Lord, but when we saw you crucified, we assumed that you had left us for good. The few of us who remain here are determined to carry your message to the people, but with you still to lead us, surely, we cannot fail."

"I'm sorry, Pedor," said the master. "But I won't be here to lead you. At least, not in the flesh, but I will be with you in spirit, and for you my friend, which will be enough. Because you will build my church and

344

others will follow where you will now lead."

"Master, I don't understand, surely…"

"Pedor, I died to save you all, and I have risen again so that you shall have hope for the future. But though I have conquered death, my father needs me and my time in this land is now very short. To be practical, if I were to stay, all Thoria would be hunting us for all time, looking to slay me and all those who follow me. But if they cannot have me, what they are left with is simply an idea, a philosophy which you will preach, and which they cannot kill."

Simeon could see the simple truth in what the master was saying, and he knew from experience that he would do as he wished him to do, no matter what anyone else might say.

"Is this goodbye then, Master?" he asked.

"In one way, yes. But in a most important way, no it isn't. It's not an end, but a beginning. One by which you and others will change the world. And I will be with you always because you'll do it in my name. Be ready to meet with Paul, whom I am sending to you for guidance. You and he will spread this gospel further than you ever thought possible.

"You will find the strength of purpose, Pedor, and all the things we have done together will never be forgotten if you stay true to that purpose."

In all the commotion, few had noticed that they had been joined by Andrew, Jespeth and Marin, who came right up to Empas and hugged him.

"Hello, Mother, Jespeth, Andrew," he said calmly. "I'm glad you are here. It would not have been right to leave without saying a proper goodbye."

Despite herself, Marin could not help shedding the tears. She had known this was coming but still she couldn't help herself. Jespeth stepped beside her to give support and comfort. Andrew looked at Empas quizzically.

"What will happen to us all now?" asked Andrew.

"I rather think that is entirely up to you," said Empas. "If you follow me, the road will not always be easy, but you will find a closer communion with God."

Andrew simply nodded. The right words just would not come to his lips.

Empas continued to speak to each of the remaining disciples in turn and finally to Jespeth, asking him to look after his mother and knowing that he need not have bothered to ask. Finally, he looked around, searching as if something was missing. Turning to look back towards the village, he saw a small squad of Thorian soldiers approaching, led by a familiar face.

When they were only a few paces away, the septim halted his men and walked forward to speak to Empas.

"We can speak, Boran," Empas reassured the man. "Your men will not hear what we say."

"Master, the Thorian governor has already set the entire garrison of Tevalem to search for you and he intends to mobilise the whole army if he does not find you," said the officer with concern evident in his voice.

"Then we must ensure that he hears the news that he wants to hear, mustn't we?" said Empas.

"How do you mean, Lord?" asked Boran.

"You and your men will witness my departure. It will be unequivocal and so obviously final that you will all be able to tell your governor, without fear, that I have gone for good. Ascended into heaven, and I cannot possibly present any further threat to him. Your men will remember only that. They will not recall any of these others gathered here, nor our conversation. So, whilst he may have his doubts, he also has multiple proof of what you say. This will stay his hand until sufficient time has passed.

"By the way, Boran, here is the man I told you to seek should you need him. Andrew, once known as Al Barab, here is a friend."

Andrew approached carefully and raised an eyebrow.

"You are one of us?" he asked.

"If you will have me, brother," replied Boran.

They shook hands then, beginning a friendship that would last a lifetime.

Then all those assembled watched as Empas moved away from them and seemed to step up onto thin air, standing there suspended as it were. Slowly he lifted away from the ground, rising higher and higher into the sky, until finally they lost sight of him altogether.

Boran turned to his squad of soldiers.

"Did you just see what I saw?" he asked of them.

"Yessir," said one. "The man we were chasing. He just rose into the sky and disappeared."

"And you, soldier," he asked another. "What did you see?"

"The same thing, sir," he answered. "It's a shame we couldn't catch him with his followers but no doubt they'll be hiding somewhere. But unless we learn to fly like the birds, we'd never catch him. Personally, I think he's gone, and I don't think that man's coming back."

"No, I don't think so either soldier," said Boran. "Come, we'll return to the village yonder and find somewhere to eat and drink before setting off back to the city. No point in searching any further out after what we've just seen."

Epilogue

The great ship sank slowly and gently to the soft, lush ground beneath, making hardly any noise as it did so. But that was the nature of the huge bio-technological miracle, for that was how it seemed. Only a few had survived that fateful event which destroyed an entire civilisation, almost an entire species really. The only survivors of the sudden supernova had been the crews of those ships that escaped. The warnings had come too late to save the rest. The inhabitants of two thriving planets, wiped out in a flash. And the great ship remembered that day in great detail.

The doctor turned to the old man standing beside him and smiled.

"What are you thinking, old friend?" asked the director.

"You mean you don't know?" joked Gaveri.

The director chuckled along with his lifetime companion.

"I was thinking," said the doctor, "that you chose a hell of a long-winded way to solve the problem of sterility among our males."

"I agree," said the director. "But it also has the benefit of giving others the opportunity to achieve what we did, hopefully without the dreadful cost."

The two continued to stare out of the window the ship had created for them and marvelled at the beautiful scenery that greeted their eyes. Nature, in all its glory and diversity, was thriving here on this planet, the presence of a sentient, human lifeform seeming to bother it not at all. Hardly surprising, given the current infinitesimally small numbers.

The huge, silent craft settled gently, and after a short while, a man-sized opening appeared at its base where, before, there had been only a plain shell.

The two old friends made their way slowly out of the opening to stand before the ship. They could feel the soft, cool grass beneath their feet and the warm, gentle breeze against their skin. They walked away from the ship, towards the small group of people who were waiting for them.

"I am glad you managed to come up with the macro-inoculant that protects us," said the director. "Otherwise, we would never have enjoyed an experience such as this ever again."

"Well, it works for this planet at least," said the doctor, pleased at the compliment despite himself.

The old man could not help smiling broadly as they got closer to the little group of humans. The adults stood silently and with dignity, but the children danced and played happily, unaware of what was going on around them.

At last, one of the men, obviously the oldest in the group, stepped forward with his arms extended towards the two travellers.

"Welcome to New Eldor, Father," he said with a smile.

"Empas," cried the old man. "It is so good to see you again, along with some of my grandchildren. And I see your half-brothers, Setram and Bensamin, have brought their families too. This is indeed a pleasure."

At this the other adults moved to greet the visitors, first Bensamin and his wife, Suren, and then the youngest, Setram, and his partner, Lisel.

"My goodness," said the old man heartily, "It does me good to see you all again, especially you ladies. The ship is not the same without you — not to mention the extra duties the remaining crew members have to perform!"

They all laughed at the director's joke, knowing full well that the ship virtually ran itself and life on board was very relaxed, even for a reduced crew!

"But where is Maikel?" asked the director looking around. "I don't see her anywhere."

"Oh, she'll be along in a while," said Empas with a grin. "The twins are playing up again. They didn't want to come and greet their grandfather. They would much rather play in the mud!"

"I'm deeply hurt," said the old man with mock sadness.

"Can you stay for long, Father?" enquired Empas, as they walked slowly back towards the small village.

"Long enough for us to enjoy a feast with you all this evening," his father replied. "And then Gaveri and I must return to our monitoring post."

"I must say, you show the most remarkable tenacity to be able to do this time and time again," said the son.

"And each time we do, we give another civilisation a shot at redemption. Let's hope it pays off at least once!"

"I hope so, Father," said Empas. "I know that is, along with the founding of this colony, your great dream. So how is this effort going?"

"Well," said the director enthusiastically. "Very well. The mother, a beautiful and dedicated woman, has given birth to a baby boy. Young Gabriella oversaw the birth for us."

"Not in another stable I hope!" said Empas jokingly.

"Actually, yes it was," answered his father. "In a little place a long way from anywhere. The inhabitants call it, Bethlehem."

END.